Black Mythology
Volume 1

WAR OF
THE
FROZEN FIRE

Happy holidays Pat

J Robertson

By Jay Earl Robertson

Dec 14th 2013

"War of the Frozen Fire," by Jay Earl Robertson ISBN 978-1-62137-285-1 (Softcover) 978-1-62137-286-8 (eBook).

Libray of Congress Control Number: 2013908523

Published 2013 by Virtualbookworm.com Publishing Inc., P.O. Box 9949, College Station, TX 77842, US.

Manufactured in the United States of America.

For my wife Stephanie,
who makes everything possible.

For my daughter Shayla,
who is my world.

CHAPTER I

The Abyss of Terrible Things

TASKICA WAS STANDING at the west end of the Bone Bridge of Broken Beliefs, which stretched for more than two hundred feet over the Abyss of Terrible Things. She waited a long time, while the foul breeze struck the dark strands of hair that curved over her forehead towards her eyes and along the cowl of her dark cloak. Her hazel eyes were hard, but lacked the sparkle one would expect from a face as appealing as hers. Instead, her gaze of iron shone with an unforgiving shine, replacing that absent sparkle.

The land surrounding the Abyss of Terrible Things was especially barren, just like the rest of The Underworld. Constant wars between overlords, warlocks and orc tribes over scarce resources and for power had scarred the land.

Taskica, staring straight ahead at the opposite side of the bridge made of bone, listened as eerie, tormented cries rose from the sea of blackness below the bridge deep into the Abyss of Terrible Things. She had never seen the creatures that she knew dwelled within the darkness, but their terrible, inhuman screams made their existence evident.

To Taskica's left was Borin Saken, a human like her, and one of the greatest of her companions. His face, a mask of overlapping scars, bespoke his violent past. His eyes were the color of steel. Scar

1

tissue prevented the growth of hair on most of his head. To her right was another one of her power weapons, the temptress Draxeen.

Draxeen appeared to be human, but was not. She was what many men would describe as a living dream, as she was more than beautiful. Her manipulating mind had as much edge as her beauty, and her body perfectly matched both. Her long red hair reached down to her waist. She had large breasts that were kept enclosed with her black leather armor, and her eyes were almost teal, a strange new blue that the gods never used to paint the seas or skies of Krynesia.

Borin rarely took his eyes off Draxeen. Her beauty was unmatched by that of any woman Borin had ever dreamed of, and her perfect body within the tight black leather armor teased and taunted him, and provoked his wildest sexual desires. She had the unfailing ability to tempt any man into her own private doom before making him one of her own. Her unnatural and immortal charm toyed with Borin's mind, but Taskica, as were all females, was immune to it.

At the opposite side of the bridge, a single figure appeared. Taskica's eyes lit up almost as if a hidden fire behind them had suddenly sparked back to life. The beast looked much like a large brain with several tentacles hanging down from its brain like body. Several fleshy stalks sprouted up from its body as well. The beholder had finally come.

"Are you insane?" Borin asked. "You're here to strike a deal with a beholder? You know how powerful these blasted beasts are!"

"Silence," Taskica ordered raising her hand almost in front of Borin's face. The Beholder's approach was cautious and slow, but it was finally close enough for them to see its face in greater detail. It was easily eight feet tall from the tip of its dangling tentacles to the tip of the sprouts which all contained eyes. Its body resembled a brain and contained one small mouth with many small, but sharp teeth. A large single red eye rimmed with gold was centered on its body right above its mouth.

It stopped within several feet of Taskica and looked the three of them over, paying particular attention to Draxeen. Her beauty had already begun to tug at its heart, but her powers did not seem to take serious affect on the beast of tentacles.

After a long moment, the beholder spoke. "I have come as you asked, Taskica."

"You are Tybiss Pylimdor, the beholder from the Tower of Seven Walls," she guessed, her voice rougher than her sweet appearance had led him to expect.

"I am," the beholder admitted. Its voice was strange and muddled.

"This is Borin and Draxeen," Taskica introduced the two accompanying her.

"You promised me a secret of great power," Tybiss began impatiently. "I am waiting, Taskica."

"I have knowledge of a spell, perhaps the greatest spell ever created, Tybiss, and certainly the most destructive ever created," Taskica explained. "It is so powerful that it will require us both to cast it. To cast it alone is not possible."

"Perhaps you judge me by my appearance. You have no idea how powerful I am, Taskica," Tybiss spat.

Taskica nodded. "I know that beholders are powerful beings with exceptional intellect, but I do know that alone you cannot cast frozen fire."

"Frozen fire," Tybiss said, and he went silent for a moment. "A spell with two elements that work as opposites?"

"The spell will work, I assure you; I need it for my plan to succeed."

"And where did this spell come from?" Tybiss asked.

"I cannot tell you such things, Tybiss. There is nothing stopping you from betraying me once you have access to the spell. How the spell was created, and by whom, will remain a secret known only to me and its creator."

Tybiss snickered, "Why doesn't the creator use the spell himself?"

"He has great knowledge, Tybiss, but he simply does not have the energy needed to cast such a spell. Neither of us alone has the energy needed to cast the spell either. However, two of us together do."

The beholder said nothing, but he appeared to be interested. Taskica took a step towards the beast and peered down into the Abyss of Terrible Things. "You are a warlock. Warlocks are known to collect spells and scrolls and add them to their libraries. You can't refuse a spell as promising as this one. Can you resist using frozen fire, Tybiss?"

Tybiss said nothing, but the expression on his face told Taskica that he would not be able to deny himself access to such knowledge.

"I want to attack Mystasia," Taskica said a moment later.

Tybiss frowned, and hovered towards Taskica. Borin moved closer to Taskica to warn the beholder off.

"Are you mad, Taskica?" Tybiss spoke harshly. "Mystasia is said to be a rich country, not to mention the alliance that exists there between humans, elves, dwarves and trows. Have you forgotten that the fairies are a part of that alliance as well?"

"Silence!" Taskica bellowed, and her anger echoed through the area like a ripple of hatred. "I have full controls over the Blacklands, Redlands and the Shadowlands of The Underworld. All the orc tribes within these lands have united with us. Now that I have full control over the lands, we will attack the country directly above us, using the frozen-fire spell, my new army, and the talent of another one of my companions, whom you have yet to meet."

Tybiss protested, "What about the watch towers and garrisons? We will be seen before we can get anywhere near the Mystasian castles."

Taskica smiled. "I have a companion who has a talent that will prevent that from happening. We can conquer Mystasia in just a few days. Their armies will be crushed, and their castles either destroyed or under our control, all in just a few days."

Tybiss Pylimdor began to turn away from Taskica.

"Remember the spell, Tybiss," Taskica called out to the beholder. "My plan will work, I assure you. I just need the two of you to cast the spell, and then you can maintain control over the Infernolands as you have for the past twenty years."

Tybiss turned back around to face Taskica. "Suppose I want control over one of your territories?"

"Which one are you interested in?" Taskica inquired.

"The Redlands," the beholder answered.

Taskica seemed surprised by this. "That is one of the most violent areas of The Underworld. It seems strange that a warlock would select such a place over the other areas."

Tybiss explained, "I have great interest in Bone Root Forest, which is located within the Redlands. That forest contains plenty of plant life I need for spell crafting."

Taskica nodded, "Very well, I have little use for that area. It is yours. You will find that the overlords and other powerful beings is that area are loyal to me, and now they will be loyal to you as well."

Taskica reached into her cloak and pulled out a scroll. She waved it in front of the beholder.

"The words needed to be spoken to activate the frozen fire are on this scroll, but it mentions nothing about how to create it, or who created it."

She stretched out her arm, and Tybiss was quick to snatch the scroll from her hand. "If you decide to betray me, be cautioned now. If anything happens to me, or if you spoil my plans even slightly, you will never know the secret of the frozen fire. Once we divide The Underworld between us, and once I have conquered Mystasia, we will live in peace."

Tybiss began to read the magic words to himself. "And afterwards you will trust me with such a spell? I could claim The Underworld for myself with a spell that powerful."

Taskica was quiet for a moment before answering, "I trust that we have an agreement and that there will be peace between us."

Suddenly, several feet behind Taskica, Borin and Draxeen, a crimson light appeared, edged with dark red flaps of light that looked like triangular flags being bullied by the wind, flickering and moving like fingers of flame. The light split open in the center, and a single figure stepped through. It was an orc, dressed in a black robe with a hint of yellow along the sleeves. The orc had a flat nose, and his bottom incisors cut into his upper lip. He carried a battle staff in his right hand. Once he was through the portal, it closed behind him.

"This is Olselg, a portal mage," Taskica said. Now you have met all three of my greatest agents, and now you know why it will be easy to attack the Mystasian castles. Olsegg has been given information that will allow him to open portals in key locations in Mystasia, including inside the castles themselves. None of the Mystasians will see us coming!"

The warlock smiled. "Your plan seems flawless, Taskica. When do we begin?"

"My source from above tells me that King Krendale will be traveling to the Hall of the Silver Shield tomorrow. We will destroy him before we do anything else. Tomorrow night, we will invade Quartz Wall Fortress."

Taskica made a strange gesture at Olselg, and the portal mage opened the portal once more.

"Read the scroll over, and meet me at Shade Deep Dungeon. Olselg will open a portal to the hall where we will eliminate the king of Mystasia." She entered the portal first, followed by Borin, Draxeen and Olselg, and the portal of crimson light vanished behind him.

The four wandered through the Naga Gardens of Praxia. They passed by trees such as bile brambles, which leaked strange poisonous green sap. The spider skin trees were infested and covered with spiders. At their feet, plenty of flowers grew such as ice blossoms and blood roses. In every direction, hundreds of nagas slithered and hissed. Some of these species of snake like humanoids had one pair of arms. Others had no arm at all while others had two pairs. Traveling through this beautiful but deadly garden was the only way inside Shade Deep Dungeon.

They entered Shadowdawn Temple, which sat at the edge of the gardens not far from the Abyss of Terrible Things. Taskica entered her chamber followed by Borin.

In the center of her chamber was a pedestal, which supported a dark orb. The wall to the far left was merely a wall of several strange mirrors made out of the same crystal as the orb. As Taskica approached the orb, different images appeared on all the mirrors.

"I have eyes and ears everywhere now," Taskica announced. "Not just here in The Underworld. To the far left you will notice Quartzwall Fortress. Beside that is the Cleric Temple of Ku'Lee. Nothing can escape my attention now."

One mirror showed a cottage at the edge of a village in a forest. "What is that place?"

Taskica turned to the mirror Borin referred to. "That is just a cottage of a young witch. There is no importance in that village. One of my apprentices must have animated a rock and left it alive for whatever reason."

Borin watched as a young woman walked out of the cottage. "She is beautiful, who ever she is." "Keep your mind on the tasks I have given you, Borin. She is a witch and has possession of nearly every herb one can think of. The one who helped me create the frozen fire spell stole some ingredients from her. She is young, but a powerful witch. Since we have what we need form her, I no longer feel that she is important."

"I don't understand what happens after you get what you want, Taskica," Borin said still watching the mirror closely. "What will keep Tybiss from destroying us once we secure victory over the Mystasians?"

Taskica flashed a baneful smile. "The frozen-fire spell is the most powerful spell ever created, Borin. Every time anyone uses it, they will weaken. Eventually, he will be too weak to use the spell and defend himself. When that happens, he will be easy to kill." Taskica turned to face Borin.

"He is too intelligent to fall for that," Borin warned Taskica.

"We will see," she said plainly. "Tomorrow, King Krendale will die; And Quartz Wall Fortress will be under our control before the night is over."

CHAPTER II

Birth of the Frozen Fire

IT WAS 1314 AG, a promising year for coalition, as the rune masters had claimed in the first month of the year, but the year had not yet been named. It was day twelve of the tenth month of Yhen'Nakk, known to the English speaking as 'The Great Fall,' which had descended on Mystasia and transformed its green forests into a blend of colors. The nights were getting colder as winter's shadow fell over the land, ruling the season with a frosty fist.

King Krendale the first rode his grey steed Atruses. He was a somewhat awkward, but nevertheless imposing man and had been king of Mystasia for twenty years now. To his left rode lance knight, Sir Nario Pureheart, who was specially assigned to ride with the king during any journey to ensure his protection. His posture was stout and attentive, even on his mount while not in battle. His narrow face sported green, daring eyes and a nose with a scar chiseled into it on either side.

To King Krendale's right was the knight, Sir Apponus Riskskin. Like most of the knights, he wore a barrel helmet, which revealed only a fraction of his oval face, which was thin and hairless. He had a small mouth and green eyes that matched the green needles of the pine trees. The three on their mounts were followed by a supply wagon pulled by four draft horses, and an army of one hundred strong, all on horseback, surrounded the wagon.

The army rode along the road known as Way of the Warrior, traveling south through the Jade Coin Forest approaching the Mongbat Mountains. Apponus glanced over at the king for a moment, studying his face with its frosty brown beard. It resembled the trees that surrounded them. They were white with snow and sparkling with ice crystals, but King Krendale's beard was frosted with white hairs because of age, not the chill of the approaching winter. The king's eyes were grey and warm, reminding Apponus of the rocky shores of Jade Lake, not far from the druid keep. The smooth, grey rocks gathered the heat from the sun during the summer months. He wished it were summer now. Memories from a time deeper into his past began to play through his mind, the time when he had fallen in love with Nario's sister, Riannon Pureheart. From across King Krendale's mount, Nario could see that Apponus' mind was not on the journey, but had wandered elsewhere.

"What are you thinking about, Apponus?" The knight asked.

Apponus smiled, "About your sister, Sir Pureheart." Apponus turned his gaze away from the king and the knight to the Mongbat Mountains ahead of them. To Apponus, the land was a little less exciting than the forest he and Riannon had been in three years earlier, during the late spring.

"Your sister and I were near the edge of Silver Timber Forest, where the eleven silver trees grow, not far from the town of Annalos," Apponus began, reviewing the evening he had spent with his love. "The blue moon had yet to rise, but could already be seen behind the silver trees. Sunset had just ended, painting the sky red and purple, but it was still light enough to see Herb Tooth Falls in the distance."

"I have heard this story before," Nario said curtly.

"I am sure you have, Sir Pureheart, but you seldom speak of your sister. You have told me little about her."

"I am sure you know her better than I do by now, Apponus," Nario muttered, studying the plains ahead.

The king cleared his throat before offering his own knowledge of the paladin lord. "She has a strange interest in gargoyles."

"She certainly does," Apponus said, nodding, "but…"

He was cut off when Sir Pureheart raised his hand. "The Guild of the Flaming Fists," the knight muttered.

King Krendale sighed, "For centuries no one knew where the guild was, and now we see it in ruins. It has been four months since the guild burned down, and we still don't know what happened to my brother or any of the other ninjas in the clan."

Sir Pureheart brought his horse around to face the ruin in the distance. "I was one of the knights who investigated the matter with Jherlom, your highness. We only found two bodies. We have no knowledge how many of them there are in the guild."

"Don't count any of the others out yet," The King said. "My brother's ninjas are experts at remaining hidden during times of danger. I wouldn't be surprised if those unfound are still alive somewhere."

King Krendale sighed again as he looked back at the ruins of the guild. "One of them should still have been able to get word back to me about what they found. Now they are missing along with the artifacts they disappeared in search of."

King Krendale took one last look at the blackened skeletal remains of what was once part of an underground structure where the flaming fist ninjas lived. A moment later, he continued to ride south-west.

The small army traveled to the village of Wistyrn where they spent the night. At first light, they continued south up the steep slopes of the Mongbat Mountains. There was only one season all year around in the high white pine forests, but for the rest of Mystasia, autumn had settled in. Recognizing the steep banks of the hills on either side of Cause Way, King Krendale took a deep breath. Breathing in the cold crisp air, which hinted at the coming of winter, the king sighed. "Just up the hill," he mumbled to Apponus, not looking at him.

Apponus nodded, stroking both sides of his narrow face in an attempt to keep the frost from settling in. "Amazing that there isn't a flake of snow at the Cleric Temple of Ku'Lee," he stated. "After all, we are only about miles south of the temple."

King Krendale turned to Apponus, "The cleric temple is not high up in the mountains, Apponus." King Krendale returned his gaze ahead. "Did you give Abadon his gifts?"

"All of them," the lean, cloaked man assured him. Apponus pulled his cloak closer to his body, trapping the warm air.

With difficulty, the four horses pulling the wagon dragged it to the top of the hill, where the forest slopes leveled out, and straight ahead was the Hall of the Silver Shield.

The hall was a single-floored structure, mostly composed of emerald and obsidian gem stone. The wagon came to a stop a few dozen feet away from the entrance.

"Remain here," the king ordered the soldiers as he approached the entrance of the hall with Apponus and Sir Pureheart at his side. The heavy door opened, and the king was greeted by four knights.

King Krendale smiled, "Sir Acinn, Lady Yal'Tonnica, and Sir Pyrelance".

Sir Pyrelance stepped forward, offering his hand to the king, who took it in his own. Exchanging firm handshakes, Sir Pyrelance nodded at the wagon, "What brings you here, My Lord?"

"A special ore, just discovered by dwarves in Hollow Haven. It is much stronger than any of the metal ores we have used up till now. I insisted on personally bringing you a load."

The king entered the hall, followed by Apponus and Sir Pureheart. He turned to the soldiers for a moment and signaled for several of them to begin unloading the metal ore from the wagon.

As King Krendale began to help himself to the roast, which sat, already prepared, on the table, Nario Pureheart and Apponus remained standing. Nario smiled as he continued the earlier conversation, "You are the first to have truly won my sister's heart, Apponus."

"After three years of trying, she finally surrendered to me, which is why I have come to see you," Apponus retorted, grinning, as he seated himself at the table.

"You want to know how to reach deeper into her heart," Nario guessed.

Apponus, swallowing a mouthful of honey ale, nodded.

"Being her brother, I wouldn't know the answer to that question, but I can offer you some advice. Maybe even a secret or two," Nario said.

Apponus said nothing, but the gleam in his oak-brown eyes bespoke keen interest.

"Although she often leads our armies, Riannon is a peacekeeper. Her specialty is diplomacy, and you may find it difficult to win her heart completely over her duties, but it's not impossible."

Sir Xzar Pyrelance closely observed the barrels of ore being carried into the hall.

King Krendale smiled as he watched the knight grab a piece from the closest barrel. "It's so light," the knight said.

"Yes," the king retorted with a chuckle, "Stronger than other ores we use for our blades and armour, but much lighter."

The king turned to Nario Pureheart, "Your sister will be the first to get plate mail crafted out of this ore. I have a wagon delivering more to each castle."

Sir Pyrelance grinned, and placed the piece of ore back into the barrel. "Our blacksmiths will enjoy working this ore," he said as he watched the soldiers unload more. "It has a strange purple color to it."

The king shrugged. He took a glass of honey ale offered to him by Sir Ackinn. "The magi of the Guild of the Blood Moon have seen the ore, and they say there are magic properties in it that they can detect. The dwarves that mined it call it mohenmar."

As the king handed Sir Ackinn his empty glass, a strange light appeared at the far end of the room. It swelled and glowed brilliantly at its center. Intrigued, the knights and the king stared at it. Apponus and Xzar moved from their chairs, clearly uncertain and uneasy about the light's sudden appearance.

Then, without warning, four orcs, armed with crossbows, stepped out from the light, which the knights suddenly realized was a portal. Before anyone could move, the orcs fired their crossbows. An arrow struck Sir Acinn in the throat, and he fell from his chair onto the floor. Sir Xzar Pyrelance grabbed the king by the arm.

"Follow me quickly, your majesty; this way!"

Xzar shoved him through the doorway, where three more arrows struck the edge of the door, missing the king and the knight by no more than a couple of inches.

"Protect the king," Lady Yal'Tonnica ordered.

Nario and Apponus obeyed and followed Xzar.

Drawing out her long sword, Lady Yal'Tonnica engaged in combat with several goblins, armed with short swords, which had followed the orcs out of the portal. Lady Yal'Tonnica kicked one goblin in the face. She quickly armed herself with a kostral dagger in her other hand. Her sword made contact with the face of one goblin and the sword of another.

Blocking her initial attack, the first was unable to defend himself as she brought her dagger to his throat. In a matter of seconds, two goblins lay slain at her feet. Yal'Tonnica beheaded another, and her sword clashed with yet another goblin's blade twice before besting him. An arrow struck her in the right shoulder, but she continued to fight, brushing aside the pain that shot through her arm. Another arrow struck her in the back, piercing her dilapidated breastplate. Her sword fell from her hand, and she dropped to her knees. One of the goblins raised its sword, ready to make the final blow, then stopped.

The goblin turned to the portal just as Taskica stepped through. The cowl of the dark cloak hid her face well, but Lady Yal'Tonnica could clearly see that she was human. Taskica ordered some of the goblins and orcs to pursue the king and gestured to others to return through the portal. A moment later, Lady Yal'Tonnica was alone with the cloaked figure and three orcs armed with jagged swords. A smile spread across Taskica's face as she watched one of the orcs strike the dame hard in the face, nearly cutting halfway into her head.

Outside, on the hills that surrounded the Hall of the Silver Lance, the small Mystasian army found themselves closed in by orcs and goblins. The dozen soldiers who had been unloading the ore from the wagon had finished, and the goblin archers fired arrows upon them until the last of them was dead. The orc infantry destroyed the king's army at the cost of sixteen orcs.

As the battle continued, Sir Nario Pureheart ended the lives of four goblins and two orcs. Then, from a room to his left, a new danger entered the room. Four sword nagas slithered towards him, hissing with rage. Their six-armed human torsos were armed with six long swords, and their serpent bodies ended in a blade of bone.

A hole swelled open from the beneath the floor as if an unknown mouth of the earth had opened. Three of the nagas fell to their deaths as the width of the newly formed hole completed but the depth continued far into the earth. Nario Pureheart fought the sword nagas with his own sword. They proved to be a formidable opponent, but, after a short test of each other's combat skills, Nario finally chopped off one of the nagas' arms, nearly beheaded the creature, and finally jabbed his sword deep into its torso. Pulling it out, Nario brought his foot up to the naga's body and pushed it into the hole that had formed on the floor.

More goblins entered the room, attacking both Nario and Apponus. Apponus fought them off with his falchion, while Nario battled against twice as many goblins. Apponus slayed two more goblins with ease.

Nario, continuing the battle, suddenly realized that the hole that had formed was beginning to enlarge. Nario's broad sword met with the throat of one goblin and the chest of another. As they fell, lifeless, into the deep pit, Nario lost his footing. More goblins entered the room. Holding his sword with one hand, Nario held on for dear life, pressing the fingers of his other hand tightly against the floor. His grip on the floor weakened. A moment later, Nario fell to his death, screaming.

Apponus fled the room, with four goblins, only interested in finding the king, ignoring him. The wall across the room transformed into ice, then suddenly shattered as a wall of blue flame crawled towards the hole that was changing back into an unbroken floor, only to be destroyed a moment later by the freezing fire.

Standing by a dozen dead bodies, Sir Xzar Pyrelance listened to the fading howls and growls of the goblins and orcs. Silence followed for a moment.

"Be still, My Lord," Sir Xzar Pyrelance whispered. Hiding in a storage room directly behind the knight, the king said nothing.

Two orcs kicked the braced door open and entered the room, savagely attacking the knight.

"Black orcs," Sir Pyrelance said, loud enough for the king to hear. Highly combative, as their reputations had hinted, Sir Pyrelance could only fend them off for a moment, but he killed one of them. His sword pierced the orc's heart even as the other orc cut off his head. It rolled across the room until it came into contact with Taskica's naga scale boots. Angrily, she kicked it aside and surveyed the room, saying nothing, while the orc stood perfectly still, waiting for orders.

A moment later, followed by seven orcs, Borin entered the room, reporting to Taskica.

"All the soldiers outside have been destroyed, Master. We left none alive!"

"Search the room!" Taskica yelled at the orcs. "Arval Krendale is in here somewhere!"

King Krendale burst from the storage room, armed with his yahol sword, a sword which had been crafted especially for him. Its hilt was the shape of a bat, and the blade was long but thin, except for near the end, where it broadened before tipping off. It brought quick death to one of the orcs, but before any other could attack, Taskica raised her hands and signaled them to stop.

King Krendale caught sight of their leader immediately after she stopped the attack. "Har… Harmonia?" He stuttered, "It… it can't be!"

Taskica removed her cowl to reveal her whole face to the king and took two steps forward.

"It can be, Arval. I am as real as the death that you are about to suffer!"

With that, two orcs swung their swords at the king. The first attack, made at abdomen level, was blocked by the king, but he was not quick enough to fend off the second attack, which was aimed at his throat. It was cut three quarters of the way, and his head folded backwards, the bottom half of his throat became a fountain of blood. King Krendale fell to his knees, then over on his side.

For a moment, Taskica looked intently at the slain king, as if making sure he was dead. She stood smiling for a while, admiring what had been done, and then the portal that had spawned her and her minions swelled open once again. Borin entered the room from behind it.

"We searched all the rooms, Master, and found no one else."

"It is done," Taskica whispered. "Arval Krendale is dead."

"Something you have wanted for twenty years, Master," Borin said, grinning.

Taskica nodded. The goblins and orcs began to return to the portal.

"Wait!" Borin ordered. "Take the barrels of ore through the portal, too.

It will serve us well."

Each of the barrels was carried by two orcs until all of them were taken through the portal.

"The year has not yet been named," Borin thought to himself.

"It will be known as the Year of the Frozen Fire," Taskica muttered as he stepped through the portal. She passed through next, followed by eight orcs, and the portal vanished.

CHAPTER III

New Shaman of Ku'Lee

THE AUTUMN AIR WAS CRISP outside the Cleric Temple of Kulee, which was situated near the sand bar at the edge of Temple Lake. Jherlom Morderum was there to witness the graduation of Prince Krendale. The cowl of his deep purple cloak hid his large, pointed ears, but a fraction of his large, humped nose protruded from the shadow.

Under the teaching of High Priestess Eradia Novah, Prince Abadon Krendale had finally become a cleric, just as he had always dreamed. Eradia carefully placed a golden amulet engraved with clerical symbols over the head of the prince. The amulet's fine gold chain nearly got caught in the tight curls of the young prince's dark hair as she placed it around his neck. Before stepping back from the kneeling prince, Eradia delicately kissed his forehead. Abadon rose and turned to face the fifteen clerics standing behind him, cheering for the new member to their temple. His hard, hazel eyes sparkled, and a broad smile spread across his lightly freckled face. There was thunderous applause from those who witnessed the first noble lord in Mystasia's history to become a cleric.

"I have something else for you as well, Prince Krendale," Eradia offered gently.

Abadon turned around to find her palm open. Centered within was an emerald ring studded with a single ruby.

"A gift from your father that Apponus brought here late last night," the high priestess informed him as he took the ring from her.

Jherlom congratulated the young prince with a pat on the back. He removed the cowl of his cloak, his deep-set, forbidding eyes resting on the younger man's. Long, raven hair fell loosely about his shoulders. His cleanly shaven face showed almost no emotion. His nose twitched, and he placed his left hand over his long, pointed chin as he spoke.

"I always knew you would become a cleric, Your Highness," Jherlom said in his low voice.

Eradia Novah smiled at Abadon, then turned her back to him as she returned to the cleric temple. Her slender elf body moved gracefully, and a gentle breath of wind lifted her long, silver hair from her back.

"Much of this is because of you, Jherlom," Abadon said modestly. "It was you who sparked my interest in the art of healing."

Jherlom shook his head and placed his hand on Abadon's shoulder, tapping it with his long, narrow fingers.

"It was you, Your Highness," he replied dryly. "It is your own accomplishment that took place here. I am a druid, not a cleric. And although druids and clerics often start out on the same path, they lead completely different lives."

In grand admiration, Jherlom gazed at the bands of red, pink and orange that the setting sun created in the sky to the west. "I must be returning to the druid keep, My Lord," he said, and he turned his back to

Abadon and the sunset. "I congratulate you on your success here."

"Wait, Jherlom," Abadon said sharply. "I want to come with you. My parents do not expect me home for another two days, and Royal Amon is along the way to the druid keep. My father should already be on his way from the Hall of the Silver Shield."

"Very well, My Lord," Jherlom accepted. "However, we will be traveling by foot. As you know, elves do not use mounts in their travels. Royal Amon is about sixteen miles from here."

Jherlom looked up again, examining the evening sky. The eastern horizon discharged the enigmatic essence of evening, and the stars were as bright as polished jewels.

"The skies are clear, and all three moons are already rising," Jherlom said, grinning.

Abadon examined the sky for himself. The moon Shaurhez was a purple orb just separating itself from the eastern horizon.

"Shaurhez is almost full, so there will be very little light, even though the skies are clear," Jherlom said as the two began their trek north. Abadon shrugged without a reply. He enjoyed the company of the druid immensely.

The two set out down North Cause Way Road. The autumn air was frosty, but manageable. Abadon wrapped his fur coat around him tightly, but the chill did not seem to affect Jherlom. The three moons provided them with enough light to see the road a couple of dozen feet ahead. It was littered with tattered and torn leaves of various colors. The moon Nuibris was a yellow sliver in the sky, and the blue moon Yubanen was a waning crescent. However, the nearly full moon of Shaurhez dominated the skies, and its dark moonlight beamed down upon them. Abadon and Jherlom listened to the crickets as they celebrated the return of the night. The songs composed by birds hidden in the partially bare branches lifted their spirits even further.

Abadon followed closely behind Jherlom. He watched Jherlom's breath as it exited his mouth. His visible exhalations were like a soul escaping the flesh shell of a body once it is dead. His breaths were occasional, unlike his own. Abadon shivered as the cold autumn air made its way into his bones, but Jherlom simply ignored it – as though he were immune to the chill.

"Doesn't the cold bother you, Jherlom?" the young prince asked. His teeth were chattering.

"Not at all, Your Highness," the druid replied casually. He turned to face Abadon, but kept walking. The night and the cowl of his cloak shrouded his face with shadow.

"Druids are one with nature, My Lord. The conditions of the weather or the terrain we walk upon are never a burden."

Abadon frowned at Jherlom's remark, then he smiled. "Perhaps I should have become a druid instead of a cleric then. What do you think, Jherlom?" the young prince joked. He twitched slightly in reaction to the vicious bite of the cold as he waited for a response.

The druid stopped and turned to face the prince. His face was still shrouded in shadow, but Abadon could feel his eyes resting on him.

"I think you will do fine as a cleric, My Lord," Jherlom said softly, and then resumed his course.

Abadon pondered Jherlom's remark. Then he lifted the cleric amulet from his neck, staring at it as he walked. This new identity as a cleric was what Abadon had always wanted. Because he was Prince of Mystasia, his name carried heavy weight around the country, but it was his identity within the cleric temple that he was proud of most. He had the ability to heal others. What abilities did he have as prince? He knew nothing of war craft or leadership. He knew even less about diplomacy or the true needs of the people of Mystasia. His parents often lectured him about how he would one day be King of Mystasia, but he did not want that responsibility. What he wanted was a true belonging among people who shared his ambitions. He wanted to explore the lands neighboring Mystasia, and the lands within his own country as well. Abadon sighed. He knew that his time as king would eventually come, and he feared that it would be sooner rather than later.

A shuffling sound from the brush to Jherlom's right caused the druid to stop dead in his tracks. Abadon heard it as well and stopped behind Jherlom.

"Stay directly behind me, your highness," Jherlom whispered. Abadon obeyed. Jherlom was rarely spooked, but Abadon was afraid. He shook violently with cold and fear, like a tree bough in a sadistic storm.

Jherlom raised his hands, as if he were lifting something invisible. A short cry came from behind the brush, and a small figure materialized out of the darkness. The unidentified form was entangled in roots Jherlom had snared it with the use of druid magic. The roots he had woken from the earth carried the little being to the side of the road, where Jherlom then had them release it. They retreated into the woods, and Jherlom's slender frame blocked the moon from sight as his shadow smothered the creature, which was smaller than he was.

"Gathus," Jherlom said sharply. "Gathus-Kur-Zamigy." Abadon slowly approached the stranger, and Jherlom introduced them to each other.

"Your highness, this is Gathus," the druid muttered, a hint of anger in his voice. Abadon said nothing. He watched as Jherlom helped the trow up from the ground. Like any other trow, Gathus was about three feet and six inches tall with yellowish skin, very large ears, large eyes that often protruded and course hair often black, brown or white on top of their head. The trow race often reminded him of trolls, but they were much smaller.

"What are you doing hiding around here?" the druid asked angrily.

"I have been detecting some strange things around this area. I just thought I'd come and investigate," the trow replied, brushing the dirt off his fur clothing.

"Detecting?" the young prince muttered, confused by the trow's words.

"Gathus is a diviner, Your Highness," Jherlom explained. "He can detect many things within a certain distance: large life forms; the use of magic; hamlets; traps."

Abadon stared at the trow in awe. He had heard tales regarding diviners, and that mercenaries and common folk often sought out their ability to detect things.

"What kind of strange things have you been detecting?" Jherlom asked with great interest. Gathus licked his lips excitedly.

"Early this morning, I was looking for herbs about twelve miles north from here. I watched as the king rode past with a supply wagon and an army a little smaller than one hundred strong. Some time later, I detected many more life forms, and a large concentration of magic use. It was a very strong presence of magic, such as I have never detected before."

Abadon and Jherlom were now concerned for the safety of the king.

"Father!" Abadon gasped. "What else did you detect?"

"In a few minutes, all of the life forms vanished, except for one. The strong presence of magic ended."

"But that means that my father may be dead," Abadon blurted out. "His army trekked down Cause Way!"

"That is correct, your highness," Gathus retorted, nodding. "Not very far from here."

Jherlom hunched a little so that the trow could hear his words over the wind. "Could it be possible that the king may have been the one of the life forms that suddenly vanished? Could he be in a prison somewhere, Gathus?" The druid's words were hopeful, but accented with doubt.

Gathus shook his head. "I suppose anything is possible, Jherlom, but the life forms that suddenly appeared did not actually join with the others."

The three stood silent for a moment before Gathus continued, "I heard that you were at the cleric temple, so I decided to wait here for you. I knew that you would pass by, and I was hoping that whoever used the magic I detected would pass this way, too."

Jherlom patted the trow's shoulder. "You were right to wait for me, Gathus. And now I must travel to Castle Blackburn." Turning to Abadon, Jherlom said, "I have to go see your mother. She could be in danger as well, your highness."

Abadon threw his arms up into the air. "But that is more than forty miles from here. It will take more than a full day to get there!"

"I have a quicker way of getting there, Your Highness," Jherlom said, glancing up. Thousands of stars sparkled in the night sky. Jherlom slipped his hand into a hidden pocket inside his cloak and pulled out a strange, wooden whistle. When he blew into the whistle, it produced a loud, foreign sound such as Abadon had never heard before.

A moment later, the gentle breeze turned into a gale wind. It was the first breath the autumn air had taken in many hours. The three waited, but for what, Abadon did not know. They stood perfectly still in the middle of King's Way.

Abadon had repeated visions of his mother meeting with a gruesome demise, and he shook his head violently in an attempt to clear his head of the horrific vision. The leaves continued to dance with the wind, and Abadon began to sob. In the interval between the wind dying down and picking up again with a powerful, chilly gust, Jherlom could hear him. Sympathetic to his plight, he turned to Abadon. "My

Lord, I share your sorrow, but we have little time to waste. It appears as though your father is dead, although we cannot be certain of that. I must reach your mother quickly in the event that someone is actually planning an assassination."

"I understand," Abadon sobbed, wiping the tears from his eyes with the sleeve of his fur coat.

The cold wind increased in strength, and even Jherlom lowered his face a little to avoid direct contact with the icy current. The chilly air stung Abadon's eyes. In an attempt to avoid its sting, he turned his face towards the south.

The three of them waited in silence, and, a moment later, a shadow appeared above Shaurhez, moved across the moon downward, then disappeared. It had wings; perhaps it was a dragon. Then the creature, which Jherlom had summoned, appeared from the darkness above them and landed before them on King's Way. It was a large wyvern with a wingspan of at least twenty feet. Its leathery skin appeared to be brown with shades of green. The dragon-like beast lowered its long neck as Jherlom approached it.

"I need you, my friend," Jherlom muttered as he stroked the beast's neck; then he turned to the others, smiling. "This is Utopia. He will take me to Castle Blackburn to see the queen. The two of you must wait here and build a camp."

"I want to come with you, Jherlom," Abadon replied.

"No, your majesty, I am sorry. It would be unsafe for you to ride aboard Utopia. In the event that the queen is in danger, I would be endangering you as well if I were to take you with me," Jherlom explained sternly. "With Gathus, you will be safe for a while. He will be able to detect anyone within miles of here. I will not be long."

Abadon sighed with disappointment. Gathus shook his head. "There is nothing within the radius of my detection, Jherlom; no human-sized life forms at all, not so much as a deer."

Jherlom nodded and turned away from his companions. He began producing strange sounds with his mouth. For two minutes, his outlandish call echoed and mixed with the whining of the wind.

A little later, four sets of yellow-glowing eyes appeared from the darkness of the forest to the west. As the eyes got closer, Abadon could see that they were dire wolves. Yet Jherlom showed no fear and petted the wolves gently when they approached.

The druid then reached into the secret pocket of his cloak and pulled out an obsidian ring with a wavy orange line in the center. He took Abadon's hand palm up, gently placed the ring in it, then forced it closed. Jherlom turned away from Abadon and mounted Utopia's back, which held a large saddle, awaiting the druid.

"It's a magic ring; my father gave it to me as a gift when I was thirty-six years of age, My Lord," Jherlom said. "It is called 'The Obsidian Oracle.'"

"What does it do?" Abadon asked, admiring it.

"It causes displacement, My Lord. Once you place it on your finger, Gathus and I will be able to see you, even though you will actually be standing a few feet away facing a different direction. It has been over one hundred years since I last wore this ring, and it has been sitting unused in my pocket ever since. It will serve a better purpose worn by you."

Abadon slipped the ring on his left index finger and stared at it intently. He felt no different than before, but in the eyes of Jherlom and Gathus, his position shifted slightly. Gathus reached out to touch him, but the trow nearly fell in the attempt. Abadon's image was not solid.

"I will be back soon," Jherlom promised, satisfied with the defense the ring provided Abadon. "You may build a fire, and the wolves will guard the camp so that the two of you may rest."

Without further delay, Jherlom and Utopia disappeared into the night sky. Abadon shivered, imagining how cold the wind would be higher up in the air.

Gathus collected some firewood from the nearby woods, careful not to stray from Abadon or the wolves. Once the fire pit was completed, Abadon moved his hand over the wood, and a fire blinked to life. The four wolves laid themselves down within the rim of the fire's light. Two of them lay licking their paws, and the other two gazed off into the forest. Abadon and Gathus sat around the fire, silently awaiting Jherlom's return.

CHAPTER IV

Assault on Quartz Wall
Fortress

THE QUEEN WAS INSIDE HER QUARTERS. Outside, the cold wind howled, but the roaring fireplace within the room warded off the chill. Unaware of the world around her, Queen Krendale concentrated on her journal, scribbling swiftly at her oak desk. From somewhere, a slight breeze wandered into the room and extinguished one of the three flames of the candelabra at her desk. Her deep-blue eyes darted towards the candle, and she turned to the window accusingly, but it was completely closed.

Queen Krendale placed her feathered pen back in its ink well, took one of the red wax candles from out of its holder, and relit the flameless candle. She brushed her long, reddish orange hair away from her eyes and eyebrows. Her full-blooded lips were pressed together tightly as her pen toughed the paper once again.

A knock at the door startled her, and the pen strayed off course, scarring the paper with a fine black line almost across the desk top.

"Enter," the queen called out annoyed.

A conscript, dressed in leather armor, entered the room, and the guards outside the room closed the door behind him. The queen turned around to face her visitor, but he did not appear as she expected. He was in panic, and his face was nearly as white as snow at first snow fall.

The conscript knelt down before the queen, bowing his head for a quick moment, then peered up at her. "My Queen, the Hall of the Silver Shield has been invaded!"

The conscript's voice cracked. He was clearly distraught and nearly sobbed as he spoke.

"How?" The queen asked with a whisper. That was all she could say. Her heart pounded against her chest as if trying to escape a prison.

Trying to hide his tears, the conscript lowered his head again. "It was terrible, My Queen! I saw it all happen from the Devil's Paw Watch Tower!"

The conscript archer lifted his head once more. His face was wet from the tears he no longer fought to hold back. "I watched the king's wagon arrive at the hall, and soon after, they were all destroyed. The wagon was raided and burned down! I didn't see them enter the hall! It was as if they were already inside when the king arrived!"

The queen's face went cold, and she returned to her desk. For a moment, she brought her hands up to her face, and then let them fall to her lap.

"Please continue," the queen requested. "There have been no reports from any of the garrisons of any army sightings other than our own. How did they get to the hall?"

The conscript did not reply, but he continued to sob. The queen was bewildered by his tale and found herself unable to speak. The conscript archer finally calmed down. His eyes were red and irritated, but there were no more tears.

Turning away form her desk, the queen sauntered to the window. "You may leave me now, I have much to think about," she said softly.

The archer obeyed, rose to his feet, and left the room closing the door behind him.

Queen Krendale sat alone at her desk. Could the conscript have misinterpreted what he saw? No doubt, such devastation as he described could cause a man to become hysterical and confused. She rushed to the door of her quarters and opened it. The two guards on duty stood on guard at both sides of the door.

Queen Krendale turned to the guard on the right. "Bring me Field Marshall Devordes at once," she ordered.

The guard left his post as instructed and walked down the hall and disappeared down the stairwell. The queen returned to her desk. She waited helplessly, biting savagely at her finger nails. Terror had posted an encampment of mystification and horror in her heart. Mystasia had not been at war with any country in three decades. Who would have reason to invade the country now?

Suddenly, a strong breeze extinguished the three flames of the candelabra. Unexpectedly a prisoner in darkness, the queen rushed to the door of her quarters. Then, suddenly, a series of screams arose from the outer-ward of the castle. There was a faint flash, and her room was filled with a red aura of light. She rushed to the window to see the reason for the glow. In the center of the outer-ward was a portal. Its frame flickered with a strange crimson radiance that moved like fingers of flame, and a single figure stepped out of the portal. It was a serpentine figure with snakes on its head instead of hair. Just outside the castle gatehouse, a great wall of azure flames appeared.

The queen watched as her forces gathered and proceeded to attack the figure, but it was safety centered within a square of more blue flames preventing them from reaching its sinister form. The great wall of azure flames began to rush towards the castle gatehouse. She watched in terror as the gate house appeared to transform into ice. The guard in the gate house froze still as well. As the azure flames made physical contact with the gate house, it shattered into pieces, and then melted into nothing. The outlandish fire was strange mix of contradictions. It was both hot and cold. Its approach froze everything within ten meters until the flames melted whatever it touched into nothing.

Queen Krendale's heart began to pound as she realized she was trapped inside her own castle. She rushed to the door and opened it. Light from the torches that lined the corridor flooded her room. Field Marshall Devordes was at the end of the corridor accompanied by the guard she dispatched to get him. Then, from behind her, came a thud. Queen Krendale turned around and found the guard posted outside her door lying on the ground. His blood drained from his body onto the floor and rolled towards the queen's feet. Taskica stood over the body holding a long sword.

Queen Krendale turned to run, but Taskica raised her unarmed hand. A wall of stone separated the queen from everyone else. She was forced to face Taskica.

"Who are you?" The Queen demanded.

"Your past has come to haunt you, Mordana," Taskica said coldly. Taskica reached into a pocket of her dark cloak and pulled out an acorn. She threw it at the queen's feet. Queen Krendale turned and raised her hands in an attempt to shield herself, but was engulfed in green flames. Queen Krendale screamed waving her arms frantically as the flames chewed away at her flesh with intense, wicked heat greater than that of a regular fire. The pain was unbearable, but it only took seconds for the flames to kill her. A blackened skeleton was all that remained of the queen. With a gesture from Taskica's hand, the stone wall collapsed and fell onto her skeleton crushing it.

A second wall of azure flames was crawling towards the fortress from the opposite side of the first wall. Both walls moved towards the other forbidding escape from anyone inside Quartz Wall Fortress. The strange biting cold of the fire slowed their efforts to find escape. Within seconds, the soldiers still outside the castle turned into statues of ice. Vygoulia folded her arms and chuckled madly, clearly amused by their helplessness. The hag erupted in an uncontrollable fit of laughter as she witnessed their terrifying deaths.

Moments later, from the clear sky, Jherlom arrived. As he approached the fortress, he immediately noticed the colossal walls of blue flame close in on all sides of the castle preventing escape. He cursed himself for being too late. The blue flames were bright like any other fire. Although it gave off heat, this fire was somehow different. It had the ability to freeze anything close to it. Jherlom watched horrified as the fortress walls crackled in numerous places, and then shattered into pieces.

Utopia continued to circle above the disordered castle as Jherlom watched helplessly. Jherlom softly stroked the neck of the wyvern. Shaking his head in disbelief, he whispered, "Take me back to the prince, Utopia. We are too late! The queen is dead!"

Although it was possible for her to still be alive, there was nothing he could do to help her. Yet how could he leave and allow her death to occur when she might still be alive? Jherlom was seized with guilt, which filled him with agonizing regret. He had never felt so guilty in his six hundred and forty three years of life. The power of the strange magical fire below was much more superior than his own powers.

Utopia began to fly south. Jherlom never looked back at Quartz Wall Fortress. He would never forgive himself for his crime of leaving the queen and the citizens of Royal Amon to die. His helplessness was no excuse.

CHAPTER V

Invisible Death

WHEN ABADON AWOKE from his shallow sleep, thousands of brilliant stars bejewelled the sky, and the air was crisper than it had been earlier. The campfire had died while he slept. Shaurhez was almost directly over the camp, its blue moonlight overpowering the light of the other two moons, and set a dark purple hue upon the camp, reminding Abadon of Jherlom's cloak. An uneasiness rose within him as he gazed at the moons. He could hear three wolves rustling about somewhere in front of him in the darkness. The wolf at his side growled. Abadon unfolded his arms and sat upright. The wolf growled again, and Abadon realized it was the wolf that had awakened him. Slowly and silently, he got to his feet and readied himself to cast a sudden spell. Crawling towards Gathus, he heard the rest of the wolves growling as well.

"Gathus," Abadon whispered, immediately wanting to suck the word back in once it had left his mouth. Whatever was out there could hear him. He listened carefully, but the wolves produced the only noise, and there was no attack.

"Gathus," Abadon whispered again, risking detection. A suspicious silence was the only reply. Abadon found the trow sleeping just the way he had been before he had fallen asleep himself. Searching for any clue of danger, he scanned the darkness around them, but he found none. Only the wolves'

39

uneasiness warned him of danger, and that it was near.

There was no longer any wind, and no night birds chirped; there was only a solid silence that rang in his ears. Abadon struggled to adjust his eyes to the darkness. A weak image of what appeared to be a human moved in front of him, but what seemed real could just as easily be a deception created by the night.

Abadon slowly turned to face the wolf closest to him, and something landed on the ground next to him. He saw nothing, but he heard the crunch of the leaves that littered the forest ground. Searching for whatever it was, Abadon stumbled and fell right on top of Gathus, who woke screaming at the sudden disturbance of his sleep.

Hastily scrambling to his feet, Abadon bellowed, "Watch yourself! Something is here!" Fearful and confused, they scanned the area.

"Gathus, can you detect any intruders?" Abadon whispered hoarsely.

"I detect only the two of us, My Lord; the wolves are too small to detect," Gathus said, failing to hide his fear. His voice was thick with it. Abadon searched for the four wolves. All of them remained only a few feet away from him.

"That's impossible, Gathus! Something just attacked me!"

Again, a thud sounded next to Abadon, and again there was no one there. Then came a shriek from the sky, and, a moment later, Utopia landed next to Abadon and Gathus, and Jherlom slid off the wyvern's back.

"Someone is here, Jherlom!" Abadon cried. "I

keep hearing noises, and the wolves are growling."

Jherlom scanned the woods around them. "I don't see anyone, My Lord, and my night vision is better than yours."

Abadon suddenly remembered the ring. He caressed it with his finger, and the realization suddenly penetrated the fog of his mind. The ring caused displacement: no one could determine his true location.

"There is someone here, and I think, whoever he is, he is invisible," Abadon exclaimed, aghast.

The three circled around each other waiting for evidence that Abadon was correct.

"That would explain why I cannot detect anyone other than us," Gathus explained. "I cannot detect anything that is invisible."

"Not even if they are human?" Abadon gasped.

"Not even then, your highness," Gathus groaned in reply.

At Jherlom's inaudible command, the wolves surrounded Abadon. Abadon exercised his magic, and a blade of ginger flame formed in his right hand. It flashed fiercely, but its roar was barely perceptible.

"The wolves have a greater sense of where the intruder is than we do. Watch the wolves!" Jherlom ordered.

Abadon and Gathus did not reply, but did as the druid instructed. Moments later, the intruder attempted another assault and again missed Abadon. Jherlom released a large stream of fairy fire in the direction of the thud, and they heard a brief cry. The bright blue flames continued to spew from Jherlom's narrow fingers, then ceased. Abadon held his mace in his hand tightly waiting for another attack. Long moments passed, and there were no additional attacks. Satisfied that the intruder had left the area, Jherlom turned his attention to Abadon. "I believe he is gone, Abadon. I think my fairy fire injured him, but he will be back. I think it was an assassin sent to seek you out and destroy you."

"What about my mother?" Abadon said.

Jherlom did not reply immediately, but he could not avoid the question forever. "I was too late, your highness. Quartzwall Fortress was already under attack when I arrived. I could not help them." The feelings of regret and guilt returned to Jherlom, and he turned away from Abadon.

Tears welled up in the young prince's eyes. "But why?" was all he could say.

Jherlom shrugged, "I don't know, but I suspect that you will be the next target. We must leave here immediately." He turned to Utopia and began to whisper to the wyvern in a magical dialogue that neither Abadon nor Gathus could understand. The wyvern soared high into the air a short moment later, and Jherlom turned to his companions once more. "We all have to get as far away from here as possible. Follow me; I have a place in mind."

The two followed Jherlom down the road towards the town of Risamol. Jherlom dismissed the wolves, and they returned to the forest. Meanwhile, Abadon was busy formulating more questions about his family's attacker.

"What puzzles me, Jherlom, is how the assassin found us without a campfire lit."

Jherlom shook his head and muttered, disgruntled, "I am also at a loss to understand how you were so easily found, Your Highness."

"What about the rest of the nobles, Jherlom?" Abadon asked, concerned. "Have any of them been attacked?"

Jherlom shook his head. "Not to my knowledge, Abadon, but the entire country will soon learn what happened here today. With your parents gone, Lord Pureheart now possesses the highest noble rank. She may be the next target, and then you!"

Gathus snorted, "Other than being able to detect things, I'm afraid that I am of no use to either of you."

Jherlom whispered into Gathus' ear, "You are wrong, my little friend. You may lack combat skills, and you may not be very big. You do, however, possess a very important power – your ability to detect. In time, you can become more powerful than someone who wields a weapon. The power of detection should never be underestimated!"

Jherlom began to lead Abadon and Gathus away from the road and into the woodland of Jade Coin Forest. For a couple of hours they walked swiftly and without resting until Jherlom decided to stop.

"There will be no campfire," Jherlom informed them. Abadon and Gathus did not protest. Only a short time passed before they drifted off to sleep. Jherlom wandered a brief distance into the woods. He found what he was looking for almost immediately – a cold, stony brook. He drank greedily and then refilled his water skin.

Jherlom returned to the camp, where he rested against a large oak, gazing up at the stars. The purple moonlight was fading, and the eastern skies were slowly beginning to brighten with the birth of a new day. Jherlom closed his eyes and drifted off into shallow sleep as well.

Abadon slowly raised himself from his meagre, uncomfortable bed of moss.

Jherlom and Gathus were gone. Fear clutched at his heart. He was completely alone in the woods, three hundred feet away from the road. Suddenly, an unseen hand gripped his throat. Its enormous strength kept Abadon from removing it, even using both of his own hands. Abadon tried to scream for help, but the tight grip of the hand blocked his airway. He struggled to breathe, squirming desperately, like a snake caught in the jaws of a crocodile. Something long and cold pierced his chest, then retreated. Pain shot through his body like an electric current. The weapon struck his chest with another sharp jab, then another, and another. Blood was everywhere.

Screaming, Abadon tried to jump to his feet, then paused when he found himself staring at Jherlom, several feet away. He could hear Gathus breathing next to him, and the druid awoke at Abadon's cry.

"It's okay, Abadon. You just had a nightmare," Jherlom comforted him.

"Try to go back to sleep."

The young prince glanced around. The darkness of the night seemed to be crawling away from him slowly, much like a slug lost in the spring rain. A flood of sunshine melted the immense canopy of night. Realizing suddenly that it had been just a nightmare, and that Jherlom was still with him after all, Abadon laid himself back down on his moss bed. The stars were now barely visible, and the night no longer seemed endless and impenetrable. Abadon closed his eyes. His heart was still pounding from the illusory attack he had endured. He thought of his parents, and his heartbeat slowed. A smile brightened his face as images of his parents continued to appear in his mind's eye. Still drugged with sleep, Abadon then forced himself to his feet.

Jherlom was studying the forest around him. He extended his arm and allowed a butterfly, stained pink and purple, to perch on his crooked index finger for a moment.

"Jherlom, you have to tell me the truth," Abadon said as he slowly approached the druid. "How do we defeat an invisible enemy?"

Jherlom lifted his finger, and the butterfly disappeared back into the woods.

"I may be more than six hundred years old, My Lord, but even those who are my age do not have answers for everything. As long as you wear the Obsidian Oracle on your finger, you will not be harmed. Unless, of course, the assassin figures out why he cannot strike you and makes a lucky guess as to where you are actually standing."

Moving his index finger back and forth, Abadon rubbed the ring. "But he won't stop until I'm dead," he muttered.

Jherlom sauntered slowly over to the sleeping body of Gathus, and nudged him with his foot. "We will find a way to destroy this assassin, Abadon. Allow me some time to figure out a way. I myself have never had something invisible threaten my life, so I do not have any suggestions to offer you."

Gathus moaned as Jherlom nudged him once again with a gentle touch of his soft leather boots and rolled onto his back.

"Daylight already," the trow complained. "It can't be."

Jherlom said, with a soft chuckle, "You're so tired, Gathus, you would have slept through a typhoon created by the goddess of air herself."

Abadon offered his hand to Gathus, who accepted it, and Abadon pulled him up to his feet. Gathus rubbed his eyes with his small fists.

"How far is Skull Moat Castle from here, Jherlom?" the trow inquired groggily.

"At least three days travel on foot, I'm afraid," Jherlom retorted.

Abadon looked around the area and sighed. "We need food, Jherlom. Do you know where we might get any?"

"The Diamond Cluster River is about three miles east from here. A part of the river branches off into a deep pool. There are shallow areas, where fish can be easily caught." Jherlom turned to them. "Would that suffice?"

"Yes, Jherlom, that would be great," Abadon replied.

Jherlom began to lead them deeper into the woods and farther from any of the roads. A thick blanket of dead leaves kept the forest floor hidden. The forest was cold and slightly damp from the thick layer of mist that drifted in the air and clung to the tree trunks. It grabbed onto their clothing as well, and the autumn air bit even more viciously into their skin.

As promised, the pool branching off from Diamond Cluster River provided a frenzy of fish, leaping out of the water in pursuit of flies. Clustered in a few areas of the calm pool were leaves, propelled there by the current of the river.

Abadon crouched down and cupped his hands together. He dipped them into the pool, flinching from the icy touch of the water. He brought some up to his mouth and drank. The water was far colder than the air, and he decided not to drink more.

Jherlom crouched next to Abadon and lowered the opened water skin into the pool. Water flowed in, and Jherlom passed the skin to Gathus, who drank from it greedily.

Abadon stood up and watched the water flow in from the river and into the large pool. "Where do you recommend we fish, Jherlom?" Abadon asked, the chilly air stinging his wet hands.

Jherlom pointed towards the shallows that dropped suddenly into deeper water.

"There, but you don't have the equipment necessary to catch them, Your Highness."

"Then how do we get them?" Abadon asked impatiently. He had disturbing visions of starvation.

"Magic," Jherlom said, leisurely strolling to Abadon's side. He made a couple of strange gestures, extending his hands towards the pool. Jherlom dropped his arms to his side and watched. A few seconds later, the water churned. Resembling an angry liquid trapped inside of a cauldron, the pool began to bubble. The stony and sandy bottom of the pool was lifted above the water, and a short moment later, inside the original pool, a smaller pool was formed inside a ring of rocks and sand.

Jherlom smiled as the trapped fish flipped helplessly in water only a few inches deep.

"Fetch the fish, My Lord," Jherlom said, grinning. "In a few minutes, I will return the pool to its usual shape."

Abadon and Gathus rushed forward and scooped up as many fish as they could. Gathus found a tree branch to serve as a solid club, and they clubbed ten fish of various sizes. Gathus carried them in his arms, and Abadon exercised his own magic, creating a campfire. He fed the fire with pieces of wood Gathus fetched from the nearby woods. Abadon inserted small, wooden spears into the center of the fish, which he had carved from small branches, using a dagger Gathus provided. The fish began to cook, and Jherlom finished restoring the pool to its natural form.

"Thank you, Jherlom," Abadon said as the druid passed by him. "Do you want any?"

Jherlom shook his head. "No, thank you, My Lord, I usually eat vegetation, and only occasionally fish. I will pass for now."

Abadon shrugged; he did not believe that Jherlom was not hungry. When the fish had finished roasting over the campfire, Abadon and Gathus dined on them, hastily – they were ravenous. Jherlom watched them with a grin on his face. He thought they looked like ravens pecking away at a dead animal. The druid glanced up at the sky to observe the position of the sun. It was far past its zenith and already descending towards the western horizon.

"We will camp here tonight," Jherlom announced, slightly disappointed. "To waste a day that could have been spent in travel normally irritates me, but you both needed rest." He was unsure if his hungry companions even heard him.

The slight breeze occasionally shifted into a strong gust of wind, and then took a short recess before ripping several more leaves from the branches of the trees surrounding the stony and sandy area where the water did not flow. Before long, night spilled across the sky. It was so thickly overcast that the moons and stars disappeared only an hour after the sunset. A few winking stars peeked through and sparkled like little diamonds studded on black leather, like on the armour he had worn on his first hunting trip with his father. The autumn chill grew stronger, and the breath of the wind steadied at the strength of a light gale.

Abadon and Gathus huddled together around the flickering fire. Jherlom leaned against a cedar tree several feet away from them. Utopia returned and landed next to the druid, who welcomed him warmly. He listened as Abadon and Gathus shared some of their childhood stories. The three of them would be safe here. The assassin would not find them so far from the roads. They were at the mercy of the wilderness and nature now, two companions Jherlom knew all too well. The campfire burned brightly, and somewhere in the darkness beyond its light, the river roared as it carried its possessions to the east. Jherlom closed his eyes. The sounds of the wilderness filled his ears, and he drifted off to sleep.

CHAPTER VI

Unexpected Enemy

THE CRIMSON SUN SOON CHASED the three moons away and flooded the skies with sunshine. Clusters of white clouds scattered across the blue sheet of sky as the party of three readied themselves for travel.

Abadon crouched next to a pool that had offered them fish the previous day. He gazed at his reflection in the undisturbed water, staring at his dark curly hair, which was very much like his father's. The rest of his face belonged to him and him alone. There was no physical resemblance between him and his mother. Abadon also stared at his birth mark. It looked much like a strange symbol on the right side of his neck. Neither of his parents had a birth mark as strange as his. As he gazed into his own eyes, the mirror of water rippled, and his image was spoiled as Jherlom refilled the water skin.

Jherlom returned to the cedar tree that supported him during his sleep the previous night. He grabbed a rock from the ground next to the tree and walked over to Utopia.

As the druid passed Abadon, he could see that there was something etched into the stone.

Jherlom stroked Utopia's long neck. "Take this message to Duchess Pureheart. Be sure that she gets it."

Acknowledging the druid, the wyvern lifted his right leg and opened his clawed foot. Jherlom placed the stone inside it, and the enormous winged beast took flight and soared to the northeast.

Jherlom watched Utopia until he disappeared into the clouds. "That message will allow Riannon to know that you are with me, Abadon."

"So what do we do now?" Abadon asked.

Jherlom pointed his crooked index finger to the southeast. "We travel to Lord Pureheart, to Skull Moat Castle. I cannot think of a safer place to be at this time. I do not believe it is safe to use the boats at the Slipper Fin Shipyard to cross Temple Lake. It is very possible that enemy forces have taken control of the shipyard, in hopes that you or another noble lord will risk crossing there. It is best to continue off road through the forest until we reach The Blind River. There is a shallow area in the river that will allow us to cross without using a bridge."

Jherlom led Abadon and Gathus northwest through the Frost Eagle Forest, until they finally reached the river known as Holy Oak Wash.

Abadon began to ponder the situation, and a concern formed within his mind.

"Jherlom," Abadon began. "Won't Duchess Pureheart be a target? With my parents dead, she has just as much right to the throne as I do."

Jherlom gave the words of the prince some quick thought and nodded. "Yes. However, Skull Moat Castle is located about ten thousand feet up in the Ice Crown Mountains and is nearly impossible to reach. It was deliberately built there, and unlike most castles, it has no city within its walls. This is why most of her army is stationed at a garrison a short distance inside one of the mountains."

Abadon remained silent for a moment. "History speaks of Skull Moat Castle once belonging to the undead. It was not originally a Mystasian stronghold."

"You speak of the undead army that was led by the first death knight ever to exist. His name was Morgg Bloodskull. He was once a paladin named Okenn Halflight. Morgg had the castle built. The castle that belonged to the Pureheart family was destroyed by the undead army. It was once located somewhere in the Jade Coin Forest, only a couple miles away from the town of Risamol. Most of Pureheart's forces were killed during the first siege against Skull Moat, which was called The Stronghold of Skulls back then. The corpses were resurrected into an army nearly doubling the size of Bloodskull's forces. Eventually, a second siege against the castle was successful, and the Pureheart family defeated Bloodskull and reformed the castle, calling it Skull Moat. Stryll Pureheart decided to use the skeletal remains as a warning to future armies attempting a siege against the castle."

Above the tree line, they could see the Jewelfang Dragon Mountains to the west. The highest peaks were shrouded in clouds. Abadon looked up at the sky, gazing past the multi-colored leaves of the trees. Images of the river entered his mind. The river would be jammed with red, brown and orange leaves. The trees in the forest were half-naked, reminding Abadon that winter was less than two months away. The air was warmer than yesterday, but it still had a crisp to it that warned of cold nights to come. The proximity of the mountains only amplified the chill. Abadon noticed that the forest animals were less lively. They were preparing for their winter sleep.

There was no path, but Jherlom led them with confidence. He appeared to know exactly where he was going. Nevertheless, Gathus asked apprehensively, "Jherlom, are you sure you know where you are going?"

"I am a druid, Gathus," Jherlom replied. "Of course I know where I am going. Druids never get lost in the wilderness. Our relationship with nature and its children is both natural and magical, and religious in its own way as well."

Several butterflies hovered around the wood elf as he paused quickly to examine their surroundings and calculate the distance left to the mountain passage. Many of them clung to his green robe, and he whispered to them softly, speaking words that neither Abadon or Gathus could understand. Then Jherlom appeared to notice something, and he gently touched the wings of one of the butterflies.

"What's the matter, Jherlom?" Abadon asked.

"One of the butterflies had a broken wing, and I healed it," the druid answered, watching it detach from his green robe and return to the air.

Gathus giggled. "Being a druid must be exhausting, looking out for the well-being of animals, insects, and the gods know what else."

"Perhaps that is why there are many of us in the country," Jherlom said with a weak smile. "Elves in general are always looking out for the well-being of others. Druids enforce peace and good will between humanity and nature. That, of course, includes animals, and even insects."

"But why are insects so important?" Gathus asked. "Especially wasps and locusts. All they do is sting and destroy crops."

"Even the smallest of creatures have importance in the circle of life. They serve a purpose to nature far greater than most know."

Abadon considered Jherlom's words carefully, and related them to a king and his relationship with his people. Without lower-class people, the country would be dysfunctional. Abadon was suddenly seized with an overwhelming storm of emotions and panicked within himself, as he realized that he would now have to be king.

"I can't believe the fate of Mystasia rests in my hands," Abadon blurted, sharing his thoughts.

The butterflies floated away from Jherlom as he turned to face Abadon. Abadon studied Jherlom's elvish features. His green eyes always seemed to be searching for something within his own.

"You will probably find that your skills as a cleric will help you succeed as king, Abadon. You must also have an open mind to everything, to see everything."

"But how will I know what decisions to make? How will I know a good decision from a bad one?"

"You will know in time, Abadon," Jherlom retorted. "Lord Pureheart will be much more useful explaining such things to you. I am not a noble lord, I am just wise."

Abadon nearly tripped on a rock. He'd noticed that Jherlom never seemed to trip over a branch or rock, or any other obstacle the forest presented to them. It was as if he knew the woods better than he knew himself. It seemed almost as if he knew exactly where every tree and rock stood.

"I am glad that I have you at my side, Jherlom," Abadon said suddenly. "I am glad that you are my godfather."

"That was the proudest moment of my life, Abadon," Jherlom said, smiling. "My proudest moment of all was the day your father asked me to be your godfather."

Gathus realized he was trailing behind the others and ran to catch up. "Even greater than the day you became a druid?" Gathus inquired.

"Definitely," Jherlom retorted smugly. "Although that was a great day as well."

"Where are your parents, Jherlom?" Abadon asked. "I have never heard you speak of them."

Jherlom seemed bothered by the question. "There is little to speak of, Abadon. They are both in the Moat prison of Xhanduraz."

"Xhanduraz?" Abadon exclaimed. "That is the one prison in Mystasia where escape is impossible by any means. It is also where they send the most dangerous of criminals. I did not mean to offend you asking you that question, Jherlom."

"Of course you didn't," Jherlom said, knowing well that Abadon meant no offense.

"I am afraid that my ancestors and my family line are not as great as yours," Jherlom said with a sigh. I was the first to break the birthright of my family line, which has been passed down for many generations."

"What birthright, Jherlom?" Gathus asked with great curiosity. Abadon could see that the topic pained Jherlom, but the trow's curiosity was always strong. It was so strong that the trow always failed to notice when such questions should not be asked. With a sigh, Jherlom decided to share his dark secret.

"I am not entirely a wood elf," the druid began. "My great grandfather was a blood elf. Their traits are powerful, and even now this many generations later, their savage blood burns in my veins. Blood elves are not from Mystasia, but my great grandfather came here to start a new life. He met my grandmother, who was a wood elf.

"My great grandfather brought his family's tradition with him when he came here. He arrived in Mystasia nearly twenty eight hundred years ago. I believe it was the year 1476 BG. Blood elves came from a country known as Ormtinia, a place mostly comprised of tropical rain forests. The Blood Talon Rouge Clan was started there. It was a criminal clan that included several races. The Mor'Derums were one elf family that developed a birthright that guaranteed their kin a place within the clan, which controlled much of the Ormtinian society. While some of the clan duties included theft, one of the duties was also assassination.

"The clan here in Mystasia was destroyed in the years leading up to the War of the Gods. Some members survived, including my parents, who began a new clan. When the time came for me to join the clan, I refused. I turned to the druids for a new home and a new way of life. I entered the druid guild and disclosed the location of the Blood Talon Clan Guild to the Mystasian King in the early 700s. The alliance between the races had already been formed by then, and King Polgra Awgar, a dwarf, was the king in those days. It was King Polga Awgar that sent an army to destroy the Blood Talon Rogue Clan. A very resourceful bounty hunter captured my parents and brought them to justice."

"I am sorry," Abadon said sadly upon hearing Jherlom's tale.

"Don't be," Jherlom insisted. "I see these current times as an opportunity to be a greater father to you than my father was to me…"

Jherlom's voice trailed off. He was starring into the woods behind Abadon. Abadon and Gathus stopped as well, and searched the forest for the danger they knew Jherlom sensed was there.

"What is it, Jherlom?" Abadon cried.

"Silence," Jherlom hissed, and then listened very carefully. "Something is wrong. We are being followed. I can sense it in the air and by the way the animals are behaving. They are timid and acting cowardly. I will be back shortly."

Jherlom then proceeded to transform his elven body. His elvish features changed, and his slender body shrunk. It only took ten seconds for the transformation to be complete. Jherlom was now a blood hawk.

"Wait here. I will be back," Jherlom ordered as he took flight and flew past the nearest treetops.

Abadon and Gathus waited apprehensively. They realized suddenly that the forest animals had stopped making their usual noises.

Abadon turned to Gathus. "Do you detect anything?"

Gathus closed his eyes and concentrated. "I can detect a few things scattered throughout the forest, but I think they are just deer. Most of them are not moving."

Abadon struggled to control his fear, and took a deep breath.

"Wait!" Gathus cried out. "I do detect something. There is a large group of beings, perhaps twenty strong, five miles away from the northeast!"

"Can you tell who they are?" Abadon asked desperately.

"No, your highness, I can't actually see them. I can only detect their presence, and they are traveling fast!"

Helplessly, Abadon searched the forest hoping for a clue to their identity. If only Gathus could identify them as allies, enemies or a herd of animals.

Gathus frowned. "Your highness, I am detecting another group coming from the north!"

Abadon's heart pounded with intense fear. He swore he could feel just as much fear pumping through his veins as he did blood.

Then Jherlom returned. He landed next to his two frightened companions and resumed his natural elf form. "We have a problem," he informed them. "We have an army of nearly two dozen comprised of orcs, frost fang nagas, four ettins and two medusas coming this way."

Gathus shrieked, "Jherlom, we have another group coming from the north!"

Jherlom cracked a weak smile. "That is a Mystasian army. Quick, run north! If we can reach that army, they can fend off the one in pursuit of us."

The three began to run through the forest toward The Blind River. Gathus, with his short legs, tripped a couple of times, but Abadon and Jherlom quickly helped him to his feet.

"Run! Do not stop. Run!" Jherlom barked at them. After a while, the trow's short supply of stamina forced the others to stop as well.

"But Jherlom," Abadon cried, "How do you know that the group from the north is a Mystasian army?"

"Duchess Pureheart has a small army posted at a garrison in the area that Gathus detected life forces."

Jherlom turned to the diviner. "How far away are the armies now?"

Gathus was leaning against a tree, trying to catch his breath. "The one from the north is two miles away, and the one from the south is four miles away."

Jherlom nodded his head. "We are safe now. The army from the north will get to us before the south army does."

Abadon and Gathus took the time to rest against a large boulder. The Blind River was only eight feet away from them, and about fifty feet down. Little time passed before the army from the north reached them. Twenty-five Mystasian soldiers gathered at the nearest trees, stopping at the small clearing where they found the three travelers. A twenty-sixth soldier entered the small clearing and passed the others. He removed his mytril helmet to identify himself.

"Captain Tor'Albus," Jherlom exclaimed, recognizing the elf at once. I am so glad to see you. There is an army on its way from the south. I think they are after the prince."

Captain Tor'Albus' expression did not change. Jherlom's news of the south army did not appear to surprise him.

"Worry not, Jherlom," the captain replied plainly. "They will not harm you. You have much greater problems on your hands."

Jherlom's eyebrows shot up, and a look of profound confusion appeared on his face. "What are you talking about, captain? What other problems are there?"

Captain Tor'Albus pulled a long sword out of its sheath and pointed it at Jherlom. "Surrender the prince to me now, Jherlom. Do that, and you and the trow will be allowed to walk away from here. I will have the southern army turn back."

Jherlom looked over at the soldiers. He realized suddenly that they were not Mystasian. They were orcs dressed in Mystasian armor. Undoubtedly, they had slain all the soldiers at the nearest garrison and taken their armor.

With one hand behind his back, Jherlom motioned Abadon and Gathus to back away toward the river. They took two steps back and turned around to find that the river's edge was almost directly behind their heels. The river was far enough down that the drop might cause their deaths.

"What in Ninantu's name are you doing with orcs, Tor'Albus? I will do no such thing," Jherlom snarled.

"Then you will die, druid!" Captain Tor'Albus turned to the soldiers. "Kill them all, except the prince. Take him alive."

The soldiers charged forward without hesitation, but Abadon and Gathus had already leaped into The Blind River. It was a long fall, and the river's current was strong. Abadon plummeted into the river first, and Gathus landed right behind him seconds later. The Blind River began to carry them southeast.

Captain Tor'Albus swung his long sword at Jherlom, but the druid was already shape shifting back into a blood hawk, causing the blade to miss him. He soared into the air and flew into the forest. Tor'Albus stared down into the canyon and watched the river carry the prince and the trow south.

Abadon struggled to find something floating in the river to climb on to, but there was nothing. Its deep azure waters were cold as ice. Gathus was lighter in weight, and was now several feet in front of the prince. He was struggling even harder to stay afloat.

A moment later, Gathus disappeared beneath the rapid waters.

"Gathus!" Abadon screamed. He tried to search for the trow, but the river was too fast, too deep and too dark to see anything. Twice the river pulled him down beneath the surface. The murky water blurred his vision, and he suddenly rose to the surface again before the might of the river pulled him under once more. The bottom of the raging river was indiscernible as Abadon searched to see if the trow was below him somewhere. The depths pulled at him, and he looked up at the racing water as death rushed to take what little time he had left away from him.

Jherlom circled overhead in search of the prince. He made four circles, and Abadon failed to resurface. Believing Abadon had drowned, Jherlom let out a loud cry, and he flew to the west.

A moment later, the river's current forced Abadon back to the surface, where he snatched a quick breath of air. He was only seconds away from passing out. The current bullied him along with its rapid force, making him bob up and down like a fisherman's float. At last, Abadon was able to grasp a branch of a tree partially in the river. For a moment, it kept the river from sweeping him further downstream. But then, the strength of the river broke the branch, and Abadon was sent hurtling once again.

Abadon felt some relief. He now had a float which would keep him from sinking any further. Once he had a secure hold of the branch, he searched the river for Gathus, scanning the waters around him. Gathus was gone. Exhausted, Abadon slammed his head down onto the large branch and allowed the river to carry him away, whereever it would take him.

CHAPTER VII
Guide to Nordach

THE SUN WAS ALREADY touching the Mongbat Mountains to the southeast, causing a bright orange, fiery glow. The river waters were finally calm enough for Abadon to swim to the steep, muddy banks. He let go of the branch that kept him from drowning. Using a large root from a nearby tree, he began to pull himself out of the river.

He sauntered aimlessly into the forest. The canyon he'd leapt into the river from was an unknown amount of miles behind him. He studied the forest, but there were no clues to indicate exactly where he was. Swampskin birch, green willows and scale bark cedars made up the majority of the forest trees. The forest floor itself displayed some moss, diamond moon flowers and dart petal roses.

Abadon looked to the bulky mountains to the southeast. It was then that he realized where he was. Terrible fright and an icy chill all struck his heart and soul at the same time. He was in the Jade Coin Forest, not far from the Mongbat Mountains. Worse than that, he was near the border of The Haunted Forest.

He found himself looking up at the sky and high up in the trees for any hint of his friends' presence, but he saw nothing to indicate that any were around. He laid himself down on his back, breathing heavily, trying to gather his thoughts. The chill of the autumn night and his wet clothing worked together to create a greater chill. Hypothermia was already setting into his body. The cold was unbearable, and there was no escape from it. He wrapped his arms around his upper body and hunched over next to a green willow.

Alone, cold, frightened and defenseless, Abadon began to weep softly. So much had happened over the past couple of days, he had not had a chance to mourn the death of his parents. With that heavy sorrow weighing on his mind, he wept even more. The autumn air dried his tears quickly, and the chilly air caused them to feel like tears of molten fire.

Some time passed before Abadon forced himself to stand. He began to walk without direction into the forest. It was relatively flat, with gentle slopes and fallen logs scattered about. Soon he could no longer hear the rushing water of the river, and the forest began to look the same in every direction. He began to recall tales his father told him of the gargoyles. He was warned during childhood that if he wandered too far into the Jade Coin Forest, the gargoyles would take him and make a slave out of him. He would never see home again, and if he worked poorly, they would make a meal out of him.

Exhausted and aggravated with his lack of success navigating the forest, Abadon dropped to his knees and rolled over onto his back. Part of him wanted the gargoyles to discover him. They would bring him a quicker death than the eventual one that hypothermia promised him. He began to wonder how he would survive on his own. He had never been on his own, and he quickly realized that he would probably die overnight.

There was no doubt in his mind that hypothermia would claim him. He felt as though he was dressed in armor crafted out of ice. Even if he survived the night, how could he keep going on his own? He did not have the wisdom Jherlom possessed, especially knowledge in forest lore. He did not have sufficient skills in combat, like the impressive skills Sir Braveblood possessed.

Abadon looked around at his surroundings, and then he realized he did have a great knowledge. His greatest skill was that of healing, particularly with the use of herbs. The forests of Mystasia were all treasuries of remedies that he knew more about than almost all the other clerics of Ku'Lee.

He closed his eyes. He was too numb to think anymore. The cold had beaten him. It was only a matter of hours before death came to him.

A moment later, Abadon felt something wet touch his cheek. He opened up his eyes and found a nyhor face to face with him. Screaming suddenly, alarmed by the large frog-like creature's sudden appearance, Abadon sat upright and backed up against the closest tree. The nyhor gazed at him with both of its large magenta eyes. Its smooth black and green skin glistened in the small fraction of light still left in the sky. The nyhor leaped toward him, twice exposing its large human-like tongue, which came out of its mouth between two fangs that grew from its bottom jaw.

He reached for his pocket, but realized his dagger was missing. He quickly snatched a large branch from the ground and waited for the nyhor to attack him.

A voice suddenly spoke from behind a tree somewhere to his left. "I hope you don't plan on killing that nyhor, stranger."

Abadon turned to his left, startled to find another man in the forest with him.

The man stepped out from behind the green willow tree. He was very muscular, and dressed scantily in quilted armor. He had an oblong face with a broad jaw, and pine-green, almond shaped eyes. His hair was mahogany and shaggy, with some black streaks. His moustache and beard were untidy, and his nose was curved and beak-like.

Trembling in fear, and fearing that he was showing it, Abadon demanded identification from the stranger, who was clearly human.

The man took one step closer to him. "My name is Gafnan Northchill. I am a beast master. The nyhor will not harm you, I promise. You can drop that branch and relax."

Hesitantly, Abadon obeyed and allowed the branch to slip from his hand. Rustling in the tree behind Gafnan stole Abadon's attention. He watched as something much larger than Gafnan approached him from behind. Whatever it was caused large branches to break under its heavy weight. From the trees emerged a saber bear, which was twice as tall as Gafnan and nearly twice as broad. Its silver fur was thick, but its greatest feature was its fangs. The top incisors were each easily over one foot long.

Abadon tried to warn the beast master, but he found himself unable to speak.

Gafnan smiled as the saber bear joined them, lowering itself onto all four legs.

"This is Sabre, a saber bear," he announced with pride.

Abadon stared at the large animal in awe. "Like druids, you have the ability to bond with animals of all kinds."

Gafnan corrected his comparison. "A druid's bond with animals is mostly magical. Mine is completely natural."

He walked toward Abadon until he was only a few feet away. "You look familiar to me. Who are you?"

Abadon studied the muscular human. He noticed a faint smell of dung, which did not surprise him. The man was filthy with dirt and apparently lived in the wilderness. Could he trust the beast master? Apparently, some of his own people were against him. Who could he trust? He decided that a delayed response may cause suspicion, so he blurted out the truth.

"I am Prince Krendale," Abadon announced, but then his throat muscles tightened. He already regretted making that statement.

"Prince Krendale?" The beast master looked him over from head to toe. "What are you doing here so far from the capital?" The intimidating voice of the large man was now a voice of compassion.

Abadon shrugged, realizing he didn't appear to be in any danger with Gafnan. He began to feel comfortable with the beast master. "You wouldn't believe me if I told you what has happened over the past couple of days." He looked around at the forest surrounding him. "Where is the closest town from here?

Gafnan folded his branch-like arms over his hairy chest. "We are about twelve miles west from a village known as Nordach, in the Obsidian Peaks Territory."

The beast master noticed that the prince was completely wet. He also recognized that hypothermia was well established within him. Abadon was no longer shivering. He was deep enough into hypothermia that he was numb to the winter wardrobe he was wearing.

"We need to get you some warmth, Prince Krendale," Gafnan recommended. "Very soon, you won't be able to walk."

"I need to keep hidden," Abadon insisted. "I need to avoid any civilization for now, even a settlement as small as a village."

"You're in luck," Gafnan said. "I know these woods better than I know myself. But trekking through these woods is difficult. There are many canyons and ravines. First we need to build a fire and get you warm, Prince Krendale," he insisted.

"A fire will attract attention," Abadon protested. "Someone invisible is searching for me, and even if they don't find me, the gargoyles will spot us."

"The gargoyles do not come down this far from their mountains," Gafnan informed him. "I have lived in these woods all my life, Prince Krendale. In all that time, I have seen exactly two rangers, one druid, and another beast master in Jade Coin Forest. No one comes here. They are too frightened of the gargoyles."

Abadon took a long moment to think, and then nodded. "Go ahead and build a fire.

Gafnan began collecting pieces of loose wood scattered about over fallen leaves and the plenty of green moss that grew there. There were large patches of mushrooms in the area. The blackness of the night swelled in the sky. Abadon sat down next to where Gafnan accumulated a pile of wood. He felt comfortable with the presence of the saber bear.

As Gafnan constructed the fire, he questioned the prince. "How did you come to be here in Jade Coin Forest?"

"I got separated from Jherlom Mor'Derum," Abadon explained. "I am hoping he'll track me down using communication with forest animals."

Gafnan paused for a moment. "Jherlom, yes, I know of him."

Abadon continued, "There are many in search for me, and if they find me, they will kill me. They already killed my parents two days ago."

Gafnan stopped what he was doing and turned to Abadon. "The king and queen are dead?"

"Yes, Gafnan," Abadon said, barely audible. "I guess as a beast master, you avoid civilization, and the news has not reached you yet."

"I have never been to a city," Gafnan informed him. "I have been to a village once or twice. I do not hear of such things in my travels."

"I need to risk going to Nordach," Abadon persisted. "From there I may be able to get word to Riannon that I am alive. I could also wait here in the forest until Jherlom or one of the other druids comes to get me."

"Traveling in these woods is dangerous for someone who doesn't know the terrain well," Gafnan explained. "This is especially true in the autumn, when all the snags, roots and tripping hazards are covered by the leaves."

Chill continued to set into Abadon's body. The fire was not yet warm enough to stop the hypothermia, and he cursed himself silently for leaping into The Blind River. Then he remembered the orcs that were dressed like Mystasian soldiers. He had no choice but to make that leap.

Nothing that had happened over the past few days made any sense. It would take plenty of time for Jherlom to find him, and Gathus had surely drowned in the river. Now he was alone with a stranger, who had yet to earn his full trust and confidence. Gafnan was a man who found life in the wilderness and apparently rejected city life. Yet the beast master did seem sympathetic to him and his troubles. He was not a commoner, and likely lived without following Mystasian laws, just like the ninjas of the flaming fist.

Once Gafnan disappeared into the darkness of the forest, but Abadon could hear him moving. Twice he heard a branch snap underneath his weight. Soon, the beast master returned with a fist full of grubs. He offered one to Abadon, who quickly shook his head, resisting.

Gafnan sat next to the fire and began to chew the grubs one at a time.

"How can you stand to eat something like that?" Abadon asked.

"As a beast master, I do not believe in eating meat, or killing mammals for food. In fact, I only eat meat when I come across an animal that has recently died."

Abadon's face went sour when he returned his gaze to the camp fire, which spewed cinders around its perimeter. Certain elements of Gafnan's personality reminded him of Jherlom. It was their passionate affection toward nature and its animals. The crackling fire continued to send smoke up Abadon's nostrils. Strangely enough, it relaxed him and offered him a sense of security. Abadon turned to Sabre, who was sleeping next to Gafnan. He realized suddenly that the nyhor was no longer in the area.

"Is Sabre your pet, Gafnan?" the young prince asked.

Gafnan answered with his usual rough, scratchy voice, "He is more of a companion of mine. A beast master has no pets, only friends of nature. There is a dire wolf that often travels with me, but she is caring for her young right now. You may notice a frost eagle with me from time to time. The nyhor you saw earlier travels with me often. Her name is Nerhion."

Before long, the three moons were visible. Rhosha was half a red orb in the black sky. Shalamar displayed itself as a waning gibbous, and Yubanen was a full moon. The mixture of moonlight created a strange, dark green hue of light beaming down upon them.

Gafnan finished the last of the grubs and relocated his weapon, which was a maul, next to Sabre. The large man then turned to the prince.

"You mentioned that someone invisible is after you. Who is it?"

"I don't know," Abadon replied. "I suspect that it is an assassin. I do not know how he makes himself invisible. I only know that whatever or whoever it is has been stalking me.

He nearly killed me last night, but Jherlom frightened him off."

"Jherlom is a powerful druid," Gafnan remarked.

"I was in the company of a diviner, but even he couldn't detect the invisible intruder," Abadon cried out, showing signs of stress.

"Perhaps you should get some sleep before we leave this area," Gafnan suggested.

"We have all the security we need with Sabre around."

Abadon silently nodded and laid his head down on the soft fur of the saber bear. The large bear didn't seem to mind. He ignored the prince and licked at his immense paws. They were both a few feet away from the fire, where the coals it spat out wouldn't reach him. Distant wolf howls, owl hoots and loon calls echoed through the forest, joined by the singing of crickets. Together they created a beautiful chorus of night song. The forest was peaceful. But the peacefulness didn't stay long. Eventually, Abadon's paranoia returned with great strength. The crackling fire sounded much like a cackle to his ears. In his mind, nature was warning him to leave the area immediately.

A moment later, Sabre began to growl. The crackling of a branch in the woods not far from them made Abadon take a deep breath and sit upright. Again, a crackling was heard, but it came from a different spot, and much closer.

"Gafnan, do you hear that?" Abadon whispered.

"Yes," Gafnan whispered back. "Look at Sabre, he's looking to the east."

Abadon peered at Sabre. The saber bear could sense the intruder as well, and pinpointed his general direction. A moment later, a family of rabbits hopped into the camp, and both Abadon and Gafnan gasped in relief. Abadon did not drop his guard. His right hand still clutched a large branch tightly, and he did not ease his defensive stance.

"What's the matter, prince?" Gafnan asked. "It's a family of rabbits."

"He's out there somewhere, Gafnan." Abadon spoke bitterly, staring to the east. "He's nearby. I can feel it."

The prince slowly turned to Gafnan. His face was hard, and his throat tightened as though he was about to snivel. "He found me once before, Gafnan, and he'll find me again. He found me in the woods, far from any roads and any hamlets. He seems to know where I am and where to find me!"

Gafnan found Abadon's strange, upsetting behavior unsettling. "Prince Krendale, I tell you, no one ever comes into these woods. You are safe in this area," he said sincerely. "The river carried you many miles downstream. Even if they know where you are, it'll take them time to get here, and when they do get here, you'll be gone."

Abadon's hard hazel eyes met with the pine green eyes of the beast master.

"I don't know who they are. I don't know what they want. I know nothing!" Abadon bellowed in a furious display of anger.

Abadon tried to calm himself, but the stress of the situation and the death of his parents all overwhelmed him. Fear and confusion were the only emotions Abadon was not numb to. The young prince dropped the branch from his hand and knelt next to the fire. Gafnan approached the prince and placed his hand on his shoulder, but his hand went right through him as if he was an illusion or an apparition. Gafnan was on the ground staring at the image of the prince.

"What just happened?" Gafnan demanded an explanation.

Abadon managed to display a weak smile. "I am wearing a ring that causes displacement. I am not actually sitting where you see me, Gafnan."

Gafnan starred at the image of Abadon, and a smile slowly stretched across his face. "A gift from Jherlom, no doubt," the beast master assumed. "We will leave soon, just as soon as you are warm enough to travel. I don't think either of us will sleep much tonight."

The fire eventually warmed Abadon enough to enable him to travel. Gafnan led the young prince southwest, toward the village of Nordach. The forest had become much thicker than the area he was in earlier. The obscurity of the forest frightened Abadon, even in the company of the beast master. Mystification always filled the Mystasian forests in the autumn. Many of them were still largely unexplored. The chilling season of autumn was proficient in hiding things, and the dying nature of the forest only increased its enigmatic disposition. Though the forests were beautiful with the multiple colors of the leaves, autumn's cold temperament seemed suitable for the previous three days.

Sabre remained several feet behind Abadon at all times. It took a long time for the prince to trust the saber bear. Abadon only had knowledge of healing and a few defensive clerical spells to use in his defense. But then he realized that if Gafnan wished harm upon him, he would have done so by now.

CHAPTER VIII

The Damned

STILL IN BLOOD HAWK FORM, Jherlom soared over the Diamond Cluster River, but there was no sign of the prince. Two hours of searching forced Jherlom to believe that Prince Krendale had either drowned, or he had simply lost track of him.

Jherlom soared over the Northguard Province. The druid began to descend down into the Cardinal Forest, not far from the village of Imayb. He landed on a moss-infested log and whistled bird song and chipmunk chatter. Almost at once, small forest animals came to the druid's aid. Speaking their languages, Jherlom stressed to the animals that Prince Krendale might still be alive. He instructed them to keep a look out along the banks of the Diamond Cluster River. Once his instructions and their importance were explained, the animals left in search for Abadon.

Now it was time for Jherlom to turn his attention to the unexpected problem. Mystasia appeared to have a traitor within its lands. He could think of no motive for a Mystasian captain to seek out the prince in the manner that Captain Tor'Albus did that morning. Jherlom would track down and speak to each noble lord until he found the traitor. It had been four hours since Abadon had leaped into Diamond Cluster River. It had only been two days since Abadon was in his care, and already he had failed.

Jherlom flew toward Trosll. Nearly midway between Iamyb and Trosll was a garrison known as Bramble Brick Garrison. He landed on a branch of an elven seeder a short distance from the garrison, where he was hidden from view. He monitored the forest, studying the behavior of the animals, but the nature of the woods was undisturbed there. He reshaped himself back to his natural elven form and began to communicate once again with the forest animals. This time he gave them instructions to search for anything unusual.

As quickly as they came to him, they scurried away into the woods. He smiled as he watched a blue butterfly glide with the wind across several wildflowers that grew in the shadow of elven seeder and butter burr trees. Withered ferns protruded from behind the boulder he had selected as a temporary chair. He turned to the trees themselves. The ovate leaves of the elven seeders were now orange instead of purple.

Jherlom began to ponder Tor'Albus. The elf captain served Countess Pamel'Lourn, but were his actions against them earlier that day for his own purposes, or was he following her orders? Pamel'Lourn had been a noble lord in Mystasia for seventy-four years. She was an elf of high morals, and one of King Krendale's most trusted noble lords. It was primarily she and Duchess Pureheart that put a stop to the gladiator arenas that were once used for the purposes of entertainment within Mystasia. What would she want with Abadon? What would Captain Tor'Albus want with the prince? Why was Captain

Tor'Albus accompanied by twenty-five orcs disguised as Mystasian horsemen?

Jherlom began to walk through the forest toward the road known as White Pine Road, toward Bramble Brick Garrison. As he passed through the brush, butter burrs and thorns clung to his green cloak, but they did not tear the fabric. Jherlom located White Pine Road and began to walk north. Occasionally, a bird, squirrel bickering, or insect debating caught his ear.

Nearly a mile up the road, Jherlom trudged around a bend in the road and came face to face with the White Pine Garrison. The structure was intact, but blood smeared the walls of the garrison, and about twenty bodies littered the road. All of them were missing their clothing save for their undergarments. The horses at the nearby stable were also missing. Jherlom had found the location where the orcs had stolen the Mystasian outfits. The enemy had been here less than two days ago. The carnage provided him with evidence that either the elves or humans played a part in the violence that took place here. The slaughter was the work of orcs, but his confusion grew stronger still. Why did Captain Tor'Albus take part in the bloodshed here?

To Jherloms' surprise, he noticed that the body of boyer warden Thal'Rodrinn was also present at the grisly scene. His archery skills were beyond respectable. The enemy had been great enough to bring death to him as well.

Jherlom analyzed the bloody scene for a moment, until a chipmunk scampered across his foot. Jherlom looked down at the bushy-tailed rodent, which ran back into the woods east toward the Eighth Glade River. He followed the chipmunk for about three hundred feet

A bird landed and perched on Jherlom's shoulder. It began to chirp into his ear.

Listening to the bird, Jherlom walked another one hundred feet. He came to a very small clearing, where a group of boulders sat clustered together on the far side of the clearing. Within them was an old well. Jherlom leaned forward and looked down the well, but darkness was all there was to see. An old rope offered possible passage into the well. A lumber mill once existed nearby, and the well was abandoned when logging of the trees in the area was no longer required.

Jherlom turned around and screamed surprised with what he saw. Hunched over a boulder next to the well was another body, lying face-down. He feared the worst. The hair of the body almost matched that of the prince. He slowly lifted the head and gasped, stunned with what he saw next. It was Captain Tor'Abus.

He looked over the captain's body as well. There were four punctures marks on the left side of his neck—two next to each other, and another two side by side about three inches below the top ones. 'Vampires', Jherlom thought for a quick moment, but then he excused that thought. Vampires left only two marks, and The Bloodstone Forest was well over one hundred miles from there. They were bite marks, but not by any being he had encountered before.

Jherlom turned to the well. It was a perfect hiding place for whoever was responsible for the murder of Tor'Albus. He sauntered over to the well and looked down into the darkness. He listened very carefully, but he heard nothing. He took one more look around the forest surrounding him. Other than forest animals, he appeared to be the only one around. He decided to climb down the well, using the rope to aid his descent.

The darkness of the well swallowed the light of the woods he considered home. The rope was rough on his elven hands. He was surrounded not just by darkness, but a very strong earthy smell, though it was not at all dank. The well was dry.

As he descended down the rope, he broke through sheets of cobwebs that clung to his green druid cloak. Occasionally, he came across large roots of forest trees that broke through the stone wall of the well on all sides. His slender form was able to squeeze through them, but then one of the roots he touched moved slightly, and the wall of the well to his left slid open. Jherlom jerked his head back in reaction to the sudden movement. He had accidentally discovered a secret passage triggered by one of the roots.

He stared at the opening for a moment. He hesitated to enter, but realized almost at once that who he was looking for was likely to be located somewhere behind the darkness of the secret passage.

He looked up at the top of the well. He was about one hundred feet down. Cautiously, he used the rope and the other roots to help him to the left side of the broad well, and climbed into the passageway. He paused for a moment and listened very carefully, but there was no sign of anyone nearby.

He snapped off the end of one of the roots, touched the tip of the piece of wood, and lit the root on fire, constructing a torch. The cavern bent to the left, and then to the right. It declined slowly to the left, and then the passageway forked, offering routes to the left or right. He looked down both passageways, but neither of them promised any interest.

Before Jherom could take a step to the left, whispers from the right caused him to pause. He quickly extinguished the torch in the golden sand of the stony tunnel. He listened carefully, but the whispers died off. Without torch light, he wandered into the darkness in the direction the voices came from. Eventually, he heard them again. The gossip became louder as he got closer to the source. It was the voice of a female, a voice that Jherlom had heard before, but he couldn't identify it.

"We will use the ore we took from the king's wagon," the voice said. "It has magical properties that cause some magic resistance. The orc blacksmiths are already using it to create some new armor."

"I have murdered one of the Mystasian captains," another female voice said.

"Good, proceed with the assassins to kill the others," the familiar voice demanded. "Nagh Shann has installed some more traps. He has provided Shade Deep with plenty of security."

A crimson glow came from around the corner, and the conversation discontinued. Jherlom could still hear shuffling from around the bend in the passage. Someone was still there, and they were walking toward him.

He turned to escape detection from whoever was approaching, but he bumped into several figures. The torch light in the room behind him was strong enough for him to see their physical appearance. They were black-skinned beings that stood at the level of his neck. Where their eyes, noses and mouths should have been, there were indents outlining their probable location. Thin, stick-like arms ended with three fingers tipped with dagger-like claws, and both their legs ended with two feet each.

Realizing that they appeared to be blind, Jherlom tried to shove his way past them hoping they would mistake him for whoever was approaching from behind, but his plan failed. The strange beings began to claw at his flesh. He hastily transformed into a blood hawk to escape their penetrating grasp, and flew past them back into the well.

As Jherlom soared up the well to the world of light, he felt himself go cold, and felt strangely weak. He crashed into a tree next to the cluster of boulders that surrounded the well. His reactions were slow due to the strange chill within him. He barely had the strength to lift up his head.

Weak, cold and fatigued, he waited perfectly still in the branches of the partially naked tree. A beautiful woman with fiery crimson hair climbed out of the well. She was dressed in black leather. Behind her, a green hag also climbed out of the well. Her green flesh appeared wet with some indication of slime. Her nose dripped, and her hair was black and wet as well.

The green hag began to walk toward the tree that Jherlom remained hidden in. The ugly woman was almost upon him when she stopped and began to study the tree. Fear knotted in his stomach. She had discovered him!

A short moment later, the green hag turned away from him. She had likely dismissed him as a regular blood hawk, failing to realize that it was him who was eavesdropping on their conversation about assassinations.

"What is going on?" the woman in black leather asked.

"There was an elf in the well passage, Draxeen," the green hag informed her with a high-pitched voice.

"You let him get away?" Draxeen asked, bellowing at the green hag. "He may have heard every word that Taskica and I said!"

"That elf will not survive the night," the green hag snapped back. "The Damned clawed at him. Their cursed touch causes their victims to slowly transform into one of them. Until such time, he will not be able to move at all. The curse works fast."

Jherlom trembled slightly as he listened to the sinister crone describe his fate.

He glanced down at his arm, where the scratches from The Damned were located. Not only was the wound still bleeding, but it was getting bigger. It was already twice as large as it was five minutes earlier. His vision was beginning to haze, and his hearing was less effective. A moment later, Jherlom could no longer hear what they were saying to each other as they returned to the well.

Soon, the druid was alone as sunset approached. The overcast sky would allow only a fraction of moonlight to touch him. Jherlom closed his eyes. He found himself wishing for death to end his suffering. Intense pain had spawned from somewhere deep inside him. 'I am dying,' he thought to himself.

As much as he wanted death, he refused it. He had to warn the entire country and the rest of the nobles about the assassins, and that a powerful plot had already begun against Mystasia. Jherlom battled against the curse that housed itself inside him like a virus. The curse was a parasite, and he felt his strength slipping away minute by minute. He was quickly losing his strength, his mind, and his battle against the strange curse. His flesh was slowly turning grey as the wound continued to grow, spreading up to his fingers and upper arm now. Before long, everything went black.

CHAPTER IX

War Guild of Serpent Slumber

THE BROAD TOWER KNOWN AS the War Guild of Serpent Slumber leaned slightly to the east. Its battle-worn structure was clearly failing with the passing of time. Haz Rhon blinked his single dark eye at the war guild. It had yet to be disturbed by the mysterious attacks on Mystasia. He walked deep into the Amethyst Moss Fields in southwest Northguard, until he reached the building.

He pushed the double doors of the guild open and stopped. Warlords Toleb Boneshed and Haerigorn Tuskgern waited for him at a large rectangular stone table in front of a glowing fireplace. Along the walls of the guild was a display of weapons, helmets and armor. The table was littered with maps of the provinces of Mystasia, and battle plans.

The two warlords stared at the Cyclops. Haz Rhon had an angular build with a pear-shaped face, his high forehead framed with light, sandy-colored brown hair. He stared back at them with the chocolate-colored eye deeply set on his face, which served as a canvas for plenty of scars.

"Your ears will be sore with the dire new I bring you tonight," the Cyclops said to them as he approached the table and sat down. Haerigorn scratched at his orange-bearded face nervously. His broad but short dwarven form was stiff and intense.

The old, bald human warlord was equally as scarred through decades of violence.

Haz Rhon continued. "Castle Blackburn has been captured, suffering some damage to the outer walls. The Hall of the Silver Shield has taken heavy damage, and all the knights present at the time of attack are dead. Sir Pureheart was one of them."

The other warlords hung their heads in sorrow, muttering miserably underneath their breath. They both shook their heads in denial.

"The king and queen are dead, and the prince is missing," Haz Rhon added to his report.

Both the other warlords continued to shake their heads in disbelief. They had only heard bits and pieces of half-truths through gossip rotating through the country.

Haerigorn spoke his opinion. "We are likely the next targets. If they attacked the Hall of the Silver Shield, they will certainly attack us. We are warlords, and will be a threat to anyone planning an invasion against Mystasia."

"I agree," Toleb spoke, watching Haz Rhon lean on his large war hammer. "This is why we must leave here tonight. We need to accumulate what forces we have left, and plan an attack against whoever is doing this."

"Leave?" Haerigorn protested. "We need a plan of action first, before we leave here!"

"Magic is at work here," Toleb roared. "What can we plan? We don't even know who the enemy is! We need KelycArthLor."

"Kelyc-Arth-Lor was the greatest warlord who ever lived," Haz Rhon nodded. "But he is dead now, and there is no point in even speaking his name. He cannot help us. The three of us are the only Mystasian warlords left, and we have to plan a counter-attack ourselves. Kelyc-Arth-Lor's presence overshadowed everyone on the battle field, but his spirit was destroyed with him three months ago, when that avalanche occurred due to that terrible earthquake. His strength was impressive indeed, but we have to plan this without him."

Frustrated, Toleb slammed his fist on the table. "We need to figure out why certain places are being attacked. The capital is obvious, but why the Hall of the Silver Shield? Why the hall and not us, or any other Mystasian stronghold?"

"It could be the ore that was transported there," Haz Rhon suggested. "It is a special ore with magical resistance. The king was also there, and that alone may be the reason. Whoever is behind the attacks is slowly destroying the Mystasian leaders, and I am sure we are the next targets. The three of us have much more tactical knowledge and an understanding of war than any of the noble lords."

"Hollow Haven holds most of the mines in the country," Haerigorn muttered. "That may be another target."

The dwarf warlord looked down at the Mystasian map. "The Trow Flatlands' only importance is the farm land there. Wishwater is home to the wish water, which is a very powerful healing agent."

"Wish water is a myth," Toleb bellowed. "There is no proof that the magical water evens exists. I don't know why that territory was even named after those ridiculous rumors!"

"None of the garrisons reported any signs of an invasion, or any traveling on Mystasian roads other than our own people," Haz Rhon reported. "It is still a mystery how the enemy reached their destinations to make their assault. A conscript did say he saw the Hall of the Silver Shield being attacked by orcs. They were never seen entering the hall, but they never left either."

Toleb thrust the left side of his face into his fist and tapped the fingers of his other hand on the table irritably. "Has anyone gone there to see for themselves whether the enemy forces are still inside?"

"I was there yesterday," the Cyclops responded quickly. "There is no one there."

"Then it has to be a portal," Haerigorn replied suddenly. "How else could they have done this?"

"What countries have orcs?" Toleb asked.

"Bikelpar has orcs," Haerigorn recalled. "So does Turr'Ocko."

"The Underworld," Haz Rhon replied slowly. "I think they are coming from The Underworld. Bikelpar and Turr'Ocko do not have reason to attack us."

"What reason does The Underworld have?" Toleb said, infuriated.

"I don't know," Haz Rhon admitted. "But for orcs to arrive in Mystasia from countries as far away as Bikelpar and Turr'Ocko through a portal just isn't practical or realistic. Citizens and beings from The Underworld, however, would use such a means of transport."

"But are any of the dungeons down there powerful enough to wage war against an entire country?" Toleb asked. "That doesn't seem very likely, either."

"It's difficult to say what goes on down there in that dark, forsaken world," Haerigorn said scornfully.

Toleb was no longer listening to the others. He was mesmerized by the Mystasian maps on the table, which were calling out to him.

"The answer is here somewhere," he said suddenly. "How strong are our remaining forces?" Haz Rhon sat back in his chair and began to calculate the strength of the entire Mystasian army. "Some of the elf soldiers were killed in the earthquake that occurred three months ago. The elven army is still two thousand and one hundred strong, and seventeen hundred of those are archers. The rest are pikemen.

"The humans have been struck hard by the strange attack on the capital, as well as the earthquake. Currently, it is only fifteen hundred strong. The trows have six hundred, and the dwarf army is currently the strongest with four thousand and eight hundred."

"The armies are useless," Haerigorn roared, suddenly angry. "Even if one of us led them, they will all die. Our greatest enemy is not orcs, but this strange frozen fire witnesses have spoken of. You have to fight magic of that magnitude with magic, not with men and swords and numbers! A higher number of soldiers sent to fight against it will only result in higher numbers of casualties."

"If the enemy is using portals, how do they know the correct coordinates to get inside?" Haz Rhon pointed out.

Both the other warlords went silent and exchanged glances. Haerigorn frowned. "What are you suggesting?"

"I am suggesting that there may be someone in Mystasia helping the enemy," Haz Rhon explained. "I know nothing of magic, but it makes sense to me that if you use a portal to grant entry into a place, you need to know the layout of the structure you are entering. Otherwise, a portal might open in solid rock, trapping whoever travels through it."

Both warlords slowly nodded in agreement. "That does make some sense," Toleb said. "But who in this country would assist anyone in destroying it?"

Again, Haz Rhon shrugged. "I don't know. It is just a theory."

"At any rate, we need to handle this on our own," Toleb decided solitarily. "Involving other countries in this won't do us or them any good."

The old human turned to the dwarf. "You said it yourself. We are dealing with magic. There is no army large enough to fight this with. Perhaps at desperate times, reinforcements from neighboring countries like Alyshia and Avenhauk would offer some aid."

"And you don't think this is a desperate time, Haz Rhon?" Haerigorn blurted out, slamming his fist onto the table. "Do you think the enemy is being hospitable by sending us a cold fire? Do you think they are keeping in mind that winter is around the corner?"

"Silence yourself, Haerigorn!" Haz Rhon demanded. "I was a warlord in Avenhauk for many years before coming to Mystasia. Alyshia is a peace-keeping country, and there is little the Avenhauk armies can do for us. We are dealing with powerful magic."

Directly in front of the double doors, a portal flashed into existence, blocking the only way out of the guild. Six goblins stepped out of the portal carrying short swords. They were followed by three medusa archers. Behind them was the portal mage, Olsegg.

Before the other two warlords could react, Toleb cut down the six goblins with ease—but as he slaughtered the sixth goblin, a barbed, poison-tipped arrow struck him in the throat. Toleb dropped to his knees, clutching his throat, and then fell face-down onto the floor.

Haerigorn grabbed his battle axe and tipped the stone table over onto its side, using it as a shield. Three poison-tipped arrows struck the wall behind him, where he stood only two seconds earlier.

Haz Rhon sprinted to the table next to the staircase leading up to the next floor. Grabbing four throwing axes, he began hurling them at the medusas. One struck a medusa in the forehead. She hissed and thrashed about, striking another medusa with her tail as she struggled to fight the pain, and then the thrashing stopped abruptly. As she died, she released another arrow that struck a wooden pillar only one inch from Haz Rhon's head. Before the Cyclops could take cover completely, another arrow struck him in the shoulder. He dropped to the floor and decided to pretend that he was dead.

As the two medusas slithered closer to the table Haerigorn hid behind, the dwarf warlord suddenly rose up from his cover, swinging his battle axe. His axe met with the neck of the closest medusa, sending her head rolling past Olsegg to strike one of the double doors before it came to a stop. Before Haerigorn could take cover again, his eyes unintentionally made contact with the eyes of the last medusa. His flesh began to turn grey, and the soft texture of his flesh began to harden. He froze, perfectly still. He was now a statue with fear etched into his face, holding his axe as if ready to strike at something.

The medusa noticed a gash in her serpentine body. One of Haz Rhon's throwing axes had struck her, doing moderate damage.

"Through the portal, quickly," Olsegg ordered. The medusa slithered into the portal. As she passed through its azure light, her wound healed instantly. This time, Olsegg had opened a portal of healing. The orc took one last look around the war guild. Satisfied with the deaths of the warlords, Olsegg deliberately tossed a lantern onto the floor. Fire erupted and immediately began to burn at the structure of the guild. Olsegg took three steps backwards until he entered the portal, and it suddenly vanished.

Immediately after the portal closed, Haz Rhon crawled to the table closest to him. Death was perhaps less than a minute away. The poison had already begun to enter his system. He pulled himself up to the table, grabbed a thin bottle, and poured the teal liquid into his mouth. The liquid had a waxy surface. It tasted salty and contained the smell of cedar trees. He could feel the toxicity of the venom weaken. As the guild began to burn around him, he slowly fled to the double doors of the guild as the potion neutralized the venom within his body. He realized that the barbed arrow was still stuck in his shoulder. It was a triple-barbed arrow that would make it either exceptionally painful or impossible to remove.

Haz Rhon snatched the broken wooden handle of an old war axe and fled to the grey grassland beyond the guild. He joined the battle beast, which never moved from its grazing site since the warlord had arrived.

He watched the guild burn as he bit down hard on the wooden handle. He snapped the arrow's shaft in half, and he focused on his teeth sinking into the wood rather than the pain that echoed through his shoulder as he began to push the arrow through. He could feel the barbs ripping through flesh and muscle. With his other hand, he pulled the arrow out, holding it by what was left of its shaft.

Once out, Haz Rhon spit the wooden handle from his mouth and took a deep breath of relief. He examined the arrow head. It was indeed tipped with poison, and it had three barbs. It was constructed well enough that even if a weak poison was used, it would enter the target's system before they could remove the arrow. It was an arrow that almost guaranteed death, yet he had escaped it.

To stop the bleeding, Haz Rhon sauntered slowly towards the war guild, which was still burning. He grabbed a piece of wood still on fire at one end. Without hesitation, he pressed the flaming piece of wood against his wound. A single scream echoed through the Amethyst Moss Fields, and he tossed the flaming wood aside. He had stopped the bleeding.

Displaying very little strength, Haz Rhon fled the area. 'We have to warn the nobles,' he thought to himself. The pain of his recent wound still stabbed at him and echoed within his body. The warlord walked straight ahead to the southeast. He never looked back at the war guild.

CHAPTER X

"Death Comes In Many Forms"

GWAN EASTFIRE TREKKED THROUGH the Jade Coin Forest in search of Prince Krendale. His intent was to kill him. Gwan was fully aware that he was one of the only remaining ninjas of the Flaming Fist Clan, and that the prince's own uncle was once his master until he was killed in The Underworld a few months ago. The awareness of his past still did not stop him from achieving the quest that Draxeen had bestowed upon him. She had used her talents as a temptress and bestowed a curse upon him that caused the ninja to fall desperately in love with her. Gwan would do anything and everything that Draxeen asked of him. He ignored his past. His past was no longer relevant to him. Draxeen and what she wanted was all that mattered. He had completely forgotten the reason why he and the rest of his clan had gone down into The Underworld. It no longer mattered.

Gwan's lean build was realized even through his black ninja robes. He stood perfectly still for a moment in his typical elaborate stance. His suspicious eyes peered about for the danger he sensed was there.

Gwan turned around to find a very large mouth with multiple rows of teeth appearing from the thick gloom. The mouth was large enough to swallow them whole. The gigantic beast was armed with ten tentacles, which all ended with hooks of bone, much like a grappling hook.

A young woman watched in terror from the window of her as one of the tentacles nearly struck the ninja. "Metaughlas!" the woman cried out.

His katana cut through one of the tentacles, but there were still nine more. Three of them swung at the ninja, but he dodged two of them. The third tentacle struck his side, knocking him back with a minor wound and a loud gasp.

The woman shouted, "I'll cast witch wind!" Seconds later, a powerful wind emanated from the young witch, directed solely toward the three metaguhlas. The spell slowed down their advance greatly. The young witch's arms were raised above her head. The flesh of the closest metaughla began to peel. The spell was more than a very strong wind—it also caused the destruction of flesh of those it was directed at. Their muscles began to decay until they collapsed. The spell ended, leaving two piles of bones where the closest two metaughlas died.

The third metaughla still approached, lunging forward with its great bulk toward Gwan and the intruding shadow that had been stalking them. Both Gwan and the cloaked figure were too quick for the beast, and he chopped off another tentacle.

The young witch pulled her wand out from her belt and directed it at the metaughla. She spoke a few words of magic, and the creature suddenly became still. Gwan watched intensely as the witch slowly approached the metaughla, which appeared to no longer be interested in attacking them. Although injured, Gwan moved swiftly toward the creature, as if to attack it.

"No!" the witch shouted. "It's okay," she said to him as she began to pet the creature. "This one is under my control. I cast a charm spell upon it."

The ninja stared at the creature, and then at the witch. The witch examined the wounds on the beast. Gwan looked down at his left hand and realized to his amazement that he had lost two of his fingers. The ninja looked around the ground for them, but no splash of blood he found contained fingers.

Gwan turned to the young witch. "For how long will you be able to control it?"

"At least several hours," she replied. "My name is Epona Crimsonfire. I am a witch. You're a ninja," Epona said, merely as a comment.

"Yes," the ninja replied. "My name is Gwan Eastfire. I am from the Guild of the Flaming Fist. Thank you for saving my life out there. It is not normal for me to be caught off guard like that."

Epona noticed that the ninja was wounded on his left arm. "Come inside immediately. I have a special stew that will help your wound heal."

Epona led the ninja inside her home. There was a single bed and a water table, but most of the cottage was filled with bookshelves and shelves containing jars of herbs.

The man sat at the table staring at Epona. The stare was not one of admiration, but rather curiosity. He noted her features in full detail. Her eyes were nearly the same color as cedar bark, her round face was that of a young woman, perhaps eighteen years of age. What he noticed most was her wavy, raw umber hair.

Epona fixed the ninja a bowl of the stew and sat down across from him. "Why are you here in the Jade Coin Forest?" she inquired.

"I'm on a quest, a quest which I cannot speak of," Gwan replied. "I can only tell you that Draxeen has sent me on a special errand."

"Who is Draxeen?" Epona asked.

"I'm in love with her," Gwan replied. "I must do everything she tells me. I have no purpose without her."

The ninja's words seemed strange to Epona. Gwan was either madly in love with the woman Draxeen he spoke of, or he was under a strange spell. The ninja did seem a little mesmerized when he spoke of Draxeen.

Epona left the table and returned to her cauldron set over a blazing fire. She returned with a bowl of thick, yellowish-brown soup with swirls of red.

"Please eat this," she instructed him. "This will help heal your wound."

Gwan began to eat the soup, and Epona questioned him some more.

"Why must you do what Draxeen tells you?"

"She is my life," Gwan replied. "I am still a ninja, but my loyalty now lies with her. I believe I will die without her nurturing and without her order over me."

"I see," Epona said, pretending to understand his obsessive behavior concerning the woman he called Draxeen.

Gwan finished his soup, but continued to act withdrawn. "I'd best be going," Gwan said a moment later, as if mesmerized by some strange disturbance from within. "Thank you for your help," he said again at the door, and then left Epona's cottage.

Epona walked swiftly to the window and watched Gwan disappear back into the Jade Coin Forest. "Strange," she said to herself.

Gwan had walked less than a kilometer into the forest before he discovered a familiar face dressed in the same black robes.

"Grim Crimson," Gwan spoke, not surprised to see the ninja.

Grim Crimson said nothing. He almost appeared to almost be lost. His blizzard blue eyes darted about the forest aimlessly, and then he turned to Gwan. "You have to tell me about my past, Gwan. You need to tell me who I am."

Gwan seemed confused by his behavior. "I don't understand."

He turned to the south and asked out loud to himself, "Who am I?"

"Your name is Grim Crimson," Gwan told him. "You are a part of the Flaming Fist Guild, the same guild I am a part of. Don't you remember?"

"I remember nothing," Grim told him. "All I know is that I serve the manticore master, Borin Saken. I have the same quest as you, to hunt down and assassinate Prince Krendale and all the Mystasian nobles."

Gwan frowned. "You mean to tell me that you have amnesia?"

"I don't know," Grim replied, shrugging. "The first thing of my life that I remember is standing in a barren wasteland in The Underworld, wandering aimlessly about with no purpose. Eventually Borin

Saken found me and gave me a new purpose. He told me that I served him. With no memory of my life prior to a few months ago, I followed him to Shade Deep."

"You were a ninja of the Flaming Fists," Gwan explained. "You have a celestial belt in the martial art of Whal-Chys-Seut, which is a very graceful form of martial arts."

"Yes," Grim nodded. "I am familiar with my knowledge of martial arts, but I have no memory of the guild, any other members, or being trained to learn martial arts."

Gwan shook his head. "That does not matter now. We both have the same purpose—to kill Prince Krendale and the other noble lords."

"But how?" Grim asked. "The prince is protected with a ring that causes displacement."

"I will remove my ring to become visible, and I will befriend them and figure out a way to kill the prince."

A few feet away, a portal opened. Borin and Olsegg stepped out of the blue light.

"Have you killed the prince yet?" Borin asked, wasting no time to get to the matter.

"Not yet," Grim answered. "He is wearing a ring that causes displacement. We cannot find his exact location to make the kill."

"We think we have found a way," Gwan added.

"Make it soon!" Borin ordered.

"Master, I have encountered a witch with great power and a vast library of knowledge in witchcraft. It occurred to me that Taskica may find recruiting her useful."

Borin stood there wordlessly, as if thinking the suggestion over. Finally, he nodded. "I will look into this witch and visit her myself. Continue on with your quest. Taskica does not realize it, but Abadon must die before she can claim the throne."

Grim scowled. "The frozen fire, and these assassinations we are performing, are all so Taskica can have the Mystasian throne?"

"Yes," Borin replied. "But there is a much deeper personal issue here. Vengeance is also involved. She wants no harm to be brought to Abadon, but he must die along with the other nobles. Hunt them all down and destroy them, and continue training the orcs I have sent you as assassins. The construction of the twin guilds has been completed."

"Yes, Master." Grim bowed. Gwan bowed as well, although it was Draxeen who was his master, and not the manticore master.

CHAPTER XI

Pureheart's Sorrow

DUCHESS RIANNON PUREHEART STOOD in the northwest tower of Skull Moat Castle. She pulled her fur coat close to her body. Her long, chestnut brown hair was tied back to prevent the wind from molesting it. Her sea blue eyes searched the sky as she waited for her companion to return. White clouds were scattered throughout the sky in all directions. A moment later, what she waited for appeared from the south. It was a white-winged creature prancing in front of the closest cloud; a winged horse with a single horn spiraling upward from its forehead.

The beast landed next to her master, who greeted her by patting her left side.

"Angelwing, where have you been?" Riannon asked, placing her hand into a pocket and producing an open hand of oats for the pegacorn.

While the pegacorn feasted on the oats, Riannon heard the footsteps of someone climbing the stairs to the top of the tower where she stood.

She turned her head and found Apponus standing at the stairwell.

The pegacorn had finished its treat of oats, and Riannon rushed into his open arms. "Apponus," she said in almost a whisper.

His arms held her close, and he kissed her forehead. "You have heard the news, then?"

"Yes, I have," she retorted, keeping her face pressed against his chest.

"The druid keep and the mage guild appear to be deserted, but the cleric temple seems to still have some clerics within it," Apponus reported.

"What about the dwarves in Hollow Haven?"

"In general, they seem to be staying right where they are. It doesn't seem that many of them have fled their territory yet. I think Count Kruxceedor plans to make a stand there. I know nothing about Shardridge Fortress or Castle Wishwater, but the trows have remained in The Trow Flatlands. The country rests in your hands, my love."

Riannon kept silent for a moment, and then she pulled away from Apponus. "The prince is dead?"

"Rumors say he leaped into The Blind River, and he has not been seen since. It appears he drowned, Riannon. The throne of Mystasia is now yours. I have heard rumors that Captain Tor'Albus and orcs tried to capture Prince Krendale."

Riannon's mind echoed with exertion. Facts were mixed up with speculation, rumors and confusion, and for the first time ever, she felt lost and did not know what kind of action to take. The well being of Mystasia and its people were her responsibility now.

Apponus sauntered over to the pegacorn. He stroked the beast's face delicately.

The pegacorn nuzzled his open hand. "Is she ready to ride yet?"

"Very soon," Riannon retorted with half a smile, and wrapped her arm around his and began to lead him down the spiraling staircase of the northwest tower. Angelwing trailed behind them. She guided the elementalist down a corridor into the castle tavern. It was just as crowded as Apponus had ever seen it.

"I can see that you are just as stubborn as the rest of the nobles," Apponus stated, clearly surprised with the castle's population.

"None of us are leaving, Apponus," Riannon said firmly as she stopped at a round table just large enough for them both. Angelwing sat underneath the table and nuzzled Riannon's leg. "A few have left the castle, but most of us are staying. We can't run from this enemy, Apponus. Besides, this castle is probably the safest of them all, because of how high up we are in the Ice Crown Mountains."

The tavern maiden delivered their usual drinks to them. She placed a cherry cider in front of Riannon and a black lotus drink in front of Apponus. Apponus reached across the table and pulled her hand toward him, taking it into the gentle grasp of his own hand.

"I missed you, Apponus," Riannon said sweetly.

"We're not safe here, Riannon," Apponus said softly, not charmed by her smile for the first time ever. We don't know for sure how the enemy is getting inside the castles and halls undetected. Just because we are thousands of feet above sea level, doesn't mean they can't reach us."

"I will not leave, Apponus," Riannon repeated. "I will not abandon my people or my castle."

"But what can you do for them here, other than watch them die and wait for your own death as well?"

Her infamous stubbornness held out.

Apponus reached for his black lotus drink, which was black and frothy. There was a black lotus flower floating on top. He removed the plant and began to chew on it before taking his first sip.

Riannon stared into his cocoa brown eyes. "I am thinking about approaching the gargoyles for an alliance."

Apponus nearly spat out his drink. He set his glass back down on the table instantly. Her suggestion was less than reasonable.

"It can't be done!" he blurted sharply.

"Are you questioning my skills in diplomacy?" Riannon asked defensively.

"Not at all, Riannon," he said. "But even one as highly skilled in diplomacy as you cannot achieve an alliance with any of the dark races. You'll be killed trying."

They both took a mouthful of their drinks, and Apponus continued his lecture. "Are you forgetting how our kind betrayed them during the War of the Gods?"

"That was during a different age," Riannon persisted. "I, of all people, know how things have changed since that time. I am a paladin lord, Apponus. Only a historian knows more than I do about such times. It was paladins who had to restore the country after that insanely chaotic time. There isn't a day that goes by when my fellow paladins ask when the gods and goddesses will forgive us and set aside their anger. It's not just the paladins, Apponus, it's the clerics and magi too. It's anyone who turns to a god. I am sure the druids also feel the intensity from the goddess they pray to."

"They don't listen anymore, Riannon," Apponus argued. "They don't listen, and everyone has stopped believing. If you know much about history, then you also know that no one has the same level of talent as those who lived prior to the War of the Gods. It's because since that war, no one who prays to them has the same level of belief and enthusiasm as their predecessors. My faith, for one, has never been so absent from my heart. Look around you, Riannon. The world is slowly dying. The gods have refused to grant us the same power as they granted to those long before us."

"You are wrong, Apponus. They are listening to us. It is us who is not listening to them. Our lack of faith has caused them to abandon us. The world just needs to adjust," Rianon continued, persisting with her optimism. "A few of the lesser gods and goddesses were destroyed in that war, and others lost their children. Of course they are angry. You are blind to the truth."

"Perhaps, but I am not blind to your beauty," he said with a smile, changing the subject. Riannon was forced to smile as well.

"Is this how you are successful when forming alliances, with your charm and persistence?" Apponus' ill effort to force a change of mind in Riannon had failed.

Riannon nodded. "I think it runs in the family. My great grandfather is the one who more or less created the alliance of the races in Mystasia, shortly after the War of the Races."

"Mystasia has come a long way," Apponus said, nodding. "Nearly all the provinces were countries of their own."

The half smile on his face disappeared, and his face became grave and no longer blissful. "Riannon, I have some bad news for you, some news you may not have heard yet."

"Has something else happened?"

"Have you heard what happened at the Hall of the Silver Shield?"

"I heard that the king was killed there, but I don't know the details on which of the knights were present. Was my brother there?"

"Yes, Riannon, he was," Apponus said softly. "I didn't know how to tell you this. I was hoping you had already heard, but as we talked over the past ten minutes, I could tell that you haven't."

Riannon lowered her head. Tears spilled onto the table as she listened some more.

"I was there, Riannon, but I couldn't help him. I was the only one who managed to escape the hall that day. I saw your brother die, but I couldn't help him."

Riannon continued to sob softly. Angelwing laid her head on her master's leg, sensing her sorrow.

"How did he die?" Riannon asked, barely able to get the words out of her mouth.

"He fell into a hole that opened up below him. We forced many orcs and sword nagas back into the hole, but Nario lost his footing and fell in as well. After that, I fled the scene. The king and I got separated. There was nothing I could do for him. He was killed somewhere else in the hall."

Apponus waited for Riannon to pull her hand away from his, but she didn't.

"You're not angry with me?"

"Of course not," Riannon said, wiping away a tear from each eye. "You did what you could, and my brother's death is not your fault."

"I am sorry, Riannon," he said. The two become silent. The only noise came from the fifty others that shared the tavern with them.

I spoke with the arch druid Vadamar and the arch mage Dranus before coming here," Apponus announced. "They believe this all has something to do with the dark druids that caused havoc three months ago."

"That is quite possible, but I have heard rumors that the enemy might be using portals to get inside the castles when they attack. Druids do not know anything about portals, Apponus. They do have knowledge about the earth. They can manipulate the earth. Could they have entered somehow through the underground?"

"No," Apponus shook his head. 'I am an elementalist of earth, so I understand everything they do in regards to how the element of earth works, and there is no one powerful enough or energetic enough to enter that way."

"There shouldn't be anyone strong enough to use the frozen fire, either, Apponus. Judging by the rumors I am hearing, even Vadamar and Dranus couldn't use such powerful magic on their own."

"That is true," Apponus nodded. "That means every time the frozen fire appears, there is more than one person creating it. However, such a strong spell would drain anyone's energy down quickly, even if as many as three were gathered together to share their energy in an effort to use the frozen fire."

"Who can use such magic, Apponus? Who else other than druids and elementalists?

"Possibly a mage or an enchanter," he informed her. "Dranus and Vadamar agree that even a fairy could create such a spell. It can be anyone who knows plenty about the element of fire, and how to make such a spell work as a contradiction. The fire is apparently both hot and cold."

"But why would a fairy create something like that?" Riannon protested.

"They are the most peaceful beings in the country, even more peaceful than elves."

"I know that, Riannon," Apponus said. "But the source of druidic magic came from fairies. That is who the druids learned much of their magic from. It seems most likely that a druid or an elementalist created the spell, but no one is powerful enough to use it on their own."

"It has to be the dark druids," Riannon decided. "Who else can it be?"

Apponus nodded. "That is likely who it is. Maybe the druids didn't destroy all of them in their battle against them three months ago. There must still be some lurking about."

Unexpectedly, Riannon stood up from her chair. "Where are you going?" Apponus asked.

She turned and looked down at him. Her eyes were red from crying, but they were no longer leaking tears.

"It is more important, now than ever before, to establish an alliance with those everyone calls the dark races. I have always been interested in the gargoyles, so I will start with them."

"Riannon…"

Apponus was not given a chance to finish. "They might be in danger too, Apponus. Someone has to warn them about this frozen fire I have been hearing about. We may not share our society with them, but we all live in the same country.

Riannon left the tavern, and Angelwing followed her. Apponus watched her leave without any further words. He knew better than to try and stop her once her mind had been made up.

CHAPTER XII

Evening in Nordach

THE VILLAGE OF NORDACH, a settlement at the edge of Jade Coin Forest, was quiet.

Twenty-two citizens lived here, and all but one of them were sound asleep in their beds.

Epona Crimson checked on the cauldron that burned in her fire place. A knock sounded at her door. It was not common for her to receive visits from clients so late at night. She grabbed her wand from the table and slowly opened the door. A bald, heavily scarred man with eyes of steel stood there with a smile.

"I am in desperate need of some rock weed," he said. "I was told that there isn't an herb in the world you do not have here in your cottage."

Epona smiled. "That statement is nearly accurate. I have almost every herb you can think of." Epona opened the door wide and allowed the man to enter her home.

Borin Saken sat down at Epona's table, and she joined him.

"I have been told that you are a witch. One of the best known witches in the country," the man said, watching Epona pull a jar down from a shelf.

"I am a witch," Epona admitted. "I like the privacy this village offers. I need lots of privacy for my work."

"Why is that?" the man asked.

"I create spells," Epona said, returning the jar to the shelf. "I am cautious about who may overhear or obtain my work."

The young witch placed the rock weed on the square wooden table. In her right hand, she still held her wand. "This will cost you three emerald shillings."

The man reached into his pocket and pulled out a gold coin. "I am afraid I am out of shillings of any kind. Will this suffice?"

"Sure," Epona said, taking the gold coin. She turned her back to him for a moment. When she turned around, she placed three silver coins, one ruby shilling and two agate shillings on the table. The man collected them with a smile.

"What is your name?" Epona asked the man.

The man hesitated for a moment, but maintained his smile. "Brom Tkel," he said. "I am from Gareth."

"What troubles you?" she asked.

"Is there something that should be troubling me?"

"You're here to collect rock weed," Epona pointed out. "When someone comes here in search of an herb, it's usually because they are sick with something."

"True," Borin said. "My brother is ill with something. An herbalist told me that he knows of a cure that may be able to save him. He didn't have any rock weed, so I csme to you."

"You came a long way for an herb that isn't usually difficult to find in any herb shop," Epona declared. "What is your brother ill with?"

"An insanity," Borin said, sighing. "He suffers from megalomania. He believes that he is greater than anybody at anything. He is rather delusional. He is weak, and has always had support from everyone around him, unlike myself."

Borin stood from the table. Epona could sense that he held back plenty of anger, but he maintained his smile, and he had a gentle polite demeanor.

"You look like you could use some company, perhaps for the night," Borin stated.

"Is that what I look like to you?" Epona asked.

"Well, perhaps not," he admitted. "But you do live in the middle of nowhere."

"I love it here," Epona said, forcing a smile. The man made her nervous, but he also brought her a strange comfort. He seemed like a man who would fear little, if anything. He was also broad and muscular.

Borin took one step toward her. "Aren't you afraid of living in the middle of nowhere in this area? The Obsidian Peaks are very near here, after all, and that is where the gemstone gargoyles live."

"I have never had a problem with them," she said, taking one step back. "The gargoyles usually stay in the mountains. I have only heard of two sightings of them in the sky, twice in the past ten months. Any children here know better than to stray away from the adults."

Epona began to think his question over. There had been gargoyle sightings every day for the past three days. Their increased activity did cause her some concern.

She was up against the water table now. There was no more room to back away from Borin, who continued to approach her.

"I am in need of some healing myself," he said. "But what I suffer from is a lonely heart. Is a witch of your infamous caliber able to cure such a thing?"

"Perhaps," Epona said. "On another night."

"I am afraid I leave for Gareth early tomorrow morning," he pleaded. "There are no women there, no women of any beauty or interest."

"That is a shame," she said, suddenly holding up her wand. "Please stay where you are," she said, speaking normally. His advance did not cause her to panic.

Borin stood still. "I am not here to hurt you. I am lonely as you are. I am not even armed."

Epona could see for herself that he wasn't armed. His strength was greater than an average man. Physically, against her, he would need no weapons.

"You could take my life with your bare hands if you wanted to," she said.

Borin's smile disappeared. "I see now that you do not trust me. I will leave you now, and return to Gareth."

He turned away, opened the cottage door and left.

Epona waited for moment, and then ran after him. "Please wait," she called out. "I mean, please stay for a lemon spice tea before you leave."

Borin smiled and returned to the cottage. He sat down at the table and watched as Epona hung a kettle over the fireplace, and then turned his attention to the hundreds of books she had collected.

He noticed that most of them were about herbs and witchcraft, but the second most popular topic on the shelves was vampires.

"You have a great interest in vampires?" Borin asked.

"I have a great curiosity for them, almost an obsession, really," she replied still standing at the fireplace.

"That is highly unusual," he said. "Nearly everyone fears them."

"I suppose I may be frightened if I came across one, but they fascinate me and I would like to meet one."

There was a knock at the door. Epona frowned and turned to Borin. "Did you bring someone to Nordach with you?"

"No, not at all," he said. "Would you feel better if I answered the door?"

"Please, go ahead," Epona insisted.

Borin opened the door. A woman with long, fire-red hair, a triangular face and small teal eyes stood at the doorway. She held a close helmet in her right arm, and was dressed in elven steel mesh armor.

"Dame Bloodweaver," Epona gasped in surprise. "Please, come in."

Borin returned to the table and watched as the female knight entered he cottage, set the helmet down on the table and sat down in front of it. The woman seemed distressed.

"What can I do for you?" Epona asked.

"I have been wandering around the woods that border the Haunted Forest for the past few days, looking for the werewolf that raped my mother," the dame said, clearly disturbed.

"I still can't find the werewolf responsible."

Epona frowned. "You mean to tell me that you have been approaching werebeasts?"

"No." Pontyia shook her head. "I have been to all the towns and villages that are near the Haunted Forest. I have been questioning villagers about werebeast sightings, applying the knowledge I have about that night, and sharing it with villagers in hope that it'll trigger a memory or force them to bring up another occurrence similar to that which happened to my mother."

"What do you plan to do when you track down the werewolf you are looking for?"

"I don't know," Pontyia shrugged. "Part of me wants to kill him, but another part of me forces me to realize that I am his daughter."

Borin quirked an eyebrow, "You're the product of the rape you speak of?"

"Yes," Pontyia nodded.

"But wouldn't that make you half werewolf?" Borin asked.

"Possibly," she admitted. "But I am twenty-five years of age, and I have never experienced anything strange about myself. They say that the three moons each do something to the werebeasts. I have heard that the red moon Rhosha causes them to become savage and extra hungry on nights when Rhosha is full. Nothing has ever led me to believe that I am part werewolf at all, at least not yet."

The dame turned to Epona. "I am still worried that I am at least a carrier of the lycanthropy disease.

I was hoping you might know of a cure that would rid my body of it."

Epona shook her head. "There is no cure for lycanthropy, Dame Bloodweaver. I am sorry. Perhaps you don't even have it. I am sure that if you had lycanthropy, you would experience the growth of hair on your body that is not ordinary for a human woman. If I had to make a guess, I would guess that you do not have it."

"Thank you, Epona. Your words are very comforting," Pontyia said softly.

"I do feel guilty about what happened at the Hall of the Silver Shield. I would have been there, if I wasn't searching for my father."

"Yes, you would have been," Epona agreed. "And you too would be dead. I have heard that what knights were present were outmatched by the enemy forces that stormed the hall."

Borin brought his hand up to his chin, cupping it. He seemed to drift into heavy thought at the mention of the assault on the hall.

Pontyia Bloodweaver grabbed her helmet and walked over to the door. "Thank you for your kind, wise words, Epona."

"Any time, Pontyia. Good luck with your search, and be careful out there.There are a lot of strange things happening lately." Pontyia nodded and closed the door behind her.

Borin turned to Epona, who rushed to the kettle which now howling to be removed from the fireplace. She brought the kettle over to the table and poured Borin someone lemon spice tea, as well as a cup for herself.

"That was a strange story that dame told us," Borin said after a moment of silence.

"Yes," Epona nodded. "I am afraid that she has become obsessed with finding out who her father is. The question is, is it for revenge, or for a reunion? I don't think she has even decided that for herself yet."

"It doesn't seem so," Borin agreed.

The two drank their cups of tea. Epona began to crave his company. His presence offered her comfort, and the fear she felt from him was trivial. Eventually, they moved from the table to her bed, where they sat next to each other. Outside her window, crickets took part in a late night choir shared with the howling wind and the calls of owls.

Soon, the howl of the grinding dark winds made it impossible to hear anything else outside.

"You seem to be very resourceful," Borin said to Epona. "How is it that a woman as young as you knows what she knows?"

"I read plenty of books. Crafting spells, crafting wands, and reading is all I do here," she said. "I was once the leader of a coven. There were five of us. One of the witches, Lispa Redspell, decided to leave. She abandoned all that she learned with us and turned to a different path of magic. Soon afterward, the others left as well. I do feel that there was envy on their parts. The three that left after Lispa were much older than her and myself, yet they didn't possess the same level of skill and knowledge that Lispa and I possessed. I left the Fairy Fern Forest and came here."

"Fairy Fern Forest?" Borin said questionably.

"That is where the coven was located," Epona explained. "In Fairy Fern Forest, right next to the Witch Trees of Viduria."

"Forgive me," Borin said softly. "I know little of magic. All I have ever known is the power of iron. My axe is my closest companion."

"What do you do?" Epona asked.

"In a sense, you can say that I am a beast master, but the only beasts I can communicate with and call are manticores. I am a manticore master."

"That sounds exciting," Epona said, smiling. "It would be great to have such beasts as companions."

"I know little of witches, but don't witches have familiars?"

"Most of them do," she said. "Mine is a leprechaun who is in Fairy Fern Forest right now. He comes by once a week to check and see if I have any tasks for him."

"I see," Borin said, nodding. "May I please have some more tea?"

"Certainly," she said, sitting up from the bed. As she walked toward her collection of spices and teas, Borin reached into his pocket and sprinkled a pale yellow powder into her cup of tea. It dissolved immediately without the aid of any stirring.

A moment later, Epona returned with a fresh cup of tea for him, and she continued to sip from her cup. "Tell me more about manticores."

"I'd rather hear more about you, Epona," the man insisted. "Tell me how wands work. What is involved when you craft a wand?"

"Well, the type of wood the wand is made out of is what determines how many charges a wand has, and how many spells you can store within a wand."

"I don't understand," Borin said, shaking his head.

"My wand, which I call Blood Branch, is a wand I made out of black oak. I don't entirely understand it all myself, but different wood seems to have different powers. I suppose druids have a much better understanding of it. The fact that my wand is made out of black oak allows me to store ten spells on Blood Branch, and Blood Branch has a charge of seven, meaning I can cast seven spells with it. Wands channel a witch's energy. Any spells we cast with them do not drain any energy from us. Witch spells require us to speak or read out our spells, which takes time. A wand is more or less a shortcut. We do not need to speak any words when using them. So casting a spell with a wand is quicker than casting one without, and there is no energy drain on us when we do it."

"That is very interesting," he said, smiling. "It is very strange how different paths of magic are so different from others, in terms of how magic is learned and performed."

"It is, indeed," she said. The young witch was beginning to feel light-headed. She dismissed the feeling with very little thought or concern about its origin.

Borin was not particularly an attractive man, but he interested her.

He folded his right arm around her and slowly pulled her toward him. Epona did not fight the stranger. His left hand brushed her face gently. It was as if she was being caressed by a compound, a compound of several magical elements all related to love. It was as if the touch was a chemical she had already become addicted to. That night, loneliness was finally suspended. She felt herself slipping away, perhaps subconsciously. He had come to her looking for medicine, but who was offering who medicine? Was this the cure for lonely nights?

She closed her eyes and surrendered herself to him. She was kissed by darkness as he explored her body. He had awakened a dormant part of her, and she had crossed over a margin she had never crossed before.

Unknown hours passed before she opened her eyes. The darkness wasn't as dark anymore. Her cottage was swamped with the light of sunrise, and a familiar voice kept calling her name.

"Epona. Epona! Wake up. It's Abadon!"

Epona woke and shook her head. She starred at the prince disbelievingly. "Abadon? Abadon, what are you doing here?"

"Gafnan and I have been here for a few hours now. You know that. You invited us in. What is wrong with you?"

"I guess I am suffering from some sort of memory lapse," Epona said slowly as she looked around the room. She saw the man who Abadon identified as Gafnan, but until that moment, her memory registered never seeing him before that very second.

"Where is Bram?" Epona asked.

"Who is that?" Abadon asked. "There was no one here when we arrived."

Epona was very confused. She continued to look around her cottage for evidence that the man was there. She noticed two tea cups resting on the table.

Epona shrugged. "I guess he left early in the morning, before you two even got here."

"You don't remember inviting us in last night?" Abadon asked.

"No," Epona said, shaking her head.

Abadon reintroduced Gafnan to Epona. "This is Gafnan Northchill, a beast master. This is Epona Crimsonfire, a witch. Epona and I have been friends since childhood. We spent some time at the Peach Page Monastery together in our youth."

Gafnan nodded at the witch. Epona's eyes narrowed as she looked the beast master over. "Interesting, a beast master. A client came to see me last night who claimed to be a manticore master. Brom Tkel. Perhaps you know him?"

"No," Gafnan said, shaking his head. "I never heard of him."

"It doesn't matter," Epona said. "So, what brings you here?

"I suppose Nordach doesn't receive much news, but to make a long story short, my parents are dead. A strange frozen fire has been threatening the country, and someone invisible is chasing after me. I am sure Jherlom Mor'Derum is looking for me. I am surprised he hasn't been here yet, actually."

Epona offered both men some buttered bread and pea soup. Both men took it gratefully as Abadon summarized the last four days in greater detail.

Abadon looked around the cottage, which looked more like a library.

"This is my home and my workshop of witchcraft," Epona said with gratification. "The frozen fire you speak of is not a spell that a witch would create."

"Who would create such a spell?" Abadon asked.

"Well, of all those who practice magic, warlocks and witches create spells more than anyone. Warlocks tend to research a wide variety of spells. Magi sometimes create spells. It's very rare for a druid or an elementalist to create spells. They usually learn what has already been discovered…"

Epona trailed off. She starred at Abadon's bare throat. "Abadon, where is your cleric amulet?"

For the first time, Abadon realized he was no longer wearing it. "I guess I lost it when I jumped into The Blind River."

Epona then turned her attention to the rings Abadon wore. "Tell me when and where you got all your rings."

"Why?" Abadon asked. The young witch did not reply verbally. She gazed at him with a hard stare.

"I got the obsidian one from Jherlom only a few days ago. That is the one that keeps me displaced. The other two are gifts I received for my promotion from brother of the Grey Faith to a cleric shaman in the Ku'Lee Clergy."

"I am sensing alien, but powerful magic from one of them," Epona informed him.

"When I say alien, I mean that it's a magic unlike any I have come across before. I need you to take those rings off and give them to me one at a time."

Epona opened up her hand, and Abadon placed the ruby ring studded with a blue agate into her palm first. She closed her eyes and her hand. Seconds later, she shook her head. "This is just an ordinary ring. Give me the other one."

Abadon gave her the obsidian snowflake ring, and repeated the process. With her eyes closed, she began to describe the ring's power to them.

"This ring does contain magic. It has perhaps the greatest area of effect I have ever encountered before."

"What do you mean?" Abadon asked.

"I cannot describe the specifics of this ring without using a spell called Bazgul's Eye. With that spell, I will know everything it does."

Epona closed her eyes again and held the ring against her forehead. "Bazgul's eye, open for me. Tell me what it is that you see. Lend me your power this very hour. Tell me of this ring's power."

Epona repeated those words three more times, and then she opened her eyes.

"My theory is correct. This ring is indeed magic, and it is linked to two other rings.

You said earlier that someone has been following you. I submit that there are two individuals trying to track you down. They are wearing rings as well, that are linked to this one. That is how they know where you are, Abadon. As long as you wear this ring, they will always know your location. We need to get rid of it. It is cursed!"

"But why would my father and Apponus give me a cursed ring for a gift?"

"Perhaps they found it in a shop, decided it was beautiful and bought it for you. It is a beautiful ring, Abadon, but it is cursed."

"So who is this ring linked to?" Abadon asked, excited that he was about to learn who was after him.

"The spell doesn't tell me that. It only tells me the details of this ring. It is linked to two other rings, but I do not know where they are or who is wearing them."

Epona placed the ring in a pocket of her cloak. "The clerics in your clergy should have been able to sense magic emanating from it. Couldn't you feel something when you wore it?"

"A little," he confessed in anger. "But when you're wearing more than one magical ring, it's a little difficult to pinpoint such things. Besides, you are highly sensitive to magic. You would notice such a thing before anyone else I know would."

"We need to leave Nordach immediately," she insisted. "We need to throw the ring away into the forest."

As Epona began to pack important belongings, Abadon questioned her some more. "You mentioned that there are two rings linked to that one. Are you saying there are two people after me?"

"Yes, Abadon," she said, rushing to gather her belongings. "I do not know if both of them are invisible or not, but it seems probable that they both are. They are probably both wearing rings that grant them that special power."

"So where are we going?" Gafnan asked.

"The Haunted Forest," Epona replied.

"Are you mad?" Abadon gasped. "The Haunted Forest is probably more dangerous than two invisible assassins. Why would we go in there?"

"It may be the safest place right now," Epona concluded. "You are being followed by two invisible assassins, and there is a powerful apocalyptic spell destroying the country. Hopefully, the assassins won't follow you there, and I doubt that whoever is behind this frozen spell has any interest in The Haunted Forest, either!"

Abadon thought about Epona's suggestion. His mind tried to resist it, but logical thought caused the prince to agree with her. "You're right. It is the safest place for me to be right now."

He opened his hand. "Give me back the ring. I am displaced, and the assassins might not attack the two of you at all while I have it. Once we are deep in the forest, I will throw it away."

Epona placed the ring on the table. Abadon grabbed it, and both men exited the cottage. Epona waved her hand over the door knob of her cottage.

"Perfect. I have my cottage locked up with magic. No one will be able to get in."

The witch began to trek south. Abadon and Gafnan followed her, and Sabre lumbered behind them.

CHAPTER XIII
Between Life and Death

SOMEWHERE BETWEEN LIFE AND DEATH, Jherlom lingered on the final threads of life in the very same tree he waited death. The length of time that had passed was unknown, but death was not coming quickly enough. As much as he wanted to live, he wanted death. A quick death would suffice, as long as the tormenting pain ended. His wound continued to grow, and the bleeding did not stop.

He wasn't just dying—he was already in the process of transforming into one of those hideous beasts that attacked him, known as The Damned. The blood racing through his veins was no longer his own. His thoughts were no longer completely his own. His warm-hearted nature toward life and all living things was being replaced with hate. His knowledge was slowly erasing, and emptiness and feeblemindedness filled the void that was once his mind. His breath was sour, and he quaked from inside, trembling with both fear and tremendous hate. He shook so much that he occasionally vomited. Bile and blood dripped from his chapped lips.

He prayed silently to Ninantu, the goddess of Nature, for an end. Ninantu denied him death. Instead, she granted him a great deal of strength to last longer without food and water, and enough resistance to slow down the effects of The Damned.

Suddenly, the branches surrounding Jherlom blossomed. It was as if a fresh breath of air had breathed autumn in, and breathed spring back out. The new leaves filled Jherlom's nostrils with a heavenly natural perfume he had come to enjoy ardently. Jherlom managed to crack a smile. "Ninantu is still with me," he mumbled.

The Damned were armed with the greatest and most unimaginable torture at their fingertips. It was like drowning in death. He could feel life slipping away from him, and every ounce of strength he had left was used to keep him from slipping away into permanent darkness. As he slowly opened his swollen, bloodshot eyes to look at the leaves around him, he heard a familiar sound. It was a screech from the sky.

"Utopia," Jherlom muttered feebly. He waited for the favorable sound of his wyvern's call to funnel through his pointed ears once again, but it did not. Jherlom's newfound hope died instantly. The air around him seemed to darken suddenly. He began to choke on breath that was no longer his.

A moment later, the screech repeated. Jherlom was unable to lift his head to view the celestial bodies up above. In a fraction of a second, he realized that his wyvern had found him. What he had heard a moment before was not part of his imagination brought on by his grave illness.

Utopia descended from the sky and gripped his master with his clawed feet, lifting him up from the tree, which had been his home for nearly two days. An image of the Cleric Temple of Ku'Lee flashed within Jherlom's mind before it went blank. The image was enough for Utopia to know exactly where to take his master.

The autumn air in the skies was nightmarish compared to the chill below. Utopia used the force of the whipping wind to push him south to the Cleric Temple of Ku'Lee. Sometime later, Utopia dropped down from through white clouds. Everything went white for a brief moment, and then the half-naked forest appeared below them.

Utopia gentle laid his master down on the ground next to the temple. He was no longer conscious. A building of gold and silver glittered in elaborate form, almost like a dream. A moat of clear, azure water surrounded the temple, provided by two silver dolphin fountains on either side of a silver bridge with snake railings.

Standing on the bridge was Ormela Bloodblend. The human cleric recognized the druid immediately. Her long, stringy auburn hair remained undisturbed by the wind. Her sea green eyes watched Jherlom very carefully for any sign of movement. Her diamond-shaped face was reddened by the chill of the autumn air, and she folded her arms around her slender figure in protest against the cold.

Ormela crossed the bridge swiftly and entered the temple. The great double doors were already open. She walked quickly through the great hall of the temple, where colossal pillars stood erect on either side. Passages of elegance stretched onward to the left or right between some of them.

Ormela rushed through the great hall hurriedly before stopping. There was another cleric there, the gnome cleric Khon'Tenn'Nul.

"What is wrong?" the gnome asked, puzzled. Ormela looked down at him. He scratched the patch of black hair that topped his head, trying to overcome the confusion caused by Ormela's stress. His round face supported large russet eyes, large ears, and a wrinkled forehead.

"Jherlom Mor'Derum," Ormela cried out. "There is something wrong with him! Where is the high priestess?"

"Eradia is in her chamber," Khon'Tenn'Nul replied. The gnome followed Ormela to the opposite end of the seemingly endless great hall of the temple. At the end of the hall, two great double doors appeared. Strange cleric symbols marked the doors, and Ormela pushed one of them open. They were in a room as equally elegant as the rest of the temple. A shiny wooden table sat centered within the room, surrounded by a dozen chairs. The room was filled with candles, and was rich with fine things. A crimson rug led them straight to the table. To the left and right of the room were two more doors, which were silver. At the far end of the room were great statues of infamous cleric priests and high priests, both male and female. Sitting in a chair in a small section of the room, on an elegant golden chair, was the high priestess, Eradia Lear'Novah.

"Jherlom is in great need of aid," Ormela declared at once.

Eradia stood up from her chair. The high priestess was wearing a glittering silver gown.

"What kind of services does our druid friend need?"

Both Ormela and Khon'Tenn'Nul shrugged, but it was Ormela who answered.

"I don't know. His wyvern brought him here. I have never seen anyone in as grave of a state as he is!"

"Follow me," Eradia said softly and with a calm demeanor. The two clerics followed the high priestess to where Ormela left Jherlom. With her instructions, the clerics brought Jherlom to a special chamber, and laid him down on a cushioned altar.

He was now blind and deaf, but what instincts he did have left proved to him that he was still in fact alive. Jherlom was unable to speak words. His voice was merely a muffled growl. His mind was barely still his own. He did not have enough energy to cast even the simplest of spells. His insides burned with a fury that no mortal man could understand with experiencing the hell that burned at the very core of his being.

His elf form was spoiled and broken, and exposed to all varieties of harm. Death would not wait much longer.

"I need a few things," Eradia requested. "Bring me some silver leaves, pine mint, egaro, xandorgan, a potion of healing, and powdered blue blight."

Ormela left the chamber to get the requested items. Khon'Tenn'Nul watched as Eradia collected a few items within the chamber. Before long, Ormela returned with the supplies.

Eradia turned to Ormela, handing her a container. "Crush three silver leaves, and place two pine mints in this container with the crushed leaves."

Ormela did as she was instructed and waited for further direction.

"Now, put one egaro into the same crystal dish, along with a handful of xandorgan."

Ormela sprinkled some strange brown powder known as xandrogan into the dish with a strange purple plant.

"Now pour an entire potion of healing into the dish, with a handful of powdered blue blight."

Ormela made haste with the last two ingredients that would end Jherlom's internal torture. Eradia placed one of her thin hands over Jherlom's forehead, and with her other hand, she forced Jherlom's mouth open.

"Pour the mixture down Jherlom's throat," Eradia ordered.

Ormela obeyed, and Eradia pinched his nose as she did. Once the mixture was in his mouth, Eradia also forced Jherlom's mouth closed.

"I am uncertain if this will work," Eradia announced. "I have never seen a curse as serious as this before."

Jherlom swallowed the mixture, and Eradia began to chant twelve words and repeat them over and over again. Ormela and Khon'Tenn'Nul could not comprehend the words the high priestess was speaking. A moment later, the natural color of Jherlom's flesh began to return as the grey slowly faded away. His senses were becoming attuned, and his memory was returning to him.

Eradia turned to the gnome cleric. "Get me a potion of restoration from my chambers."

Khon'Tenn'Nul left quickly, and Eradia and Ormela watched as Jherlom slowly returned to normal. His typical melancholy gaze returned, and so did the green of his eyes that matched the color of asparagus.

Khon'Tenn'Nul returned with a flask of glowing yellow liquid. Eradia poured the flask into Jherlom's mouth slowly, allowing the druid time to swallow without choking.

Jherlom asked no questions. His mind was still numb. The liquid tasted nearly like butter, and it was warm and went down his throat smoothly. His recovery was hastening now. He shifted as if meaning to remove himself from the restoration altar.

Eradia pressed her hands down on his chest and forced him back down, indicating to him that his recovery was not complete yet.

The high priestess helped Jherlom roll onto his side, and she placed a bowl beneath his chin. A moment later, he began to vomit grey ooze into the bowl. Ormela and Khon'Tenn'Nul stared at the druid in disgust.

"The last of the curse is leaving his body now," Eradia explained to them. "This is the last of the evil that has been poisoning him."

A few minutes later, the vomiting stopped, and Eradia removed the bowl. The entire curse that had spawned within him had completely exited his elven body. Jherlom rested back down flat on the altar. He was no longer ill, though exhausted and still physically weak, but his mind was his own again.

"How long?" Jherlom asked with his eyes closed.

"We don't know, Jherlom," Eradia told him. "Utopia found you and brought you here."

Jherlom sat upright immediately. "Then the prince is…"

"Not here," Eradia finished his sentence for him and eased him back down flat.

Jherlom sighed, recalling what he saw. His memory was still blurry. "I am not certain, but I believe the prince drowned when he leaped into The Blind River."

"There have been rumors about it. I have been praying that he survived the fall, but you must rest now. In your current condition, you will be unable to help the prince if he is in trouble. The curse in you is now gone. I have never seen one like it, but you still need a few days of rest to recover."

Jherlom silently nodded. He knew that the high priestess was right.

"Khon'Tenn'Nul will tend to your needs, Jherlom," Eradia told him.

Eradia left the restoration chamber. Khon'Tenn'Nul offered Jherlom a drink of water. He took it quickly and thankfully.

"I sent a pack of dire wolves to search for the prince," Jherlom told the gnome cleric. "They might have something to report by now."

"The other druids will receive word if they search something, won't they?"

"Yes," Jherlom said, staring up at the ceiling. "I just feel so helpless here, when I could be out there doing something."

"You've done plenty," the gnome assured him, taking back the glass from Jherlom. "You have wolf scouts looking for him. Your forest friends will find him quickly. He is skilled enough in survival and herb medicine that I think he is better off in the wilderness somewhere. The enemy will have difficulty finding him far from civilization."

"That is true, Khon'Tenn'Nul," Jherlom muttered. "However, the graveness of the situation is greater than you know. One of the noble lords may be involved in this frozen fire plot. Captain Tor'Albus tried to take the prince a few days ago. I discovered later that it wasn't Tor'Arbus, but an imposter. Someone with the ability to change their form to look like someone else is definitely involved."

"Only an illusionist can do such things," the gnome retorted.

Jherlom did not respond to his suggestion. "I do not have great evidence proving my theory, but I strongly feel that someone we know is involved with this strange attack on Mystasia."

"Who can it be?" The gnome asked, mostly to himself.

"Someone with a great understanding of the elements," Jherlom advised him. "It is someone who knows how to make two opposites work together. It seems likely that it is a druid or an elementalist. Fairies simply do not behave in such ways, but I do not know anyone who would create such a destructive spell. I do not know anyone capable of causing so much death, especially against people they have come to know."

"Nor do I," a voice said at the entrance of the restoration chamber.

The arch druid Vadamar Oakfounder, along with Drabel Thunderthumb, entered the chamber with their hands folded in front of them. Jherlom recognized the ruddy-skinned face of the arch druid at once. His bushy eyebrows, his long mustache and his eyes, which looked much like pools of mercury were all there on his round face, just as Jherlom had last seen him. Drabel's sturdy form was directly beside their master. His long sepia hair fell upon his shoulders. His square face was home to those infamous glossy indigo eyes everyone frequently commented on.

"Vadamar," Jherlom said, smiling. "It is good to see you, master. You too, Drabel."

Vadamar approached Jherlom, and they touched hands, their palms flat against the other for a brief moment. Drabel and Jherlom did the same. It was an interaction that the clerics had never seen before.

"I have a plan in motion," Vadamar announced. "I have spoken with the arch mage Dranus, and we feel there is a chance to defend ourselves against the frozen fire spell." Everyone listened intently and surrounded the arch druid.

"Legend speaks of a lost lake somewhere in the County of Wishwater. Nearly everyone regards this as a myth, but the lake does exist. I have been there, and only myself is permitted to enter the forest that surrounds it. This is because of the deep secrets that nature has there. The water in the lake is wish water, which has extremely powerful healing agents within it. The lake is invisible, except on nights when the blue moon Shalamar is full. As you know, this only happens once a year."

"Yes," Jherlom recalled. "I have come across this story a few times in the druid archives. But how will the wish water help us against the frozen fire?"

"We can make rings," the arch druid suggested.

"The Forge of Soulfire," Jherlom exclaimed, and Vadamar nodded. Jherlom already knew what he and Dranus had planned.

Jherlom, sitting upright in the bed, looked up at Vadamar. "You mean to forge rings at the Forge of Soulfire, and then travel to the lost lake to cool them. You believe that the ancient magic in both of those locations will craft rings strong enough to resist the frozen fire spell altogether."

Vadamar nodded. "But there is a great danger with the Forge of Soulfire."

"What is it?" the gnome interrupted.

"The forge is located three miles down in the Red Oubliette, where there is a broad tunnel known as Hell's Mouth. It glows red and is very hot. Some molten fire sits inside of this broad cavern. The Forge of Soulfire is inside Hell's Mouth. It is the only known entrance into the hells below, but the paladins say that route has been destroyed or cut off. However, legends say that there is still a demon lair within that cavern."

"What kind of demons?" Khon'Tenn'Nul asked quickly.

"The legends speak of blood demons," Vadamar replied.

Khon'Tenn'Nul silently cursed himself for not remembering the mythological tale. Like the prince, he had chosen the grey path of the cleric temple. The red path was the path demon slayers chose. However, clerics of both paths were well educated on demon lore. The Forge of Soulfire was a legend that Khon'Tenn'Nul had nearly forgotten.

The gnome turned to the arch druid. "You will need blacksmiths and demon slayers to travel to Hell's Mouth."

Vadamar nodded. "Dranus and I must also travel to both locations to oversee the proper completion of this quest. Only I can enter the forest to the lost lake. Only I know the way to get to its pristine silver shores. Even if someone else found their way there, which is impossible, the water will be invisible. No one other than myself has to be there during a night when the blue moon is full."

CHAPTER XIV
Discussion in Shade Deep

TASKICA FOUND BORIN in the gore gallery. It was a new room within Shade Deep that both Borin and the orcs wanted for the purposes of entertainment. Behind panes of glass were body parts of enemies taken from previous battle scenes. The body parts were displayed as if they were pictures.

Taskica shook her head. "I can't say that I approve of the gore gallery, but if it keeps you and the orcs happy, I will desist in removing it."

"It excites us," Borin said. "It also motivates us for upcoming battles."

Taskica shook her head again. "You are human, but at times, I think you are somehow more orc than you are human."

"I have been down here in The Underworld all my life," Borin said, looking at one of the grisly displays. "How do you expect me to act when I know many more orcs than I do humans? The only humans I have known are you and the Cannibal King, but he isn't human anymore, is he?"

Taskica seemed upset with the new topic and lowered her head slightly. "No, he isn't. What happened to him was tragic. He is merely a shadow now. There is absolutely no humanity left in him. Sometimes I feel that way about myself."

"No," Borin said, shaking his head. "You still care about those around you, down here. You want the best for everyone down here."

A gigantic shadow appeared from the east entrance of the gore gallery. The two-headed form was ten feet tall, and as it entered the room, its brown flesh easily identified it as an ettin.

Taskica turned to view the ettin. "Ah, Nagh Shann, do you have something to report?"

"Yes, master," the ettin replied. "I have installed a fire vent trap down the hall, and I have also put a triple trap door in place. I have much more work to do, but the traps you requested for this area are done."

"Very well, Nagh," Taskica stated. She was very pleased with the progress of the trap specialist. "Take a while to relax before you engage in your other duties."

"As you wish, Master Shadowdawn." The ettin left, and a moment later, Tybiss hovered into the room.

Taskica welcomed the beholder with a question. "How do you like your quarters, Tybiss?"

"I love my quarters," the beholder replied. "It is more of a library than a place for sleeping, which I am happy about."

Borin's voice was less friendly. "Have your forces abandoned the Wall of Seven Towers?"

"It is in progress," Tybiss reported. "You'll find my ettins and erinyes an excellent addition to your army. What orcs I have had in my service have also joined your forces. I am told we have more than six hundred orcs in our army now."

"That is still small compared to the Mystasias," Borin pointed out.

"No, it's not," Taskica replied. "The earthquake that my dark druids and I created months ago destroyed three of their armories, and it killed the most notable warlord in Mystasia. We have already destroyed the war guild with the frozen fire. Half of the human army has already been destroyed as well."

"So what is next?" Tybiss asked.

"Borin will lead an attack on Jasper Oath," Taskica explained. "Three centuries ago, it was a human city, but now it belongs to the elves. It is the capital of the Wish Water County. Borin will lead our army to attack Jasper Oath Castle."

Taskica turned to Borin. "Leave none alive, Borin. Tybiss and I need some rest from this. None of my dark druids are strong enough to use the frozen fire spell at this time. This assault will be done by force, and without the frozen fire."

Taskica glanced back at Tybiss. "I know the floor plan of that castle. I have given Olsegg a map of the entire castle, and he knows where to open the portal to make the surprise attack."

"What about the fairies?" Borin asked.

Taskica grinned. "Those small beings seem to worry you even more than the dwarves, Borin. "

"For good reason," Borin exclaimed. "They are only one foot tall, and hard to strike down with a weapon. They are also very resourceful when it comes to using magic."

"The forest fairies can use magic at will, and their style of magic is the same as the druids. It is based on nature. However, I know the location of the fairy orb tree.

There are too many fairy birthing trees to destroy, but if you can manage to destroy the fairy orb tree, they will lose their ability to use their magic. That tree is the source of their power and life. Without it, their life span will shorten to mere weeks. They will continue to be born from the birthing trees, but they will die shortly afterwards. We will need the use of the frozen fire for that attack. For now, attack Jasper Oath, and leave none alive. The elven archers will be the greatest danger there, so be wary of them."

Borin bowed to Taskica. "I will take most of the army and leave now."

Tybiss continued to hover behind Taskica. "That ettin that was here a moment ago, who is he? I have never seen him before."

"His name is Nagh Shann," Taskica explained. "He is an engineer, and particularly specializes in manufacturing and setting traps. Borin found him in the town of Ihon Delgrisol, which isn't far from here. I am paying him well for his duties. He is vital to the security of this dungeon."

"Taskica, how do you know so much about the layouts of Mystasian castles, and the locations of such important places?"

"I am very resourceful," Taskica replied. "With my style of druidic magic, anything can be accomplished."

CHAPTER XV

Assault on Jasper Oath

THE SUN PEEKED OVER the horizon with compelling curiosity. It reflected off Jerymia Braveblood's plate armor brilliantly. He stood on a catwalk on the west side of Jasper Oath Castle, named after the solitary almost at the center of Agate Cluster Lake in Wish Water County.

To the west, Jermyia could see Frog Water Anemone Lake, which was connected to Agate Cluster Lake and the Lake of the Woods. His short, pale blonde hair looked dull compared to his shiny armor. He was a handsome man, even with the 'L' shaped scar on the bridge of his nose. His indigo eyes stared into the grassy plains absently as he brought his hand up to his chin and pondered thoughtfully. His sturdy, broad form turned around once he heard footsteps approaching from behind him. Count Sedor'Dyr was only a few feet away.

"Something troubles you, Sir Braveblood," the elf noble lord said, taking two more steps until he was at the knight's side.

"It's Nadja, isn't it?" the elf noble continued. "You don't understand the science of magic. And yet you love that woman terribly. The situation is a tug-of-war with your heart, Sir Braveblood."

Sedor starred into Jermyia's eyes. Their color remained him of the ocean waters that crashed onto the west coastal shores of the Wish Water County.

Jermyia sighed. "Yes, my lord, you are right. It is Nadja. But the problem is not that I don't understand magic. It's just that I believe magic does more harm than good."

"You live by your sword," Sedor'Dyr said, gazing off into the same direction as Jermyia.

"I live by my shield," Jermyia corrected the noble. "A man without defense is a dead man."

Sehor'Dyr nodded and placed his hand on Jermyia's shoulder. "Perhaps it is time you go to her, then. You are my favorite of the Mystasian Elite Knights. That is why I insisted that the king send you to me, but there are other knights here. You may go home, Sir Braveblood. It seems as though the dark druids have all been killed, so I suppose I no longer need you here."

"I am a knight," Jermyia commented. "What good am I against magic?"

"You are the bravest man I know," Sedor said sternly. "Your presence here offers me security, which I need. But it's been months since you've last been home. It is time to leave here and return."

Sehor turned to face the western country once again. "Had the dark druids taken control of this countryside, they would have had access to a power that would have made them greater than the druids you and I have come to know."

"You speak of the lost lake," Jermyia said, not entirely certain.

"Yes," Sedor said nodding. "This countryside protects the lake. No one knows where it is. It is safe from everybody, but the dark druids may have found it, had they not been destroyed."

"I will leave now," Jermyia said as thoughts of Nadja filled his mind. "I have everything I need back at home, and my horse is down below."

Both men exchanged hands in a strong handshake, and Jermyia started down a flight of stairs down from the catwalk. Sedor watched him as he approached his horse, Sorrel. The horse's sorrel color and lean build gave the knight the idea for naming his horse. Sedor watched as Jermyia collected his horse from the stables. Before long, the knight was out of sight, riding toward the south side of Willow Wall.

Sedor sighed. A large part of him did not want Jerymia to go, but the Wish Water County was not Jermyia's home. Sedor watched Jermyia become visible over a distant hill, and then disappear over another. The elite knight was gone.

"Count Sedor'Dyr," an elf screamed. Sedor turned around to find the sergant-at-arms, Boh'Ogren, rushing toward him and pointed at the outer ward of the castle.

A single portal opened. Sixty medusa archers, more than three hundred orcs, and sixty ogres exited the portal. One hundred feet in the air above the northwest tower, another portal opened, making way for one hundred and ten harpies.

The harpies attacked the archers in the northwest tower immediately, before they even knew that the savage vulture-women were there. Their claws were equally as sharp as the blades of the elven pikemen below, and scraped and clawed at their faces and eyes. This maneuver allowed the medusas, ogres and orcs to get out of the portal with very little harassment from the elven archers.

Sedor'Dye and Boh'Ogren watched in disbelief as the castle was stormed from the inside. The medusas were the biggest threat. They were armed with triple barbed arrows dipped into poison. Those who survived their arrow strikes would have to face them up close, and their gaze caused petrifaction. Anyone close enough to them would be turned into stone. The strategy was perfect. Whoever led the attack seemed to know that the elven archers were the greatest archers in the land, and that eliminating them from the battle first would bring the odds heavily to their favor.

The archers of all four towers of the castle only managed to shoot down fourteen harpies. Their attack was not only a surprise from above, but incredibly savage—enough to overwhelm the elven archers. Many of them panicked.

The skills of the elven pikemen, and their thin bodies, were no match against the brute ogres and the merciless combat skills of the orcs. From behind the ogres, the medusa archers carefully continued to fire their battle bows made out of bone. Their range was not as great as the elven archers, but they continued to target the elf archers. The harpies attacked from the sky, while the ogres and orcs concentrated on the elf pikemen.

"Aim the trillistas at the medusas!" Boh'Ogren ordered. Unlike a ballista, a trillista had three colossal arrows. All three arrows were fired from the three trillistas, and many of them penetrated both an ogre and a medusa behind them. A couple of them missed their targets, and three others only killed an ogre each. Sedor'Dyr could see that they were losing the battle, even though they outnumbered the enemy.

Stepping out of a freshly made portal was Borin Saken. Behind him were two manticores. The winged, lion-like beasts followed their master as he joined the battle, slaying every elf pikeman that was in his chosen path.

The enemy began to make its advance far below the inner ward of the castle. They had bypassed the city of Jasper Oath. The outer ward of the castle was about two hundred feet above sea level. The enemy would have to climb about seven hundred feet to the outer ward, and then another five hundred feet to the castle itself. A series of archer towers and a single curving steep stairway was all there was between the enemy and Jasper Oath Castle.

"They have a long way to go before they reach us, your highness," Boh'Ogren stated with confidence.

"But why are they here?" Sedor'Dyr queried with much less doubt.

"They are poorly equipped," Boh'Ogren shouted to Sedor'Dyr, moving farther to the left for a better look.

Sedor'Dyr frowned. "They don't have to be equipped! Those ogres are merely machines of muscle and flesh. The medusas are a lethal nightmare! We may have the numbers, but an army like this can turn the tide quickly, Boh'Ogren."

One hundred and twenty elven pikemen descended the stairs toward the outer ward to greet the enemy, giving the archers more time to eliminate as many as they could before they reached the castle. The greater range of the elven long bows gave

Sedor'Dyr's forces a great advantage over the medusa archers. The bone battle bows of the medusas had less range, and the elves had the high ground. The elven archers concentrated most of their fire on the medusa archers, who slithered as fast as they could to reach the inner ward.

Borin smashed his forehead into the nose of an approaching elven pikeman, and then flipped the elf over his head and back, and swung his axe down over the elf's body, splitting it in two.

Several pikemen jabbed their pikes at one of the manticores, creating puncture tears in its wings, and one in its chest. The second manticore landed behind the pikemen. Together, with savage, bloodthirsty fury, the manticores clawed up the pikemen, snapping their jaws occasionally over their arms and stinging some of them as well with their scorpion-like tails. Both manticores suffered minor injuries, but they were eager to taste more elf blood. One of the three arrows of the trillista struck down a medusa, killing her immediately.

The harpies continued to harass the elven archers, clawing at their eyes and faces with savage hatred. Some of them gripped the archers well enough to pull them off the archer towers, sending them more than one hundred feet below. Almost all the archer towers were unattended now, allowing Borin's forces to climb their way to the top with very little resistance.

More quickly now, Borin's forces pushed their way up to the inner ward of the castle. The ettins were much slower than the elves, but many of the ettins dropped dead only after eight or more arrows struck them. Any blows the ettins landed with their colossal war hammers killed the elves instantly with one crushing blow. Some of the orcs used throwing axes. Others relied on a sword or battle axe, but all of them fought with berserker rage, which easily overwhelmed the elves.

Boh'Ogren fired several arrows at an ettin approaching the castle entrance from the stables. Three of the arrows struck the ettin in the head, and it fell to the ground, knocking nearby orcs onto their feet. An average ettin weighed about the same as eight orcs.

"They are getting too close, your highness," Boh'Ogren said to Sedor'Dyr. "You need to retreat to the castle. I will hold them here."

Sedor'Dyr didn't argue. The sight of thirty or more medusas slithering up the stairs, and the destructive raw power of the ettins, was enough to convince him to leave.

One trillista took out two ettins, but the third arrow missed. The medusas were now within range, and their poisoned tipped arrows began to strike down the elven archers. Some medusas were close enough to petrify the unsuspecting elven pikemen, who were already engaged in battle with orcs. Sedor'Dyr opened fire on a few harpies swooping down toward him as he fled to the castle. His arrows knocked down three of them, which all crashed uncontrollably into the castle wall.

Boh'Ogren pulled an arrow out of his quiver and released it. The arrow struck a harpy in the wing, sending it crashing into the inner ward. However, he failed to notice the medusa to his right. He turned, catching a glimpse of something at the corner of his eye, but once he made eye contact with the slithering beast, it was too late. His skin turned grey, and his flesh hardened. He had become petrified. An ogre slammed his war hammer over the stone figure of Boh'Ogren, shattering his lifeless body into many pieces of pebbles.

The scent of blood was plentiful and fresh, and overwhelmed any other smell in the inner ward. The elves could hear laughter and jokes through their foreign speech of hatred.

Borin's forces had conquered the inner ward, and the final leg of the climb had been reached. The elves in the archer towers of the castle were the only resistance left, save for three more elven pikemen and another three hundred elven archers stationing themselves on the catwalks of the castle, desperate to stop the enemy.

The airborne attacks from the harpies made the archers' attacks difficult. They distracted them, forcing the archers to fire at them instead of the approaching enemy. Sedor'Dyr slammed his fist into his open hand in frustration. The attack was well planned. Almost every obstacle the enemy faced had been countered extremely well.

The archers had eliminated more than sixty of the enemy forces, but their advance was too quick to eliminate enough of them. Arrows tore through muscle like a ripsaw, but Borin's forces continued ignoring their wounds and the pain that came with them.

The battle moved into the castle through the great hall, and through the elf knight quarters. One knight blocked Borin's path from entering Jasper

Oath Castle. One of the manticores pounced at the knight, who managed to cut into the face of the manticore.

The manticore roared at the injury the knight caused, but before it could attack again, Borin Saken engaged in battle with the knight. The battle lasted thirty seconds when Borin finally bested the knight. The battle ended with Borin's sword going through the throat of the knight.

Sedor'Dyr watched in terror at the surprise assault within the walls of his own castle. He muttered to himself, "Sir Braveblood, I should never have sent you back to your love. I need you right now."

Sedor'Dyr entered the battle, surprising an ogre in the stables from behind. The noble lord appeared from within a stack of hay and slit the ogre's throat from behind.

The clever maneuver caught the attention of Borin Saken, who followed Sedor'Dyr.

Most of the resident quarters down the corridor were empty, but those inside hoping that the enemy would pass by without opening the doors of their quarters paid the price for their wrong judgment. They met their deaths with crushing blows from war hammers, or the stinging steel of the swords used by the orcs.

Outside, screams continued as the harpies finished off the elven forces that either refused to enter the castle, or were unable to retreat inside. The medusa archers began to slither inside as well. Only a few stray elven archers remained, trying to find a place to hide, but the enemy was everywhere. There was nowhere to hide.

The lance of an elven knight pierced the leg of an ettin, making it all the way through its brownish flesh. Angry with the injury, the ettin raised its war hammer and crushed the knight. The knight's armor was no match for the weight of the weapon and the strength of the ettin.

Sedor'Dyr fired three more arrows. All of them slivered deep into an approaching medusa's torso, and one struck her in the forehead.

Some of the elves began to freeze in battle. Their nerves festered with fear of the blood hunters that had come to destroy their beautiful city and everyone in it. Metal melodies continued as swords clashed with pikes, and war cries and screams of agony added to the sound.

Sedor'Dyr witnessed an elven knight pulled his sword out of the body of an orc. Seconds later, the knight grasped his throat. The arrow of an accurate medusa was able to strike the knight in the throat, avoiding both his helmet and his chain mail.

Sedor'Dyr fled the great hall, retreating into one of the knight's quarters.

An ogre entered the room and grinned at the noble. His green skin was soaked with the blood of elves he had already killed. Blood dripped from his war hammer at regular intervals. The ogre raised his right leg, and sent Sedor'Dyr across the room with a powerful kick to the face. Sedor'Dyr suddenly felt cold, as if someone had opened winter upon him. The powerful blow left him stunned. The elf noble was motionless, but the ogre ended his life anyway. His war hammer swung down hard onto the noble lord's chest. Jasper Oath Castle fell to the enemy shortly after.

Taskica waited in the portal room for the return of Borin and the army. She waited for quite some time before anyone stepped through the portal. She noticed that several orcs made exit from the portal with one or two arrows driven deep into their green flesh. A moment later, Borin stepped out of the portal.

"Were you successful?" Taskica asked.

"Yes," Borin said, nodding, "But the layout you gave us was wrong. The layout of Jasper Oath was different than the plans you gave Olsegg. We lost many more than we had intended to. Their direction you gave us placed us in the outer ward of the castle, and not inside the castle as you had planned."

Taskica lowered her head thoughtfully. "They must have changed the layout of the castle. I knew the layout twenty years ago, but the elves must have reconstructed parts of the castle since then."

Olsegg stepped out of the portal and stepped aside to make room for more to come through.

"I could have used my healing portal," Olsegg suggested. "But the arrows would be harder to remove from those who have been struck by them if I'd used such a portal."

"We will tend to the injured the old-fashioned way. We will remove the arrows by normal means, and the injured can drink healing potions that Tybiss is brewing right now. The two of you have done very well. Go rest yourselves."

CHAPTER XVI

Doves of Fire

NORDACH WAS LESS THAN A MILE behind Abadon and his followers. They traveled south out of Jade Coin Forest and into the natural garden forest of Serenity Swan Forest, in the most northern region of the Fairy Fern Forest Territory.

Its beauty tempted the weary travelers to forget The Haunted Forest and to enter the Fairy Fern Forest instead, but they rejected the temptation.

They were in the northern portion of the territory that the forest fairies, sprites and dryads called home. The forest folk reminded Abadon of Jherlom.

The druids had once told him that they adapted their magic from such folk many centuries ago, long before the War of the Gods, during times when gods and goddesses and their worshippers maintained healthy communications and a respectable relationship with one another that was practiced constantly.

"I think it's safe to assume that Jherlom might be dead," Abadon blurted out, breaking the silence of the morning. "If he was alive, I think the forest animals would have found me on his behalf and reported my location to him by now."

Gafnan disagreed. "Your highness, Mystasia is a very large country, and forests easily cover more than three quarters of the land. It will take time for him to locate you."

Abadon looked up at the tops of the oak trees. Somewhere behind him, a branch snapped. Abadon, Epona, Gafnan and the two beasts accompanying them froze still. Sabre growled, looking in the direction that they had come from. The metaughla did nothing. It waited as well, but did not have the sharp senses the saber bear had.

The three travelers turned, but there were no animals behind them. Another snap sounded, and it was closer to them this time.

"Someone is here," Abadon whispered. Everyone remained silent, waiting for the intruder to make another move. Epona, Gafnan and Meta looked around for themselves. Sabre began to backtrack toward the paranoid prince.

Suddenly, three feet to Abadon's left, a thud sounded and a twig on the ground was abruptly split in half, without any obvious reason. Seconds later, a branch from a shrub three feet behind Abadon was chopped from its parent branch.

"He's here!" Abadon screamed, running away from the strange activity.

Epona closed her eyes and clenched her fists. Something struck the beast master at his side, causing him to bellow out in pain and fall to the ground.

Several seconds later, the young witch opened both her eyes and her hands. A dove of fire formed in each of them and flew from her palms. They circled in the air, seeking the invisible intruder. Epona closed her eyes again, concentrating hard, and both doves joined nearly as one and soared toward Abadon. The doves of fire crashed into the invisible intruder, who was only a few feet away from Abadon. For a quick moment, the intruder appeared visible as the doves crashed into him, but he disappeared again two seconds later. They could hear the intruder screaming in pain as he fled the area, running to the northwest. His moans of pain continued to ring out more distant from them, until they couldn't hear him anymore.

"That was incredible, Epona!" Abadon gasped. "What was that spell?"

"Doves of fire," Epona said with pride. "Whoever it was is obviously still alive. I concentrated too much in making the doves find him, rather than make them powerful enough to kill him. I designed the spell to track invisible objects, and it obviously works." She sighed in relief. "This is the first time I have actually had a chance to use the spell."

"But he is injured," Abadon said, his voice was strained with desperate hope.

"Yes, he is, but so is Gafnan."

Abadon rushed to Gafnan's side. After a moment of examination, Abadon concluded the nature of the injury.

"His right lung is ruptured. He was struck by something incapable of piercing or cutting flesh. The wound was likely a club, or even a strong punch or kick."

Abadon placed his right hand on the beast master's chest. Like Epona, no words were spoken to perform the magic. Sabre was at his master's side, nuzzling him, trying to get movement out of the big man. Epona watched with mild interest.

"I thought clerics get their power from their gods and goddesses," she stated.

"We do," Abadon replied, concentrating on repairing the ruptured lungs. "All clerics of the Temple of Ku'Lee have faith in Iona Pawl, the Goddess of Healing. As a result, we possess steady power, supplied to us by her. However, like anyone else, if we use too much magic in a short period of time, its effects weaken. It takes longer to heal."

"Magru is the god of witchcraft," Epona said, for the sake of conversation. "How is he, Abadon?"

"I used so much of my energy healing Meta that it'll take quite some time to heal Gafnan. I am afraid that the healing process is working slowly."

Epona walked up to the creature and began to pat its body next to one of its eyes. The metaughla opened and closed the eye occasionally. It appeared to enjoy the treatment it was receiving. Abadon watched as Epona petted the creature.

"Fascinating, isn't it, Abadon? To be this close to something so large and normally very aggressive without having to kill it," Epona said softly, but with great curiosity. "To be able to actually gaze upon the beast, and get to know it for what it is."

"It is a destructive beast, that's what it is," Abadon muttered. "How long do you plan to keep it?"

"Just until tomorrow," the young witch replied. "While it is still under my charm spell, I have commanded it to travel away from us before it wears off."

Abadon nodded that he approved. "An excellent plan, Epona, but how long do your charm spells last?"

"I cast one of my more powerful charm spells, which will last for at least another several hours before I'll have to cast it again," Epona assured him.

Eventually, all three of the humans were asleep. They woke up sporadically during the night. Abadon rolled over to his left side, drifting on the edge of sleep. With his eyes closed, he continued to drift in and out of sleep, on the border that separated consciousness from deep sleep. He opened one eye, and then quickly opened both eyes. Skyline was standing only several feet away from him staring straight at him.

Abadon quickly shut both eyes. The image had disturbed him greatly. Nothing was stopping Skyline from feeding upon them during the night. The intense fear that Abadon felt suddenly turned into a realization that sparked hope. He realized that Skyline was clearly watching over them, like a guardian. Soon, the fear he felt became a feeling of warm security. Nothing would disturb any of them, as long as Skyline was there to watch over them. Once that realization was locked within Abadon's mind, he finally drifted into a deep sleep and never woke again until Epona screamed hours later. The metaughla was gone.

"By the gods, I fell asleep and didn't get the chance to send metaughla away!"

Epona turned to Abadon, who suddenly rose up, startled by the hysterical behavior of the witch. A terrifying look masked Epona's face as she turned toward Abadon. The metaughla was right next to the young prince. Epona wanted to warn Abadon, but as she realized that a warning was too late, she also realized that the metaughla was simply standing there. The charm spell had expired, but it made no aggressive movements to threaten Abadon, or anyone else. Its ten tentacles waved harmlessly around.

Abadon quickly got to his feet and backed away from the beast. Epona walked slowly toward the beast and placed her hand on its body. The metaughla jerked back slightly, and Epona pulled her hand back. The creature still did nothing. Epona tried again to pet the creature, and this time it let her. The metaughla seemed to enjoy the special attention, just as it did during the night.

"Cast the spell again, Epona!" Abadon screamed. "Cast it now, before it eats you!"

"It won't attack me, Abadon," Epona stated. "I think it likes me."

"But how is that possible, if the charm spell wore off?" Abadon asked.

Epona shrugged. "I don't know, Abadon. I've never had this happen to me before. When my charm spells wear off, the creature under its influence always returns back to normal, but this metaughla likes me."

"Can you explain that?" Abadon inquired as he watched Epona and the metaughla begin to bond.

"Perhaps it got attached to me last night," she said. "Maybe the healing you did for it last night caused it to want to stay with us. Maybe my spell has somehow caused a permanent effect. Either way, the metaughla seems as tame as any animal Gafnan travels with."

Abadon stared at her, and his voice hinted slight anger. "You mean to keep it, then?"

Epona did not answer right away. She looked into one of the creature's eyes. They were like smooth, obsidian beads with a special shine. She could see her reflection in them. Skyline watched calmly as everything transpired before his eyes. He did not seem to be threatened at all by the creature's presence.

"Why not, Abadon? I can't just let it wander into the wilderness in this state. I might as well take it with me," Epona decided.

"What if it attacks one of us?" Abadon asked in protest.

"As long as none of you make aggressive or hostile movements toward Meta, I don't think he'll attack," Epona said.

"Meta!" Abadon exclaimed out loud. "You already named it?"

Epona nodded with a large grin, and began to talk to the creature.

"Epona, you are unbelievable!" Abadon stormed away from the witch in denial.

Gafnan led them across shallows in the River of Copper Cedars, which continued south from Griffin Lake. As the three approached The Haunted Forest, Epona began to question the beast master about it. "Do you know your way around The Haunted Forest, Gafnan?"

"I have been in some of its regions a few times," he replied, nodding. "Very few who enter, return. The spirits and ghosts that haunt the forest can kill you in numerous ways. Some by fear alone, others go insane, and others are physically tortured. It seems no one victim dies the same way."

Fear had become their worst enemy as they approached The Haunted Forest. The thick gloom drifted sluggishly past the trees, concealing some of them. Even the saber bear Sabre seemed reluctant to enter the forest. The four stood there, half a mile away from the terrifying border that separated the Royal Province of South Guard from The Haunted Forest Territory.

"We have to go on," Epona said.

"But how will Jherlom find us this far away?" Abadon said hysterically. "He'll never suspect that we went into The Haunted Forest."

"He is a druid, Abadon," Epona blared. "He has eyes and ears everywhere. You know that! I am sure he'll discover your location, even while in The Haunted Forest."

Frustrated with the arguing, Gafnan began to walk toward the forest. Sabre followed closely behind him. Fixing each other with glares, Abadon and Epona began to follow as well, setting their differences aside.

The forest was a mix of red cedars, black oaks, bramble braids and ghost willows. They crossed over the invisible border of woodland splendor and into the woodland of obscurity and death. The fog was thicker than the forest itself, offering the least amount of visibility possible.

"We need to travel south," Gafnan insisted."

"Are you sure?" Abadon asked.

"I am very sure," Gafnan persisted. "To travel farther east from here is very dangerous. We need to travel south for a while before continuing east."

Abadon and Epona nodded in agreement. The forest sloped downward slightly, and they soon encountered a very small lake. Though the fog was less thick here, it still denied full visibility of the lake. The fog drifted and clustered together like ghosts reuniting and touching. The chill of the forest was greater than any night any of the three had experienced that year. Abadon bent down and cupped his hands to drink from the lake. As his fingers made contact with the water, he jerked his hands back as the cold liquid surrounded his hands.

Gafnan dipped a water skin into the lake, and shared the water with the others. Gafnan assessed the area. The forest was quiet, save for the call of a few birds that Abadon and Epona had never heard before. Their spooky cries echoed with the calls of loons that were sailing on the small lake.

Gafnan stretched out his neck and squinted, looking toward the opposite side of the lake, which was barely visible through the fog.

"What is it, Gafnan?" Epona asked, failing to hide her fear.

"I don't know," Gafnan replied. "I thought I saw a shadow move on the other side of the lake."

Sabre was looking across the lake as well, but he didn't growl. Gafnan tilted his head back and inhaled the air. There was no smell in the air. It was just thick and clustered with cold. The four continued on, looking over their shoulders every ten seconds.

After a long time of traveling, the weary travelers remained undisturbed. Gafnan began to lead them east and shortly after slowed his pace. Something large and black vaguely outlined through the fog snared his attention. It was about his height, but three times as wide. The top of the figure was uneven and sharp. The fog continued to drift to the south, and as Gafnan approached the figure, he realized that it was the broken tree stump of a black oak. A large opening was visible on the east side of the tree trunk.

With slow, cautious steps, Gafnan walked toward it, and a figure in black dashed out of the trunk with a swift kick to Gafnan's chest, knocking him back. Sabre stood on his hind legs and roared. As Abadon and Epona rushed to the beast master's aid, Gafnan had already recovered from the assault and raised his broadsword, ready to attack.

Epona shouted, "Gwan? Gwan, is that you?"

Both Gafnan and the black figure froze, and Abadon recognized the man in black robes as well. "Gwan, it is you," the young prince exclaimed.

"You know this man?" Gafnan asked, surprised.

"Yes," Abadon said, nodding. "It's Gwan Eastfire. He is a ninja of the Flaming Fist Clan that my uncle was the master of."

"I know you," Epona said, suddenly realizing that she recognized the ninja.

"You do?" Abadon asked.

"Yes," the witch told the prince. "He was the one who was attacked by Meta the night you guys showed up at my cottage."

Abadon turned to Gwan. "What happened to you, Gwan? My father asked you and the rest of

163

your clan to enter The Underworld in search of Fire Fern Keep. All of you entered The Underworld about four months ago, and never returned. What happened to you?"

"I remember very little," Gwan said, shrugging. "Most of us were killed off by the orc tribes and other dangers of The Underworld your nightmares wouldn't dare dream of. We survived for a while down there, and we found the keep, but I believe I am all that's left of my clan."

Abadon interrogated the ninja further. "Did you find the artifacts that were in the vault of Fire Fern?"

"No," he said, shaking his head. "They had already been taken when we found the keep. I eventually found a well that happened to be the bottom of the Saffron Moss Well, and I climbed up and found myself in the Diamond Aster Gardens."

Abadon's voice was grave. He was desperate to learn what had happened since the Flaming Fist Clan entered The Underworld.

"Where are the others, Gwan?"

"Dead," he exclaimed. "They are all dead, I am sure of it! Some of us got separated from each other, but I am sure everyone except me is dead."

Gwan lowered his head for a moment. Remembering what had happened down there seemed to be very difficult for him.

"You don't know what it's like down there," he said somberly. "It is a world so alien compared to ours. There are dangers that minds are incapable of imagining, your highness."

"Well, you're safe in Mystasia now, Gwan," Abadon said softly.

Gafnan brought up a different matter. "Why are you here in The Haunted Forest?"

Abadon turned immediately to Gwan. He was so concerned to learn what had happened to the rest of the ninja clan that he had forgotten how uniquely rare it was for anyone to travel into The Haunted Forest.

"It's you, isn't it?" Gafnan accused the ninja. "You're the one after the prince, aren't you?"

Gwan stared at the beast master. "Are you insane? I am hiding here because someone attacked me last night. It was someone that I couldn't see."

"The assassin after me," Abadon mumbled, and then he defended Gwan. "This can't be the assassin, Gafnan. My uncle was the master of the Flaming Fists."

Abadon's gaze fell back onto Gwan. "What happened to my uncle, Gwan?"

"I don't know," Gwan said, shrugging. "I got separated from him and most of the others. I can only tell you that he is likely dead. If he is alive, I do not know where he is. If he is dead, I cannot tell you where, why or how. I know nothing"

"What about the guild? Abadon asked. "The Flaming Fist Guild was destroyed shortly after you entered The Underworld."

"I haven't been back there yet," Gwan said. "Perhaps the assassin who's after you destroyed the guild, to be sure that all of us are dead. I am probably almost as important a target to the assassin as you are, your highness."

Gwan took a few steps toward Abadon. "I don't believe the assassin followed me into these woods."

"What's to stop him? He is invisible," Abadon declared.

Gafnan offered some comfort. "Many of the ghosts and spirits in these woods can apparently see anything that's invisible. Being invisible will be no advantage here."

"Let's be on our way, then," Epona demanded impatiently. "We are wasting time in a place that we are not welcome."

Gafnan took the lead once again, and Gwan brought up the rear. Occasionally, Abadon and Epona turned back to the ninja. For whatever reason, they did not trust him completely.

A short time later, the heavy gloom combined with the thick night prevented them from traveling any further. The small party settled for the night.

"Fire will attract attention," Gafnan pointed out. "I know it is cold, but I do not think we should light one."

"We will freeze without fire," Epona protested. "We'll have to take the chance of detection."

The beast master stood his ground. "Do you know what these spirits are capable of doing, Epona?"

"Do you know what hypothermia does, Gafnan?" she said. "My witchcraft should be able to handle any ghosts that bother us."

"As you wish," Gafnan submitted. "Build a fire if you like."

Even with Epona's witchcraft, a fire was difficult to build because of the cold, damp nature of the forest. A long moment later, Epona was able to create fire, and the four surrounded it, greedy for its warmth. The fire helped, but was almost useless against the cold, which caused the air itself to seem nearly solid. The air seemed heavy, and its chill made it difficult to move, and slowed their movements down considerably.

Abadon looked up at the sky, but none of the moons were present. Very few stars were visible through the overcast. Sleep would come in fractions that night, he was certain of that. He allowed his mind to ease, and then he began to think about Jherlom. What was taking him so long to find him? Did Gathus drowned? Abadon shook his head. What a stupid question. Abadon was much stronger than Gathus. The trow had surely drowned in the Diamond Cluster River.

He began to think about the cleric temple. How could Eradia have given him the very ring that led the invisible assassins to him? She would have never have given him such a ring intentionally.

Abadon jerked at the biting cold. He wondered if the burning hells would be hot enough to ward off such cold. The damp chill seemed invincible and permanent. The colossal shadow of the night seemed to be as equally impregnable. The flickering fire created the illusion that the night was trying to shatter the rim of light, to snatch him away from the others and deliver him right into the hands of the enemy searching for him.

As Abadon had predicted, sleep did come, but in fractions. They slept no more than fifteen minutes at a time, disturbed by both the cold and brutal fear never felt before. Surprisingly, there were no attacks during the night from ghosts or spirits. The nature of the forest promised them the presence of terrible spirits. Fear was tangible here. It lived and it breathed, just like them. It fed on the uncertainty that grew stronger within each of them. The darkness spawned shadows that neither approached nor retreated. They simply stalked the rim of light created by the fire, watching them. Sometimes the shadows melted before their eyes, and they were left wondering if they had actually been there at all. Nobility and strength did not matter here. Uncertainty and immortal fear ruled the woodland. Those who entered became slaves to fear. The more brave they pretended to be, the more the fear grew. Each of them knew it, and pretending to be fearless around each other soon became irrelevant.

Time seemed to be slow, or had stopped itself. Morning was not coming quickly enough. The gigantic eye of the night watched them closely. When daylight did return, forcing night's shadow to retreat to the west, their fear grew stronger still. Gwan Eastfire was missing.

CHAPTER XVII

Speculation and Blame

JERMYIA BRAVEBLOOD ENTERED the Forest of Wounded Sands wearily. He stopped suddenly and listened. Only the creatures of night replied with cries and calls. He adjusted his course to the southwest. The mage guild seemed to be absent. There was no sign of any attack on the guild, but no sign of the magi that studied within the establishment, either. He felt fear for Nadja Kost, the woman he loved, who devoted endless hours of study to the guild.

Abruptly, his nose caught the scent of a burning fire, which was still hidden from view behind a wall of wicker elms and bearded elm beard trees. The forest was bleak, and Jermyia began to wonder how the druids could feel at home in such a place that seemed unwelcoming. A long moment later, he found the clearing that the others had fled to. Myra Southstorm was the first to greet him.

"Sir Braveblood," the mage said brightly. Nadja perked up and ran to the knight. Jermyia dropped his long sword and held out his arms, waiting for Nadja to fall into them. Her wavy white, shoulder-length hair tickled his face as she thrust herself against him, ignoring the hardness of the armor around his warm flesh that she preferred to be against. Jermyia kissed her forehead, and the young magi looked up at him with her blue eyes, which were almost the same color as the blue roses in the Fairy Fern Forest.

"I've missed you," Nadja said, pressing her face against his chest once again.

"Me too," Jermyia replied, loud enough for only Nadja to hear.

"You found us," Myra said, smiling.

"It wasn't easy," Jermyia admitted. "I am not one who belongs in the woods."

Myra stood there smiling, holding her long silver pine staff in her right hand. Her face was roughly heart shaped, with her curly, tan-colored hair slightly parted downward at the center of her forehead. Her small periwinkle eyes with a glow of bliss rarely seen in Myra. Her refined appearance did not match the cold disposition she was known for.

As Jermyia and Nadja let go of one another, Myra shoved two slices of roast into the knight's hand, leaving him with no choice but to accept it. Jermyia noted the large sapphire gem attached to the end of Myra's staff. The gem was the in the shape of a half moon. He recalled that the shape of the gem at the end of a mage's staff represented their rank in the mage guild.

Nadja led Jermyia to a large pot resting over a fire. Surrounding the pot were the majority of the druids from Agate Hedge Keep, and the magi that studied at the Guild of the Blood Moon, where Nadja studied, researched and practiced spell craft.

Myra returned to dishing out beef stew into bark bowls crafted by the druid, Loamus Earthmend.

The arch druid Vadamar greeted the elite knight. "Welcome, Sir Braveblood. I am glad to see that you have made it here."

"It would have been easier if you have sent animals to guide me through the forest," Jermyia replied in a half-serious matter.

Vadamar shook his head. "I am sorry to say that the animals have not been behaving in normal manner. Mystasia is in chaos. Even the animals seem to be aware of the frozen fire, and are afraid of it."

Vadamar's ears were slightly pointed, indicating that he was half elf, half human. He had ruddy skin, bushy eyebrows, and a long mustache the color of chocolate. The most apparent feature on his round face was his eyes, which resembled pools of mercury. The arch druid's pine staff was thicker at the end, which was carved into an owl. His staff seemed almost more like a long club than a staff in the knight's eyes.

Jermyia spotted his brother at the edge of the camp, bending low as if trying to grasp something behind the tall, orange flowers known as flame feathers. Seconds later, Galum Braveblood carefully pulled out a snapping serpent. The serpent was a dull iron color, and large snapping jaws made its species obvious. Galum brought the iron snapping serpent back toward the campfire.

Galum grinned. "Jermyia, how about a game of serpent slap, if you dare?"

"I'll have you a game," Jermyia agreed quickly. Both brothers made it a point to live up to the family name, Braveblood. Galum was the elder of the two, and taunted Jermyia often in tests of might, courage and skill with a sword. Galum would always be the one to challenge Jermyia, and Jermyia never turned down a challenge. Both men were very brave indeed, but there was one great difference between the two. Their combat skills and preference in battle were opposite.

Jermyia watched Galum assemble a small fire that flickered only a couple of inches up from the ground, and then place the snake in the middle of the ring of fire.

Galum explained the rules of the game to his younger brother. "I have seen barbarian dwarves play this game in a tavern more than once. Normally, the game is played on a table without a fire. I am using the fire to keep the snake from escaping. The object of the game is to slap the serpent. You wager however many gold coins you wish, and if you can slap the serpent without getting bit, you earn those gold coins. You lose the wager if you are bit, and are often out of the game to seek attention from a healer."

Jermyia looked around the camp. His eyes finally spotted Ormela Bloodblend within the light of the fire. Jermyia nodded. "We do have a cleric here in the camp to heal us if either of us gets bitten. I have twenty-four gold coins on me. I am game."

Caprigus Flamefinger approached Drabel Thunderthumb on the opposite side of the large campfire from the two brothers. Drabel was reading through three scrolls with torn edges, and resting his sturdy frame against an oak tree. His long sepia hair fell over his shoulder as his glossy indigo eyes swept over the pages with vast interest.

Trying to get a glimpse of what the druid was reading, Caprigus inquired, "What are you doing, Drabel?"

Drabel looked up at the demon slayer cleric. His prominent olive green eyes and long raven hair with triple braids were his most noticeable features, along with his inverted triangular face.

"Sprite literature," Drabel replied. "Learning how to read and speak sprite is much more difficult than other forest folk. I imagine clerics have plenty to read in the cleric temple."

"Followers of the grey light and the red light have much to read. As a demon slayer, I follow the path of the red light," Caprigus explained. "I read analytical demonic writings more often than anything."

"Demonic writings?" Drabel mumbled incredulity. "I know little about demons, but I didn't think they were intellectual enough to have literature of their own."

"Many of them are," Caprigus corrected the druid's knowledge on the matter. "Studying such things is what I am best at, and it's my hobby."

Drabel thought heavily on the demon slayer's words. "I didn't realize that demons developed their own writings."

"Their intellect works differently than ours," Caprigus confirmed. "They do have their own literature, but it is one of a primitive and ancient style."

"I hate anything with teeth," Myra commented, straying off topic slightly. "I don't like anything that has a tendency to bite or is infamous because of its teeth."

"You mean dragon fish?" Caprigus said, smiling.

"Anything, including dragon fish," Myra said bitterly.

Growls and the cracking of tree branches began to echo into the night from the woods to the south. Everyone in the camp froze, waiting to see the source of those sounds. The disturbance was getting closer.

A family of ape-like creatures with red fur and a single eye began to flee hysterically from the south. They rushed past the trees just outside of the camp.

"It's a family of darkens," Vadamar said, identifying the creatures easily. "Something from the south has disturbed them. All the animals in the woods can sense the frozen fire and the new presence of danger in Mystasia."

Dranus focused his energies of detection to the nearby south. "Whatever disturbed them is not near us. I am not detecting any use of magic within ten miles, but I suppose an enemy army could be in the wilderness nearby."

Jermyia shook his head. "Why would they travel this far into wilderness?"

"It doesn't seem likely that they would," Dranus said, turning to the knight. "However, many Mystasian citizens have fled their towns and homes, fearing that the frozen fire will come for them. Great uncertainty has plagued this country from the cities right into the wilderness. Nothing is safe as long as that destructive magical fire burns."

Drabel looked at the two brothers in disgust. 'What you are doing is cruel!"

Galum shrugged. "It is only a serpent."

"Even the smallest of creatures deserve to live!" Drabel was in fury. "All creatures deserve to live, regardless of how dangerous or unimportant they may seem."

Galum glared up at the druid, remaining seated on the ground. "Don't lecture me with druid philosophy. Druids and elves take nature too seriously. Elves are the worst!"

Drabel snapped, "The wilderness is what is keeping you hidden from those who are invading our country, Braveblood!"

Drabel snatched the serpent quickly enough to avoid being bit. The druid held the serpent's head in place by holding his thumb directly behind its head. He disappeared into the darkness of the woods with the serpent.

Galum frowned in protest that the game had been interrupted.

"Let him be," Jermyia said, placing his hand on his brother's shoulder. "I have heard that Drabel is very much in tune with nature and has a strange understanding of it. He may very well be the most faithful of all the druids to the druidic religion."

"So be it," Galum argued. "My faith is in my sword and my ability to use it. Let the elves and druids have their wilderness. All I have ever needed is in my hands right now!"

Galum looked down at his broadsword. It was made out of red iron, which was the strongest ore used in crafting weapons of metal. The hilt was black, and the guard reminded of a wing of a bat.

Both brothers turned to their right. A frost eagle was perched on the shoulder of the arch druid

Vadamar. The arch druid tilted his head to the bird, as if listening to the bird whisper to him. The arch druid nodded, and the frost eagle returned to the night sky.

Vadamar shook his head wretchedly. "There is no sign of Jherlom, but Frost believes he got a glimpse of the prince."

"Where?" Jermyia yelled out desperately. "Where is he?"

"It seems he is traveling south toward The Haunted Forest with a woman and a very large, muscular man," Vadamar reported. "I saw what Frost saw, and I do not recognize the two that the prince is traveling with, but it is definitely Prince Krendale."

"The Haunted Forest," Jermyia gasped. "Why would he travel there, unless he was being forced by the two he is with?"

Vadamar shook his head. "It doesn't seem like he is a prisoner to the company he is with. He seems to be acting in accordance with his own will. There is no hostile activity or interaction between the three. I do not know why he is traveling toward The Haunted Forest, but he is not a prisoner."

"If only our young prince had the understanding of a blade, and the skill to use it," Galum muttered.

"He doesn't need either of those," Jermyia retorted bitterly.

"You still believe that great defense is what defines a man in battle, don't you, Jermyia?"

"That's because it's true," Jermyia defended his beliefs. "What good is a man without solid defense?"

"A knight is defined by his knowledge on the battlefield and his arsenal of skill with a weapon. Your offensive skill on the battlefield is what wins battles, Jermyia. A shield will win you nothing," Galum argued with his younger brother.

"Except your life," Jermyia argued. "I will never agree with you, Galum. You will never persuade me to agree with you on the matter."

"Then you are a fool," the first of the elite knights cursed Jermyia.

"Perhaps in your eyes I am," Jermyia said plainly with a shrug. "But you will die before I do."

Galum's face soured, and without a word, he stormed off away from the campfire, into the darkness of the woods.

The tension between the two brothers had ceased, and the Griffin Lilly Forest had become relatively quiet. Vadamar watched as a family of chipmunks and bluebirds gathered seeds and nuts, and carried them to their oak and birch homes in preparation for the winter.

"How I love the wilderness," Vadamar said to Dranus, who was standing next to him. Before Dranus had a chance to respond, Myra approached them both from behind." "Master, it is time to train the apprentices, but it will be difficult without normal means."

"I have it all figured out," Dranus said, smiling. "I only need you to assist me for the next several weeks. I have arranged another way of training them with some inspiration from Vadamar."

Myra frowned at the mention of Vadamar. It seemed strange to her that an arch mage received inspiration from an arch druid. Druids and magi explored completely different walks of life. There was nothing similar about their way of magic.

Dranus Drathiso trotted toward the two apprentices. "These lessons will be based mostly on lectures of magic."

"Dranus is very idealistic," Vadamar said to Myra.

"Sometimes our master has too many ideas," Myra replied miserably. Her miserable attitude caught the arch druid by surprise. He watched closely as Dranus began his teachings.

Dranus was astounded to find Remko Slayskull standing next to Tethus and Gekmon. "Remko, you are no longer an apprentice. You have reached the second circle of magic within the guild. You are now a scripter of sorcery."

"Yes, master," Remko nodded. "But with the threat of the frozen fire, I feel that I should learn more. Nadja often tells me that practice makes perfect."

"There is no such thing as perfect," Dranus said, shaking his head, "But practice always creates improvement. Like Nadja, you are very devoted, but you already know everything that I will be teaching tonight."

Dranus turned to the twins. There were two types of magi that shared the mage guild. Some studied to be moon mages, and others studied to be gem mages. Dranus maintained his gaze on Tethus, who was practicing to become a moon mage.

"Tethus, you have selected your core interest in divinatory academics. It is needless to say that the three moons play the most vital role in our lives as moon magi. For you, however, it will play an especially important role in your line of study."

Dranus turned to Nakon. "You have chosen to have a complete understanding of low energy magic. As a gem mage, you will find that gem stones will last longer before they crumble while using your magic."

Dranus turned to Remko suddenly. He realized that Remko could participate in the evening exercises. "Remko has devoted himself primarily to the philosophy of energy. I have an exercise for all three of you tonight, and they will all be different from each other."

Dranus took a step back and addressed all three of his students. "First, I want to review with all of you the power of the three moons. Each of you draws your energy from the moons, regardless of what your specialty in magic is. They are the source of your magic, and each of the moons has a different benefit. For you, Nakon, gem stones have different benefits."

Galum suddenly appeared next to Vadamar. "What nonsense," the knight muttered. "Do you understand any of this rubbish?"

"No," the arch druid admitted. "Druids have little interest in the moons, but I do find it interesting."

Dranus continued his teachings. "When joining the guild, each of the moon magi picked one moon in particular to rely on for our source of power. Remember that the more full the moon is, the greater its influence will bestow itself upon you. The red moon Rhosha is the moon of spell power and strength. Remko has selected this moon as his energy reserve. This means that when Remko casts a spell, it will be more powerful than when any other magi relying on a different moon casts the same spell. The yellow moon Yubanen is the moon of endurance. This allows the effects of Gekmon's spells to last longer before they expire. The blue moon Shalamar is the moon of greater magical reserve. This allows Tethus to cast more spells without being drained of energy. His energy reserve is greater than normal."

Dranus turned to Nakon. "Gem magi make use of all gem stones, but certain gem stones are required to draw energy from to cast certain spells."

Dranus turned his hooded teal eyes to Tethus. "When it comes to divinatory academics, it is important to understand the concept of divine power and the source of magic. Do you know where magic comes from, Tethus?"

Tethus blinked his closely set olive green eyes nervously and brought his fingers up to his strawberry blonde, sheep wool textured hair.

"I am not sure," Tethus said a moment later.

"It comes from the stars, Tethus. Astrology and astronomy are both important aspects when it comes to magic.

Vadamar shook his head. It was apparent to Galum that the arch druid disagreed with the arch mage's statement.

Dranus looked up at the stars. "The stars shed magic, and that raw power falls upon us like unseen rain. It is invisible energy that we are able to focus on and channel through our minds and bodies. That is what makes magic divine, but with magi, it is also divine because of the way we use such energy. Knowing the source of that energy, and the measurements in which it absorbs into us, is the first step in divinatory academics. Divinatory academics are generally the study of numbers and measurements of the energy we use."

Something began to drift into the camp from the southern regions of the forest. It was something that only the druids noticed. Drabel Thunderthumb reacted to it first, and Loamus seconds later. The two druids exchanged glances.

"Something doesn't feel right," Drabel said.

"I sense it, too," Loamus exclaimed. "Something from the south."

"Let's see what we can find," Drabel suggested.

"Can I come with you?" Jermyia asked.

"Why not?" Loamus invited the knight.

Drabel led Loamus and Jermyia into the forest. Only Nadja noticed them leave, and she watched them silently, realizing that the druids had probably sensed something and wanted to investigate.

Dranus turned his attention to Gekmon. "Focus hard on that rock next to Remko, Gekmon." Gekmon concentrated on the rock as Dranus instructed and continued to listen to the arch mage.

"Focus hard on it, and try to heat the rock," Dranus demanded.

"How can I heat the rock just by…"

"Dranus thumped his staff hard onto the ground to silence the sorcery student.

Gekmon began to focus hard on the rock, and Dranus looked at Remko.

"Why does magic exist, Remko?"

Remko began to recall his earlier teachings. "It is a balanced combination of the stars, their positions in the celestial map, and their relationship with the gods and goddesses."

"Excellent," Dranus said, smiling. "I would not have been able to explain much better myself."

"Master," Remko said, pointing to the rock that Gekmon was focusing on.

"You're doing it, Gekmon," Dranus cheered. "You have learned to focus your energies on a single object."

Gekmon smiled, realizing that he had potential.

"The magic that magi practice is the most unpredictable of all magic," Dranus stressed.

"Focus is vital. Otherwise, we may lose control of our spells and harm ourselves or others."

Caprigus watched as the magi apprentices practiced various spells. He noticed almost immediately that Remko was casting two spells.

"Why is Remko able to cast two spells at once?" the demon slayer asked. "Isn't that something only a higher mage can do?"

"No," Dranus replied. "He is using a spell known as 'moon minutes', which allows him to cast two spells at once for several minutes, but only spending the energy normally spent casting one spell. Moon minutes gathers more energy from the moon he relies on for casting spells."

Caprigus nodded. "Very impressive, but what if there is a new moon?"

Dranus shrugged. "Since there are three moons, there is only one night a year where there is no visible moon in the sky. On that one night alone, our powers are useless. A moon magi can draw powers from any moon, but they receive greater benefits drawing power from the one moon that they have chosen to draw their strength from."

Dranus recognized confusion on the dwarf's face and explained further.

"There are different types of magi. Battle, blood, shadow, gem and moon magi, to name a few. Only moon magi draw their strength from the moons. Gem magi need gems to use their magic. A blood magi needs blood to perform his or her spells."

Caprigus smiled. "All a cleric or a demon slayer needs is a very strong belief in their religion and their goddess. For us at the Cleric Temple of Ku'Lee, that goddess is Iona'Pawl, the goddess of healing."

The arch mage leaned on his oak battle staff. "It seems rather simple compared to the life of a mage, doesn't it?"

"It seems that way," Caprigus said, nodding. "But I doubt cleric life is any more simple than the life of a mage. Our lives and beliefs are completely different."

Caprigus took two steps back, pondering the arch mage's words, when he tripped over a stone and fell into the campfire. Dranus rushed to the demon slayer's aid.

The dwarf rolled out of the fire in a serene manner. He did not appear to be in any pain or to have sustained any injury.

Dranus was at the demon slayer's side. "Are you okay?"

"Yes," Caprigus replied, showing the arch mage his hand.

Dranus studied the demon slayer's hand, but there was no injury. He failed to hide his confusion. He shifted his gaze to the prominent olive green eyes of the dwarf, and then back at his uninjured hand.

"That is my specialty," Caprigus explained. "I have a strong and very strange resistance to fire. I have practiced and studied protection from fire for many years, but I was also born with this ability. Seers and astrologers tell me that it is a part of my astrological sign."

"What is your astrological sign?" Dranus asked.

"Ancestral Flame," Caprigus replied. "And yours?"

"The energy geyser," Dranus retorted, turning his attention to his students.

Deeper in the Forest of Wounded Sands, Jermyia seemed to slow his pace. Drabel and Loamus turned back to the young knight, who was infamously well known for being afraid of nothing, just as his family name suggested.

"What's wrong?" Drabel asked.

"It's the black oaks," Jermyia responded sheepishly, but showing some signs of nervous tension.

"What about them?" Loamus asked.

Jermyia hesitated to answer, feeling shame swell within himself. "I am afraid of black oaks. It's a childhood memory, just forget about it."

Drabel smiled as he turned to the west once again. "I have never heard of anyone fearing trees before." The druid found humor in the situation and maintained his grin.

"Only black oaks," Jermyia said, almost snapping at them. The young knight was irritated that his company failed to drop the subject.

Drabel continued to lead them west. "Does he even know where he is leading us?" Jermyia asked Loamus.

"Of course," Loamus retorted brightly. "It's impossible for druids to become lost in the wilderness, or in any forest. Even if we did, we can communicate with the forest animals, who would then guide us out."

"So as druids, you feel that society is controlled by nature," Jermyia commented.

"We care much less about society than we do about the wilderness that surrounds societies," Loamus replied dryly. "It would be more accurate to state that druids believe nature controls everything in life. How do you see it?"

"I don't," Jermyia said, shrugging.

"You must have some sociological view on life," Loamus urged the matter.

"Society is society," Jermyia said plainly. "I don't agree with any of the sociological views. Why can't things be as people see them?"

"Because they're not," Loamus argued. "Naturalism is the true sociological view."

"There is no true sociological view," Jermyia protested. "Things are as people see them.

Loamus took a deep breath as he inhaled the scent of red pines and smiled. "I love red pines," he said dreamily. "They are without a doubt the greatest species of tree I have had the privilege of protecting."

Both druids turned to the west, and Drabel took a single step in that direction. "I sense a change in the woods," he mumbled gravely.

Drabel took two more steps and nodded. "Yes, it's getting stronger with every step I take to the west."

"You are right," Loamus said, mimicking his fellow druid. "Of all the druids in the keep, you are the one most in tune with nature. You would be the first to notice any change in the woods, but I sense it, too."

Jermyia strayed to the left and watched as Drabel reached for a mushroom, but before the druid could grab it, it erupted in flames.

"Fungal fire," Drabel blurted, pulling his arm back. "Another plant thought to be a myth. It is a plant that does not belong here in this forest."

Drabel sighed, feeling saddened by the unnatural change in the forest. He looked up at Loamus. "There are several species of plants that are very dangerous and unnatural, and do not belong here. Can you restore the forest?"

Loamus nodded. "I can, but it'll take quite some time. It'll take an exhausting amount of energy to correct this."

"What does this mean?" Jermyia asked, cutting Loamus short.

Drabel explained, "It means that the forest has been altered, probably by powerful magic.

We encountered what we feel were the first dark druids ever to exist in Krynesia a few months ago, but we thought we destroyed them all in the battle that took place. We may have been mistaken. This alteration suggests that there are still some dark druids at large."

"This could have been done before we destroyed them," Loamus pointed out.

Drabel disagreed with a nod. "I am now convinced that some of them still exist, and that they are the ones behind the frozen fire spell."

"The frozen fire would be the work of a very powerful dark druid," Loamus exclaimed. "One even more powerful than Vadamar."

Loamus began to focus on repairing the forest. "Some of the physical properties and chemistry of things here in the forest have been altered, just as they were months ago."

Just outside the camp from behind a nearby elm beard tree, Shardana Ebontear watched the arch mage continue to teach his pupils. Their faith in their magic was as solid as the boulder next to her emerald gemstone gargoyle form. Her ruby eyes gleamed in the moonlight that stroked her eyes from the jeweled sky with imperceptible fingers. She watched Dranus praise his students for their success in their practices that night. She saw Dranus exercise a spell of his own. She watched as he hurled a lightning bolt at a boulder, faster than any she had seen sent from any stormy sky.

The lightning bolt was followed by a strange sphere of energy that surrounded the arch mage. He asked his students to attack him, but none of their spells could penetrate the defense of the sphere Dranus had formed around himself. Dranus chuckled, but it was not a mocking chuckle. He began to praise his students once more with arm and comforting words of kindness. He was a powerful man who did not raise himself above his students. Dranus could clearly destroy them all in seconds, but he wasn't the type of man who would abuse his power for personal gain.

For the second time in her life, Shardana smiled. Since the birth of her hatchlings, this was the happiest moment of her life. She realized that she had begun to fall in love with the arch mage. She was attracted to both his magical power and his compassion. His humanity was pure. He was a garden of soft soil flourishing magic, and she was merely a body of stone. His faith in magic was more solid than any mountain she had called home.

She watched Dranus until the last cinder of the campfire died. Happiness transformed into sadness. The gargoyles would never be a part of Mystasian society, and even if one day they were, it was not likely that the arch mage would ever be attracted to her. His human love was out of her reach.

CHAPTER XVIII

The Haunted Forest

THE HORRIBLE HAUNTING MANNER of The Haunted Forest lingered even during the day. Eerie evil tormented them with cruel cold and a tormented essence that never shifted. It seemed to be the source of the lesser evils that the party could feel staring at them as they traveled southeast. Though Gafnan did not seem as fearful as the others, Abadon and Epona regretted their decision to enter The Haunted Forest, especially after Gwan Eastfire had disappeared. Night or day, it did not matter. The evil was always there, stalking them. The evil never rested, and neither did they. Sleep tried to overtake the three, but fear chased it away. None of them noticed when exactly Gwan had disappeared from the camp last night. There was no trace of the Flaming Fist ninja, and he left no tracks.

The second coming of daylight within The Haunted Forest came to them with no attacks at all, and before long the black ink of night spilled upon them, bringing extra evil and icy chills. They were still somewhere in Dark Wood, and Gafnan promised them that if they traveled southeast, they would cross over Whip Weed River and stumble on the edge of Jade Swamps, and enter the very forest the territory was named after.

They crossed Whip Weed River, which crawled south with a gentle flow. The three knew what waited in the water, but they gambled that some of the evil spirits might not follow them across the river. The gentle current of the river never threatened to drown them, but the weeds below the surface of the water whipped at them. Lashing pain struck them again and again.

Gafnan was in the lead, followed by Abadon. Epona was trailing several feet behind Abadon when one of the whip weeds wrapped itself around her right leg, and pulled her down beneath the surface of the water. As she was pulled down, she could see that both men were unaware of her attack, and kept swimming to the eastern banks of the river.

Epona looked down at her assaulter. The bottom of the river was entangled with countless whip weeds. She grasped at the one wrapped around her leg, but there was no use. The whip weed was much stronger than it looked.

Epona looked upward. The surface of the river was at least fifteen feet above her, and suddenly, she was released. She looked down as she quickly made her way up to the surface and saw Sabre below her. The saber bear had cut her free from the whip weed's grip.

Breathing heavily and snagging a quick breath, Epona continued to swim toward the east side of Whip Weed River. Sabre was right behind her. Both men had just reached the other side. The whips from the whip weeds below continued to whip at her with painful lashes, but none of them made an attempt to pull her below again. Both Epona and Sabre had reached the eastern bank, where Abadon helped Epona out of the river.

Although common sense cautioned them all not to do so, they reached the far end of Jade Swamps and passed through it with great difficulty. Every third step they took caused them to splash down into the swamp. The difficult trek stole two hours from them before they finally reached drier land and set up camp for a second night, just outside the Jade Swamps. They slept better that night, despite the fact they were officially in The Haunted Forest. The night brought them nightmares and additional eerie sounds that they had not heard before. Nothing attacked them that night, but they slept without fire. Their lack of sleep got the better of them, and although cold, they slept for a few hours anyway.

They woke up and began their third day of trekking since they entered The Haunted Forest Territory. There was still no sign of Gwan. Surely the evil spirits had snagged and destroyed the lone man by now, after an entire night of torturing him. The spirits here seemed to be amused by watching the suffering of the living.

The wind whipped at them the entire day, and a very thin layer of frost had developed over the night. The cold was unbearable. Abadon was much colder now than he had been when he climbed out of The Blind River. The first sign of winter had arrived, and it was enforced by an icy strong gale wind. The three had little choice but to stop prematurely and build a fire.

"A fire will be less noticeable now than during the night," Gafnan told them.

They agreed and succumbed to the cold, taking a chance on being noticed by something they did not wish to find them. The cold was just as bad as being found by the two invisible assassins—or worst yet, the evil spirits that lived in the forest. At least the assassins would provide them with a quick and likely painless death. The spirits merely killed you with pain that seemed everlasting.

Gafnan produced a fire, and the three gathered around it voraciously for the heat. The trees in the forest were completely naked now, and they swayed back and forth, as if bowing to the evil that dwelled around them. All three moons had the courage to peer down at them that night. Shalamar was still not quite full, but Yubanen was full. Its yellow form seemed much like a giant yellow pupil gazing down at them, surrounded by the blackness of night. Rhosha was still a half moon. The dominating yellow and blue moons created a strange green moonlight, as the previous few nights had.

Abadon looked over at the beast master. Gafnan had changed slightly over the past two days, but the young prince could not identify what it was about the big man that had changed. His constitution seemed to have become far superior to theirs. Abadon and Epona still showed markings on their bodies where the whip weeds had whipped them. Gafnan showed no evidence at all. His welts had completely disappeared.

Gafnan forged for food in the perimeter of the camp, where the light of the fire guided him dimly. He managed to find roots and shrubs appropriate for feasting. The three chewed the food that Gafnan had provided for them. Much of what they ate was bitter, but they all accepted it.

Abadon glanced around at the trees that surrounded them. "How did this forest come to be?"

the prince asked. "I mean, how did it come to be haunted?"

Epona shrugged, but Gafnan offered an explanation. "It always has been haunted. It was haunted before the War of the Gods. Tales of an old cemetery and a dark cathedral that once existed in these woods have been passed down to children in villages that I have visited."

Epona cleared her throat. "I have no idea how or why the forest is haunted, but I do know that the House of Candles is somewhere in The Haunted Forest."

"The House of Candles," Abadon uttered, mystified.

"Yes," Epona said, continuing her story. "The vampire lord, Lure Vesper, lives in it."

"But the vampires live in the Bloodstone Forest," Abadon recalled. "Why would their lord live in The Haunted Forest?"

"The dark races have respect for one another," Epona replied. "Apparently, the vampires once lived here in these woods before they moved to the Bloodstone Forest."

"Only a vampire would be crazy enough to live in a haunted forest," Abadon muttered, nibbling reluctantly at the shrub.

Epona sighed. "I do research on vampires, and I have come to respect them. They are not as horrible as the tales told over dozens of centuries portray them as. They deserve respect."

"Respect, Epona?" Abadon gasped. "Vampires drink blood and feed upon our kind! Are you crazy?"

Gafnan remained strangely quiet, as if he was hiding information from them, but the others dismissed it, believing that the eerie nature of the forest had brought out the worst in all their personalities.

Finally, Gafnan spoke. "Epona is right, Prince Krendale. Vampires are not as bad as what many believe. I have had some experiences with vampires, and all of them were pleasurable ones."

Abadon cast a glance of irritation upon the beast master. "Are you insane? Gafnan, are you aware that three hundred Mystasians are killed annually due to vampire attacks? There are probably more victims than we know."

"They need blood to live, Abadon," Epona shouted out with a sudden burst of anger. "Are we much different? We slaughter cattle for beef. They live in their own little corner of this country! Isn't that good enough for you?"

"We don't bite cattle and drink their blood, and then convert them into human beings, Epona! There is a very big difference between us and vampires."

"I can't believe I am hearing this," Abadon said, shaking his head and lowering it into his hands with great frustration.

"Dark tales," Gafnan muttered. "That is what you grew up with as a child, Prince Krendale. There are limitless tales of vampires, gargoyles and werebeasts. It is not true that they are all evil. In fact, very few of them are."

"I know that they are not all evil, Gafnan," Abadon cried out, showing some rage, "But they feed on blood and flesh and are dangerous to humanity!"

194

"I tell you, young prince, they are not," Gafnan argued back, but without raising his voice. "They are no more dangerous to us than you are to them."

"You?" Abadon and Epona said almost simultaneously. Gafnan let out a very shallow sigh. Abadon and Epona barely noticed it. Gafnan lowered his head, as if he had been caught red-handed performing a serious crime.

Gafnan suddenly rose to his feet, staring at the prince with a strange smirk never seen on his face before. His body began to change. His muscular form was becoming more slender. As seconds passed, his flesh became covered with golden-brown feathers. His nose transformed into a grey beak. His limbs were now a little longer and converted into wings. About one minute later, Gafnan had transformed into a were-eagle.

Both Abadon's and Epona's jaws dropped. They stared at the beast master.

"You're a were-eagle?" Epona gasped.

Gafnan nodded. "It is a secret I have kept from everyone all my life, except for my own kind, of course."

"Then why did you reveal your true self to us now, Gafnan?" Abadon asked, bewildered.

Gafnan shrugged and retorted softly, "To show you that I am a part of one of the dark races. To show you that I am one of those that man is afraid of. To prove to you that we are not as bad as the tales make us out to be."

Abadon noticed that his voice did not change, just his physical appearance.

He looked up at the sky and noted that the yellow moon, Yubannen, was full.

Gafnan spoke as if reading his mind. "My were-eagle form has nothing to do with the phase of the moons. That is all myth, passed down with the dark tales of my kind. We can change into our were forms whenever we please. Day or night, it doesn't matter. The moons do offer us special abilities when they are full, though."

"What do you mean?" Epona asked.

"When Yubanen is full, like it is now, werebeasts heal faster," Gafnan explained.

Abadon's face lit up. "That is why the whip marks on us are still present. All the injuries you suffered when crossing Whip Weed River have already healed on you!"

"Exactly," Gafnan said with a smile. "Rhosha causes us to become more savage and hungry. Sometimes it even causes us to go into an almost berserker rage. Shalamar heightens our senses very effectively."

Gafnan sat back down next to the fire across from the others. "I have met Lure Vesper once before, years ago. Vampires and gargoyles suffer from the same fate werebeasts do. We suffer from isolation from mankind."

Guilt stabbed at Abadon. He suddenly felt very ashamed. "I apologize deeply, Gafnan," he said. "I am terribly sorry. I should not be so judgmental of your kind."

"I don't blame you at all," Gafnan said. "Children grow up believing the stories that their parents pass down to them. Your generation, and the few before it, didn't know any better. You have done no harm."

Gafnan began to stare at the flickering fire, and educated them about Mystasian history. "Shortly before the War of the Gods, what you call the dark races were actually a part of human society. There was a peace between us all, but the War of the Gods changed that. My people live here in The Haunted Forest. I lied to you earlier when I said I knew little about this forest. I was simply protecting my identity. The vampires hide in the southeast corner of Mystasia, ands the gargoyle find solitude in the mountains of obsidian. Those three races went into hiding, but it wasn't really hiding. We simply fled to the areas of the country that humans, elves, dwarves, Halflings and fairy kind did not populate vastly."

Epona shuddered slightly in reaction to the cold, and then spoke almost in a whisper. "As king of Mystasia, you could change all that. You could reunite all of the races."

Gafnan nodded. "Before the original alliance, things were as they are now. But none of the races were in an alliance then. The alliance you know today occurred following the War of the Races. A little more than a century later, empathy and understanding came between the Mystasian people and the ones you refer to as the dark races. Such an alliance can happen again, but I am afraid that ignorance on both sides has remained strong since the War of the Gods."

"Yes," Epona agreed. "Abaltor the Third brought the races together following the War of the Races. You can repeat history and do the same with the vampires, werebeasts and gargoyles."

"I don't know if I can," Abadon said, breathing out a deep sigh. "Two thousand years ago, it may have been possible, but not now! Not with the way things are. There is no trust to muster in this world, and there is little faith left in the gods and goddesses because of the War of the Gods."

Abadon stood up from the fire. "That war nearly destroyed Krynesia, but instead it changed it. It left critical wounds that will scar this world forever."

"But someone like you who has kingship can change all that," Gafnan argued. Your name would be etched onto the pages of history books."

Abadon's fingers curved inward, turning his hand into a fist. A throng of thoughts tore at his mind like claws. He displayed a sign of slight anger.

"This is something that I am going to have to think about over the years. There are many who will not be happy with the alliance."

"But there will be some, like Gafnan and myself, who would be," Epona urged the matter on.

"Indeed," Abadon said casually, as if an idea sprang into his mind. He no longer appeared to be angry or frustrated with the idea. "Do either of you know where the House of Candles is?"

"I have an idea where to find it," Epona replied.

Gafnan nodded. "I have been at the house once, about ten years ago."

"How far is it from here?" Abadon asked.

"About ten miles southwest of here," Gafna exclaimed. "It is basically in the same direction we are heading in now."

Abadon looked at the beast master. "Are you certain we'll be welcome there with your presence? Is the relationship between werebeasts and vampires stable?"

"There is no official alliance," Gafnan explained. "It's more of an understanding. It's an alien empathy between us. Each of us are still locked in isolation with our own kind. I am not certain my presence with you will persuade Lure Vesper to agree to any alliance with mankind..."

Gafnan trailed off slowly. A suddenly strange noise ended the conversation. A strange moan escaped the darkness of the woods from the northeast. It was impossible to elude the evil that became a natural part of the forest. For a short while, it recoiled, but it came back about two minutes later. The same immortal fear that had been stalking them since the first day they entered the forest was back at full force.

A face of fear materialized out of the darkness next to Abadon, but it was part of the darkness. It was as if night had shown its face for the first time in history. The outline of its eyes proved its existence, but its mouth remained unseen. Seconds later, the nose could be seen as well. Its mouth opened, and strange grey light appeared, as if a grey sun had ripped the fabric of night and spilled through. Harsh cold struck all three of them as the mouth appeared, as if the night face had the breath of winter. It hovered toward them. A morbid madness raged from it, and it hated them.

The three slowly backed away from it. Sabre growled, warning the spirit off, but the warning had no effect. Behind them, another spirit joined in on the terror. This newcomer was clearly a ghost. It was merely a floating skull of bright white mist that glowed with almost the same luminosity as the yellow moon. It gazed at them, forcing their stomachs to churn with unbearable fear. The night spirit laughed at them mockingly. The ghastly laugh almost sounded as if the wind was playing tricks on their ears. The ghost and the spirit circled them for a moment, and then they attacked.

Abadon dropped to the ground in a fetal position. One of his greatest fears struck him. Dozens of large centipedes, each three feet long, crawled all over his body. They bites were hard and painful.

Epona began to hallucinate as well. Dreadful visions replaced the true image of the forest. The trees were bleeding, and Abadon and Gafnan were merely shadows. Blood dripped from the bare branches of the trees, and their trunks were soaked in blood as well. She looked down at herself and realized in terrible horror that it was her own blood. Her insides were hanging out of a large gash in her stomach. She screamed at the dreadful sight. The horror and fear were so great that she never noticed that she felt no pain at all.

"Get them off me!" Abadon screamed. "Get these things off me! They're all over me!"

Gafnan froze in fear. He was unable to move at all. The fact that he was a were-eagle, and that were-beasts lived in the forest as well, did not matter to the evil spirits. Their pure evil and frightening forms prevented the beast master from performing any action against them at all. The evil that surrounded them was so thick that it seemed to be as solid as an object. What they saw and felt seemed as real as anything that they had encountered. Sabre swiped twice at the ghost, but his claws simply went through its glowing mist, making no injury at all. The spirits were real, but physically, they were not entirely there.

Suddenly, the glowing mist shaped like a skull faded away and disappeared. The night spirit shrieked, and appeared to melt back into the night. Gwan Eastfire had returned, and the evil intensity seemed to decrease down to a bare minimal.

Breathing heavily, Gwan stood before them, holding his katana in both of his hands.

Abadon jumped back to his feet. He searched the ground for the giant centipedes that covered his body, but there were none. Epona examined her body, but with astonishing surprise, she found that it was untouched and still intact. Shadow shrouded the trees, but there was no blood on them at all. The fear that left Gafnan immobilized was gone as well. It took a long moment for the three to gather their thoughts and realize that, for now, the danger was gone.

"Where have you been, Gwan?" Abadon demanded an answer. The ninja didn't appear to hear Abadon. Gwan was staring at the were-eagle. It took Gwan a moment to realize that the were-eagle was Gafnan.

Gwan returned his katana to its sheath and shrugged. "I heard a woman screaming for help late in the night, so I left the camp in search for her. I ventured too far and got lost."

"Did you find her?" Epona asked.

"No, I did not," Gwan said, lowering his head as if a little embarrassed.

"That's because there was no woman," Gafnan growled. "It was just another trick from the evil spirits to lure you away from us. The spirits can create illusions that are so realistic that you can usually feel pain. You can see injuries that are not even there. They baited you away from us so that they could destroy us!"

"But Gwan has been missing for two days," Abadon stated. "Why didn't the spirits attack us last night?"

Epona blinked her green eyes. "All I can think of is that Gwan was never very far away from us. He was close enough that they decided not to attack us. Perhaps they can detect his weapon, and know that it can destroy them easier than they can destroy us."

"Then why did they attack us when they did?" Gafnan asked. "Gwan was obviously close to us when they attacked us just now."

Epona shrugged, shaking her head a little. "I have no answer."

"Neither do I," Gafnan mumbled, showing a little confusion.

The four circled the campfire, and Gwan confirmed that he found nothing of interest in the forest. Before long, they gathered what sleep they could, but it wasn't enough. Several days with very little sleep led to fatigue and irritable attitudes. Only the fear of the forest and the spirits that dwelled within it kept them in order.

As the birth of a new day came to them, Epona interrogated Gafnan, who was in his human form now.

"Gafnan, if you live in these woods, why were you so afraid of the spirits last night? Shouldn't you be used to them by now? Has your kind not found a way to co-exist with them?"

"Werebeasts primarily live in the northern region of this territory. The spirits are generally in the south. Not as many of them reside in the north. I rarely come face to face with them. This is my second encounter with one of them."

A smile appeared on his face as he asked the young witch a question. "Why didn't you cast a spell on them last night?"

Epona fixed Gafnan with a gaze of provocation. "I just froze in fear. I was unable to react. I just can't believe were-beasts live in the same territory as these spirits."

"We don't have much choice," Gafnan responded bitterly. "We risk war or being hunted down by mankind if we do not."

Epona hung her head in shame. She realized that Gafnan was quite correct. What choice did the werebeasts have? They were greatly under-populated. Mankind outnumbered them, and they would likely be hunted down to the last of their kind due to fear of them, and fear of lycanthropy

Epona lifted her head once again. "Is there no immunity your kind has developed against the fear this forest is thick with?"

Gafnan shook his head. "I don't think one can overcome the fear that resides within these woods, not even if you live here. The evil of the spirits is so greatly concentrated."

"But where do they come from?" Epona asked.

"It's not entirely clear where they come from," Gafnan replied. "Many believe that it is an extinct race that existed long before the War of the Gods.

You just learn to live with it. It seems as if the fear here has an irreversible magic to it. The fear is so great that you can't dispel it, and you can't overcome it with courage or in numbers, either. You die from the realistic images and pain, and perhaps even the fear itself. The illusions are so real that experiencing them simply kills you. The concentration of hate within these woods never rests."

Sleep eventually dissolved into their systems, and they drifted into a deep sleep for the first time in several days. They woke relatively late in the morning. Daylight had already stained the skies with bright sunshine, which could be seen even through the thick gloom of the forest. Distant loons sang their morning songs, and the four were relieved to find that all of them were present. The sloping hills of the naked forest were blanketed with dark grey gloom in all directions. Beneath the gloom, they could hear their footsteps. Each step resulted in a crunch of the thousands of fallen leaves beneath their feet. The cold, windless air was almost solid, and did not appear to stir.

During their trek southeast, they passed another small lake dotted with several loons and a few jumping fish of small size. Sunshine continued to peek through the breaks in the trees, but eventually was drowned out by the thick gloom. The forest became much quieter, and they climbed up the largest hill they had encountered in the forest yet. Soon, the thick gloom became a fine, light mist.

Gafnan had reached the top of the hill first. Once he reached the peak, he froze still. When the others noticed that the beast master had found something, they raced to the top of the hill as well. About five hundred feet in front of them, behind several trees, was an old wooden log house.

"The House of Candles," Gafnan muttered with mild surprise. "But I do not remember it being this close to the lake, or upon such a large hill."

He turned to the others. "It has been so long since I have been here, I have forgotten how close it was. I remember it a little differently."

"Time has a way of altering our memories," Epona commented.

"The lake below is where I met Lure Vesper," Gafnan told them. "It was ten years ago, and it was winter, the coldest winter I can remember. The spirits had chased me here, and Lure offered me a place to stay for three days, until the spirits left."

Gafnan's voice went cold suddenly as he rubbed his face in recollection. His gaze wandered to the ground and away from Epona's face.

"He told me never to return here if I valued my life. To this day, I wonder if he meant from the evil spirits, or from his thirst for blood."

Gafnan's eyes met with those of his comrades. Fear shone in each of their eyes, save for Epona. Her green eyes revealed some fear, but they mostly reflected a strange twinkle of curiosity. Gafnan stared at her for a moment. He could not decide if she was crazy or truly obsessed with vampires.

After a moment of silence, Abadon spoke in a near whisper. "We are here, so let's move on. Perhaps he will be as generous with us as he was with you ten years ago, Gafnan."

Gafnan nodded, and the four approached the House of Candles with Sabre close behind them. As they reached the door, which was on the south side of the cabin, Abadon turned to the others. "Do not mention that I am a cleric. There is a history of hatred between clerics and paladins with regard to the undead."

The three nodded that they understood, and Epona bought her hand up to the door and knocked three times. They waited, but there was no answer. Epona brought her knuckles to the wood five more times. Again, they waited, and there was still no response.

Epona turned to the others. "Maybe he isn't here."

After the young witch spoke those words, the door creaked open, and a charming yet cold voice spoke. "Enter." Reluctantly, the four forced themselves inside, leaving Sabre outside of the cabin.

CHAPTER XIX

Green Griffin Tavern

A GAP BETWEEN THE TREES ahead of Gathus was all there was to indicate that he was on a road. This disturbed him, but the snow in the mountains was deep—too deep for a trow to travel in. Even on the road, each step was difficult and knee-deep. He moaned to himself like a mumbling lost wind that couldn't find its way. He began to feel guilty for stealing the clothes he currently wore from an unsuspecting villager. He would surely be dead by now, had he kept the same wet clothes he wore when he plunged into The Blind River. The snowfall had been constant during the day. Until recently, he had been lost. He knew that he was on a road, but he had no clue at all to his current location.

He paused for a moment. He could detect about twenty life forms up ahead.

He couldn't tell if it was people or deer, but the life sources were coming from straight ahead, and the road was leading him straight to them. He turned back to where he had come from. There was no way to know if what he detected was another enemy force. What he sensed might not be people at all, but deer or other large animals. After a moment of thought, he decided he was tired of being lost, and after spending a few days alone, another would cause him agonizing loneliness. He decided to gamble, and walk on ahead.

Gathus lost his footing and fell face-first into the snow. His faith had run out. He allowed the snow to fall over him. In a moment, a passing traveler wouldn't even know he was there. He forced himself to lift his head. The heavy snowfall sent large snowflake crashing into his face, tickling him with every cold kiss they gave him. He forced himself onto his knees, and made himself to believe that what he detected ahead was friend and not foe. Part of him hoped that enemies waited up ahead. Perhaps death would have been better than living the past few days as he had.

He walked for a long period of time before falling face-first into the snow again. The blizzard blocked the three moons from guiding him. The cold began to grip him with frosty fingers. Soon, frostbite would set in. The life forces he sensed ahead were still there, but he also had the ability to detect hamlets. There was no hamlet up ahead. Who would be in this weather without shelter? Gathus decided that what he detected must be a gathering of deer. He was certain that he was far from any trace of civilization.

He looked up once more, lifting his head out of the snow. There was a faint glow just beyond where the road seemed to end before a wall of blackness. He forced himself back up to his feet. As he slowly got closer to the life forces he'd detected, he could see two more glows, well-lit windows, perhaps. There seemed to be a single structure up ahead. The fear within him weakened as he realized that the people within the structure must surely be Mystasians.

Choosing to travel the direction he had was a foolish decision on his part. He was lost and lucky to have stumbled on something. He had hoped that Jherlom would have found him by now. The well-lit windows up ahead gave Gathus new hope. At least he wouldn't be alone any longer.

As he got closer to what appeared to be a tavern, he could finally read the wooden sign over the building's entrance. 'Green Griffin Tavern', he read to himself silently. He repeated those three words in his head three more times before he realized where he was. He was deep in the Jade Coin Forest. He was already in the foothills of The Obsidian Peaks. He was in the very territory that gargoyles called home.

Gathus swallowed his fear as if he had swallowed more than he could chew, nearly choking on the new fear that spawned within him. If the blizzard had not been present, a gargoyle would surely have located him, captured him, and either tortured him or eaten him by now. The trow realized that he was in fact very fortunate over the last few days, and not unfortunate as he felt he was.

With a deep breath, Gathus pushed the door open and entered cautiously. The tavern was only half full, but the occupants were frightening to him. To his immediate left, two mountain dwarves engaged in an arm wrestling match at a table large enough for three. At the table behind him, two more dwarves and two humans played a dangerous game. Most of them wore tattered clothing, and Gathus could clearly see scars on their arms, even from fifteen feet away. At the center of the table was a blood serpent. Each of the men in turn slapped the serpent and added a gold coin from a large pile next to the serpent, to their own pile directly in front of them. The middle pile next to the serpent represented the bank.

Gathus had seen this game played once before. Those who were able to slap the serpent without getting bit were allowed to take one gold coin. It was a daring game of bravery and reflexes. Those who were bit were out of the game, and rushed to the nearest healer to rid their bodies of the poison injected into them.

He couldn't help but to think of Jherlom and his opinion of the game. An image of Jherlom frowning over the four players with his arms crossed angrily appeared in the trow's mind. Jherlom would never approve of the animal cruelty, and he would laugh if he witnessed any of them get bit by the serpent.

Gathus swallowed his nervousness and dodged his way past tavern folk, making it to the bar unharmed.

"Excuse me," he said, looking up at the bartender. He was a shaggy man, very grim in appearance. Gathus was almost too frightened to bother the balding, petulant man.

"Excuse me," Gathus said again.

The bartender looked down at the trow. "What do you want, you little worm?"

"I am looking for Prince Krendale. In fact, any cleric or druid for that matter would do."

"Prince Krendale doesn't come here. None of the nobles ever come here. Does this place look like a temple or a keep to you? This place is in the middle of nowhere, and close to The Obsidian

Peaks. It's a haven for criminals and people who do not wish to be found. Now get out of here!"

The bartender's words and actions frightened Gathus even more. He turned his back on the man and glanced about the tavern. Near the fireplace, he noticed someone dressed in a green cloak, much like the cloaks the druids wore.

"Jherlom," Gathus cried out, racing toward the green cloaked figure. He tripped over an extended foot and rolled along the floor before coming to a stop. He lifted his head and found the cloaked figure looking down at him, but it was not the face of Jherlom that peered out. It was a woman's face, with long, thick brass-colored hair, a square face, and cyan eyes. She carried a holly bramble staff, which ended with a quartz stone carved into a skull.

"I overheard that you were looking for Jherlom Mor'Derum," the woman said firmly.

"Yes," Gathus said immediately, getting back up to his feet.

"Then you have found the next best thing, little one," the woman said, smiling slightly and causing dimples to form on her cheeks. "My name is Dradia Frostfern, and I, like Jherlom, am a druid."

"I am very pleased to meet you," Gathus exclaimed excitedly. "But why are you here in a place like this?"

"I am just investigating," Dradia replied, looking around the tavern. "I can handle myself in such a rough place, and disturbing things have been happening over the past few months. This is as good a place as any to search for whoever is behind the frozen fire. The majority of the people here still haven't learned what has happened."

Gathus noticed that Dradia carried a strong smell of lilacs with her. He breathed in her scent and smiled.

"I am an evoker of the earth," she told him, resting back in her chair.

"Then you are not as powerful as Jherlom?" Gathus commented.

"Not quite," Dradia admitted. "I am not a Father of Seasons, like Jherlom is. Should Vadamar Oakfounder die, I suspect it is Jherlom who will continue to lead us druids, and take the rank of arch druid."

Dradia Frostfern lifted her glass, which contained very pale blue liquid. She drank two mouthfuls before returning her glass to the table. "Tropical rain has always been my favorite drink, even when I was a child."

She studied the trow for a moment. "It is strange to find a trow here. Most of these people are from the lost city of Jun'Tanay, which is a short distance from here. This place is a haven for those who wish to hide from society. You will find nothing but trouble here, my little friend."

Gathus heard a hiss from beneath the table. He lifted the cloth that covered the table and found a triple-tailed naga flicking its tongue at him. He let out a quick cry, released the cloth from his hands and backed away.

"Nazul will not harm you," Dradia promised him.

"Then, the naga is your pet?"

"Nazul is my friend," Dradia corrected the trow's choice of words. "So tell me, little one. Why are you here, and why are you looking for Jherlom?"

Gathus spoke hysterically. "My name is Gathus'Kur'Zaimgy. I was traveling with Jherlom and Prince Krendale when we were attacked by a Mystasian captain and a host of orcs."

"Are you sure about that?" Dradia asked leaning heavily on her staff toward the trow.

"Yes," Gathus cried out. He spoke so fast that Dradia could barely make sense of what he was saying. "I am a diviner and have been detecting very powerful magic lately," he explained. "Have you not yet heard of the frozen fire?"

"Of course I have," Dradia exclaimed petulantly. "I have heard rumors about it, but I have yet to actually see it for myself."

Gathus noticed that a man at a nearby table sitting alone was listening to their conversation. Occasionally, the man looked their way. He wore a thick dark cloak, but the cowl of his cloak was large enough to shadow his entire face. Gathus wasn't even sure that it was a man, but his broad frame indicated that the stranger was male. Once the stranger realized that the trow noted him, he continued to carve on the table, as if ignoring them.

"Come," Dradia said, suddenly standing up from the table. "We must find Jherlom and the prince."

As Dradia finished her tropical rain drink, the wind howled once again as the tavern door opened. A Cyclops with an angular build and a high forehead walked in, carrying a battle axe. He entered the tavern and closed the door behind him. He stood there for a moment looking around the tavern, as if searching for someone.

"I think I know him," Dradia told Gathus. "I believe he is one of the Mystasian warlords. He might be able to answer a few questions."

"How do you know he is the warlord you're speaking of?"

"For starters, there are not many Cyclops in this country. I believe he is the warlord Haz Rhon."

Haz Rhon began to walk toward the bar, but Dradia intercepted his path and blocked him. "Haz Rhon, isn't it?" Dradia asked.

"My name is Haz Rhon, but who are you?" The Cyclops asked with severe exasperate.

"My name is Dradia Frostfern. I am a druid," Dradia replied. "I was hoping you could answer a few questions."

"I haven't got the time," Haz Rhon said, shoving past Dradia toward the bar.

"I just came here for some food. I must travel to the Trow Lowlands as quickly as I can."

Gathus overheard the Cyclops mention his home territory. "The Trow Lowlands? What is wrong in the lowlands?"

"Nothing yet," Haz Rhon muttered. "If I get there quickly enough, nothing will happen." Haz Rhon turned to the bartender. "A few slices of beef, and some beef broth if you please."

Dradia refused to give up her personal quest to get information out of the warlord.

"Why is it important for you to reach the lowlands? Has the frozen fire reached there too?"

"Not yet," Haz Rhon snapped. "Not as far as I know. I am going there to make sure Baroness Pyhon-Ash-Pree hasn't been assassinated. I believe someone is hunting down all the Mystasian nobles. The war guild was attacked a few days ago as well."

The bartender returned with the food and beef broth the Cyclops requested. He selected a table just large enough for him to enjoy his meat, sat down, and began to eat.

Dradia and Gathus followed him. "I can help you," Dradia said. "I know the country well, probably better than you do. I may know of a shortcut to the Trow Lowlands."

"Why are you so interested in helping me?" Haz Rhon asked.

"Because the entirely country is being threatened," Dradia spoke, showing some hint of aggravation.

The Cyclops looked Dradia over for a moment while he chewed on a slice of beef. "Perhaps you will come in handy. Do you know the country to the east well?"

"Not really," Dradia admitted "But it is impossible for a druid to become lost."

"We have to travel east to avoid the Haunted Forest, unless your druid skills will come in handy there."

"No," Dradia replied. "That forest is haunted by powerful spirits, and most of them are unfriendly. The fact that I am a druid and it's a forest will not help us in any way. It is best to travel east and take our chances with the gargoyles. If we stay close to the border of the Haunted Forest, and a safe distance away from the Obsidian Peaks, it shouldn't be a problem. But we need to avoid travel in the Third Mire Swamp. It is treacherous and will slow us down greatly. I do know of tunnels in The Obsidian

Peaks that bypass the swamp. We can then travel into the Griffin Forest, and follow Skull Bottom River into the Trow Lowlands Barony."

The warlord nodded approvingly. "Yes, that sounds like the best plan."

Dradia nodded and noticed suddenly that Gathus was no longer next to her. She glanced about and noticed the trow several feet away.

"Gathus, stay close to me," Dradia ordered.

Gathus returned to Dradia's side. "That big man over was listening to us talk."

He turned around to look at the man. "I think he might…"

He stopped talking the moment he noticed that the man was gone. He was there just five seconds ago, and he vanished instantly. "He was there," Gathus assured Dradia. "I swear he was."

"There are itchy ears everywhere in taverns, little one. Don't worry," Dradia said, brushing the matter aside.

"His interest seemed more than just casual, Dradia. He was listening to us and carving something into the table. He was watching us almost right after we sat down together."

Dradia surrendered to the trow's suspicions. "Where was he sitting, Gathus? Show me."

Gathus led Dradia to the table where the man sat. The man left nothing behind, but there was a symbol carved into the table. It was a symbol they did not recognize.

Haz Rhon joined them. "What is so interesting?"

Dradia pointed to the symbol. "Do you recognize this?"

"No, should I?" Haz Rhon asked with slight sarcasm.

The warlord returned to the table, and the others followed him, but remained standing since Haz Rhon occupied the only chair.

"So, tell me about these tunnels you spoke of and how long it'll take for us to get to them," Haz Rhon demanded as he began to chew another slice of beef.

"I traveled through them once before, so I know which tunnel to take. There is a risk of running into gargoyles or were-rats, or maybe even a beast or two. It'll take nearly two days just to get to the tunnels, and about a full day to reach the end of them. If we run into any trouble, my druid magic will be able to get us out of it."

"My battle axe will likely be what gets us out of trouble, druid," Haz Rhon said rudely.

"I thought a warlord's skill was generally in knowledge of war and tactics, and not particularly combat skills," Dradia stabbed back with a harsh tone.

"We are skilled in combat as well," Haz Rhon corrected her.

Dradia and Gathus noticed the bartender approach the table that the man was sitting at.

"He was here again," the bartender sighed.

"Who?" Dradia asked, walking quickly to the bartender. "Who was here again?"

The bartender pointed at the symbol carved into the tabletop. "A great assassin called the Wind Wraith. I don't know his real name, but that is his symbol. I only know because my cousin, Drake Smokeruin, was a part of the same guild before he apparently disappeared in The Underworld about four months ago."

CHAPTER XX

Heart of Flesh or Stone?

THE SKIES WERE GREY, as they had been for several days. The different layers of clouds and the direction the different winds sent them could all be seen clearly from Dosel Den, the second city. The gargoyle city featured more than sixteen towers stretching upward from between two large peaks within the Ebony Earth Mountains, which were completely composed of obsidian gem stone.

Shardana Rubyclaw, an emerald gargoyle, looked up at the sky, but all three moon remained absent, just as they had been the three nights prior. She stood at the opening of her cavern, one thousand feet above Dosel Den. Cradled in her right arm was Jade Rubyclaw, one of her five new younglings.

Shardana moved away from the opening of her cavern and crouched low next to the cinders of a fire she had extinguished. The warmth of the coals was all she needed to be sure that her hatchlings were warm.

A noise from the mouth of the cavern forced her to turn around. Standing at the entrance to her home was Kharious Bloodwing. The glowing embers from the fire pit spared enough light for her to see the glossy obsidian form of the gargoyle. He had broad wings, thick horns, and ruby eyes that flashed when he was angry, but they always glowed with hellish radiance. He was larger and taller than most gargoyles, but several of his ruby teeth were chipped. His right wing was cracked slightly toward the middle, and there was a chip in his upper right leg. Like Kharious, Shardana had ruby eyes and claws as well.

"I know you have been in the lower lands lately," Kharious told her, crossing his arms. "You know that it is forbidden to associate with humans or any other species down below."

"The frozen fire snared my curiosity, my lord," Shardana said, ignorant to the true anger that fueled Kharious.

"It is not just the frozen fire that caused you to stray from your homeland, but the magic you have been detecting from the mortals."

"There are some down below that seem very powerful indeed," Shardana admitted. "Magic fascinates me, and I am drawn to it. You know very well that I am sensitive to the use of magic, and I can detect when powerful magic is in use. I can probably find the one who is using the frozen fire."

"The frozen fire is not our concern anymore," Kharious said, lowering his head slightly. "Those who are using it will not bother us high up here in the Obsidian Mountain Range."

Shardana gasped. "How can you say that? We lost an entire clan of gargoyles in search of the artifacts in Fire Fern Keep. That keep held several artifacts, one that belongs to us."

"Yes, we did," Kharious roared regretfully. "We lost an entire clan, Shardana! We lost the Shardskins. Thirty-two gargoyles went searching for the frozen fire, and they never returned. I do not want to lose any more of our clans in search of something that is no longer important!"

Shardana argued, "You don't think that the Black Charisma is important?"

"It is an artifact that we help create during the War of the Gods, and it's not something we need anymore. Let it go, Shardana! That artifact was made during a dying age. Let it die with that age."

Kharious began to walk to the entrance of Shardana's cavern home. Shardana lowered her head, but continued to cradle Jade in her arms. "I can't let go of the past as easily as you, Kharious. My clan, the Bloodwings, made that artifact. It offers protection against dragons, something we need to protect our young."

"Let it go," Kharious said again, looking back at her. "And keep away from the humans! Are you not educated in history? Are you not aware of their treachery?"

"As you said, Kharious, that happened during a dying time."

"Why are you so interested in the mortals?"

"It's not really the mortals I am interested in," Shadrana informed him. "As you know, I am heavily attracted to magic. I have a very strong sensitivity to it. I am curious about the frozen fire, and someone down there who uses magic in a way that I have never seen before."

"Who?" Kharious asked with doubt.

"The arch mage, Dranus," Shardana replied reluctantly.

"Kharious' eyes flashed red with hellish anger. "Keep away from them, Shardana. I will banish you from these mountains if you do not!"

A tear welled up in Shardana's left eye, and her eye cracked. Kharious stepped back with surprise. He had never seen his kind cry before. The perfect sapphire gem that served as Shardana's left eye was now flawed. Kharious took another step back from her. He had no words to counter what he had just witnessed.

"Perhaps one day you will learn that not all of us are made out of cold stone, as you are, Kharious. Not all our hearts beat to the same rhythm. My heart is not solid like yours! It is hollow, and filled with something that you will never understand."

Without a word, Kharious spread his wings and leaped out of the cavern, and flew northwest. Shardana watched him until he blended in with the horizon.

CHAPTER XXI

House of Candles

THERE WAS A SINGLE ROOM in the house. There was no furniture or windows. It was completely empty, except for about two hundred lit candles that covered the walls on little niches and candle holders attached to the walls. The only other thing in the room was a wooden railing at the far end of the room that descended downward to the right.

"A staircase," Abadon muttered, as if a little surprised. The young prince started to walk toward it, but his instincts warned him to look up, remembering that vampires could cling to walls and ceilings. Abadon glanced up at the ceiling. There were no vampires. Only two large chandeliers hung from the roof, holding at least a dozen candles each.

Epona starred at the candles as if mesmerized by their flickering light. Hundreds of lit fires burned, creating enough light to make it appear as though sunlight was flooding the room, somehow penetrating the walls. Some of the candles were red, and some were black.

"I thought vampires hated light," Gwan commented, looking at the candles.

Epona shook her head. "Photophobic vampires do, but most of them don't. They hate sunlight. Sunlight will reduce them to ashes in seconds. These candles are as close as they can get to a true sense of what it is like to bask in sunlight. That might be what this room or house is all about."

"This place is a little different," Gafnan told them. "This large room was here, but there was a wall separating a smaller room from this one. They changed this place a little."

"Were the candles here before?" Epona asked the beast master.

"Yes," Gafnan replied. "And just as many."

The four slowly made their way to the staircase at the far end of the room. Gafnan volunteered himself to go first, and the big man led the others down the narrow stairway. The staircase ended in front of a wooden door. Gafnan raised his hand, ready to knock on the door, but before he could touch it, it opened on its own.

Hesitating, Gafnan peered into the room, but only a fraction of it was visible. One at a time, the four gradually entered, fearing that fangs could sink into the flesh of their necks at any moment.

The rectangular room contained bookshelves along the walls. A crimson rug carpeted the wooden floor, and a desk rested at the end of the room. Behind the desk sat a pale figure dressed in black robes rimmed with red. He had short black hair, and his face was round. He was scribbling something down on paper, which they could not read. The desk was easily twenty feet away from them. On the desk was a candelabrum of obsidian stone, supporting three lit candles. The pale figure lifted his head to view his visitors. A strange, baleful smile appeared on his face.

'He is guessing how warm our blood is, and how sweet it will taste when his fangs sink into our throats,' Abadon thought to himself.

"Welcome," the vampire said. His mouth was small, and the tips of his fangs poked down beneath his top lip. Abadon, Gafnan and Gwan shivered when the voice spoke, yet his voice was gentle in some way. Epona stared at the vampire and offered a small smile. The vampire was very charming. He was charming enough to snare the heart of nearly any woman.

The vampire moved from behind his desk and stood several feet away from them. He did not appear to be worried that he was outnumbered four to one.

"Lure Vesper is my name," the vampire said softly. "You have somehow stumbled upon my house of candles. You are the first visitors I have had since 1302 AG, the year of the dove."

Lure Vesper turned to Gafnan. The vampire's smile remained, but Gafnan remembered what he had said the last time they met. 'If you value your life, you will never return here.' That sentence repeated in the beast master's head. It was a chilling memory.

"It was your face that I saw here ten years ago," Lure Vesper recalled. "I have not forgotten it. Until now, you were the only one who was somehow able to elude the evil spirits and trek this deep into the forest to find my house."

Lure Vesper brought his face within inches of Gafnan's bearded, filthy face, which twitched nervously.

"I see that you have not learned from last time. You have refused to take my advice," Lure whispered, his voice growing colder still. His icy breath seemed nearly as frigid as the early winter air.

Gafnan's eyes shifted to the points of Lure's fangs. He waited, shaking like a leaf being bullied by the wind, just waiting for those fangs to pierce his flesh. Instead, Lure moved away from him, walking back to his desk. He turned around to face them once he was behind it.

"Why are you here?" Lure asked them calmly, but with a stern voice.

Abadon introduced himself, trembling. "Lord Vesper, I am Prince Krendale. Please excuse our intrusion. We have been hiding in the forest for three days now. There are powerful invisible assassins searching for us. We felt that entering the forest was the only way to elude them."

"Why are you here?" Lure asked again, this time yelling at them.

"To seek your help and wisdom," Abadon replied. His voice trembled even more.

"Why would I help you, young prince?" Lure asked. "After the War of the Gods, your kind forced my kind into hiding! Vampire slayers have sought us out since then, but have done little damage over the passing centuries. You foolish humans have no idea how superior we are over you."

Lure looked them over for a moment, and then shouted. "You are weak!

The four jerked suddenly at the loud, snapping words of the vampire lord

Lure Vesper turned his back on them and sat back down at his desk. Abadon licked his lips nervously and made another attempt to make peace.

"I am not a historian, Lord Vesper, but I understand that you have suffered as much as my kind in the past. Please realize that we are of a new generation. The humans that survived the War of the Gods have long been dead. I have not only come for help, but to make peace between my people and yours."

"And why should I trust you now?" Lure hissed. "You made peace with our kind once before, and that trust was shattered! You came to us for help, and we gave you that help. Hundreds of us spilled our own blood protecting your precious monuments, buildings, farms and families."

Lure began to move slowly toward them with his index finger extended at Abadon. "And when it was all over, you slaughtered us by the hundreds. Nearly one thousand of our kind were killed by your hands."

Lure was face to face with Abadon. "My kind have come to hate your kind for more than one thousand years. We were strangers before the War of the Gods, but now we are enemies."

Abadon said nothing. He was almost in tears, hearing the devastating impact his ancestors had on the vampires. He was ignorant to how humanity had treated their kind. As a child, he was told that vampires stalked and fed upon humans. Now he knew both sides of the story. Guilt and regret tore at Abadon's heart, and the young prince dropped to his knees and kneeled before the vampire.

"Please, Lord Vesper, please accept my apology. I ask for your forgiveness. I regret the past with more guilt than I can stand. I promise you safe passage through the Mystasian territories. I promise you peace, and understanding from one race to another. I promise solid gratitude and unbreakable trust. I will create new laws that will protect both your people and mine."

Lure snickered, moving away from the bowing prince. "Your father sent you through the haunted forest just to tell me all of this rubbish?"

"My parents are dead," Abadon said softly. "What I tell you comes from my heart alone."

"You know so little, boy," the vampire muttered without forgiveness. "You cannot persuade the tens of thousands of your citizens to love us. You cannot force them to live with my people in perfect harmony. Humans have come to hate vampires as we have come to hate you. The elves and dwarves share that same hate. It cannot be reversed."

"But it can," Abadon said out loud, standing on his feet.

Lure brought his index finger up to Abadon's lips. "Silence yourself. I have heard enough!"

Epona voiced her opinion as Lure returned to his desk. "I am a human, Lord Vesper, and I have come to respect your kind. I am a witch, and anyone will tell you that my bookshelves hold just as many books about vampires as they do books about witchcraft. Please give us a chance to prove ourselves to you."

Lure's hate faded slightly, but a strong sense of it still lingered. "How do I know that this isn't some sort of trick? This could be a chance for you to destroy my kind. You must understand that I risk much more than you to accept your word."

No one spoke for a moment, but then Lure tested them. "If you are serious about this, come to my castle in Bloodstone Forest, five days from now. We can discuss this matter further there."

Uneasiness swelled within each of them. They exchanged glances, and Lure could see the uneasiness in their eyes. There was no doubt that they felt it was a trap to snare them in their own lands, and to murder each of them there.

It was Abadon who finally spoke. "How do we know you won't kill us once we're there?"

"You see?" Lure Vesper said with a strange grin of cold compassion. "There is too much trust to be gained on both sides. Empathy existed before the first alliance was formed, but now there would be hatred and distrust as a foundation to build a new alliance. It is not possible. We do not trust each other. How can an alliance be reversed back into what we once had twelve hundred years ago?"

"A gift might be a start," Abadon suggested. "I will offer you a cloak, one that my parents have kept for years. I do not know where they found it, but it protects the vampire who wears it from sunlight, making it possible to travel during daylight hours. It is a reminder that our people did trust each other once. There was a time when we shared the same society."

Abadon licked his lips. He could see a slight persuasion shifting in the icy eyes of the vampire lord. Lure listened intently as Abadon continued to speak.

"To be honest, I spoke of distrust toward your kind a night or two ago, but Epona and Gafnan made me realize that you deserve to live, just as much as we do. Your kind is different from ours, much like night and day, but the differences between our cultures should not limit us to ignorance. Your kind, although evil in the country of Shadowsa, does not mean you are evil here in Mystasia."

Abadon sighed, and then quickly made a decision. "We will come to your castle in five days, as you have asked. Please forgive any delays we may experience on the way, but I trust you enough to accept your invitation. The gift I mentioned is still at my castle, and I will give it to you another day."

Lure nodded. He rose from behind his desk and slowly walked toward them.

"I want to believe you, Prince Krendale. I dream of the day my kind can gaze at the sunless horizon and see the colors of sunset and sunrise. I have never seen a sunrise or sunset. The candles upstairs are as close as I can get to the warmth of the sun's rays, and have them rinse the darkness from me. It is something I have always wanted to experience."

Lure looked solely at Abadon. "My heart wants to believe you, but my mind cautions me to refuse your offer. I will need a few days to think this all over. I just hope this isn't a trick, or some passage to revenge."

The intense fear they had of Lure weakened, and hope for friendship sparkled in both Abadon's and Lure's eyes.

Abadon shook his head. "This is no trick, Lure. Please, call me Abadon. I look forward to spending a night at your castle."

"I will welcome you," Lure responded. His voice was still cold, but the coldness seemed natural.

"Please stay a while," Lure said as he moved toward the bookshelf to the right of the room. He moved a book from the second lowest shelf into a new place on the fifth shelf from the roof. Two parts of the bookshelf opened, as if they were doors. Behind the opening was another room. Lure entered the room and motioned for the others to come inside. The room was easily twice the size of Lure's study. A large oak table sat in the middle of the room, and two more vampires were already sitting there. Abadon and the others noticed a tub of blood in the corner of the room, and it brought chilling shivers to their spines.

Three tapestries decorated the room. The closest one to them was a mountain of skulls. The second was an infamous battle of wizards known as the war of the magi, which occurred in 224 BG. The third, the farthest one from them, was an image of the blue moon, Shalamar, while full. Two cupboards and more bookshelves were the only other furnishings in the room.

Abadon and the others turned their attention to the two vampires already seated at the table. The one closest to them was female. Long, curly blood-red hair hung down to her waist. Her fangs were thin, but sharper looking than the others. Her eyebrows were thin, and her face was younger than yesterday. She was exceptionally beautiful, even though she was undead. She was thin and had small breasts.

The other vampire was one with a face of death. Cold, piercing eyes peered at them mockingly. His face was round, and he had short black hair, but he was not charming like Lure Vesper. An aura of fear and chill seemed to surround that vampire, and it reached out to them. His fangs were longer and thicker than the others. His nose had a slight hump on it. The arrogant, intimidating face of death studied them pleasurably. His eyes could see through them. He could see their fear, and he fed on it. Their fear gave him pleasure, and he smiled almost as their fear had sparked it.

Lure motioned to his companions with a smile. "Mornia Moonhaunt is an elementalist of fire. She does much of her studying with me here. She is loyal and highly intelligent. Next to her is Skyline Shadowfrost."

The name echoed in the minds of the visitors, and it lingered like a curse that would be impossible to remove. His terrifying gaze remained, but he was no longer smiling. His cold, hating eyes watched their fear grow.

"Skyline is considered the most terrifying of all vampires. He is the one who destroyed nearly half of the vampire slayers who have lost over the centuries, single-handedly. He is an assassin, and the greatest one ever at that. He is loyal to no one, except perhaps me."

Abadon and the others could not maintain eye contact with Skyline for more than a second. His eyes and face were too chilling and too terrifying.

Gwan summoned enough courage to inquire about Skyline's assassination skills. "How good is he?"

All three vampires gazed at Gwan, as if he was insane for asking such a question. They looked at him as if he had asked something that even the most foolish of fools would know the answer to.

"Greater than great," Lure replied bitterly.

Gwan continued. "I ask because two invisible assassins are tracking Prince Krendale."

Lure snickered. "As good as they may be, Skyline is more skillful. I assure you."

Skyline continued to stare at them, as if trying to decide which of them to feed upon first.

"Just a precaution," Lure continued. "If your alliance is a trick, Skyline is the one you will have to deal with. Keep your word, and you will find him to be a useful and powerful ally. He is night itself, deadlier than death. He is silent and invisible. He fearlessly stalks evil spirits and undead as frightening as banshees, if he has such a desire."

Lure sat down between Mornia and Skyline, and he invited Abadon and his party to sit across from them at the table. All threats and warnings were set aside.

"Your names," Lure demanded gently.

Abadon introduced Epona, Gafnan and Gwan, and concluded the introductions by introducing himself. Lure began to share a fraction of his past with his visitors.

"I must admit, I have long dreamed of this day, since the death of the first alliance. I am tired of the barren surroundings we dwell in since the Mystasian society considers us beasts, and soon possibly beasts of burden. My ageless life has given me two gifts. Those gifts are immortality and great wisdom, and yet I would trade them both in for a human life of my own."

Abadon and his companions stared at Lure, unable to believe what they just heard. Epona in particular seemed unable to believe it.

"I am older than life itself, it seems. I remember the days when humanity had no knowledge of magic. I witnessed the birth of magic, and watched mankind discover it and learn to use it."

Abadon sputtered, "You're speaking of a time that goes as far back as 3500 BG!"

"Exactly," Lure retorted with a weak smile. "Yet I have no memory of a human life. My mind holds no memory of ever being human at all."

Lure suddenly became slightly angered. "You humans must think that immortal life is great. No death from illness, and no aging. Let me assure you that a vampire life is a curse. I am dead. I am trapped in a carcass that never rots. I may have no memory of a human life, which makes me perhaps the oldest of all vampires, but Mornia has spent many years watching her companions grow old and die. Everyone around you dies when you're a vampire, until finally your only friends are vampires themselves. This is a rather cruel life when you were once human."

Lure Vesper calmed down a little, but his lecture continued after a brief pause.

"I turned Skyline into a vampire a few years before the end of the War of the Gods. His love aged, and then she was gone. His love for her faded not long afterwards. Unlike me, he relishes being a vampire and would never return to a human life, even if it was possible."

Skyline slowly nodded, wordlessly agreeing with what Lure said. Then he simply got up from the table and exited the room without a word.

"Lure," Gafnan said abruptly. "What did you mean when you warned me never to return here?

Did you mean to warn me about the ghosts and evil spirits, or that you would kill me if I ever returned?"

"Both," Lure replied. "The ghosts and spirits of this forest are not to be tampered with. I may not have fed upon you, Gafnan, but others such as Mornia, and certainly Skyline, would have. The warning was for your own good. The Mystasian society has shunned gargoyles, werebeasts, and vampires, but Skyline in particular only trusts other vampires."

Lure looked at each of his visitors in turn. "It is time for you to leave. Skyline will show you out, and is already upstairs waiting for you. I will wait for you at Castle Bloodstone."

"I look forward to it," Abadon stated, stretching out his hand. Lure hesitated for a few seconds, but shook hands with the prince.

"Me too," Epona declared. Lure's face seemed strangely less cold when he looked at the young witch.

Abadon led the others out of the room. They slipped past the study and walked up the stairs. Lure and Mornia never followed them. When the party of four reached the top floor, Skyline was already waiting next to the door, smiling arrogantly. Abadon and the others approached Skyline cautiously, fearing a sudden attack. Skyline remained still as they passed him and joined Sabre outside of the house.

Once they were outside, Skyline blessed them with some advice, something that they did not expect. His voice was as cold as winter, and as low as roaring thunder when he spoke. His arrogant, chilling smile never disappeared.

"Travel south for a day, and then travel east. You will find a much lower concentration of ghosts and evil spirits that way."

Skyline closed the door to the House of Candles, shutting them out in the Haunted Forest.

CHAPTER XXII

Lycanthropy

THE ROAD KNOWN AS Cold's Weary Finger gave a hint of danger. Haz Rhon spotted it, and gripped his axe tightly with both hands. Drops of blood could be seen on the freshly fallen snow. The blood was undoubtedly only a few minutes fresh, otherwise the snow would have hidden it. Gathus began to worry about whose blood it was, but Dradia walked on ahead and didn't seem to be concerned about it.

Not long before dawn, they entered a valley between two tall peaks. Soon the night dominated the sky. There was a slight wind, but it was very quiet. There was no sound at all except for the whistling of the wind, which was normal in that region. It disturbed Gathus greatly, and the trow decided that the silence may have frightened Haz Rhon as well. Dradia knew the mountain passage well enough to know that the whistling sound was normal. The haunting wind did not disturb her at all.

Without warning, from out of the darkness came teeth and claws that ripped at Haz Rhon's torso, knocking him to the ground. Three werewolves circled the group. None of them were armed with any weapons. Haz Rhon was the closest one to them. Two more appeared from behind a boulder—they were not werewolves, but were-tigers. One of them lunged at Gathus, but Dradia pushed the trow out of the way. Thinking quickly, she spoke two words of magic and managed to dodge the were-tiger's attack.

Dradia gestured toward the cliff behind the were-tiger, and a minor avalanche of snow fell upon four of the werebeasts, trapping them. Two of them were buried deep within the snowfall. Two more were trapped from their legs down.

Haz Rhon acted fast and killed the trapped werewolf and were-tiger before they could free themselves. From behind, the only remaining werewolf bit Haz Rhon's forearm. He pressed his hand against the werewolf bite hard. Blood leaked from beneath his fingers, but at a slow rate. He looked around the area warily, searching for more werebeasts, but there were none, and the attack stopped.

"Let me see your wound," Dradia ordered the Cyclops. Haz Rhon pulled his hand away from his forearm. Dradia took a few seconds to look over the wound, and then bandaged it with a cloth.

"Come, you need aid. Perhaps we can find a cure for you in the passage," Dradia said, already walking away.

Gathus's lips quivered. "Will he be okay, Dradia?"

"No," the warlord replied. "I have been both scratched and bitten by a werewolf, and soon I will be one of them. There is no cure for lycanthropy."

Dradia turned to face the others. "Don't forget that I am a druid, and I know of such things. Only silver leaf can cure lycanthropy, but the disease acts quickly, and we have little time to stop it."

Just as Dradia was about to continue leading them to the passage in the mountains, she noticed movement from the pile of snow she had created. A were-tiger crawled out from the snow and erected himself. He stood there staring at the druid.

Dradia asked, "Why did you attack us?"

"We came from Owl's Hoot," the were-tiger roared. "The forest has changed. There are leaves of brass and trucks of iron, and the sap is poisonous."

Dradia realized quickly that the effects of the dark druids on the Mystasian forests had not yet passed. "I have nothing to do with the changes in the forest," Dradia told the were-tiger.

"Destroy him!" Haz Rhon ordered.

"I will not destroy him," Dradia said. "They had no reason to attack us, but they are simply frightened and confused with the changes in their forest. If you want this were-tiger to die, you will have to do it yourself!"

"And I will," Haz Rhon said as he threw his large battle axe toward the were-tiger, who reacted quickly and easily avoided being struck by the colossal weapon.

Haz Rhon had calculated that the were-tiger's next attack would likely to be a leap in the air, straight for his throat. The were-tiger did exactly as the warlord had guessed. As the beast aimed himself straight for Haz Rhon, he pulled a thick dirk from his boot, striking the were-tiger in the face. Dradia and Gathus continued around the corner and waited at the mouth of the passageway into the mountains. They did not wish to witness the death of the were-tiger.

The were-tiger was down on the ground, and Haz Rhon jabbed the dirk into his body three more times to ensure that he was dead.

A moment later, Haz Rhon joined at the others at the mouth of the passageway.

Dradia fixed the warlord with a sour gaze. "Warlords are cold. Almost as cold as assassins. You bring death to others well, don't you?"

"Spare me your emotional blunder, druid," Haz Rhon snickered. "I am a warlord, and I have seen for myself how harsh life and death and war can be. Nothing is fair, and life is cold. Nothing sorrows me anymore. I have seen firsthand how harsh reality can get."

Dradia turned her back on the Cyclops and decided to drop the matter.

The floor of the tunnel was made up mahogany sand, and the walls were natural stone generally made of granite stone and obsidian. A frog-like creaturehopped along behind them aimlessly.

"What a strange creature," Haz Rhon said, watching the creature.

"She is a nymyr," Dradia told him. "Her name is Skoria."

Just ahead, there were holes in the walls of the tunnel. Crawling in and out of the holes were dozens of cave nagas. Haz Rhon slammed himself up against the wall of the tunnel and lifted his axe.

"Calm down," Dradia said, raising her hand. "They are just cave nagas. Their poison is weak, and they do not normally attack unless provoked."

Haz Rhon lowered his axe. He watched as the nagas slithered about. They did not seem interested in them at all. Like all nagas, they were snake-like beings. They had human faces and fuchsia hair, but they lacked limbs completely, just as most snake species did. They were striped with red and green, and had two small fangs protruding from their top lip.

Dradia led them onward, but Haz Rhon still kept his distance from the cave nagas.

"Listen," the Cyclops spoke softly. "Are you sure that this is the quickest way to Trow Lowland Barony? I have good reason to believe that one of the Mystasian noble lords is responsible for what is going on."

"This is the quickest and safest route," Dradia said. "There is always a risk of running into gargoyles, but we risk that outside of the mountain as well."

The tunnel curved and descended downward, and then branched off into three different directions. Dradia studied them for a moment, as if trying to recall which tunnel was the correct way. She turned down the right tunnel, which sloped upward slightly. Not far ahead, the druid spotted something on the sandy floor of the tunnel. Dradia knelt down next to it.

"What is it?" Gathus asked.

"Spider dung," Dradia replied, "But I am not entirely sure what kind."

Dradia continued onward, passing a few patches of purple stringy vegetation. She ripped a few strands of the strange plant out of the rocky wall of the tunnel, and slipped it into a pouch she carried.

"What is that?" Gathus asked, abiding his inquisitive behavior.

"Rabannic," Dradia answered, showing no frustration with the trow's questions. "It's a plant I sometimes use for healing purposes."

"Will it help me?" Haz Rhon asked.

"Possibly, but I doubt it," was the druid's reply.

Dradia made a sharp turn around the bend of the tunnel and came face to face with a flame fang spider. It was a giant spider with bright orange and red patterns on its round abdomen. Its fangs were not made of flame, but their bite burned, and they were bright orange. All eight of the spider's eyes were green.

The flame fang spider took one step toward Dradia, who muttered a word of druidic magic, and the spider began to walk in front of her as if scouting ahead for them.

"What did you do to it?" Haz Rhon asked with his hand on his battle axe, ready to use it.

"Druids can communicate with animals," Dradia explained. "I merely asked it to scout ahead for us."

Haz Rhon followed the druid closely, realizing that the extent of her powers and druidic skills were beyond what he had initially thought.

"Perhaps magic does have a place in the world," the warlord said.

"What do you mean?" Dradia asked without turning back.

"My opinion of magic is small, and more or less those who use it as well."

"In other words, you have no use for magic or those who use it, and think the world is better off without it," Dradia summarized the warlord's true thoughts.

"That was my prior opinion on the matter," Haz Rhon confessed. Suddenly, Haz Rhon leaned over and grunted. He was reacting to the changes in his body. The transformation into a werewolf had begun within.

"It's started," the warlord moaned. "Even my senses are changing. I can actually smell the spider that you sent up ahead."

Dradia watched the warlord for a moment, unsure of what to do. Using caution, she kept her holly bramble battle staff clutched in her hand. A moment later, Haz Rhon was back on his feet, exhaling deeply.

"I am okay," he ensured them. "The transformation has stopped."

"For now," Dradia added with a hint of worry mixed in with her voice.

After much travel, the three travelers had become fatigued. They found a reasonable sized natural chamber in the tunnel, and they set up camp together. Sleep for all of them that night was shattered into fractions of rest. Haz Rhon continued to experience changes from within his body, making comfortable sleep impossible.

Dradia and Gathus were too worried that Haz Rhon would transform, and that his personally would transform as well, and that he might kill them during the night if they were asleep during his complete transformation. The flame fang spider that scouted ahead for them was nowhere in sight, but Skoria rested nearby. Dradia found it strange that the spider did not return to report its finding to her. The druid kept her weapon within reach, in case Haz Rhon did attack them during the night.

Haz Rhon never transformed into a werewolf during the night, and eventually the three woke and continued their journey down the tunnel in search of its end in the northern region of the Trow Lowlands.

Soon after leaving the natural chamber where they built camp, many holes could be seen in the walls and on the floor of the tunnel.

"More cave nagas?" Haz Rhon asked.

"No, these are from spyavani," the druid replied.

"Spya… what?" Haz Rhon asked.

"Spyavani. Earth eels," Dradia told them, looking back at them for a quick moment. "They are harmless. Don't worry about them. Tell me more about the frozen fire."

"I only know what I saw," Haz Rhon reported. "I didn't see the fire, but I heard that it is strange. It is a cold fire of highly destructive power. A portal is what allowed the small Underworld army to enter the war guild. I only saw goblins and medusas. The frozen fire was never used against us at the war guild."

"Medusas." Dradia said the word with uncertainty. "They are such a powerful enemy. They shoot arrows tipped with poison, and if they get close enough to you, they turn you into stone. I certainly hope that The Underworld doesn't have many of those in its ranks."

"Jherlom has seen the frozen fire," Gathus said out loud. "When it was used against Castle Blackburn."

"I don't know anyone powerful enough to cast such a spell," Dradia told them. "Not even Vadamar or Dranus are powerful enough to use the amount of power that would be required to cast a spell of that magnitude."

"Speaking of druids," Haz Rhon mumbled. "Are any of them inside the keep guarding it from these attacks?"

"I don't know," Dradia shrugged. "Possibly, although it's not necessary. The keep has a special stone within it, and when that stone is pressed, it triggers the keep to seal itself shut. It basically becomes a giant rock. When it is in that state, there are only five of us who know how to reopen it."

"Are you one of them?" Gathus asked.

"Yes, I am," Dradia replied.

Dradia passed by white frosty ferns. "Be sure not to touch these," she warned the others. "They are frost ferns and cause serious freezing when touched."

"A nice winter plant," Gathus said teasingly. "I bet it's a great ingredient for a recipe for a cold spell."

Dradia nearly dropped her staff. The trow's last sentence echoed strong within her mind. "By the gods, Gathus, that's it! I bet the frost fern is one of the ingredients used to create the frozen fire spell!"

Haz Rhon leaned on his battle axe. His words were thick with sarcasm. "You mean to tell me that none of you druids have already thought of that?"

"I have been much more focused on who might be creating the spell, rather than how it was made," Dradia admitted almost sheepishly. "If we can figure out how it was made, we might be able to discover who created it."

"Maybe…"

Haz Rhon was cut short as Dradia raised her hand. "Shhhhh! I hear something moving ahead of us."

Haz Rhon raised his battle axe, and the three waited. Gathus secured himself behind the cyclops. The flame fang spider was approaching very slowly. Haz Rhon eased himself and slowly lowered his weapon.

"It might not be the one I sent out," Dradia warned him.

Haz Rhon raised his axe again, taking the druid's warning very seriously. Once the spider got closer, Dradia realized that it was the same spider that she had sent scouting ahead, but it wasn't responding to her. As it got closer still, she could see its wounds. The spider took two more steps, and then collapsed on the tunnel floor. Dradia inspected the spider. It was dead, and its wounds very critical. She was surprised that the spider had even made it as far as it did. She noted that strange white bones embedded in the spider's abdomen, where the wounds were located, and her face changed. The face she wore was normally highly confident, but uncertainty masked it now.

"What are those?" Gathus asked.

"Teeth," Dradia replied nervously. "They are raz'kaktal teeth."

"raz ka…" Haz Rhn gave up trying to pronounce the name.

Dradia got up from her knees and turned to the others. "Raz'kaktal is elvish for beast of teeth," Dradia said gravely.

CHAPTER XXIII

Barbarian Encampment

THE SKY OFFERED THE SMALL BAND plenty of sunlight hours to easily set up camp ten miles southeast of the House of Candles. They slept well that night, and the ghosts and evil spirits of The Haunted Forest did not bother them. They were relieved that their lives were spared. They were just as equally relieved that the vampire lord had considered a possible alliance with Mystasia.

Epona seemed sad as she looked about the area.

"What is the matter?" Abadon asked.

"Meta is gone," Epona replied with a near sob. "I guess the charm spell did wear off, and Meta left without harming any of us."

Abadon placed a hand on her shoulder. "Meta will be fine, Epona. He probably went home." Epona nodded wordlessly.

When the black skies faded to a dark blue, Abadon woke facing the north. He immediately noticed a shadowy figure peering at them from just beyond the distant gloom. He turned to the others to see if any of them noticed, but they were all still asleep. He turned back to the north, but the figure was gone. The grey gloom ringed around them, but there was no trace of the shadow.

A moment later, the others began to stir as their sleep shifted to awakening.

"I saw a shadow," Abadon told them, breaking the morning silence and still waiting for the figure to return. "I saw something staring at me."

"It could be the forest playing tricks on your eyes," Epona suggested.

"No," Abadon replied. "Something was there, but it wasn't a ghost or a spirit. It was something real, something with a definite physical shape."

Epona, Gafnan and Gwan all scanned the forest around them, but the shadow remained absent from view. Shrugging, Gafnan made a startling announcement to the others.

"I am going to attempt to persuade my people to join the alliance. I do not know how they will react. There is a strong chance they will reject me, or even imprison me."

"Then why take the chance?" Abadon asked.

"Because the risk involved is worth what may become of the attempt I make," Gafnan replied quickly, almost cutting the young prince off.

"Good luck, Gafnan," Abadon said, offering his hand. The beast master shook hands with Abadon, and then turned to the others, who each offered him a nod of approval. Gafnan nodded back, and he began to walk to the southwest. Sabre trailed behind him, but the beast master quickly pointed to the others.

"No, Sabre. Stay with them. They will need you," Gafnan ordered.

Sabre let out a roar of protest, but listened to Gafnan. Sabre and the others watched until Gafnan disappeared behind the closest trees to them.

A moment later, Gwan began to lead them to the east. Abadon trailed behind Epona and Gwan, looking over his shoulder to where the shadow had materialized moments earlier from the gloom. There was nothing there. Unsatisfied that whatever or whoever it was could still be in the area, Abadon trekked east, keeping a close watch over his shoulder. A part of him wished that Gafnan had not left them.

Daylight decayed much sooner than they had expected, and the creeping night forced them to set up another camp for the night. The three moons returned to the sky, casting a purple hue down on them. A short time after the camp was set up, a scream echoed into the night. It seemed that everything around them, including themselves, froze, startled by the alarming scream. Silence stained the air, and another scream echoed, followed by more.

After a few minutes of reoccurring screams, the silence stayed. The three waited silently for a long time, exchanging glances but never saying a word. They waited for whatever caused the screams to attack their camp, but nothing came to them.

A long time passed before Gwan made a suggestion. "Perhaps we should go see what happened."

Abadon and Epona exchanged uneasy glances, but said nothing.

Gwan shook his head. "It is difficult to know exactly what direction those screams came from. I think it came from the southeast. I will go have a look for myself."

"No," Abadon protested. "I have full trust in your skills as a ninja, but we need you here. We'll investigate first thing in the morning. I don't want any of us separating from each other. Besides, it definitely wasn't Gafnan that we heard, and we don't know who else is out there."

Gwan's eyes hinted disagreement with the prince's decision, but the ninja sat back down next to the fire Abadon had constructed.

"Remember what Gafnan said," Epona cautioned the ninja. "The ghosts and spirits sometimes lure people away from camps. What we heard might have been false echoes created by them. You can't believe everything you see or hear in The Haunted Forest."

There were no more screams in the night, and the three were soon asleep. Only the silence and the cold kept a strong presence. The three remained undisturbed, and they woke with the rising sun the next morning. Abadon and Gwan watched Epona extinguish the fire that had not been entirely successful at warding off the chill of the early winter night.

Abadon was the first to form an opinion of direction. "The screams sounded like they came from the southeast, but it may have only appeared that way."

"It could be a trap," Gwan said, showing little interest in investigating the matter.

"But what if it's not?" Epona asked, thrusting her wand beneath her belt of black cloth. "Last night you wanted to see where they came from."

"Last night we had time to spare," Gwan said. "Now we need to get going to reach Castle Bloodstone, in time to meet with Lure."

"You do have a weapon that slays ghosts just as easily as birds can fly through air," Epona said, as a means of reminding Abadon of the nature of the weapon Gwan armed himself with.

Abadon let out a very faint sigh, as if he made his decision reluctantly. "We will travel southeast and see what we can find," he said.

As they traveled, the cold fog clung to their clothing like ghosts, molesting their bodies with frigid fingers of cold caress. It seemed about two hours had passed, and they had not found any evidence revealing the source of the screams. A moment later, the three noticed what appeared to be a clearing just beyond the misty collection of fog to the east, which seemed finer and less solid than the fog they had encountered earlier that day. The smell of smoke polluted their nostrils, and got stronger with each step they took.

Carefully, they entered the clearing, which was broken up with occasional bramble hollies and ghost willows. The clearing was also a clutter of night crown carnations. Smoke was rising from the still-burning fires, and it caused their eyes to sting and forced them to cough. The fires continued to chew at the six skeletal and blackened frames of what were once buildings. Blood carnage was scattered through the clearing, and was almost as plentiful as the night crown carnations. They examined the bodies of men cut down and broken, almost like scarecrows. Abadon's heart saddened when he saw the bodies of women, and a few children as well. What or whoever attacked them left no one alive. Some appeared to be human, but some were werebeasts.

"Oh no," Abadon began to say. "This is the werebeast encampment that Gafnan was going to, isn't it?"

The young prince turned to Epona for comfort, but she did not answer. Instead, she began to search for Gafnan's body.

"This is not the main werebeast encampment," Gwan said a moment later.

"How do you know?" Abadon asked.

"What we are looking at is what remains of the Moonmuzon Barbarian Tribe."

"Gwan is right," Epona said, realizing that they were not in the main werebeast encampment. The young witch recalled looking at a map of the area. "The encampment Gafnan went to is anywhere from fifteen to twenty miles from here.

"Look at the weapons lying around, and what is left of the buildings," Gwan advised them. "This was a barbarian tribe."

"But why would..." Abadon was about to speak, but he was cut off. A loud moan through the heavy fog to their right caught their attention, and they all rushed through the fog to find its source.

About thirty-five feet to their right lay a barbarian werewolf. His bloody state made it impossible for them to see the color of his hair, or the structure of his face. He was merely a bloody mass of flesh.

"Be careful," the barbarian warned them. Abadon crouched low next to the barbarian and began to study his wounds. After wiping away some of the blood, Abadon discovered three vital wounds.

"What happened?" Epona asked as Abadon began to heal the barbarian's wounds.

"I don't know," the barbarian puffed, barely able to speak. "Some of us were attacked by orcs, but some of us were attacked by something we could not see. However, invisibility was not the only skill my attacker had. He also had abilities too great for him to have been a man. The gods must be angry with us."

"It wasn't any god who did this, my friend," Abadon said to him softly, still struggling to heal him in time before the seriousness of the wounds claimed his life. "It was an assassin armed with a powerful weapon."

"But why attack us?" the werewolf asked. Blood poured out of his mouth as he spoke.

"I don't know, but be silent and still," Abadon ordered him. The barbarian obeyed, but several seconds later, he croaked something that none of them could understand, and he died.

Abadon sighed as he took his hands away from the chest wound. He rose to his feet, turning to Epona.

"The assassin knows that we are somewhere in this forest. I think he came here with a party of orcs, seeking information about our location. When they didn't get that, they slaughtered the tribe."

"But that's ridiculous," Gwan exclaimed.

"What else would they have slaughtered this tribe for?" Abadon asked Gwan. The ninja said nothing.

Abadon looked down at another corpse. Epona placed her hand over the slain barbarian's forehead.

"What are you doing, Epona?" Abadon asked.

"I'm performing a spell called 'death's eyes'," Epona replied, heavy in concentration.

"With it, I'll be able to see the last several minutes of his life."

Abadon and Gwan watched as Epona performed the 'death's eyes' spell. She closed her eyes. "I can see several tribesmen being cut down by orcs. I see a few others being slain by something invisible."

Abadon inquired, "Do you see anything that is not ordinary at all, Epona?"

"No," Epona replied. "Now I see the ground. It seems the barbarian I am using this spell on just died. He turned quickly to see his killer, but no one was there."

Epona pulled her hand away from the barbarian's forehead. "This man was killed by the invisible assassin who has been stalking you."

Gwan nudged the prince and pointed. "Look!" The shadow that Abadon had seen the previous morning had returned. Fog drifted around the shadow, and then it was gone.

"It has to be the assassin," Abadon cried out hysterically. "Who else could it be?"

"No, my lord," Gwan shook his head. "I don't think so. I didn't see his face, but his posture did not match anyone from my clan."

"If it's not someone from your clan, then who is it?" Abadon demanded.

Epona shrugged, staring into the gloom, "Well, whoever it is, they obviously don't mean us any harm. Unless of course they are waiting for the right moment to strike."

"We'll travel on," Abadon urged. "That's the second time I've seen that shadow. It'll return again later."

The three went on, but with every step they took, they waited for something to attack them from the gloom that edged the trees just behind the closest trees to them. The trek continued for a long time, leaving the ruined barbarian encampment more than twelve miles west. The trees ahead disappeared, and the forest opened up to another clearing, much smaller than the clearing the Moonmuzen Barbarian Tribe had located themselves in. Something stirred within the mist ahead—something much larger than Sabre.

Gwan looked over his shoulder and jumped back when he found the shadow that had been stalking them, standing only a few feet away from him. His movements were swifter than shadows. He was now close enough to be identified. It was Skyline Shadowfrost.

"That shadow stalking us was you the whole time?" Gwan asked.

Skyline nodded. "Lure sent me to make sure that you arrive at Bloodstone Castle safety, much to my dismay." The vampire's voice was cold and conceited. The three ignored the vampire's comment.

Seconds later, something large thrashed through the forest. The adventurers all armed themselves, but Epona was quick to lower her wand.

"It's the metaughla that I charmed days ago! The one that attacked Gwan."

Epona rushed to the beast.

"No!" Abadon warned her.

Epona gave the beast a hug, and nothing happened. The metaughla did not react hostilely toward her at all.

"It is still under the influence of my charm spell," Epona exclaimed.

The others said nothing. They simply did not trust the beast.

Epona walked toward Abadon and made a plea. "Abadon, I want you to heal the metaughla."

Abadon was silent in disbelief for a moment before responding to Epona's absurd request. "Are you serious? That large monster would require an extreme amount of energy to heal, not to mention that it will eventually attack us!"

"Please try, Abadon," Epona nearly begged. "It is under my control with a charm spell. It will prove to be useful to us."

Abadon stared at the large beast, which stood perfectly still, staring back at him. What a dumb, awkward beast, Abadon thought to himself. It was probably trying to figure out what type of creature he was.

"Oh, okay," Abadon moaned. "I suppose I could heal it, but perhaps not entirely. I still think it's a waste of energy that could be better spent doing something else."

"Like healing my arm," Gwan complained.

"Your arm is healed, Gwan," Abadon informed him. "Sometimes the pain lingers for a moment or two after the healing process."

Abadon knelt down next to the metaughla. He hesitated for a moment before touching the beast. Although he was confident in Epona's abilities in witchcraft, he still did not know the measure of her power, or how long the metaughla would be under the influence of her charm spell.

"This may take a couple of hours," Abadon informed her.

"Thank you, Abadon," Epona said, smiling, and she kissed the prince on the cheek.

As Abadon healed the metaughla, Epona and Gwan created a campfire. Eventually, Abadon joined the others by the fire. Sabre and the metaughla were uncomfortable with one another at first, but eventually the two befriended each other as the night hours passed. Skyline always remained in the shadows where the fire light barely reached, just him enough to display his form to the others. All eyes were on Skyline. The warmth of the campfire did not benefit him in any way, and the cold, early winter air did not burden him.

Gwan questioned the vampire in an attempt to involve him with the rest of the group. "Are you part of an assassin guild, Skyline?"

Skyline glared at the ninja and said nothing at first. It almost seemed to offend him that Gwan had even dared to speak to him.

"I do in fact have a guild of my own, in the Bloodstone Forest," the assassin informed them. "There are seven members who are all vampires. The greatest of them is Eifel Fatalfang, whom I taught everything I know. He is a lethal instrument who, like me, can assassinate any target."

Gwan frowned at the vampire's comment. An arrogant grin of his own formed on his lips. "Any target at all, Skyline? Even several magi?"

Skyline nodded. "If I was placed against several magi, I would prevail." He began to smile, but his smile was more than arrogant. It was dangerous. None of them trusted the vampire.

"What can't you beat?" Gwan asked conceitedly.

Skyline slowly approached the ninja, who was still sitting around the fire. When he reached Gwan, he bent low until his face was only two inches away from his. Gwan trembled slightly in fear, and began to wish that he had not been so hostile to the vampire. In a quick flash, Skyline reached for a dagger in a pocket of his cloak, stabbed Gwan in the right thigh with it, and returned it to his cloak. His movement was so fast that even Gwan's quick reflexes were not enough to prevent the assault. Gwan bellowed once he was stabbed and stared down at his wound in disbelief.

Abadon and Epona leaped up from the perimeter of the fire. Epona screamed, "What is wrong with you?" Abadon rushed to Gwan's side to heal the wound.

Skyline walked back to where he had been standing before and turned, smiling at Abadon. "I think your healing abilities will be in constant use in the near future, young prince. Especially if your companions anger me."

Abadon ignored Skyline's words and focused on Gwan's wound.

"I thought you were sent to protect us, not terrorize us," Epona commented on the situation.

I am, my lady," Skyline hissed. "A stab wound isn't going to kill anybody, unless I want it to. A nick in the neck would be perfect. The sweet nectar you humans call blood would taste sweet to my tongue. The warm fluid pouring down my mouth. I can taste it and feel it now."

Skyline closed his eyes as he tilted his head back slightly. His bottom lip quivered slightly twice. There was no doubt in any of their minds that Skyline was imagining drinking their blood that very moment. A moment later, he opened his eyes and gazed at all of them.

"I doubt Lure would approve of your behavior, Skyline," Epona said bitterly.

Skyline retorted with even more bitterness. "I do what I like, when I like. Lure is not my leader. I am my own master. You will soon learn this to be true."

He paused for a moment, and then leaned against the closest tree to him.

"I respect Lure Vesper for only one reason, and it is not because he is the greatest of the vampire blood lords. It is not because he is the most ancient of us all in Mystasia. It is because he gave me the greatest gift anyone could have given me. He gave me what no one else could—immortality. The moment his fangs left my throat, he gave me immortal strength and took away all my weaknesses. You have no idea just how weak humans really are. I know, because I was once human prior to the War of the Gods. Not even one million gold coins would persuade me to go back to a human life."

Abadon let out a sigh that was barely audible. He had returned to healing the metaughla, but it was taking too much time to fully heal the beast. As time passed, the three humans slept in shifts. Throughout the night, they occasionally glanced at Skyline. He was a shadow of death, and his icy eyes were so cold and piercing that they stabbed at them every time they looked at him.

Gwan looked down at his leg where Skyline had produced a puncture wound. Not even a scar remained. It was as if Skyline had never assaulted the ninja at all. He looked up at the vampire. "Are you sure you can defeat both the invisible assassins searching for us? Have you murdered anything invisible before?"

"Nothing invisible has ever dared to attack me," Skyline said proudly. "I destroyed a band of eight ogres once, about fifteen years ago. They ventured too far into the Bloodstone Forest, and I destroyed them all in a matter of seconds."

Abadon, Epona and Gwan all exchanged glances, but they remained silent. They were not sure if the vampire spoke the truth or not, but they decided that it was probably best not to anger the assassin that Lure promised them was the greatest ever. They were beginning to believe his stories. As frightening as Skyline was, he was also mysterious. With the exception of his assassination stories, Skyline mentioned nothing else about his past, except that it was Lure Vesper who had transformed him into one of the living dead. They knew nothing at all about his life prior to being a vampire, except that he was once in love with a woman who had been killed during his absence from her. The three decided to leave the vampire alone for a while.

Skyline never once spoke to them unless they spoke to him first.

Abadon glanced over at the metaughla. He could hardly believe that he was in the same camp as that massive, fleshy bulk of destruction. He moved to the beast and finished healing the fifth wound, and moved on to the sixth and final lesion.

He looked up at the others. "Does anyone here know anything about metaughlas, other than that they have large enough mouths to swallow an ogre whole?"

Epona nodded at Abadon and looked the beast over for herself. "There are many types of these creatures, Abadon. This one is full grown, so it is called a metaughla.

"I certainly hope it's full grown. How much bigger can it get?" Abadon asked sarcastically.

"A cyughla is what you call a hatchling," Epona educated them. "They have only one tentacle at that stage. They grow into biguhlas, which have two tentacles, until they eventually become a metaughla, which has ten."

Gwan yawned. "How many years does it take for them to grow into a metaughla?"

"I am not sure," Epona said, shrugging. "I only know about their stages of growth and that they gain more tentacles as they age."

The party of four soon traveled west with Sabre and Meta trailing behind them. A single thought was on Abadon's mind now. Would Lure Vesper be as welcoming to them as he was at the House of Candles, or was this all just a conspiracy to trap them in their own territory before feeding upon them? Skyline's presence certainly seemed to prove that Lure was at least considering an alliance. Skyline could have easily murdered them all during the night, but he didn't. However, Abadon still did not completely trust the assassin, and he was not completely convinced that he could trust any of the vampires, including Lure. His offer to form another alliance with the vampires just seemed too easy, but Lure Vesper could still say no.

CHAPTER XXIV

Werebeasts of Moonmire

THE CAMPFIRES OF OWL'S HOOT were dim and barely penetrated the gloom. Gafnan approached the werebeast encampment from the east. The trek through the Jade Swamps slowed the beast master down, adding a few hours to his journey home. The late autumn gloom kept the tops of the trees from being seen, as if the approaching winter had decapitated them. It was as if they had been executed for bearing witness to the frozen fire that no one still knew anything about.

Gafnan felt strangely constrained as he approached his home encampment. There was a shift in the air, as if something was different somehow. Gafnan shifted back into were-eagle form just before he entered Owl's Hoot. Only a few eyes bothered to look at him as he entered the encampment. Passing a few eerie trees, Gafnan found the chief werebeast, Kalim Evernight, in were-bear form. His fur coat was frosty brown, and his powerful muzzle contained fangs pointing both up and down from his jaws. His eyes flashed bright green as he noticed Gafnan draw near.

Gafnan greeted Kalim with a nod, and Kalim returned one.

"Brave Gafnan," Kalim began to say. "I was hoping you'd return soon. Bhyrhon has reported strange events taking place to the north, just outside the borders of the Haunted Forest Territory." The were-bear towered over Gafnan's were-eagle form. "These events may affect us as well. Forest animals from the north have fled into these woods, woods that are normally avoided at all costs."

"The frozen fire may affect us more than you know, Kalim," Gafnan reported.

The were-bear's face became shadowed with conjectural curiosity. "What are you talking about, Gafnan? Where have you been over the last two weeks?"

"Something unexpected has happened, Kalim," Gafnan deciphered boldly. "Not far from Nordech, I came across Prince Krendale. He was lost in the forest. The king and queen of Mystasia are already dead."

"I have heard," Kalim spoke grimly, appearing to already disapprove of Gafnan's involvement.

"An invisible assassin has tried to kill him twice," Gafnan continued. "I was with him for the second attempt."

"Why did they not succeed, Gafnan?" Kalim inquired impatiently.

"The prince has protection given to him by the druid Jherlom Mor'Derum. It is a ring that causes displacement. They could not strike him down."

"And you have been traveling with the prince?" Kalim's question was stated more like an accusation. His bulky size caused Gafnan to take a step back from the brute chieftain.

"He asked for help, and I led him to Nordech," Gafnan admitted, standing his ground.

Kalim continued in rage. "You know why I do not approve of interaction with those who are not one of us, Gafnan! Vampires and gargoyles are one thing. They share the same conflict as we do. They are outsiders to Mystasian society, just as we are. Why do you trust any of those races so much?"

"I never meant to form friendships with anyone outside the camp, Kalim," Gafnan apologized truthfully, "But my explorations have taken me to places much more beautiful than our home forest. I have met interesting people on my travels that I have come to trust."

"Where is the prince now?" Kalim roared.

"He is on his way to Castle Bloodstone," Gafnan stated. "We visited Lure Vesper at the House of Candles. Lure agreed to consider a possible alliance with the Mystasians and invited the prince to their castle. I came here with a request from the prince, Kalim. I have come to ask you to consider an alliance with the Mystasians as well. United, we may survive the mysterious frozen fire that will eventually burn here, and destroy us all."

"How dare you come to me with such a request?" Kalim roared, shaking a fist at Gafnan. "After everything the Mystasians have done to us at the end of the War of the Gods! I can't believe you would even think that I would agree to such a thing."

Gafnan refused to show the were-bear that he had instilled any fear in him.

"Think, Kalim," Gafnan forced the issued further, but was cut off by the were-bear's temper. "I don't need to think!"

"But you do," Gafnan insisted. "Once the frozen fire has conquered Mystasian civilization, it will come here! It won't stop there, Kalim, I promise you that."

"Seize him!" Kalim demanded. A nearby werewolf and were-tiger pounced on Gafnan before he could react. A were-tiger from behind Kalim, armed with a spear, pointed it at Gafnan's face.

"I did not return home to shed blood," Gafnan squawked. "We too live in Mystasia, and we have to help them! If we do not unite to defeat this new enemy, we will fall to them alone."

"Do your human companions know the location of this encampment, or any others?" Kalim asked.

"No," Gafnan replied, offended by the were-bear's distrust. "Of course not. I would never give them such information, whether I trust them or not."

Kalim stood still with his arms crossed starring at Gafnan. A moment later, the were-beast chieftain sighed. "Cage him up."

Gafnan lowered his head, discontent with the results of his return home. He went willingly along with the guards to a wooden cage less than one hundred feet away. Gafnan entered the cage, but it felt more like a casket to him.

Kalim chuckled uncontrollably. "You can't possibly believe that the vampires will side with the Mystasians. It is a trick," the werebeast chieftain said. "They will never agree to such a thing, not after the betrayal they suffered those many centuries ago. The very same betrayal we suffered. He will likely be killed once he arrives there."

A new fear awakened within Gafnan's soul, chilling his blood. He began to believe what Kalim was saying. Abadon probably was walking into a trap. The prince would likely die in their castle, and the frozen fire would eventually burn within the Haunted Forest, destroying all of werebeast kind.

CHAPTER XXV

Noble Funeral

THE PASSAGE DESCENDED, and its path was rough and very uneven. Dradia held her bramble battle staff tightly in both hands. Haz Rhon towered over her from behind, holding his great axe in an offensive position.

"The blood stains are getting larger," Dradia said, observing the blood that the flame fang spider had left behind. "We must be getting closer to the site of the attack."

"What should I expect from this beast of teeth?" the warlord asked.

"Death," Dradia replied without showing even the slightest hint of mockery.

Just ahead, a scraping sound could be heard. Gathus kept himself in between both Haz Rhon and the battle beast, where he was most safe from this beast Dradia promised them would be terrifying. The scraping sound continued, as if something was scraping its claws against rock. Dradia stopped before advancing around the corner. Haz Rhon risked a peek around the corner and snapped his head back and pressed himself flat against the uneven stone wall of the tunnel with Dradia.

"By the gods, that thing is hideous," Haz Rhon whispered. Hair and teeth was nearly all the Cyclops saw. It was a monster larger than his battle beast, and he thought he saw four hands, armed with claws several inches long.

"I didn't see any eyes," Haz Rhon whispered.

"I am not certain they have any," the druid answered, pushing Gathus and Skoria behind her and out of harm's way.

"Then we have an advantage over the hellish beast," Haz Rhon murmured.

Dradia gripped the warlord's forearm and cautioned him, shaking her head. "Sight is but one of five senses, warlord. Surely you know that. There are things of great danger out there that have no eyes," Dradia mocked him.

"Hearing or smell is obviously not any of the senses it uses either, druid, or it would be on to us by now," Haz Rhon snapped back.

Just as the warlord finished his sentence, four claws at least two feet long cut nearly a foot into the rocky wall of the tunnel, barely nicking Haz Rhon's arm. A moment later, the rest of the raz'katal's hairy bulky view came into view from around the corner.

Three gaping jaws opened and snapped shut, again and again. No legs were visible, but there were four arms, all featuring the same lengthy, thick claws that nearly struck the warlord.

Dradia began to retreat, muttering words of druidic magic. Vines from below the earth began to snare the beast, but its claws cut through them with ease. Seeing that her druidic magic failed, Dradia made another attempt. She muttered additional words of magic, and stalagmites from the ceiling above the raz'katal fell, spearing themselves into the beast. It screamed out loud in reaction to its two new severe injuries, but its rage increased, and it did not slow down. It came toward them with alien fury. Great fear jolted through Haz Rhon, and for a moment, he froze in fear.

Reacting to fear that he was not accustomed to, the warlord threw his war axe at the beast, which struck it in between the two clusters of small eyes. The beast shrieked again.

Dradia continued to mutter several words over and over again, opening and closing her eyes in an attempt to both focus and watch the beast for any sudden advances.

The right side of the tunnel began to crack, and seconds later, collapsed. Tons of rocks slid onto the raz'katal, burying it. All that could be seen of the crushed beast was one extended arm, and several claws that were only one foot away from striking down the Cyclops.

It took a moment for Haz Rhon to relax. Dradia reversed the spell, and then located a large boulder to rest against. She was greatly exhausted from excessive magic use.

"I hope there are no more of these up ahead," Dradia puffed. "I will not have the strength to repeat this spell again for many days."

"Just get me out of these mountains and cured," Haz Rhon requested wretchedly.

Dradia nodded. "Let me rest for a moment, and we'll continue."

Many hours later, the saw the jeweled sky once again. They had exited the mountains and entered the northern region of the Trow Lowlands. A combination of flat grasslands and rolling hills extended beyond.

Gathus pointed to the south. "Udarshen is the closest town. We can get some rest there."

After a while, Dradia and Gathus noticed that for about a mile, the grassland was mixed with a strange crushed powder, but it wasn't actually powder. The substance was too sharp and brittle.

"What the hell are we walking on?" Dradia asked after a while. To her surprise, the answer came from Haz Rhon, and not Gathus, who was native to the land.

"A great war was fought here once," the warlord said, smiling.

"The War of the Races?" Dradia guessed.

"That is correct," Haz Rhon nodded. "That was the war that made Mystasia the country it is today. The very same war brought the races together that are now in alliance within its borders. These skulls are mostly trow skulls, and some human skulls as well. The battle that occurred here was between humans and trows. So many bones were left behind here that they are merely crushed and part of the ground now. What we are walking on is what is left of about eight thousand bodies' worth of bones, as a result of that war."

Gathus frowned. "Who were the victors?"

"Surprisingly, the trows," Haz Rhon recalled. "They won that battle, but they were the first race eliminated from the war. The humans entered the battle underestimating the trows."

Gathis sighed, imagining thousands of his own kind dying in battle. The trows were a peaceful race.

He couldn't even imagine his own race having any participation in the war at all.

The trow mumbled thoughtfully, "What makes Mystasia today rested on thousands of deaths?"

"Ten of thousands of deaths," Haz Rhon corrected the small being. "And..." Haz Rhon stopped his speech, and the muscles in his face began to twitch. Seconds later, he began to twitch everywhere, and his physical form began to change. He started to become hairier, and the structure of his face began to change as well.

Dradia pushed Gathus back and armed herself with her staff. Still armed with his war axe, the transformation was complete. Haz Rhon was no longer a Cyclops. Now he was a werewolf. The savage bites were more severe than the druid had thought. The transformation came more quickly than she had anticipated.

"Haz Rhon, remember that it is me, Dradia," she said, trying to reason with him.

Haz Rhon was now the tallest werewolf she had ever seen, and the only one she had ever seen with a single eye.

"You promised me a cure!" Haz Rhon roared.

"There is no cure," Dradia retorted, nearly sobbing. "There is a rumor of a recipe that might cure lycanthropy, but it has never been tested or proven. That is what I was trying to do for you!"

Haz Rhon took two steps toward the druid.

"Do not attack me, Haz Rhon! I will fight you and use whatever druidic magic I choose against you."

"You're weak, remember?" Haz Rhon took another step toward her. "You said that you need some rest before you dare use any more magic, and my combat skills are far superior to yours."

"I still have enough energy in me to doom you, Haz Rhon! Do not attack me, or you will die."

"I am not me anymore," Haz Rhon growled. "I am a werewolf now! What makes you think I don't want death?"

"Please don't," Dradia pleaded. "If you fight me, it won't just be you against me. It'll be you against nature. I can call upon any animals and beasts I wish to defend me. You are not a match against that."

Haz Rhon took another step, and then stopped. He turned to Gathus and then back to Dradia. He fought against the new rage he felt rushing through his bloodstream. A moment later, he cautioned Dradia. "Don't cross paths with me ever again!"

Suddenly, Haz Rhon fled to the forest to the west, barely within eyesight. Dradia sighed in relief and lowered her staff. "Come, Gathus. Let's continue on to Udarshen."

Two hours of additional travel brought them to the trow town of Udarshen. As with any other trow town she had seen, Udarshen was composed of plenty of shops and houses. Many of the houses were built into hills. Gathus seemed concerned with the behavior of the townsfolk, and Dradia noticed. "What is wrong?"

"The pipes they are playing are not a good sign," Gathus mumbled.

"Trows are infamous musicians. Music has an important role in trow culture. What is wrong with the pipes?"

"Everyone is playing funeral pipes," Gathus said, pointing to one group performing outside of a tavern. "The only time the entire town does this is when someone of high importance has died."

Dradia's face saddened. "Then we are too late. It seems likely that Pyhon-Ash-Pree has been assassinated."

One of the townsfolk recognized Gathus and greeted him with the dire news.

"Gathus'Kur'Zaimgy," the trow spoke hysterically. "Where is your pipe?"

"I have just returned home, Nysab," Gathus replied. "What has happened?"

Nysab pulled Gathus away from Dradia. "What I am about to tell you must stay between us. Promise me! Do not even tell your human friend. We do not know who to trust."

"I promise," Gathus said, nodding. "Now, what happened?"

"Someone poisoned the twin sister of Baroness Pyhon'Ash'Pree," Nysab reported.

"Phyon-Ash-Pree is now in secret location that I do not know of, but we are pretending that the assassination was successful. Whoever it was that tried to poison her thought that her identical sister was Pyhon'Ash'Pree herself."

Gathus smiled at the good news that Pyhon'Ash'Pree was safe, but then his smile disappeared, remembering quickly that her sister still met fate.

"I promise to tell no one," Gathus assured Nysab. He returned to Dradia and nodded sadly.

"You are right, Dradia. Pyhon'Ash'Pree is dead. She was poisoned."

"But there has been no actual attack on the trow army, or the territory itself?"

"Not that I have heard," Gathus said, shrugging. "As far as I know, our army is still intact. But it is a small army."

"Of course," Dradia said. "Trows are a peaceful race. It is not expected of your kind to raise a strong army. It appears that the enemy may not consider trows a threat to their plans at all."

Dradia watched some of the townsfolk play their pipes. The music was both gloomy and soothing all at once. "When did the baroness die?"

Nysab overheard the conversation and quickly answered her question. "Three nights ago. She was poisoned, but no one knows by who or why."

Dradia produced a thin, weak smile. "Perhaps the enemy's lack of interest in your kind can be used to our advantage."

"What do you mean?" Gathus asked.

"I am a druid, not a warlord," Dradia said, patting the trow on his left shoulder. "I know nearly nothing of war or tactics. But I am sure we can use their lack of interest against them somehow. Haz Rhon did say that the humans lost their battle against the trows during the War of the Races because they underestimated them. Maybe the enemy will make the same mistake."

CHAPTER XXVI

Clash of the Assassins

THE COLD SPREAD THROUGH the air like eccentric electricity. Gwan returned with his arms full of dead wood and dropped it in front of Epona. Epona began to speak words foreign to Abadon's ears. She waved her hands two feet above the wood, and a fire sparked to life.

"I know you are proud of your witchcraft, Epona," Abadon spoke softly. "But should you waste energy on something as simple as making fire?"

"You think witchcraft is simple?" Epona scorned Abadon, taking great offense to his choice of words.

"I didn't mean to say witchcraft was simple," Abadon explained.

Abadon took note of his surroundings. Skyline was just outside the border of light and shadow, and Gwan was standing behind him and to his right. The clearing they selected to camp in was only forty feet in diameter. "I don't like this clearing," he declared. "The forest is too close."

Skyline hissed, baring his fangs, "It is the only clearing I could find within three miles, my dear prince."

Abadon turned to Epona, choosing to leave the vampire alone. "Do you have a spell that might keep the snow at bay, Epona?"

"It might be a waste of witchcraft," Epona said bitterly. Her gaze had almost as much fire as the fire that burned before them. Abadon sighed, realizing that Epona was still angry with him.

"Witches," Gwan said. "They are always proud of their witchcraft, and will take every chance they get to show off their talents."

Epona pressed her lips together hard, deciding to ignore the ninja, but Skyline seized that opportunity to mock him.

"As do ninjas," Skyline demurred, smiling. His fangs poked down from behind his upper lip. "They too believe heavily in their talents, and believe that they are the greatest assassins in the world. They are unquestionably no match when compared to a true assassin like myself."

Gwan produced a sai from his sash and pulled it out with such great speed that Abadon and Epona only saw a flash of action, but the vampire was even quicker. He blocked the sai with his dagger.

"You just proved my point, ninja," Skyline said coldly. His arrogant smile disappeared and was replaced with a grave face that promised death.

"You would have killed me by now if you could, Eastfire," Skyline continued to speak. "You will find that your skills will not be needed, as long as I am here to protect the three of you."

Gwan returned the sai to his sash, and everyone kept quiet and chose to ignore the vampire's threats. He had yet to prove that he was as skillful as he bragged, or as dangerous as Lure praised, but they did not doubt what they were told.

"Gafnan should have been back by now," Abadon said after a long moment of silence. No one said anything. There was no conversation that could take place between the four of them. The cold became increasingly cruel, and before long, the three humans could feel their fingers and toes become numb. Over time, Abadon realized that Gwan had disappeared. A moment later, Skyline disappeared as well.

Skyline began walking east, stepping over the tracks he had already made earlier. They were nearly erased by the falling snow. He took two more steps, and then stopped. There was a fresh set of tracks over his own. Someone had attempted to fool him, hoping that he would not notice. He looked around, but where the second set of tracks came from could not be detected. The tracks that overlapped his were not made by boots, but by actual footprints that resembled wolf tracks.

"Werewolves," Skyline said to himself. He continued to walk over his tracks until he found where the second set joined with his. They came from the woods to the south. Even though the clearing was small, the winter gloom hid anything farther away than eight feet. He looked into the forest. Nothing moved except for the falling snow. His night vision and keen hearing scored him no additional clues.

Then, Skyline noticed something. A small section of bark on an oak tree at the edge of the forest had been scraped off, as if something may have climbed up the tree. He looked up and saw yellow eyes glaring at him. The intruder leaped on top ofhim, but he rolled on his back and used his legs to kick the intruder off, and several feet away.

Both Skyline and the intruder were quickly on their feet.

"Who are you?" Skyline demanded. "You are the assassin I've been looking for, aren't you?"

The werewolf said nothing. He was armed with a broadsword, and circled around Skyline for a moment, and then stopped.

"You're a vampire," the werewolf finally noticed.

"I am death," Skyline replied.

"I don't understand," the werewolf said. "You are traveling with three humans."

"I don't understand it myself, yet," Skyline retorted sourly, but never let his guard down.

The werewolf lowered his sword. He looked into the clearing, and then back at Skyline.

"If you wish to feed upon them, I will not stop you," the werewolf said.

"Why are you here?" Skyline demanded.

"Business that does not concern you," the werewolf replied.

In a flash, Skyline was on top of the werewolf, and held his sword at the beast's throat.

"Your business is now my business," Skyline whispered into his ear.

"My name is Bhyrhon," the werewolf howled, terrified. "I was sent here by Kalim Evernight."

"To do what?" Skyline asked.

"To frighten the prince out of the forest, and away from our encampments," Bhyrhon said. "I am not here to kill him, I assure you."

"Then you have nothing to do with the assassination attempts on him?"

"No, not at all," Bhyrhon choked as Skyline held his unarmed hand tightly at Bhyrhon's throat.

Skyline released his hand, but kept his sword at his throat. "Return to Kalim and tell him that I will lead the humans out of the forest. He does not need to concern himself with these human beings."

Skyline straightened himself out, and the werewolf was back on his feet as well.

"Who are you?" the werewolf asked.

"Skyline Shadowfrost."

"Shadowfrost," Bhyrhon repeated. "I have heard of you, but you are the least likely vampire I thought I would find traveling with humans. You and your assassins are responsible for the death of hundreds of vampire slayers. One hundred and twelve are credited to your name alone."

"That is business that does not concern you," Skyline said sternly.

"One of our own approached us for an alliance on their behalf," Bhyrhon informed the vampire. "Have they done the same with you?"

"As I said, it is no business of yours," Skyline said once again, but his voice was much colder this time.

Two screams echoed into the night, and both Skyline and Bhyrhon jerked their heads in the same direction as the camp. They both raced to the camp, but Bhyrhon's agility enabled him to reach Abadon and Epona first. Skyline was seconds behind him.

Meta had returned, but the charm spell had finally expired. The metaughla was on top of the prince. "The ring! I lost my ring!"

Skyline and Bhyrhon acted fast. They attacked the metaughla, which crawled off from the prince. Epona rushed to Abadon's side. "Are you hurt?"

"No," Abadon replied. "But in the struggle, the ring slipped off my finger!"

Epona prepared a spell, but when she turned around, the metaughla retreated back into the forest, suffering from several light wounds.

"Do not pursue," Skyline ordered Bhyrhon. He turned to the two humans. "Where is Gwan? He should have been here to protect you while I was patrolling the clearing."

"He never returned," Epona told the vampire. She examined Abadon and nodded. "Abadon is fine. Just several cuts, and some nasty bruises are already forming."

Skyline barely heard her. He was looking into the clearing.

"My ring," Abadon cried out suddenly. The Obsidian Omen was a few feet away, and he snatched the ring and put it on his finger quickly. His position shifted. Abadon now appeared to be three feet away from Epona to her left.

"Gwan," Skyline murmured.

"What about him?" Epona asked.

"The assassin is Gwan," Skyline spoke louder.

Epona wasn't convinced. "If it is Gwan, why didn't he attack us earlier? He's been traveling with us for over a week."

"Because Abadon just lost his ring, and Gwan knows that," Skyline argued.

He turned to Bhyrhon, pointing his sword at him. "Stay with them and keep them safe!"

The werewolf nodded, deciding not to anger the vampire, and then turned to the others. "What is going on here?"

"The assassin is invisible," Epona warned the werewolf. "Be cautious and listen."

"Skyline," Abadon called out to the vampire. Skyline stopped and turned around.

"Gwan was a member of the Flaming Fist Clan," he cautioned. "That means he has knowledge of both martial arts and a few mage spells. He is a ninja magi."

"How do you know this?" Skyline asked, as if doubting Abadon's knowledge.

"I know because my uncle, Adison Krendale, was the master of the Flaming Fist Clan. The clan disappeared a few months ago. They entered The Underworld and never returned. In fact, Gwan is the first member of the clan I have seen since then."

Skyline still had doubts. "If he serves your uncle, why is he here to destroy you?"

"I don't know," was all Abadon could say. The young prince had no idea why any of the ninjas from his uncle's clan would want him dead. Skyline said nothing and disappeared into the gloom.

Epona got to her feet and closed her eyes. She began to focus, and a dove of fire appeared in each of her open hands. The doves of fire circled the area, but they made no attack.

"What's wrong, Epona?" Abadon asked. "Why isn't your spell working?"

"They can't find him, Abadon," Epona declared desperately. "I have been using too much energy lately. I can't focus enough for the doves to find him!"

Epona decided not to dispel the doves, and to allow them to continue to fly.

Skyline stood perfectly still, looking in all directions and waiting for the invisible assassin to make an attack.

"You are an invisible coward, Gwan!" Skyline screamed, trying to taunt the ninja.

"You are invisible, and yet you are still frightened of me."

A ball of fire appeared from nowhere and struck Skyline. As the flame hit him, it vanished in smoke. Several large burn holes ruined Skyline's black cloak, and much of his flesh sustained second degree burns, which were already healing.

"Is that all you have, ninja?" Skyline taunted.

Another ball of fire hit him, this time from his left. The impact sent him several feet back, and knocked him onto his back. The pale flesh of Skyline's upper body was exposed now. His black cloak was almost entirely burned from him. His undead flesh was scorched even more, but the rapid healing was already making great progress.

Skyline felt a blow at his right side. The blow would have been accurate to rupture his liver, if it had been living tissue. Another blow to his chest nearly knocked him off his feet. The blow would have stopped his heart, unquestionably. Skyline focused, and listened carefully. From behind, he heard Gwan's movement. This time, he blocked the assault.

"This is insane," Abadon gasped. "Even Skyline won't be able to defeat this invisible menace!"

"Save your strength," Epona told Abadon, sensing that he was about to cast a spell of his own.

The three watched helplessly as Gwan continued to attack, but Skyline's defense seemed to be improving. Gwan was landing fewer attacks.

Bhyrhon took two steps away from Abadon.

"No," Skyline cried out. "Stay with the prince. He is the one the assassin wants."

"I am after all of you, you fool!" Gwan spoke out loud.

His voice came from behind Bhyrhon, who was farthest away from Skyline. Skyline raced to the three and waited for the ninja to make another foolish mistake.

"Your deaths are a great enough reward for me," Gwan spoke again. This time his voice came from the edge of the forest.

Skyline whispered, "He is trying to draw me away from you guys."

"I have him," Epona whispered out loud excitedly.

The four turned their attention to the doves of fire. One of them soared down and crashed into Gwan. The ninja screamed at the impact of the spell. The second dove followed, causing Gwan to scream again, and his body glowed with fire for two short seconds. Those short seconds were enough. Skyline was on top of Gwan, and thrust his sword into his belly—but Gwan applied a strange leg lock around the vampire's neck and flung him ten feet away.

Skyline was quick to get back to his feet. "You can't last much longer, Gwan!"

A moment of silence passed, and then Gwan made his next attack. Skyline detected his movements, but not quite quickly enough. Gwan's nunchuku struck Skyline across the face, but the blow wasn't direct. The nunchuku barely made contact. Skyline began to watch the snow for Gwan's footprints, but then he noticed something even better. There was blood dripping from Gwan's wound. The size of the droplets of blood dictated not only where Gwan was, but also indicated where exactly to strike.

Skyline paid close attention to the footprints Gwan formed in the snow, and even more attention to the size of the droplets. He spiraled around and jabbed his blade into Gwan. He could feel his sword sink into the flesh of the ninja, and Gwan cried out, agonized by the bite of the sword. Skyline twisted the blade to the right and left, and then pulled it out.

The others rushed to Skyline's side. Gwan was still invisible.

"Search him for a ring," Epona suggested.

"Be careful," Bhyrhon warned them. "He might not be dead."

Skyline frisked Gwan's body. He felt no ring on the first hand he discovered, and searched for the other. A short moment later, Skyline felt a ring on the other hand and slipped it off his finger. The body of the ninja became visible. He had suffered two very large third-degree burns, due to the damage done by the fire doves.

Skyline placed the ring on his own finger, and vanished.

"Can you see me?" he asked.

"No," Epona replied. "That is the ring that caused his invisibility."

Skyline removed the ring and grinned.

Bhyrhon looked down at the body of the ninja. "How did you know where to strike at him?"

The grin doubled in size. "It's a trade secret, my friend, and one only a great assassin knows."

"You are great!" Abadon confessed with a broad smile. "Please, tell us how you defeated him. Gwan was supposed to be the best when it comes to pinpointing vital organs. He has killed many with a single punch, because he knows where to strike. How did you beat him?"

"His strikes were indeed very accurate," Skyline admitted. "Had I been human, he would have killed me twice. He struck me in the liver, and again in the heart. His hard impact would have stopped my heart, had I been a being of regular flesh, and not a undead being. I watched his footsteps in the snow, and the droplets of blood from a previous wound I gave him allowed me to know exactly where he was, and where exactly to strike him down. The droplets gave me clues as to what position he was in, whether he was standing or crouching."

"Very clever," Epona exclaimed.

"There is still another assassin out there," Skyline reported.

"How do you know?" Abadon asked.

"When I wore the ring, I could detect someone else about fifteen miles from here. That someone has a ring linked to the one Gwan was wearing."

Epona turned to Abadon. "Those two rings were linked to the one you threw away back at Nordach. That is how they knew where to find you at all times. You're only alive because of the displacement ring Jherlom gave you."

Fear overwhelmed Abadon, and he turned away from the others. His open hand became a fist, and he looked down at the obsidian ring. He had escaped many odds and should have been killed days ago.

"There is still one invisible assassin out there," Skyline reminded them again. "I will track the assassin down and destroy him as well."

Abadon turned to the north. "Do you think the other knows that you killed Gwan?"

Skyline shrugged. "I am not sure, but he would not have been able to detect Gwan's position for those seconds I took to remove the ring and place it on my own finger. As I hold this ring now, the second assassin knows that Gwan is not wearing it. Your guess is as good as mine as to what he suspects."

Epona turned to Abadon. "You said your uncle was the master of the ninja clan."

"Yes," Abadon nodded.

"The second assassin is likely from that guild as well," Epona pointed out. "Can you make a good guess as to who it is?"

Abadon shook his head. "No, I can't. None of them returned from The Underworld. They were due two or three weeks after they entered. Gwan is the first and only one I have seen since then."

Skyline's face became grave. "You best hope that the entire clan has not turned against you, and that there are no more rings like this one."

"I don't think so," Abadon said confidently. "You said yourself you can only detect one ring. I think there is only one more assassin out there with the intent to kill me. But I strongly believe that something terrible happened down there to the Flaming Fist Clan in The Underworld. Something had to have happened. These ninjas are very skilled, and yet none returned. Some of them may even be corrupted somehow, like Gwan."

Skyline nodded. "I will admit that he was very skilled, but still no match for me."

Epona frowned as she reflected back on the night she met Gwan.

"Gwan was at my cottage the night before you and Gafnan arrived. I had helped him fight off a couple of metaughlas. He mentioned a woman, but I cannot remember her name. He told me that there was nothing he wouldn't do for her."

Abadon thought hard for a moment, and recalled the names of women he knew were in the ninja clan. "Was it Starsha, Lorech or Loressa?"

"No, no," Epona said, shaking her head. "It wasn't any of those names, but it was someone who had great power over him."

Abadon brushed the matter aside and looked at the werewolf. "Where is Gafnan?"

"Back at Owl's Hoot, a werebeast encampment," Bhyrhon replied.

"Why are you here?"

"I was sent by Kalim Evernight, the were-bear who is chieftain of all the werebeasts. He sent me here to make sure you leave the woods."

Before Abadon could question the werewolf any more, Bhyrhon spoke again. "The werebeasts are considering the alliance proposal, but many of us do not trust Gafnan for many reasons. The reason your proposal is being considered is because a respectable percentage of the werebeast population were not werebeasts when they were born."

"I am not sure I understand," Abadon said, seeking a better explanation. "What you're telling me is that many werebeasts were once human, or elves, or some other race?"

"Exactly," Bhyrhon said, nodding. "I have always been a werewolf. My parents are werewolves, and so I was born a werewolf. A disease with no cure called lycanthropy is what created werebeasts. So in a sense, I guess you can say that all of us are descendants of a human. It was a human that contracted the disease, some time prior to 3200 BG. The disease spreads through bites or reasonable scratches done by a werebeast to someone who is not affected. Many of our kind remember a little of their former lives and what it was like to be human, or an elf or dwarf. They are the ones considering the alliance. Those of us who possess no knowledge of experience of being anything other than werebeasts reject the alliance."

Abadon sighed. "Where do you stand with the alliance proposal?"

Bhyrhon shook his head. "I do not trust mankind, Abadon."

"But you share your society with man," Abadon said hastily. "You said it yourself. Many of the werebeasts in your encampments were once man, or a race that associates with man."

Bhyrhon was speechless. The prince did make a point, but the werewolf formed an explanation. "Those who become werebeasts almost never approve at first. But everyone in Mystasia knows that werebeasts reside in The Haunted Forest. Most of those who become werebeasts come to the forest knowing that it is their new home. They know that the Mystasian society will reject them if they return. They become one of us, because we are the only ones who will accept them."

Abadon nodded. "There is a strong chance, then?"

"There is a chance, but allow Kalim and the others some time to make that decision."

"The frozen fire won't wait," Epona interrupted. "Time is something none of us have."

"You'll have to," Bhyrhon stated. "Kalim won't make such a decision overnight. Allow us time to speak amongst ourselves."

Abadon extended his hand. "Thank you, Bhyrhon. Please see what you can do about the release of Gafnan."

"I will," Bhyrhon promised, accepting Abadon's hand. The werewolf promptly disappeared.

The death of the invisible assassin brought great comfort to Abadon, and sleep came easy and quickly. Soon, both Abadon and Epona were asleep. Skyline watched over them, licking his lips. 'I will obey Lure Vesper,' Skyline thought to himself. 'I will bring them to Castle Bloodstone.'

As Skyline watched them, savage hunger for blood plagued him from within. He hungered for their flesh. Thoughts of sinking his fangs into their soft flesh replayed within his mind. He reminded himself that he could not betray Lure Vesper. It was Lure who gave him the gift of immortally. The one who rid him of a mortal life would be the only one he would never betray. Lure gave him the greatest gift of all, and for that reason, Skyline would never betray him—but he would never look up to Lure as his master.

Skyline turned to the southeast. The snowfall slowed down to occasional flakes. The body of Gwan could still be seen. He trekked quickly to the body of the ninja, and feasted.

CHAPTER XXVII

Research at Agate Hedge Keep

THE GREY SKY MADE IT DIFFICULT to determine the exact time of day. Only one thing occupied Vadamar's mind. He desperately wanted to know the exact location of Wish Water Lake and the Forge of Soulfire. He had read about their locations many years ago, but had forgotten it. Jherlom followed behind the arch druid.

"Only the arch druid has the privilege of knowing the location of the Forge of Soulfire and Wish Water. One day, you will replace me as arch druid, and I have decided that it is time for you to learn of the location as well."

"The way to Wish Water can't be too difficult." Jherlom shrugged off the importance. "Druids never get lost in the wilderness."

"Except for the woods that surround Wish Water," Vadamar corrected the wood elf. "The forest shifts. The trees move, and it is a thick forest that is generally unexplored. It doesn't welcome visitors. I am the only one who has stood on the shores of the enchanted lost lake, but I have forgotten the way. Tonight, I will relearn how to reach the magical waters, and I will pass that information on to you."

Vadamar's words were always words of wisdom, right down to every last word spoken, and Jherlom listened closely. His own questions would be answered by Vadamar, resulting in a great gain of wisdom.

Vadamar continued to educate Jherlom on Wish Water. "The lake is invisible except for the nights blessed with a full blue moon. For reasons unknown to even me, the blue moonlight causes the water to become visible. Then and only then can we dip the rings into the water. We must first forge the rings at the Forge of Soulfire before dipping them in Wish Water. The quest at the Forge of Soulfire will not be easy. The cavern where the magical molten fire is located was also a lair for blood demons, when it was last visited some years before the War of the Gods. The blood demons may still be living there."

The two druids passed by an opening in the agate wall that closely resembled a hedge, which surrounded the druid keep. Vadamar tapped the end of his staff on a rock within a cluster of rocks, and the stone door of the keep opened. The keep itself didn't look like a keep at all, but a tall formation of rocks fused together. A passing explorer would never have suspected that the joining jagged rocks were actually the Agate Hedge Keep. Only the agate wall that surrounded the keep suggested that there was some importance to the rocks within its structure.

Both druids entered the keep side by side, passing through a great hall. The pillars of the hall were carved into infamous druids of the past, with the exception of Vadamar and Jherlom, who had both earned enough fame to have their faces and figures etched into stone. Eventually, they came to a stairwell to the right and left. They climbed up the right stairwell to the highest floor of the keep. Vadamar unlocked the door to the druid archives. There were many shelves of stone inside, and all of them were filed with books that had collected a thin layer of dust over the years. Within the pages of the books were historical writings and valuable information that was rarely sought out.

Vadamar selected a red book with gold trimming. The font was that of an old language forgotten by many, except for many of the druids of the keep. It was a language once used by sprites and fairies. Somewhere within the eighty-two pages of writing was the exact location of the Forge of Soulfire.

"Myth and legend says that the molten fire within the Forge of Soulfire is mixed with the blood of an angry warlord god, the dwarf war god of Ardrend. This has caused anything forged there to have magical properties. These properties would be twice as powerful if cooled in Wish Water."

Vadamar found the page that related important information about the Forge of Soulfire. "The Forge of Soulfire is located one thousand, three hundred sixty feet down into the Red Oubliette, which happens to be just over the border into Avenhauk. The Red Oubliette is said to be connected to both The Underworld and hell."

Jherlom examined several books, but none of them were the books that they were looking for. One book caught Vadamar's attention. Behind a fine fabric of dust, Vadamar could see blue coloring with smudges of white. He removed the book from the shelf and wiped away the dust using the sleeve of his cloak. He had found his old dairy, which he stored in the druid archives once the pages had been filled.

He brought the book to the table. His memory suggested to him that he would find the information he required about forty-six pages in. Vadamar quickly found the page he had written about the lost enchanted lake, when he was there forty-seven years ago.

"I found it," Vadamar exclaimed. Jherlom rushed to the arch druid's side. Vadamar turned to Jherlom in a very grave manner. "Only the arch druid of the keep is allowed to know the secret of the woods that surround the lake. I cannot tell you why at this time. I am sharing a few things with you now, because one day when I am gone, you will need to know them, and I will not be here to tell you of them. Remember where this belongs, and read it after you replace me as arch druid of the keep."

Jherlom nodded. "I will, master."

Vadamar replaced the book back on the shelf, and Jherlom was sure to pay close attention to where he had placed the book. Jherlom moved away from Vadamar and began to look over other books within the druid archives.

A noise from down the hall captured Vadamar's attention. He chose to investigate the noise, and strayed from the archives. Valuable secrets were kept in the archives. Only Vadamar and authorized druids were allowed on the top floor of the druid keep. He walked slowly and cautiously down the hall. Only druids knew how to enter the keep, but his senses told him that there was a chance that something else had gotten in somehow.

Where the corridor joined with three others, Vadamar was attacked from the left corridor by two erinyes. The female furies clawed at the flesh of his forearm, but the arch druid reacted quickly. A mass of vines from the roof entangled the erinyes. The furies screamed, frustrated with imprisonment. Their claws began to cut through the vines. From behind him, two ettin approached, carrying large war hammers. The giant humanoids were so large that their bulky bodies completely occupied the corridor. Vadamar made a couple of gestures with his hands, and a large wall of thorns was erected, blocking their path. They began to hammer away at the wall. Vadamar spurted forth blue fire from his fingers. The fairy fire burned the erinyes into ashes.

Vadamar turned to the only other corridor that offered escape. A single woman dressed in a cloak approached him. She lifted the cowl from her head to allow the arch druid to identify her.

Vadamar's jaw dropped. For a moment, he was speechless. "I know your face," he finally said, gasping in surprise. "It is a face that I once knew so well, Harmonia."

"Not anymore, my former master." Taskica sneered.

"It is you who is behind the frozen fire!"

"I can only take half the credit," Taskica said, smiling. From behind Vadamar, the ettins had broken through the wall of thorns. Once again, fairy fire erupted from the fingers of both Vadamar's hands. One hand was directed at the ettins, while the other was aimed at Taskica. The fairy fire turned the ettins into a mound of ash.

Taskica erected a wall of stone between herself and Vadamar to avoid the fairy fire. Then she made a pushing motion toward the wall, causing it to fall down toward the arch druid. Vadamar did not react in time to completely avoid the wall. The stone wall fell on his legs crushing them. The arch druid screamed at the crushing pain. He struggled to crawl free, but the weight of the wall was too great.

"The great arch druid, Vadamar," Taskica said slowly. "To think that I was your apprentice is amusing."

"Why are you dong this, Harmonia?" Vadamar said, nearly completely out of breath.

"My name is Taskica Shadowdawn, and I think you know why," she replied.

"Your fellow druids have done nothing to you!"

"You didn't save me from the doom that was given to me either, Vadamar."

Taskica gestured one of her hands, and the stone wall crumbled into chunks of stone, surrounding Vadamar's broken body. The dark druid then raised her hands. Black fire roared from her hands, engulfing the arch druid and turning him into ash immediately. The black fire Taskica used was similar to fairy fire, but it was a strange new twisted version that Taskica had realized on her own. It was even hotter than fairy fire.

Taskica turned around to find the green hag, Vygouli the Damned, walking casually down the corridor with two more erinyes behind her.

"Vadamar has a diary in here, somewhere in the druid archives, with important information in it. It is information I want to keep away from the druids. We need to find it."

"We can take all the books back to Shade Deep," Vygoulia suggested.

"No," Taskica said abruptly and sharply. "I will have you and other dark druids stay here for a few days to read through all the books. If you find one of very high importance, bring it back to me."

Hearing Vadamar's screams, Jherlom grabbed the diary from the bookshelf. An ettin blocked his escape from the druid archives. Jherlom backed away from the ettin, which grinned at him. There were no windows in the archives. Jherlom was trapped. Behind the ettin were three blade scale nagas. Their black, serpentine forms slithered into the archives behind the ettin. Using fairy fire would destroy all the books in the keep, but Jherlom realized that the druid keep had somehow been breached, and vital information would fall into the hands of the enemy.

The decision was difficult, but Jherlom decided quickly. Fairy fire burned from the druid's hands, turning the four enemies into ash. He then proceeded to burn all the books in the druid archives, save for Vadamar's diary, which was safe in the pocket of his cloak. Black ash was everywhere. Everything within the druid archives that wasn't stone was completely destroyed, forever.

Jherlom could hear voices approaching the archives. Thinking quickly, he dove into a large pile of ash, hiding himself from the nearby enemies. There was more than enough ash to hide him.

Vygoulia slowly entered the archives with the two erinyes. She studied the room for a moment, and then sighed. A moment later, Taskica entered the room. Her cowl was placed back over her head, and her back was turned to Jherlom. He could not identify her.

"Blast Vadamar," Taskica cursed. "He must have scorched the place when he heard us enter the keep. He must have decided that if the valuable information in here couldn't be kept secret to the druids alone, then no one would have access."

"At least you still got what you wanted, master," the green hag pointed out. "The druids no longer have the information you wanted to keep from them, unless others know it."

"No," Taskica said, smiling. "Only the arch druid is allowed to know such things, and I just destroyed him before he had a chance to pass any vital information on to anyone else."

Jherlom recognized the voice of the cloaked woman. He could not figure out who spoke, but it was a voice from the past. He listened intently, but the cloaked woman offered no further clues to her identify.

"A portal is waiting down the hall," Taskica said to her pupil. "Let's get out of here. I have done what I have come to do."

Taskica and Vygoulia left the archives. What the druid believed was very important was gone, and the arch druid was gone as well. Jherlom lowered his head. Once again, he had failed to save someone of great importance. He would now replace Vadamar as the arch druid of Agate Hedge Keep. He placed his hand in the pocket of his cloak, as if to be sure he did place Vadamar's diary there. At least the most vital information of all was still safe. He waited silently for over an hour, until he was sure that the enemy had left the keep.

CHAPTER XXVIII

Caverns of Fear

THE SUN AND ITS GLOWING SHINE was barely prying over the Ice Crown Mountains of the Northguard Dutchy when Riannon and Apponus reached the Pegasi Stables. The two passed over the Ice Paradise River, through the Earth Moor Garden, and into the Herb Tooth Mountains to reach the Pegasi Stables.

Apponus smiled as he finally got a glimpse of the stables and the slender dame who owned them. Tacet Riskskin was a fellow elite knight, the sixth knight of the Hall of the Silver Shield. The stables were home to a dozen pegasi.

"Good morning," Apponus said, smiling.

"Good morning," Tacet responded. Her fine, night-black hair was relatively short, but hung down covering her brows, stopping right above her bright cyan eyes. She was mounted on a pegasi of her own.

"How is Lacewing?" Apponus asked.

"She is doing well," Tacet said as she patted the pegasus on the side of her neck. "What can I do for you?"

"We need a Pegasus," Riannon stated. "I have Angelwing, but Apponus needed a mount that can fly."

"Well, you have eleven to choose from," Tacet said, gesturing to the stables.

"Thunderhoof, Willowmane and Starshine are the best choices. They are the most tame."

Apponus looked over the pegasi for a moment before making his choice.

"I'll take Willowmane," he said.

"I'll get her ready for you," Tacet said, dismounting from Lacewing.

Apponus turned to Riannon, who was still mounted on Angelwing. "Where are Angelwing's parents?"

Riannon pointed to one of the pegasi in the stables. "Starshine is her mother, and the father is a unicorn in the country of Alyshia."

Tacet returned with Willowmane. "How did you come to get her?"

"She is a gift from an angel of Alyshia," Riannon told them while stroking her mane. "I am a paladin lord, and so they sometimes drop by with a gift, even though they are from a different country."

Tacet handed the reins of Willowmane to Apponus, who took them, and then mounted the pegasi.

"Where are you off to?" Tacet asked.

"You'll think we're crazy," Riannon said, reluctant to tell the dame. "We're going to the Caverns of Fear to seek an alliance with the gargoyles. None of us will last long without additional help, Tacet."

Tacet sighed, knowing that the paladin lord was right. "Is there no way I can talk you out of this?"

"I wouldn't be a paladin lord or a noble lord of Mystasia if anyone could talk me out of anything," Riannon replied, raising her eyebrows.

Tacet nodded. "Be careful then, and good luck."

"We will need it," Riannon retorted. At Riannon's command, both mounts leaped into the air and began to fly southeast. Tacet waved at them, and watched them until the glow of the rising sun devoured them.

Eventually, the two flew over the Black Mountains of Kurakas, over Black Beach River, and into the Obsidian Peaks, where they knew the Caverns of Fear existed. Nearly two hours later, they located the Caverns of Fear, and both mounts landed on the summit of the mountain that supported the caverns no one had dared to visit before. The Obsidian Peaks were glossy, and their shine reflecting the sun nearly blinded them at times. During the night, the mountains were often impossible to see.

"There are five types of gargoyles," Riannon educated Apponus. "There are ruby, lapis, obsidian, quartz, and emerald gargoyles."

"How did they come to exist?" Apponus asked, looking up at the cliff that contained the three caverns that led inside the mountain.

"An animist brought them to life about three thousand years ago," Riannon replied, looking down at the fabric of clouds that kept the land far below hidden from her gaze. "They were sculptured out of different types of gem stone, and brought to life to service the animists, but their creation got out of hand and they lost control of the gargoyles. Centuries later, the gargoyles began to mutiny and think for themselves, and abandoned the animists that created them."

Apponus was puzzled at the origin of the gargoyles. "How do they breed, if they are not actually alive?"

"They are alive, and they do breed," Riannon told the elite knight. "I am not entirely sure how, but over the passing of years, they seem to have become more like us. They actually breathe and lay eggs."

"It seems strange," Apponus commented. "How do you know what you know, if you have never actually seen a gargoyle?"

"I know what I know from books written by those who have met with gargoyles, prior to the War of the Gods."

"There are no guards here on the summit," Apponus noted. "Surely they know we are here."

"We know everything that happens on the summit," a low, growling voice said.

Riannon and Apponus looked up at the cliff. An obsidian gargoyle stood on a protrusion several feet above the Caverns of Fear. His bulky, glossy obsidian form shone in the sunlight. He had two horns that curved and spiraled, almost like a mountain goat. His eyes and teeth were made out of ruby gemstone, but his eyes glowed. His teeth were jagged and looked much like broken shards of glass.

"My name is Servion Dabendar. I am a barbarian, a beast hunter to be exact. What are you doing on our mountain?"

"Fascinating," Riannon whispered out loud. She forced her excitement aside and answered the gargoyle's question. "My name is Riannon Pureheart. I am a paladin lord and a Mystasian noble lord. I have come to speak with your leader and discuss a grave matter concerning a frozen fire. It is a threat that threatens the existence of gargoyles as well as mankind."

"Our leader is Kharious Bloodwing, and he is here, but you are wasting your time," Servion spoke austerely. "Leave this mountain immediately!"

"I won't leave without speaking with Kharious," Riannon insisted stubbornly.

Another gargoyle appeared at the mouth of the center cavern. He was an obsidian gargoyle as well, but he was larger than Servion.

"I am Kharious Bloodwing, and I will warn you no more. Leave my mountain now!"

Riannon attempted to plead. "But the frozen fire…"

"I know about the frozen fire," Kharious bellowed. "Our kind watches over your kind much more than you know. We know almost everything!"

The gargoyle's voice was low, rough and full of bitterness. "This apocalyptic spell does not concern us. Those who use it cannot reach us here on the summit."

Riannon argued, "But what about the five cities you have built here in the Obsidian Peaks? They will not be safe forever."

"All out cities are high up in the Obsidian Peaks as well. Your enemy has likely come to wipe out mankind and the other races in the alliance you have formed. You have wronged us during the War of the Gods, just as you have wronged the vampires and the werebeasts. You have enemies everywhere now, and you will find no friends here!"

Riannon and Apponus lowered their heads in shame. Their attempt to make an alliance had failed.

Hundreds of bitter years between humanity and the dark races had conquered them to nonexistence. The frozen fire would soon engulf the territories and counties of Mystasia, until every last man, elf, dwarf, trow and fairy were dead.

Riannon and Apponus turned to their mounts, but five more gargoyles blocked them from reaching them.

Riannon turned around to face Kharious. "I thought we were free to go."

"Go where, human? Back to your lowlands? Only death awaits you down there."

Riannon and Apponus turned to the gargoyles that surrounded them. They were slowly taking steps toward them.

Kharious nodded, "Yes, I think your last days will be better spent up here in these dizzy heights, where winter is the only season."

The frightening faces of the gargoyles instilled heavy fear into their hearts. Horrific images of their future tortures replayed various scenarios in their minds. Riannon's holy and noble grandeur did not matter here. The gargoyles desperately wanted solitude from humanity. Their mountain homes were evidence of this.

"Enter the middle cavern," Kharious ordered. Riannon and Apponus exchanged glances, and they obeyed. They were not strong enough to battle seven gargoyles, and fighting them would make any future alliance impossible. They submitted themselves willingly, and entered the middle tunnel of the Caverns of Fear.

A steep stairwell led them straight to a natural cavern chamber, which branched into three natural corridors of stone.

"Left," Servion ordered the two humans.

Riannon led Apponus left, and a short distance brought them to a cavern used as a prison cell. They entered the large cell. Servion pushed on a loose stone, and a dozen iron bars dropped down from the ceiling of the cave to the rocky sandy floor. They were trapped.

Servion gazed at the two prisoners for a moment, and then turned his back to them and left the prison chamber.

"Now what do we do?" Apponus asked, throwing his hands up in the air and slapping them down at his sides.

They could hear the muffled voices of the gargoyles in a distant cavern, but nothing they said was clear.

"They are probably discussing what to do with us," Apponus moaned.

Riannon agreed. They were discussing whether or not to eat them, or deciding on what form of torture to use on them for purposes of entertainment. She shook her head in shame. She knew better than to judge them. Humanity had turned them into the monsters that they had become through ignorance and banishment. Man, elves, dwarves, trows, and perhaps even fairies all contributed to labeling vampires, werebeasts and gargoyles as the 'dark races'. Man was the dark race, Riannon thought to herself. Men were the real monsters, and they were guilty of one of the biggest sins of all, which was greed. The elves and fairies primarily lived in the forests. The dwarves found homes mostly in the mountains. The trows lived on the grassy plains, and most of them were farmers or musicians. Man was everywhere, and it was man who often took for granted the land they lived on. With the exception of demons, and perhaps the were-rats, man matched orcs and goblins as one of the most menacing races in all Kryensia.

It was almost solely the forest fairies and sprites that were responsible for the alliance that brought humans, elves, dwarves, trows and fairy kind together following the War of the Races. The conclusion of that war reduced war on the continent greatly. Man contributed little to the formation of the alliance, and was the primary reason that the alliance with the dark races was shattered in the waning years of the War of the Gods.

"How could it have come to this?" Riannon said, nearly sobbing as she reflected on the past. Her words were nearly whispers.

Apponus shrugged. "I don't know what to say about any of this."

A moment later, Apponus began to ponder the past. "Riannon, who originally created the alliance between the Mystasians and the dark races?

"The dwarves approached the gargoyles, and the elves approached the werebeasts. The vampires came forward to the trows and fairies. The trows and fairies are the only ones that vampires have never preyed upon."

"Why?" Apponus asked.

Riannon shrugged, "There are no trow vampire slayers, or fairies that partook in any vampire slaying. If you look back on history, the trows and fairies have always been peaceful. They are always there to help, but have never started any conflict, ever."

"No one trusts man, do they, Riannon?"

Riannon shook her head. "I am afraid our ancestors have created a rather grim future for us by living a complicated, violent past. Man didn't really make any effort to form friendships with any race, unless he benefited from them as well. Man had nothing to do with the alliance formed during the War of the Gods, but they shattered it years later."

Riannon turned to Apponus, who sat down next to her. The uneven stone ground was very uncomfortable. "It is up to man to correct the past, Apponus, or no one will ever trust us."

Her face tightened with regret, and Apponus recognized the poignant expression.

"Man has matured since those hundreds of years ago, Riannon."

"Man has rekindled their reputation, Apponus. We still have a long way to go."

"Our time will come, Riannon," Apponus pledged. "You will be one of the first of our kind to prove to the world how wonderful humans can really be."

Riannon studied their prison cell. Everything about it was related to stone or the earth itself.

"Apponus," Riannon said abruptly. "Weren't you an elementalist before you became an elite Mystasian knight?"

"Yes," Apponus conceded. "That was fifteen years ago. I abandoned that way of life."

"Everything around us is associated with the earth," Riannon uttered despondently. "Can't you manipulate the earth, or alter the prison bars?"

Apponus shook his head. "It doesn't' work that way, Riannon. I was an elementalist of earth, and fifteen years ago, I would have been able to do what you're asking. When I abandoned my faith in earth and the elemental studies of magic, I lost all my elemental powers. I prayed often to the earth god, Lykinod. When I stopped practicing and worshipping the element of earth, Lykinod lost all faith in me. He will grant me no powers now. I abandoned him."

Riannon lowered her head hopelessly. "We have no way of escaping then. I was hoping you could manipulate the gargoyles as well, considering that they are made out of the earth."

"Even if I was still an elementalist of earth, I am not sure I would have been able to do that," Apponus said.

Unexpectedly, a dozen gargoyles began to make their way out of the cavern they had gathered in, and walked past the prison cavern that jailed Riannon and Apponus.

Apponus pressed himself against the iron bars. "Listen to me!"

The gargoyles ignored him, and kept walking. The last gargoyle stopped. Torch light allowed them to see that he was a lapis gargoyle with ruby eyes.

"Silence, human, or I will feast on your tongue. There is no one here that will listen to your words."

Apponus raised his voice. "The frozen fire is a threat to you as well!"

"Fire and cold do not affect beings of stone," the same lapis gargoyle responded. "We are creatures of magic. We do not fear magic, and the users of the frozen fire have no reason to bring their troubles this high up from the lower lands."

Apponus cried out, desperate to get through to them. "This spell can eat through castle walls! Your cavern society will have no defense against it."

The gargoyles were gone, and the two humans were left almost totally in darkness. One dimly lit torch offered them a splash of light.

Apponus joined Riannon, who was resting against the stone wall of the cell.

Riannon muttered miserably, "The frozen fire won't stop down below, Apponus. It won't stop at the destruction of man, elf, dwarf, trows and fairies. It'll eventually destroy all the dark races as well."

CHAPTER XXIX

The Twin Guilds

THE STRIPPED FOREST was almost behind Abadon and the party now. The gloom of The Haunted Forest was thick enough to keep the sun from harming Skyline, but the open grasslands beyond would prove fatal to him.

Skyline stopped suddenly, and the others came to a halt as well, and turned around to inquire why the vampire had stopped.

"I am detecting the other ring bearer," Skyline announced.

"The other assassin?" Abadon asked.

"Yes, Abadon," Skyline replied coldly. "He is about twenty miles away from here, and is moving away from us."

Abadon became stern with the vampire and decided to exercise his nobility. "Abadon is no longer my name, Skyline. It is King Krendale, or your highness."

"Not to me," Skyline said with a smirk and an even colder voice, and lowered his head slightly. The assassin then turned his back on the others and sauntered toward the darkness to the north. Abadon turned away as well, to regroup with Epona and Sabre. When he turned around, Skyline was gone.

Shortly after Skyline left them without a word, the setting sun painted the sky pink and orange.

Epona gazed in the direction that Skyline had vanished. "Do you suppose he abandoned us?"

"I don't know," Abadon shrugged. "I am sure he is nearby, lurking in the shadows and watching us."

Epona reflected on what Abadon had said to Skyline. "I thought you didn't want to be king."

"I don't," Abadon admitted. "As far as I am concerned, it is not part of my destiny. But right now, I am king."

"It is something you cannot escape, Abadon."

"I can turn the crown over to Riannon Pureheart," Abadon persisted.

Epona changed the subject. The relentless stubbornness Abadon portrayed during his years as a child remained unchanged. "You still don't trust Skyline, do you?"

"I don't know who to trust, to be honest with you, Epona," Abadon snapped back.

"Shouldn't Gafnan be back by now?"

"Yes," Abadon muttered miserably. "His attempt to persuade the werebeasts to join our cause probably failed."

Epona shook her head. "You have always feared the negative in any situation. He is probably busy discussing everything with the werebeast chief, Kalim. Surely Kalim will realize that an alliance is necessary to defeat whoever is using the frozen fire."

"They don't trust us anymore, Epona," Abadon said faithlessly. "In their minds, we may be even more dangerous than those who are behind the spell. There is much trust to be gained on both sides."

The three moons were hidden behind a midnight shroud. The mix of moonlight behind the clouds caused them to appear almost green in color. Rhosa was nearly a half moon, making its red light the weakest of the three moons. The ring bearer that Skyline sought out was still within the range of detection, but he had moved north, away from him. He decided that the ring bearer either thought he was Gwan, or that Gwan had been killed and decided to keep a safe distance away from his killer.

The middle of the night settled in when Skyline reached a clearing. Two buildings were centered within the clearing. 'Guilds of some kind, possibly thief or assassin guilds,' Skyline thought to himself.

Judging by their height, he estimated that each of the buildings had at least five floors. The guilds were roughly triangular in shape, making each floor smaller as they rose. Like a shadow cutting swiftly through very dim moonlight, Skyline blended in once again with the night and moved toward the guild on the left. Once there, he studied the building for a moment. There were four windows, and one of the windows on what could be the third floor was open.

Skyline leaped up into the air thirty feet to clutch the window sill, and pulled himself inside. It appeared as though he was in someone's sleeping quarters. A single figure was sleeping in the only bed in the room. Skyline took two silent steps toward the bed and found that the person in it wasn't human, elf, dwarf or halfling, but an orc.

He smirked at his discovery. The two ninjas had secretly built twin assassin guilds and recruited orcs from The Underworld. The vampire decided that it was another part of the plot against Mystasia to eliminate threatening key figures of the country using these assassins, before the Underworld forces finished the task of wiping out all the Mystasian armies. With the humans almost entirely annihilated, the elves would be finished off, and the dwarves would likely be next.

He moved next to the bed, and with a quick flash snapped the sleeping orc's neck. Since the orc still appeared asleep, Skyline left his victim in the bed. He moved swiftly to the door of the quarters and listened carefully. He could hear no noise from beyond the room. He slowly opened the door, and found a corridor beyond the room. The corridor was empty, but three more doors taunted him to explore.

He rushed to the closest of the three doors and tugged softly at the doorknob, but it was locked. 'This is too easy, anyway,' he thought to himself. 'Murdering orcs in their sleep is far too dull a task for me to even employ.'

Skyline returned to the quarters of the orc he had murdered. He moved to the desk next to the bed and began to search through the drawers. The first thing he found were what appeared to be personnel files on all the members of both guilds. Realizing that the papers could prove to be interesting information, he grabbed them. Just as he placed the papers in his pocket so he could find anything of interest, he heard footsteps approaching from the corridor.

He leaped into the bed next to his victim and pulled the covers over himself. The footsteps stopped at the doorway, and Skyline recalled that he had left the door to the quarters open. Silence followed for a moment, and then the footsteps came closer toward the bed and seemed to stop at the desk. He threw the blanket from his body and thrusted, and his blade met with the throat of another orc.

Skyline watched the life of the orc slip away. He opened his mouth and caught the initial rush of blood that poured out of the orc's throat before the orc fell onto the bed soundlessly. He realized that this too was a little dull. He wanted a victim that knew he was coming. Slaying unsuspecting orcs did not fuel his hatred in any way at all.

He swallowed the mouthful of blood and allowed the rest of the blood in the orc to drain from the body onto the bed. He searched the desk once again and found a set of iron keys in the second drawer.

Skyline snatched the keys and returned to the locked door he had discovers only moments ago. He opened the door after one failed attempt with the wrong key, and closed the door behind him. He was in a storage room for traps. Snare traps, net traps and jaw traps were all collecting dust. The layer of dust was thin, and it seemed that they had been there for perhaps no more than three months. He collected an assortment of traps and returned to the quarters of his victims. He jumped out of the window and assembled jaws traps underneath every window he could find on the guild.

Next to the entrance of the guild, Skyline saw an even greater opportunity. Four barrels sat on either side, and it was the only entrance. He readjusted the barrels so that they blocked off the entrance. Even the might of several orcs would fail to push the door open. The barrels contained enough weight to equal more than four hundred pounds each. Skyline reached into his pocket and pulled out a flint. He sparked a flame and ignited the doors to the guild. The building, which was primarily constructed of wood, was in flames in seconds.

Screaming from behind the door, the assassins within the inferno pushed against it, but the barrels proved far too heavy for them to push their way to escape.

Skyline patrolled the parameter of the guild, waiting for assassins to make their escapes out of the windows. Only two made a daring escape, and they landed in the jaw traps, which nearly cut their legs off at the knee. Their screams for help ended quickly once Skyline brought his blade to their heads.

He began to walk toward the second guild. The assassins within would have wakened to the screams of the first guild's members by now.

Skyline pushed the entrance doors of the second guild open forcefully. He walked toward six assassins fast and fearlessly with his sword in his hand. His pale face was not visible to his prey, due to the shadow of the cowl of his cloak, which shrouded his head. The six of them attacked, but Skyline's movements were far too swift for them to compete against. One of them began tossing throwing daggers at Skyline, but the vampire dodged them all. He leaped into the air, landed behind that assassin, and slit his throat from behind.

He crouched low, avoiding an attack from behind. The attacking assassin accidentally slashed the throat of another, and Skyline's blade met with the abdomen of the other orc.

The fourth and fifth assassin on the bottom floor fell quickly to Skyline's blade.

The sixth stood still desperately trying to calculate a plan of escape, or to defeat the vampire who seemed impossible to match skills with.

Skyline bared his fangs and hissed at the assassin. "Orc blood is bitter compared to the blood of humans. The more bitter, the better!"

The assassin charged at Skyline, screaming and fueled by desperate fear, but with one swift movement, Skyline ended his life as well.

Skyline proceeded to the second floor, and discovered that the entire floor was a training room. A vial of poisonous gas was hurled at him, but the gas had no effect on the vampire. His shadow appeared seconds later, materializing out of the green cloud of poisonous vapor. Sixteen throwing daggers were thrown, and all but one of them either missed or were fended off. One dagger struck Skyline's upper right leg. The knife was halfway in his ever-dead flesh, but the wound did not slow down the vampire.

He glared at the assassin responsible for wounding him, but the glare was a mix of hatred and respect. It had been an eternity since anyone had been able to wound him.

Skyline battled against eight more assassins, including the one who managed to injury him. He pulled the knife from his leg and tossed it at an orc, striking him in the forehead and killing him instantly. He battled against four assassins at once, and they fell dead one after another, all within seconds. The remaining three assassins backed away from him. He leaped into the air once again, splitting the head of one orc open as he landed and quickly killed the other orc. He was now face to face with the orc that had caused his injury, which the orc noted had already healed.

From behind, four more assassins rushed down the stairwell. Skyline turned to face them while bringing the back of his hand speedily to the orc's face, knocking him out.

Half a minute later, those assassins were dead as well.

One at a time, Skyline searched the remaining floors of the guild, but he had killed all the assassins in the building. None of them would have been able to leap from the windows of the highest three floors without breaking a leg.

He returned to the training floor of the guild and found that the one orc who had managed to injure him was still unconscious, but was slowly beginning to wake. He scooped up the orc in his arms and carried him down the stairwell and out of the guild. Skyline dropped the orc on the ground and produced his flint once again, and set the second guild on fire. The first guild had already nearly completely burned down to its last frames behind him. He watched for a moment as the second guild caught fire. A sinister grin spread across his face. He had destroyed one of the two invisible assassins, and now he had destroyed their twin guilds and everyone in it, save for one.

Skyline turned to find that the orc had just regained consciousness and was standing erect. Before the orc could regain all of his senses,

Skyline's fangs met with his throat. He produced a second set of marks on the other side of the orc's throat, and then the vampire bit into the orc for a third time, much higher up the right side of his neck.

Seconds later, Skyline backed away from the orc, who dropped to his knees and grasped his throat in a desperate attempt to stop the bleeding. The third set of marks was so far from the first, that it was impossible for the orc to cover all three sets of wounds.

"You cannot stop your life from draining," Skyline told the assassin. He chuckled as the orc tried to get up from his knees, but was already too weak to do so. The orc tried again, but ended up falling onto the ground, flat on his back.

Skyline began to search the orc and found a dagger hidden in his right boot.

Using the dagger, Skyline slashed his own wrist and thrust it into the orc's mouth. "Drink, or you will die."

The orc ignored the request. Skyline repeated himself with a thunderous voice, rich with hatred. "Death will come within seconds if you do not drink now!"

The assassin obeyed this time and began to sip the blood from Skyline's wrist. His sips were moderate at first, but the more the orc drank, the stronger he began to feel.

"Keep drinking until an equal amount of my blood replaces the blood that you have already lost," Skyline demanded.

The assassin obeyed, and after a long moment, Skyline pulled his wrist away from the orc. The assassin got to his feet. His wounds were already healing, but were still leaking a little.

"Am I… am I a vampire?" the orc asked.

"Not quite yet," Skyline told him. "You are only half. The last of your orc essence is leaving you now as your wound continued to bleed."

Without warning, Skyline quickly attacked the orc again, biting where he had already made the second set of puncture wounds. A minute later, he pulled his head back and grinned. "I have just drained the rest the orc blood out of you. In a moment from now, your transformation will be complete. All the blood within you now is dead blood."

"The world seems so different now," the orc said, looking at his surroundings. The first guild was a ruin of blackened, smoking wood, and the second guild continued to burn.

"It is difficult to tell at night, but all colors have a strange way of being grey," Skyline educated the new vampire. "That is how the world appears through the eyes of the dead."

The orc looked down at his wounds, but they were completely healed. It was as if he had never been injured at all. Not even a scar was left behind to remind the orc about his potentially fatal encounter with Skyline.

"You need not worry about death ever again, and age and disease will never harm you," Skyline told the newborn vampire. "Only the sun can destroy you now, or having something driven through your heart. In time, you will be a lethal weapon."

"Why have you done this to me?" the orc asked.

"I have given you a gift, and you will now service me in my assassin guild," Skyline said coldly.

"But why did you pick me out of all the others?" the orc asked.

Skyline shrugged. "Because I am the greatest, and yet you somehow managed to wound me. To injure me is a very rare thing indeed. In fact, I have only ever been struck once before, more than a century ago."

The orcish vampire listened as Skyline continued to speak. His words were much like winter. His words were like a cold wind.

"Since I am now your master, you will receive training far superior to what you have already been given. Everything you were is now gone. I know not your name, nor does it matter. From this moment on, your name will be…"

Skyline took a moment to look around. He gazed at the naked trees behind the flaming structures he had set on fire. The bare trees reminded him that early winter had almost arrived. "Your name is now Llabarus Iceseason," Skyline declared.

Llabarus kneeled before Skyline, and the vampire grinned. Suddenly, Llabarus reached for a dagger hidden within his robes, and attacked. Skyline simply dodged the attack, gripped Llabarus by his robes and hurled the orcish vampire eight feet away. Llabarus landed on his hands and knees, and slowly rose to his feet.

"Do not underestimate me, Llabarus," Skyline warned the new vampire. "Any of our kind will tell you that I am living death. If you try to kill me again, I will bring you to your end!"

Llabarus said nothing. He stood there gazing at Skyline for a moment, but then the new vampire bowed to him. "It will never happen again, master," the orcish vampire promised.

Skyline stared at Llabarus for a moment. He had never had such resistance before when transforming someone into a vampire. Perhaps Llabarus was somehow different. Perhaps this is how it was when you transformed an orc. He had never turned an orc into a vampire before. 'He will prove to be an interesting asset," Skyline thought to himself.

"For your sake, I hope you make no such attempt on my life again," Skyline said in a daring voice. "I must return to the others now. Castle Bloodstone is your new home now, which you will find if you travel for four days to the east. I will be there in such time."

"Do you not wish for me to follow you, master?" Llabarus asked.

"No," Skyline replied. "I do not wish for those that I travel with to know of your existence yet. You may be my new instrument used against them, should I decide to disagree with Lure Vesper. I need time to think matters over. For now, go to your new home. Keep in the shadows and stay out of the light, especially sunlight. It will kill you. Consider keeping yourself undiscovered until you reach Castle Bloodstone your first test, my apprentice."

Abadon and Epona were asleep when Skyline returned. A forbidding, sinister smile spread across his face. A loud crackle of the fire caused Abadon to wake suddenly.

Skyline's shadowy form caused him to gasp out loud, waking Epona.

"It is only me, you fools," Skyline said, sitting down next to the fire. "It is done," he said a moment later. The vampire almost completely blended in with the darkness of the night. "Both the assassin guilds have been destroyed."

"What of the ring bearer?" Abadon asked.

"He was not present," Skyline replied, chuckling low like the beginnings of thunder in a storm. "He fled to the north like a coward when he detected that I was coming."

Skyline revealed one of many papers he stole from the guild. "These two assassins that were after you were helped by The Underworld. The two guilds were built by orcs, and all the assassins within them were orcs. It seems that someone below wants you dead pretty badly, young prince, and the construction of the guilds was part of their reward for bringing you your death."

Abadon sat upright. "How did you defeat those assassins so easily? I don't understand."

Skyline shook his head, as if a very foolish question had been asked. "I told you before, there is no target that I can't defeat. I am death's shadow."

Skyline's cold stare was frozen upon Abadon's face. "I am already dead. I no longer suffer the living! It is me you will have to deal with if this alliance proposal of yours is a trick."

"It is not a trick, Skyline!" Abadon shouted. "Haven't you realized that yet?"

Skyline stood up over the burning fire and spat out, "For the sake of you all, I hope you speak the truth." The vampire walked away and became part of the night.

CHAPTER XXX

Bloodstone Castle

THE EDGE OF BLOODSTONE FOREST choked off the open country. The trees huddled around each other, unlike any other forest Abadon had ever seen. The forest was thick, and passage through the trees was very limited.

"This is Sunless Forest," Skyline informed them. "The trees have broad tops here, and are so tall that the sunshine never reaches the forest floor."

Both Abadon and Epona took a moment to observe the forest floor. There was very little vegetation. In fact, the higher up the trees they looked, the more the vegetation was noticeable.

Eventually, the three reached the edge of Sunless Forest. Skyline stopped and studied the sky for a moment. The entire sky was masked with overcast, but it was still too risky for a vampire to attempt travel in the open country.

"We will remain here for a few hours," Skyline told them. "Just until nightfall. It is too dangerous for me to pass through open country right now."

Epona looked around and realized that the metaughla was missing. "Where is Meta?"

Abadon shrugged. "I haven't noticed Meta for about an hour now, but where is Sabre?" They realized together that both beasts were missing.

"Forget about them," Skyline spoke out, annoyed with their foolish concerns. "They will eventually return."

Abadon and Epona reluctantly obeyed the vampire, but they silently agreed to themselves that he was probably right.

The forest was generally composed of black oaks, carrion cedars, royal oaks, wicked spire trees, whip trees and blood sprout trees. The wicked spire trees were ugly, but they were much taller than the rest of the trees. They were black and their trunks were twisted. Very large thorns protruded from their trunks and dripped with poison. The rough bark of the trees shed easily, and was just as dangerous as the thorns because of their sharp edges. The royal oaks were broader than the black oaks, and they were dark blue in color, with large ovate leaves that were blood red.

"It's so thick," Abadon said, commenting on the forest. "No wonder your kind chose to live here."

"Bloodstone Forest is much thicker than this, young prince," Skyline warned them.

Before long, the sun retreated from the sky for another night, and travel into the Badlands of Blood continued. Very few stars were visible through the overcast, and gentle, delicate snowflakes floated down upon them. The badlands was open country of tall, jagged grass with an occasional boulder coming into view. Abadon estimated that an hour had passed before they entered the Bloodstone Forest. It was indeed thicker than the Sunless Forest, just as the vampire had told them. Most of the forest was made up of royal oaks, red arch trees and bristle bark trees. The red arch trees were reddish brown with red leaves and arched wide near the top, blocking out any passage for the sun which otherwise may have found its way to the forest floor. Passage through the forest was carefully chosen by Skyline, and Abadon noticed that Skyline avoided traveling near the bristle bark trees. They were dark green with needle-sized bristles, and had very few branches and twigs. The few branches that the trees did contain were blue and heart shaped.

'Straying for even a few seconds is enough to get you lost,' Abadon recalled Skyline's warning. Large chunks of bloodstone were scattered about the forest. Their black forms were misshapen and eerie.

"I don't like this," Abadon whispered to Epona, riding alongside her.

Epona showed no concern for worry. "What is there to like?"

"I just think we're walking into a trap," Abadon expressed. "I don't trust Skyline. He is evil."

"I have had my doubts about him as well," Epona admitted. "However, I feel better about this now. He may be evil, Abadon, but those who have created the frozen fire certainly are."

Epona paused for a moment, and then continued. "If Skyline was going to kill us, he would have done so already. He killed Gwan, and he certainly doesn't need the help of other vampires to kill us. There is no reason for him to lead us to Bloodstone Castle just to kill us."

"True," Abadon said. "I feel much better now."

Skyline stopped for a moment, and turned to the southeast. "Wait here for a short while," he told them. "I will be back."

The vampire disappeared into the woods. Abadon and Epona waited for his return, but the sounds of night and the unfamiliar sounds of a foreign forest brought shivers to their spines. The cold of fear crept into them, and they constantly glanced about in all directions. After a long while, Skyline returned with blood dripping from his fangs. Bloodthirsty hunger could be seen in his icy eyes, a hunger they had never seen before, even in a wild animal.

"I have had my breakfast," Skyline exclaimed. "But I am afraid you'll have to wait until we reach Castle Bloodstone to have yours. I will not allow you to build a fire in this forest. The trees are too close to each other here."

Abadon nodded. "I understand. I think Epona and I can manage until we reach the castle."

Without another word, Skyline led them deeper into the forest. More than an hour later, Skyline stopped suddenly once more. Cold whispers that Abadon and Epona could not hear clearly spread through the forest like wind. Skyline appeared to understand them, and he stood there waiting. A moment later, two figures approached them from the east. Both figures were dressed in black cloaks similar to Skyline's.

"Welcome home, Skyline," one of the figures said. The two figures walked ahead of Skyline, and a moment later, they found themselves in a strange city made completely out of bloodstone. It was a dark city of twisted towers that did not look at all safe to step in. There were about fourteen towers all together, but the towers were only half as high as the tall trees that hid the city from the sky. The towers looked weak and ready to tumble at any time. The only source of light was that of short stone towers that burned fire about twelve feet off the forest floor, and away from any trees that the fire towers might ignite.

"This is Splendor Shade," Skyline announced. "It has been our capital city for about three thousand years. You are the very first to step into its vicinity since before the War of the Gods—the very first who are not vampires."

"This is fantastic," Epona exclaimed brightly.

"We are perfectly safe from sunlight here," Skyline said, looking over the towers of the city. "Vampire slayers never make it this far into the forest. Our scouts kill them within the first five miles they travel into the forest."

Abadon noticed that even in late autumn, the trees here never lost their leaves. Although some of them were coniferous, many of them were deciduous, which normally lost their leaves in colder weather. The deciduous trees in the Sunless Forest were somehow different.

A five-minute walk took them past the city and in front of Castle Bloodstone. The castle itself had six towers involved in its structure. The trees that surrounded the castle arched toward it like hundreds of crooked fingers that meant to grasp the castle. Most of the castles in Mystasia had a moat of water that surrounded them, but Castle Bloodstone had a moat of blood. Four gargoyle head fountains poured blood into the moat from the castle wall. A drawbridge made from a combination of wood, stone and bone lowered over the moat. The smell of fresh blood was heavy and nearly caused Abadon and Epona to vomit while passing over it. The source of such a large quantity of blood was unknown, and neither of them were brave enough to ask Skyline or learn about the truth of its source.

Splendor Shade was black, cold, and in permanent shadow. However, once the visitors were inside the castle, they were surprised. Instead of bloodstains, bones, carnage, and cobwebs, the castle was very neat and tidy. The outer ward of the castle was almost empty save for a few wooden barrels. Both Abadon and Epona guessed as to what was inside the barrels, but the contents remained a mystery. The castle itself was constructed out of bloodstone, just as they expected. They walked up ten wide stairs, leading them into the inner ward of the castle. Instead of a gatehouse, a stone bridge arched over them, and was part of the inner ward wall. Many torches were lit and were the only source of light. There were no windows at all that the visitors could see.

The castle mesmerized Epona. All her life, she had wanted to meet a vampire. Now she was inside their castle. She had spent her childhood reading books about them, but half of the books she read, she knew now were not true. Depending on Lure's decision, she would possibly be part of vampire history forever. She would be part of the birth of a new age that had failed two thousand years earlier.

Just ahead of them, a shadow separated itself from a pillar in the great hall. It was a young female vampire dressed in an elegant red dress, with long, fiery red hair.

"Welcome home, Skyline," she said.

"I am glad to be back," Skyline said. The assassin turned to the guests. "This is Mornia Moonhaunt, a fire elementalist."

"Pleased to meet you, Mornia," Epona said, grinning.

"You as well," Mornia said in a friendly manner, but without a smile. She turned to Abadon. "And this is the prince?"

"I am Prince Krendale," Abadon stated.

Mornia gave Abadon a nod and turned to Skyline. "Lure has not returned yet, but someone else is here of high importance. He just arrived from the Red Mist Catacombs."

"Shael Bloodfang," Skyline muttered.

"Who is Shael?" Abadon asked.

"He is the blood lord of the second dynasty," Skyline explained. "He usually keeps to himself and his followers in the catacombs."

Epona was baffled. "I thought Lure was the highest ranking vampire there is."

"He is," Skyline said. "Lure is a blood lord of the first dynasty. The first dynasty was prior to the War of the Gods. The second dynasty is from the War of the Gods up till now. Since Lure is older, the majority of us have remained loyal to him. However, technically, it is Shael's time to rule. He has fewer followers, and the blood wars occur less frequently now."

Epona was shocked. "Are you telling us that there is a civil dispute between the vampires? There is a civil war going on between your kind?"

Skyline nodded. "That is what the blood wars are. A civil wars between us and Shael's followers."

Skyline turned to Mornia. "What does he want?"

"He didn't say, but I think it's clear why he is here. I think he has somehow learned or suspected that the humans would turn to us for an alliance, and Shael is using this as an excuse to win over some loyalty normally spent on Lure."

Skyline agreed. "I don't know how he could know about Abadon's proposal, but I agree with you. He is here for a reason, and I doubt that it is for a visit."

Skyline addressed the human visitors. "Remain calm. The dispute between him and us is usually civil these days, and does not often lead to bloodshed."

He led the humans down the corridor, until a figure stepped out in front of them from a joining corridor. The vampire was dressed in a black robe rimmed with red. His eyes were much like large disks of ice.

"Are these the humans that Lure invited to the castle?" the vampire asked.

"They are," Skyline replied.

Shael smiled. "My name is Shael Fatalfang. I am a blood lord. Welcome to Castle Bloodstone. I am the leader of the vampires in Lure's absence."

"I thought Skyline was in charge when Lure was away," Abadon spoke.

Shael's smile broadened, and he shook his head as he walked past them and turned around to face them again.

"Skyline is a weapon, and a lethal one at that, but he is not the best when it comes to making decisions for our race. He is not a blood lord."

Skyline said nothing, but he glared at Shael with just as much dislike as he did when he first set his eyes on them back at the House of Candles.

"Please feel free to make yourselves at home here," Shael said. "You will not be harmed."

"What brings you here?" Skyline asked bitterly.

"I am here to make peace between all of us vampires," Shael said, maintaining his grin.

"I have come to speak with Lure. The blood wars must stop, Skyline. Last night I heard about the frozen fire, and I realized that we can only conquer this new enemy united."

"That is for Lure to decide," Skyline stated.

"Or myself," Shael said. "I am, after all, the blood lord of the second dynasty. I am the rightful ruler of this age, not Lure."

"But Lure is in rule, and for good reason," Skyline argued. "As a blood lord, I am forced to respect you, but just know that the respect I give you is only because by the laws of our race, I must respect you. Do not tempt me to force my blade through your flesh, Shael."

The smile on Shael's face vanished. Shael and Skyline stared at each other for a long time, until Shael backed away slowly. "I will see you soon, Skyline." Shael disappeared down the corridor.

"Mornia will take you on a tour of the castle," Skyline said to the guests. "I will back for you shortly to take you to your quarters."

Abadon and Epona followed Skyline and Mornia. The torches were dimly lit. Many of the vampires gazed at them with intense hatred, and others gazed upon them with rich curiosity. Abadon felt his skin prickle, and it felt as though his flesh would crawl right off his bones, fall onto the floor, and run out of the castle. Epona felt frightened as well, but her inquisitiveness had peaked. She was finally able to see how vampires lived, a race that she had been interested in since she was a child.

Abadon began to question himself about why he was in the one place he had always been forbidden to be. He felt as though winter had arrived within himself, and not in the lands that he was now in rule of with his amateur kingship. He decided that conversation would clear up the discomfort he was sure everyone felt.

"Forgive me for asking, Mornia, but how do you keep the blood moat outside the castle filled?"

"Your kind is always full of questions, aren't they?" Mornia said, chuckling softly.

"The truth is that some of the blood you see has come from vampire slayers and others who ventured too close to the castle over the past several hundred years. The blood moat was Skyline's idea. He stole a large pump from a group of dwarf engineers in Hollow Haven. The pump was intended for a dwarf dam, but it works perfectly for pumping the blood and maintaining the blood moat. It is a warning that mankind, and elf kind in particular, are not welcome here. It is a simple reminder that we feed off that sweet nectar in your veins."

Abadon shivered at the sight of the blood. "I assure you, no reminder is needed."

Epona realized that she had never seen a trow or dwarf vampire before. "Why not dwarves or trows? Why don't your kind prey upon them?"

Mornia replied dryly, "We do prey upon them, but dwarves seem to have more resistance than the rest of you with regard to transformation. That means they often need to be bitten three times to cause them to become one of us. We have no interest in trows, and their blood is not as sweet as human or elf blood."

"Where do vampires come from?" Epona asked.

Mornia continued to lead them through the castle as she explained. "We do not know. We know that the vampires here in Mystasia originated from Shadowsia. Lure is the oldest vampire we know, and he came from Shadowsia on a ship. He can't even remember the date he arrived here. We do not know how we came to be, but since vampires look like humans, we suspect we somehow originated from human beings."

Mornia lead them to the dining table. Several others vampire were at the table as well, including Skyline and Shael. Fruits and breads were on the table, along with a roasted boar and fine wines.

Shael smiled at the reaction of the humans. They were in awe. "Not what you expected, is it?"

Abadon shook his head. "I thought vampires fed solely on blood."

"We do need blood to survive, but because blood is a liquid, we sometimes wish to chew on more solid things. The wine is for our werebeast guests that we get here on occasion."

Mornia added to Shael's explanation. "Since we are undead, our taste buds are dead as well. As Shael says, it is strictly a change of texture concerning the food we eat. We can't taste any of it. Blood, strangely enough, is the only thing our taste buds actually pick up."

Epona was amazed with the scientific differences between vampires and humans. "That is rather strange and sad in a way, to only be able to taste blood."

"That is all we need," Shael said, smiling and allowing his fangs to show. "Those who were once human sometimes recall what bread or meat tastes like as they eat it. There are some of us who enjoy being vampires, and others who look upon it as a curse."

The vampires and their human guests dined for over an hour, speaking briefly about their cultures and how they may have changed since the War of the Gods.

Shael returned to the conversation to the reason the humans were there.

"I must admit, Prince Krendale, that there are many of us who do not appreciate the possibly of an alliance. I personally hope that it does not succeed. If I was the blood lord of the first dynasty, as Lure is, this dinner would not be happening right now."

Abadon and Epona were surprised at first at the frank attitude of the vampire, but they ignored his words and continued to eat. It suddenly became clear to them that his reaction to the alliance wouldn't be any other way. Even though he was polite to them, he hated them. When his eyes were fixed upon them, they knew that secret thoughts of feeding upon them were racing through his mind, and not thoughts of peace. Shael was warm and hospitable to them, but his face was cold and unsolicited.

"The alliance would benefit us both, Shael," Abadon said after swallowing a mouthful of winter wine. "You would never have to worry about vampire slayers again."

"You think I worry about vampire slayers, young prince?" Shael said coldly. His icy voice made both Abadon's and Epona's skin prickle. "Perhaps you failed to notice the blood moat outside this castle. There will always be those of your kind that hate us. You can't protect us from them."

"They would be severely punished if they harm any of you, in any way," Abadon promised.

Shael touched the tips of his fangs with his tongue. "Would you sentence them to death, young prince?"

"If that is your desire, then yes," Abadon retorted bravely. "As Mystasian citizens, it would be murder or attempted murder, should anyone try to take your lives." Abadon realized that there was no use in bargaining with the stale lord. Shael probably knew more about kingcraft than he did. Abadon licked his lips nervously, struggling not to lose focus due to fear. He could feel Shael's stabbing eyes fixed upon him, and they felt sharper than his fangs looked. He needed the right words.

"Mystasia is a rich county, and there are no taxes. No one is poor, and the laws I'll create for you will be strongly reinforced."

Skyline joined the conversation. "What about our freedom? Isolation is key to us."

"You can do whatever you please here in Bloodstone Forest," Abadon told them. "What you do here is none of our business, as long as there is peace between us."

"You are forgetting one important matter," Shael said, smiling. "We need blood to survive. How do you intend to supply us with blood, if we can no longer feed upon you?"

Abadon was silent for a moment. He had not considered that very important matter. "Is it possible to feed on animals?"

"We cannot," Shael replied slowly and almost in a whisper. "Fairy kind are not affected at all by our bites, so we do not feed upon them, and their blood is too sweet. We must feed on human or elf blood, and dwarf blood if necessary. We can feed on animals for emergencies only. To live off animal blood would be like humans living on only a diet of meat or vegetables, or bread. It would be like asking you to drink only milk and never water. Humans need water to live, just as we need blood to live. But you can't get blood out of milking a cow, can you, young prince?"

"Of course not," Abadon replied. "This does create a large problem, but it's a problem that was solved once before. How did you kind feed during the first alliance?"

Shael and Skyline exchanged glances, and Shael replied. "We fed on the blood of prisoners. War was everywhere in those days, Prince Krendale. There are no wars taking place these days.

"Prisoners of crime, then," Abadon offered. "Those who are on death sentence can be executed by your kind for feeding purposes."

Shael leaned toward Abadon. "Mystasia produces enough criminals deserving a death sentence to feed us all, Prince Krendale?"

"No, I suppose not," Abadon admitted. "Because Mystasia is a rich county, crime rarely occurs."

Shael laughed. "This alliance has been given good thought, hasn't it?"

Abadon stood his ground and raised his voice. "The only way either race will survive now is to join forces! There has to be a way!"

"I have an idea," Epona spoke out. "The vampires can feed outside the county. The Bloodstone Forest does border the Peppered Sands."

"That would be the same as declaring war on another county," Shael declared.

"Not at all," Abadon said, smiling. "That idea may work, because those outside of Mystasia won't know about the alliance."

"The Peppered Sands are open desert county," Shael pointed out. "We cannot venture there for food, and to rely on you to hunt for us would be foolish. We would be putting our lives in your hands."

Abadon lowered his head. "There has to be a solution. We will think of something eventually."

There was little more conversation at the dining table. Eyes darted about everywhere, looking at facial expressions for any hint of unshared feelings or thoughts. Abadon and Epona also glanced about at the other vampires that had not been introduced. Were they loyal to Lure, or Shael Fatalfang?

Eventually everyone consumed their meals and left the dining room.

Mornia led the human guests up a flight of stairs and down a dimly lit corridor. She stopped at a wooden door, three doors down from the stairwell.

"This is your quarters," Mornia said to them. She opened the door and allowed it to swing open. "You will find everything you need inside. I will come and check on you once in a while. Have a good night."

Mornia walked away from them, until darkness engulfed her at the far end of the corridor. Abadon and Epona entered the room. The room was just as elegant in appearance as the dining room. There were two beds with furs on the right of the room, and a single window on the left next to an oak dresser. A crimson rug covered the majority of the floor. On the crimson carpet was an oak table with a candelabrum on it.

Abadon shook his head. "I still can't believe I am here. Clerics have been trained to hate both demons and the undead."

"Let's just try and get some sleep, Abadon," Epona suggested. "I don't feel entirely safe here. Skyline and Mornia did seem concerned about Shael's unexpected appearance here."

"I agree," Abadon said. "But they can't hate us too much. They did give us dinner." Abadon stopped talking and gave his words some thought. "The dinner could have been to simply get information out of us, about why we are really here."

Not a single sound was heard during the hour that Abadon and Epona attempted to sleep. It was like the castle was deserted. Yellow moonlight spilled through the thin fabric of the curtains, pasting a silhouette of the candelabrum on the wall. The shadow reminded Abadon of the tip of a trident. Angry, pale faces began to trouble his mind. He could see them materialize out of the darkness and pass the moonlight with their arms stretched out, reaching for them. They disappeared and returned again at the side of the bed. Their mouths were dripping with saliva, thirsty to taste their blood. They did say that human blood was their favorite, not too sweet or bitter.

The horrifying image melted from his mind, and Abadon felt great panic from within. There was nowhere to go. If the vampires did mean them any harm, they were trapped at the core of their castle in the middle of their forest. Abadon calmed his mind, and turned to his left. Epona had already managed to fall asleep. Guilt replaced fear, and Abadon began to realize more than ever how cruel humans had been to vampires over the centuries. Humans were a greedy race, and they had accomplished little without the help of another race. If he could accept the responsibility of being king, he would change that. The drug of sleep finally dissolved within him, and he closed his eyes and was asleep in seconds.

CHAPTER XXXI
Sorrow In Fairy Fern Forest

THE BITE OF THE AUTUMN AIR was not as vicious in the Fairy Fern Forest as it had been in all the other provinces of Mystasia. Rumors of the frozen fire and the death of the king and queen had not yet passed into the Fairy Fern Forest.

The gentle wind toyed with Nadja Kost's wavy, white shoulder-length hair. The blue roses that grew in the fairy-occupied forest nearly matched the blue color of her eyes, which matched her smile perfectly.

Nadja leaned against a white seeder tree. Its ice blue branches, like all white seeder trees, were broad, and its leaves were white and serrated. She closed her eyes and breathed in the aroma of the wild flowers and the lush forest. The aroma remained throughout the four seasons.

Nadja opened her eyes and viewed the beauty around her. She stood at the edge of the Fairy Fern Forest, where it joined with the Blue Rose Meadows. At her feet were numerous mushrooms, which were tiny orange mushrooms that wood elves loved to add to their food for extra flavor. Golden glories and red roses wrapped around the trunks of the majority of the trees in the area. Blankets of jasper moss grew along much of the forest floor. Nadja watched as a pair of jadewing birds perched themselves on the branch of a prickle pine.

From the other side of the Blue Rose Meadows, Nadja could see a forest fairy approaching. It was

Namira. Like all forest fairies, which were the largest species of fairy kind, Namira was ten inches in height and possessed two pairs of delicate wings. The bottom pair was smaller than the top set. She had dark green hair, and pale green skin, but Nadja had noticed that her natural light green complexion had become more pale than normal lately.

A couple of branches snapped to Nadja's right. She turned, startled, and smiled once she caught sight of Jermyia Braveblood. Nadja quickly fell into the elite knight's arms.

"I guess Namira and I found you at the same time," Jermyia said into her right ear softly. Nadja said nothing. She enjoyed the warm and secure comfort that Jermyia offered her.

She pulled herself back away from him to look at his face. "I thought that Marquise Sedor'Dyr would never let you come back to me."

"He was reluctant to," Jermyia admitted, but his smile disappeared. "Have you heard all that has happened?"

"Yes," Nadja nodded. "Dranus sent me to speak with Auroramal. She may have additional knowledge that might help us realize who is behind all this."

"I have come to warn her as well," Jerymia said, "and to see you, of course."

The elite knight turned to the forest fairy. "How long before we reach the fairy queen, Namira?"

"She should be nearby," Namira assured him.

Nadja noticed that Jermyia seemed exhausted. "You need to rest, Jermyia. Traveling around in such heavy armor must be a terrible burden," she insisted.

"No, I am fine, Nadja. Sorrel is the one who is exhausted."

Nadja looked around, but there was no sign of his horse. "He is tied up a short distance to the north of here," Jermyia explained.

The three reached the Forest Fairy Gardens of Life. More than eighty different types of flowers made up the gardens. In the center of the garden was a single special tree.

Namira pointed at the tree. "That is the Fairy Orb Tree of Life. That is the source of our life force."

The orbs were reddish pink, and there were about a dozen of them. Jermyia and Nadja noticed many large red flowers in the garden.

"Those are birthing flowers," Namira explained. "That is where forest fairies are born."

Nadja was surprised. "You mean that sprites and fairies do not mate to produce young?"

"No," Namira replied. "The fairy queen, Auroramal, plants special seeds that grow the birthing flowers. They randomly spawn either a sprite or a fairy."

"I never knew that," Jermyia exclaimed with a bright smile. "This is amazing. I always thought fairies reproduced like anyone else."

"Then how did the queen herself come to be?" Nadja asked.

"She came from the Fairy Orb Tree of Life," Namira told them. "It is difficult to explain, and it is a science of nature that even the druids do not understand."

The area was rich with wildlife. A large population of deer and butterflies dwelled in the area. From the south, Auroramal fluttered toward them. She was slightly taller than the other fairies, and her skin a deeper teal color than the others. Her long, flowing hair drifted everywhere as it was touched by the wind, and long enough to make it pass her back.

"Welcome to Fairy Fern Forest," Auroramal greeted them with a voice that could only be described as both music and wind mixed together. "What brings you here?"

"The frozen fire," Nadja said gravely. "It is a danger to you. Dranus thought that you might know who created the apocalyptic spell."

Auroramal nodded her head. "I am aware of this terrible spell. I do not know who created it, but I do have theories."

Jermyia and Nadja witnessed one of the birthing flowers give birth to a newborn forest fairy. The infant fairy was only one inch tall. Within seconds, the infant fairy began to fly away. She had trouble flying. It seemed her wings were not yet strong enough to maintain her flight and keep her in the air, but the fairy seemed to learn quickly.

Auroramal floated to their right and continued to speak. "Forest fairies are born with knowledge of nature-based magic. The infant fairy you just witnessed the birth of already possesses that knowledge, but it will take many weeks to learn many of the spells. History shows that the first druids ever were forest fairies and sprites. It was the sky fairies that taught them how to manipulate the weather. Sprites and fairies alike taught them the nature-based spells they know. They learned spells relating to the four elements elsewhere, perhaps from elementalists."

Nadja asked, "What type of magic is the frozen fire spell?"

"It is definitely elemental," Auroramal answered. "A number of magic users could have created the spell. It could have been an elementalist, a druid, an enchanter, a witch or a mage, or even a fairy, but fairies are always creatures of peace. A fairy is not behind the creation of the spell."

"It has to be the dark druids," Nadja insisted. "This spell has suddenly appeared only months after the first appearance of dark druids."

Auroramal nodded. "It is likely their mentor that created the spell. The druids of Agate Hedge must not have destroyed them all during their battle four months ago. The spell is so powerful and so destructive that no one individual can use it alone. Perhaps together, the dark druids use the spell."

Nadja inquired some more. "But could they have created a spell like that? Druids are not spell crafters. Witches and magi often craft spells. Druids study existing magic, as do elementalists."

"That is generally true," Auroramal agreed. "I have heard that portals are being used to siege the Mystasian strongholds. It seems to me that the dark druids are behind this, but it's not likely them that created the spell. I suspect that a mage created frozen fire."

Nadja's face turned to stone with frozen emotions of both uncertainty and confusion etched on her face. "That would mean that someone in my own guild may have created the spell."

Auroramal floated toward Nadja. "Examine the members of your guild very carefully, Nadja. There is a strong possibility that someone within your guild is working with the enemy. Watch everyone very closely."

Nadja nodded, but her mind was already focusing on each of the members of the Guild of the Blood Moon. No one to her knowledge would even have a motive for befriending anyone in The Underworld, or conquering Mystasia.

Auroramal's words were sorrowful. "I only hope that the spell users don't come here."

"I thought only fairy magic can be cast within the Fairy Fern Forest," Nadja exclaimed.

"That is correct," Auroramal said. "But from what I have heard of this frozen fire, it does seem to have traces of fairy magic. There is a chance that it will work here. The orbs of the fairy trees forbid any magic that is not native to these lands to use, but I believe the frozen fire will burn here."

As Auroramal finished her sentence, a portal of blue light appeared a short distance from them. Ettins, harpies, orcs, medusas, and manticores exited the portal. The closest forest fairies and sprites began to attack the large mob. Jermyia pulled his long sword out of its sheath and attacked the closest orc.

The fairies and sprites began to use their magic. Vines entangled the enemy from the ground, and walls of stone and thorns were erected to slow the enemy's advance. Many of the sprites used stone skin to armor themselves against the sharp weapons of the orcs. The stone skin was no match for the heavy war hammer that the ettins carried. The harpies primarily drew the attention of the forest folk.

Nadja had never seen so many fairies. There were easily more than one hundred of them in the area, and at least sixty sprites. Auroramal cast some magic of her own. As an orc approachedNadja, she hurled a fire ball at him. The flames critically injured the orc in a matter of seconds. A surprise attack from behind caused Nadja to react quickly, she spoke a word of magic and caused the orc to become fearful and flee from the battle.

Jermyia's sword was already stained with the blood of several orcs. He brought an ettin to his knees by cutting deep into his right leg. He beheaded the right head of the two-headed giant, and thrust his sword into the ettin's heart.

Borin, Olsegg, Kcargia and the beholder, Tybiss Pylimdor, were the last to step out of the portal.

"Cast the spell now," Borin commanded them. "I will make sure your work is not interrupted."

Kcargia and Tybiss began to chant several words. They closed their eyes and focused hard on the fire they were about to spark to life.

A manticore pounced on Jermyia from his left, knocking the knight to the ground. The beast was too heavy for Jermyia to move. Its stinger tail struck the knight in the chest, but it did not penetrate the plate mail.

"Kill it!" Jermyia cried out to Nadja, but the young moon mage froze still. She could not bring herself to kill the beast. Instead, she hurled a fire ball at the beast, knocking it clear off Jermyia. Jermyia recovered from the attack. Before the manticore could react, the knight cut off its tail, disabling the beast from being able to poison anyone. Two vines entangled the manticore, and their thorns began to seep poison of their own into its blood stream. The manticore shredded the vines with its immense claws, but the damage had already been done. Eventually, the poison would enter all of the beast's systems in its body, and it would die.

Jermyia noticed that not all the orcs were being affected by the fairy magic. He studied the orcs for several seconds and noticed that their armour had a purple hue to it.

"The magic ore King Krendale delivered to us," Jermyia spat out. "They stole it!"

As Jermyia taunted the closest orc to him, a wall of azure flames appeared. It was easily twenty feet tall, and it rolled into the Gardens of Life.

"No!" Auroramal screamed. "If that fire reaches the Tree of Life, our existence will be destroyed, forever!"

A wall of thorns was erected in front of Borin. Its appearance was so quick that he walked into the wall. None of the thorns pierced his armor, but two of them cut his face. Displaying combustible anger, Borin destroyed the wall with four swings of his axe.

Jermyia made short work of the orc he taunted, thrusting his sword into his guts. He glanced about, trying to locate the spell user. A moment later, he spotted Kcargia and the beholder. Jermyia grinned. He began to walk toward them cutting down every orc in his path.

Borin noticed Jermyia on the battlefield. His skill with the sword attracted his attention. Borin intercepted him, and Jermyia's sword clashed with

Borin's battle axe. The frozen fire continued to destroy every fairy, sprite and birthing flower in its path. More and more of the forest folk arrived to join in the battle. Their forces began to overwhelm the forces of The Underworld. A force of one hundred and thirty had stepped through the portal, and more than forty had already been killed. While the magical ore that the orcs, medusas and ettins wore resisted one or two fairy spells, they did not resist the constant use of magic the fairies continued to cast upon them.

Dryads from the south joined in the battle. Their naked, delicate bodies made their identity easily recognized. A medusa approached Nadja from behind. A sprite and forest fairy were instantly turned to stone. They had accidently turned to face the medusa. Nadja reacted quickly with two words of magic and struck the medusa with a bolt of lightning. The medusa was thrown back with the sharp bolt, and did not move.

The ettins and medusas stopped their advance and formed a wall around Kcargia and Tybiss, preventing anyone from reaching them. Borin and Jermyia continued to battle against each other in an endless stalemate of skill. Once again, a manticore pounced on the knight, interrupting the battle. Borin smiled and moved on to slay more sprites and fairies.

The manticore's jaws snapped in Jermyia's face, but Jermyia was able to reach for a dagger and stab the beast in the belly. The manticore roared and backed away, ready to pounce again. Jermyia allowed the beast to leap onto him, but his sword was ready. The beast impaled itself on Jermyia's sword and rolled over on its side. Jermyia jabbed the beast two more times to ensure that it was dead.

The forces of The Underworld were slowly diminishing. The small size of the fairies made it difficult for the orcs and ettins to destroy them. The fairies were too quick to target.

"No!" Auroramal yelled again. Jermyia turned to his right. About three hundred feet away, he watched as the frozen fire made contact with the tree of life. The tree froze into ice, and then shattered. The multicolored gardens suddenly turned grey, and the birthing flowers began to wither rapidly.

"Excellent," Borin cheered. "Back into the portal! Retreat!"

Olsegg created a new portal, and Kcargia and Tybiss were the first to go through it. The Underworld forces made certain that the spell casters were protected, and that they were the first to leave the battle. Borin entered after Olsegg.

They returned to the portal chamber, where Olsegg kept the portal open.

Taskica was there to supervise their return. "Let as many back as possible without letting any fairies or sprites through the portal!"

Olsegg obeyed as their forces continued to file through the portal. From the chamber, they could not see what was still happening in the Fairy Fern Forest. Taskica was gambling on taking the chance of allowing enemies through. She wanted to sacrifice as little of her forces as possible.

"Let more come," she ordered.

Borin was at Taskica's side. "Close the portal! Do not let any of their forces in here!"

"A little longer," Taskica ordered, ignoring Borin.

She watched as more and more of her forces returned, but more and more of them were returning injured. The might of her forces was failing quickly against the forest folk.

"Close the portal," Taskica ordered.

Only several feet away from Jermyia, the portal closed. He slayed one more orc and allowed the nearby sprites to finish off the remaining five orcs and two harpies. The young knight turned to Nadja.

"What happened? Why were you slow to get that manticore off me?"

Nadja lowered her head shamefully. She was slow to answer. "I… I just froze. I am sorry."

"Sorry, Nadja," Jermyia bellowed. "I was almost killed by that thing!"

"I… I can't bring myself to kill. I just can't! I hate death. I was overwhelmed."

"You can't even kill in emergency situations such as this?"

"I suppose not," Nadja said, shrugging. "I am fearful of death."

"We'll talk about this later," Jermyia exclaimed, clenching his fist in anger.

The two humans turned to the fairy queen. Auroramal wept as she assessed the damage done by the frozen fire. About one third of the birthing flowers were gone. The area was now grey. Instead of flowers, trees, moss and blades of grass, there were mounds of ash and charred, stony earth. The tree of life was gone.

Nadja was almost sobbing. "What will happen now?"

Auroramal continued to weep as she answered. "With the tree of life gone, the birthing flowers will slowly die. There will be no more of our kind born."

"There was only one tree?" Jermyia asked.

"Yes," Auroramal retorted. "With it gone, there are no seeds left to grow another one. No more sprites and fairies will be born. The orb trees to the south will allow us to continue using our magic. But our kind will be no more, and our health will slowly fail over time."

CHAPTER XXXII

Death of the Blood Lord

YELLOW MOONLIGHT SEEPED into the room through crimson curtains and onto the back of Abadon's bed. He gazed at the beam of light, feeling trapped between strange comfort and uneasiness. He began to feel what Epona had described to him earlier. There was a danger inside Bloodstone Castle, but he couldn't identify it. It simply lingered in the air, like a stray breeze that somehow separated from the storm that sheltered it.

Epona was sleeping soundly next to him, facing away from him just as she was before he had fallen asleep. She almost seemed lifeless save for the blankets rising and lowering with every breath she took in and expelled.

Abadon faced the door, and darkness blinded him. The beam of moonlight had shifted and no longer offered much light within the room. It had served as a silent alarm, giving warning to anyone passing it, but no longer. If silent enough, a vampire could slip into the room undetected now. The sliver of light that was beneath the door indicating torch light outside the room was gone.

He turned to the window and jerked back as a sudden chill of fear struck him and passed a few seconds later. Mornia Hauntmoon was standing there, looking down at him. He quickly sat up and shook the young witch next to him. Epona woke, and was startled herself to see the vampire standing there silently, as if she had been watching them sleep.

Mornia turned away from them and looked out the window. The yellow moonlight stained her dress. "The moonlight looks warm, yet it feels cold when you look outside," she said in a hushed manner. "I remember that autumn was my favorite season when I was human."

Epona was sitting up next to Abadon, but chose to be quiet. Abadon attempted conversation. "How long have you been a vampire?"

"For twenty years," Mornia replied without turning to look at the humans. "It was an autumn night just like this one, when Skyline transformed me into a vampire."

"What were his reasons?" Abadon asked, pressing for more information.

Mornia brushed the question off with a shrug. "That is something you'll have to ask him."

"And Lure?" Epona asked.

"Lure has always been a vampire," Mornia told them as she turned to face them. "I suppose that is why he wishes he was human. He has never seen what you have been blessed to see. He has never seen the sun, a sunset or sunrise. All he has seen all his life is dark and grey."

"What about you?" Abadon inquired.

Mornia did not answer right away. "I have always been told how beautiful I am, but when I look into a mirror or a pool of water and see myself, I am afraid."

"Why?" Epona asked, surprised by the vampire's words.

"I see death," Mornia said coldly and with a shiver in her voice, as if possibly frightened even at that very moment. "I look at myself and I see death. I am not the beautiful woman I once was. I am dead."

"But you will forever look young," Epona pointed out.

"I suppose you're right," Mornia shrugged. "I suppose that is one positive outlook on it."

Abadon recalled Mornia's behavior earlier. "Is that why you were uncomfortable in that room of water, because you were avoiding your reflection?"

"That is part of the reason," Mornia admitted. "I am not comfortable around water."

Abadon smiled. "I overheard a vampire say earlier that you are nearly as dangerous as Skyline."

"No one is as dangerous as Skyline," Mornia said, shaking her head. "But I do like to play with fire. I am an elementalist, one who worships the element of fire. That is another reason I am not comfortable with water."

Abadon and Epona's minds froze for a moment. They suddenly felt numb. Maybe Mornia was behind the frozen fire.

Mornia leaned over them, taking one step closer to them until she was again directly at their bedside. "I have a terrible secret to share with you."

Abadon and Epona felt their skin go cold. Ice had been poured all over their souls. Mornia's eyes never blinked, and she stared into Abadon's with cold penetration. Her beauty had somehow become eerie.

"Shael plans to destroy you," she said finally. "I have come to warn you, but there is no way for you to escape this castle without him knowing about it. You do not have long."

"What about what Lure wants?" Abadon asked desperately.

"Lure is not here, and all the vampires in the castle will follow what the blood lord present wants. I feel that Shael believes all the vampires will side with him when Lure does return. He believes he can overthrow Lure. Some vampires favor the possibility of an alliance with Mystasia, and others do not."

"What do you want?" Epona asked.

"If I agreed with Shael, I would have killed you already," Mornia pointed out. A mix of fear and relief passed through both the humans, realizing that they could have been killed already in their sleep. "I can do nothing to help you. The majority of the vampires will act on behalf of Shael while Lure is gone from the castle. I will be outnumbered and destroyed. We can only hope that Lure returns before Shael…"

Suddenly, four vampires storm into the room and dragged Abadon and Epona out of the bed. Mornia stood still, taking no part in the altercation. They were dragged into the corridor from their quarters. Shael Bloodfang walked behind them, smiling sinfully as the four vampires took them down a spiraling set of stairs to what the humans guessed was the bottom floor of the castle. They were thrown into a prison cell in the castle's dungeon.

"Please, let us go. Please, you can't do this to us!" Epona and Abadon both pleaded. Their words were ignored, and the vampires left the dungeon, slamming an iron door shut behind them. Shael's laughter continued, but became less loud the farther up the staircase he climbed. A moment later, silence was their only company other than each other.

Skyline was basking in darkness in his quarters, within his coffin. A thud coming from the roof of his sarcophagus forced his eyes open. Skyline tried to lift the lid of his coffin, but he couldn't. Something heavy kept it from opening. Outside of his coffin, he could barely hear voices, and hammering began. It sounded as though metal spikes were being hammered into the lid of his coffin to prevent his escape. Skyline tried again to force the lid open, but even his great immortal strength wasn't enough to overpower whatever held the lid down, and those who had imprisoned him.

Skyline screamed, "You are all dead when I get out of this tomb. All of you!"

"What makes you think you'll ever get out?" a familiar voice said. It was not the voice of Shael Bloodfang, but rather that of his most trustworthy companion, Laronbac Redcrypt.

"When was the last time he fed?" Laronbac asked one of the others.

"Hours ago, my lord. He is not at full strength right now."

The hammering stopped, and Skyline heard something heavy scrape across the lid of his bed of shadow. They had placed something onto the lid to ensure that he wouldn't escape what would now permanently be his tomb. He listened to the footsteps of about four vampires leave his quarters. There were only about six vampires brave enough to make an attempt on his life, and he would hunt them all down once he found a way to escape.

Abadon and Epona waited for death to come for them. The dungeon was cold and dank. They clung to each other, trying to gather warmth, but the dungeon had no warmth for them to offer. Even their own body heat was failing.

"We have been betrayed," Abadon whispered. His teeth clicked repeatedly as his jaw shivered.

"I am sorry, Abadon." Epona's apology was barely audible. "Maybe if I didn't trust their kind so much, you wouldn't have either, and we would never have come here."

"Jherlom is surely dead, and Gafnan is probably dead," Abadon muttered. "My parents are dead, and we are next. Mystasia is over."

"Everything I have read in those books is a lie," Epona said sadly. "Your initial feelings toward vampires were true, Abadon. They are dead. How hospitable can they really be? They are not alive, not like us. They are the living dead. Their blood is no longer warm like ours. They dwell in shadow."

The two prisoners began to feel a new source of heat, but they could not figure out where it was being generated from. A short moment after the heat arrived, a strong presence of light appeared from around the corner of their prison cell, and a faint roar of fire could be heard. Seconds later, a being of fire appeared in front of their cell.

Abadon and Epona were on their feet instantly. Abadon demanded an explanation. "What is happening? What is going on?"

"I am a friend," the being of fire said. He spoke with a male voice, which was a strange mix of words and roaring flame with some crackles. "My name is Fluxx. I am a fire elemental. I do not have the ability to free you from your cell, but I have come to tell you that everything is going to be fine. Lure Vesper will be arriving soon, and you will be freed."

As quickly as the fire elemental appeared, he was gone, and Abadon and Epona were again in a prison of cold darkness.

For a long period of time, silence and darkness was all that surrounded Skyline. Eventually, a light began to swell from outside the cracks of the lid of his sarcophagus, accompanied by a sudden presence of heat. A moment later, flames began to chew through the wood of his coffin to the right. 'Sealing me shut for eternity wasn't enough,' Skyline thought to himself. 'Now they are going to set me on fire.'

The flames feasted on his coffin for only a brief few seconds. It was long enough to char the wood, so that Skyline could break free from the right side. He used his right arm to push the blackened wood outward from his coffin, and crawled out. Standing in his quarters were Mornia and a fire elemental.

"Good to see you, Mornia," Skyline said, smiling. "You too, Charr."

The fire elemental stood there with his arms crossed and said nothing.

Skyline turned his attention to Mornia. "I always knew there was good reason to make you one of us. Does Shael believe you to be loyal to him?"

"Yes," Mornia replied. "I am surprised you went along with this plan, knowing that you would have to be entombed within your own coffin."

"I knew you'd free me," Skyline said, smiling, but even his friendly smile was cold. "As long as my blade meets with Shael's throat and the others who imprisoned me, I will go along with whatever plan you and Lure formulate."

Charr disappeared in black smoke, and Mornia's voice became graver. "I found out why Shael is here and out from the catacombs below. Since he trusts me, he told me everything. He plans to murder Lure tonight with his four most loyal servants. He wants to claim sole leadership over all of us and began a second dynasty. Since Lure has always been our leader, a new age for vampires would begin."

"Do you think he has anything to do with the frozen fire Abadon told us about?"

"No," Mornia said quickly, "But the chaos spreading throughout Mystasia would benefit his plan. He could spread his dynasty out beyond the Bloodstone Forest if he wanted to."

"We have to send word to Lure," Skyline insisted, and was about to leave the room.

"I already did. Fluxx left the castle to tell Lure everything, and Lure is less than a mile away now. They plan to kill him once he is inside."

"Who can we trust, Mornia?"

"With the exception of the four loyal to Shael, the rest of the vampires will remain neutral until either Lure or Shael merge as the survivor of their battle. Let Lure kill Shael, Skyline. You can slay the loyal four to even the odds."

Mornia smiled and added, "And of course, to score vengeance for yourself."

"You know I will," Skyline retorted callously.

"What assassins do you have here in the castle?"

"Eifel Darkfang is here, and a new apprentice that no one knows about named Llabarus Iceseason," Skyline replied. "I will send Eifel after Lacreth Irontomb. Llabarus will destroy Tilph Nightmourn. Laronbac Redcrypt and Tolbren Duskshroad are mine to deal with."

"Then what do I do?" Mornia asked.

"Aid Lure in any way you can," Skyline said, looking down the corridor from his quarters to be sure no one was there listening. "Protect Abadon and Epona, and make sure they are not killed before Lure can get here. We both know very well that you love to play with fire, and I don't want the castle burned down by you or any of your fire elementals."

Mornia sighed. "Fine, I'll make sure Abadon and Epona are not harmed."Without another word, she left Skyline's quarters.

Something moved from somewhere in the darkness that surrounded Abadon and Epona. Their executioner had arrived. Epona managed to find a piece of cloth and set it on fire. The small fire created enough light to see a shadow move toward them. A vampiric orc stepped out from the shadows. With hungry eyes, Llabarus Iceseason stared at the two humans, who exchanged glances. They had never seen or heard of an orc vampire before.

Before Llabarus could act, Laronbec Redcrypt descended down the flight of stairs leading to the castle dungeons. Even from their prison cell, they could see that Laronbec lacked pupils. His eyes were completely white. An accident he had prior to his vampire life, perhaps?

Llabarus ambushed Laronbec from the shadows and sank his fangs into Laronbec's neck, but instead of drinking his blood, Llabarus tore a large chunk of flesh from Laronbec's throat. A generous amount of blood drained from the wound. Laronbec was emptied of blood in half a minute. Llabarus's hungry eyes turned towards the two humans again.

He took two steps towards the prison cell before his passage was blocked by two elemental beings. Mornia's figure appeared behind Llabarus.

"Llabarus!" Mornia screamed. "Skyline would not approve of your behavior. It is foolish for you to even think about disobeying his commands. You will stand guard here with Fluxx and Charr, or Skyline will destroy you."

Llabarus said nothing. To the humans, it seemed as though a different breed of savageness existed within him. He was fueled by something more than just bloodthirsty urges—something untamed and unchecked.

Blonde hair that looked like dozens of quills gave away the identity of Lacreth Irontomb, who walked slowly down the hallway. Eifel Darkfang stepped out from behind a pillar, slashing the vampire's throat. Lacreth dropped to his knees. He turned and looked up at Eifel Darkfang. Eifel raised his sword and thrust it through Lacreth's heart. With a scream that lasted only a second, Lacreth fell onto the floor of the corridor in a supine position.

Shael led Tilph and Tolbren down the corridor leading to the castle dungeons.

Tolbren pushed the jail door open, which opened up to the prison cells. Skyline appeared from behind the door. The chief assassin acted quickly, thrusting his sword through Tolbren's heart. Tolbren's long, clawed fingers stretched out for Skyline's throat, but life drained from him too quickly to get a decent grip.

Surprised by Skyline's sudden appearance, Shael fled back up the stairwell. Tilph armed himself with his own sword.

Skyline shouted, "You are a traitor, Tilph! You are the blood knight assigned to protect Lure Vesper, and here you are at the side of Shael!"

"Shael's opinion on the alliance is correct." Tilph stood his ground. "An alliance with humanity will eventually lead to our doom, or theirs."

"Your loyalty to Shael has brought you to your own," Skyline said with a smile.

Their swords clashed, but the battle was less than half a minute. The result was Skyline's sword thrust through Tilph's heart. The sword had gone through the blood knight's heart and out the back, nicking the spinal cord. Skyline pulled his sword back and watched Tilph's body fall to the floor at the stairwell. Tilph's body slowly disintegrated into a small pile of ash.

Skyline turned to Abadon and Epona. "Shael Bloodfang has the keys that will free you. I will stay here and make sure that he does not return to murder the two of you. Lure will arrive soon to deal with him personally."

"Well, I hope he doesn't take too long," Abadon said desperately.

Shael Fatalfang entered the courtyard of the castle. The absence of vampires troubled him. Screams could be heard in the distance. Another civil dispute had begun. His loyal vampires were engaging Lure's forces.

Shael listened to the cries of death. Suddenly, to his left he heard the chains of the drawbridge lowering. He turned around and found Lure Vesper entering the courtyard immediately after the mouth of the castle dropped down. The sound of blood pouring into the blood moat nearly drowned out Lure's footsteps. Lure walked slowly toward Shael.

"They say you feed on fear, and smell it as well as you can smell blood," Lure taunted Shael. "Tell me, Shael. You do not smell anything right now, do you?"

Lure stopped several feet away from Shael, who gazed deep into Lure's eyes. His face was flush with hatred.

"Your hypnotic gaze will not work on me, Shael," Lure snickered. "The same cold blood runs through both our veins. We are merely carcasses blessed with the gift of life."

"I will take yours," Shael snapped back. "I will drain you of all your blood and dine on it right after your death!"

The two vampires began to clash swords and bare their fangs in disgust and hatred. They leaped into the air and battled on the ceiling. Gravity had no effect on the vampires. The battle moved to the wall, and then down on the courtyard. Their skill with the sword was evenly matched. They fought with such great speed that a human would not likely be able to follow their movements with their eyes.

Eventually the two separated and were on two separate walls of the courtyard, staring at each other. Shael made the next move. He lunged at Lure from one wall, sailing through the air toward him. Lure guessed Shael's line of course and threw his sword toward Shael like a spear. Lure's sword went right through Shael, who descended and crashed onto the floor of the courtyard. Lure used that time to recover his sword.

Shael recovered from the attack and was already on his feet. Lure rushed toward him, and they met once again in a frenzy. Their swords met with one another three or four times in a single second, until finally one of them made a mistake.

The battle stopped, and Shael looked down at his chest. Lure's sword had nicked Shael's heart. The shock left Shael unmotivated, and Lure retracted his sword and beheaded the blood lord. Shael's head rolled across the courtyard, and his body dropped to the floor. Lure tossed aside his sword and pulled a dagger out from his cloak. He carved into the body of the blood lord until his still-beating heart was exposed. With a smile, Lure began to feast on Shael's heart. The pumping stopped seconds later, and Lure drank every ounce of blood from Shael's body in greedy victory.

Time found both Abadon and Epona being led to the same dining room Shael had feasted with them in the day before. This time, Lure was sitting at the head of the table.

Mornia sat to Lure's left. Skyline gestured to the table, inviting the humans inside, and took a seat to Lure's right.

"The Blood Wars are over," Lure announced. "I suppose in a way, I have the two of you to thank. The battles between myself and Shael Fatalfang are finished. Shael is dead, and those who were loyal to him have been destroyed as well, thanks to Skyline's assassins."

Lure lifted his glass. "I offer a toast. Let no man, elf, dwarf, or others of the Mystasian society or vampires prey on one another after this day. Let this new society bring us victory over our enemies, and preserve the newfound peace between us."

Everyone tapped glasses and sipped from them. Skyline's aloof and cold nature was considered normal. He did not share his thoughts with the others, and remained completely quiet, although he participated in the celebration. He smiled, but his smile was weak. He seemed to silently agree with the new alliance, but his cold, piercing eyes told a different narrative.

THE END

WHAT WILL BECOME of Riannon Pureheart and Apponus, who are stilled locked away in the Caverns of Fear? What will become of Gafnan, who is also locked up in Owl's Hoot? Why is it important for Taskica to conquer Mystasia, and why does she care for Abadon? Will the druids find a defense against the frozen fire? The answers to all these questions will be revealed in the next book, *Blue Moon Over Wish Water*.

CHARACTER INDEX

Abadon Krendale: Male/Human

Prince of Mystasia and a cleric; brother of the golden faith. His greatest asset to the temple is his skill with natural healing and herbal healing. He has never wanted the task or responsibility of being king of the country and has only ever been interested in healing ill and suffering people.

Apponus Riskskin: Male/Human

Apponus is one of the elite knights of Mystasia.

Auroramal: Forest fairy/Fairy queen

Auroramal is queen of the forest fairies, and ranks among the Mystasian noble lords as a Marchioness. It is not known exactly when Auroramal was born or how old she really is, but it is rumored that she is one of the oldest beings living in Mystasia.

Avor Behn: Male/dwarf

Viscount Kruxceeder is the noble lord of the Hollow Haven County. His primary interest is the mining of the mountains, which are plentiful in Hollow Haven and rich with resources, mainly gold and gemstones. Most of the forging of Mystasia's weapons is also done here under his watchful eye.

Borin Saken: Male/Human

One of only five humans ever to make a living

and survive in The Underworld, Borin is a manticore master. He was born with the ability to control and share his mind with the savage beasts. Borin is the chief of the Earth Blood Orc Tribe.

Caprigus Flamefinger: Male/Dwarf

Caprigus is a cleric demon slayer that ranks as a warrior of the red light. He has a special resistance to fire.

Charr: fire elemental

Charr is a popular fire elemental called upon by the elementalist Mornia Moonhaunt. He comes from the fiery realm known as Oblivion Wastes of Infinite Fires, which is in the elemental plane of existence. Some suspect that love exists between Charr and his summoner.

Drabel Thunderthumb: Male/Human

Drabel is a druid known as an evoker of earth, which study and practice druidic magic.His fathers have all been druids before him, but usually chose to devote their studies to storm brewing. Drabel is more in tune with nature than any other druid in his keep.

Dradia Frostfern: Female/Human

Dradia is a druid known as an evoker of the earth. She also travels with Trossk, which is a triple-tailed naga.

Dranus Drathiso: Male/Human

Dranus is the arch mage of the moon mage guild. His greatest skill is sorcery instruction.

Draxeen: Female/Temptress

No one knows where Draxeen was born or how old she is, but she looks like a human woman. Draxeen can take the form of any man she seduces into her private doom and imitate them perfectly. She was discovered by Taskica in 1299 AG in the Shadow Wastes, where Taskica saved her life from a forbidden flesh stalker.

Epona Crimsonfire: Female/Human

Epona is a witch, and a childhood friend of Prince Krendale. Her greatest ability is crafting spells, and she is the most talented witch in her coven.

Eradia Avito'Lanz: Female/Wood Elf

Eradia is the high cleric priestess from the Cleric Tempel of Ku'Lee. Highly resourceful and wise, Eradia can resurrect those who have died recently.

Gafnan Northchill: Male/Were Eagle

Gafnan is a beast master who has a saber bear companion named Sabre. He has always been a were-beast. He occasionally visits hamlets and towns, passing himself off as a human and keeping his identify as a were-eagle secret from almost everyone, and he keeps such visits secret from the other werebeasts.

Galum Braveblood: Male/Human

Galum is first of the Mystasian elite knights. Galum often lectures that offense is key in winning any battle. As first knight, he is the head knight of the Hall of the Silver Shield.

Gathus-Kur-Zaimgy: Male/trow

Gathus is a diviner, but most diviners learn how to detect various things. Gathus was born with the ability to detect human-sized life forms in numbers of eight or more. He went on to learn how to detect traps within seventy-two feet, and hamlets within eighteen miles.

Gekmon Wishworth: Male/Human

Gekmon is an arcane apprentice of the Guild of the Blood Moon. When he isn't learning about the magical sciences or reading, he devotes endless hours to learning divinatory inscriptions.

Gwan Eastfire: Male/Human

Gwan is one of the few remaining ninjas of the Flaming Fist Clan. He has a celestial belt in Seyn-Ach-Zeul, a martial arts dealing primarily with arm locks and speedy punches. Seyn-Ach-Zeul is known as the strike or conviction of the serpent style.

Haz Rhon: Male/Cyclops

Haz Rhon left his home country of Avenhauk when he was banished for refusing to serve the king in leading a battle against helpless aquatic elves. Following his morals, Haz Rhon joined the ranks of the Mystasian

Warguild of Serpent Slumber with his battle beast mount. Educated in practical engineering, Haz Rhon oversees the construction of warfare siege weapons.

Jermyia Braveblood: Male/Human

Jermyia is the third Elite Mystasian Knight, and is known within the Hall of the Silver Shield for preaching that defense is the greatest ability a fighter can have. If one's defense if not solid, you will die in battle regardless to how strong one is with their offensive talent. Jermyia has a strong dislike toward magic. This creates friction in his relationship with the moon mage, Nadja. He has a horse named Sorrel, and squire named Bruid Steelmight that he plans to apprentice into a knight.

Jherlom Mor'Derum: Male/Wood elf

Jherlom is the second most powerful druid in the Agate Hedge Druid Keep. His rank is father of seasons, which means he has knowledge of three of the four druid paths. Jherlom can shapeshift into a blood hawk, and has a wyvern companion named Utopia. He enjoys the druid life, but his greatest pride is being the godfather of Prince Krendale. His greatest skill is druidic spell mastery.

Kalim Evernight: Male/Were Bear

Kalim is grand chief of the werebeast tribes, which are all located within the Haunted Forest Territory of Mystasia. Because the forest is haunted, Kalim has spent his entire life mastering his great skill of spirit warding. His protective magic keeps ghosts and spirits away from him and the camps closest to him.

Kcargia: Female/Medusa

Kcargia was once an overlord, overpowering the beings and creatures that dwelled in the Black Catacombs of Beristaki. For many years now, Kcargia and her horde have been cut off from rations and resources needed to survive, due to a collapsing of the earth above much of the catacombs that cut them off from key areas and trapped them within from reaching The Underworld. Now she is a dark druid pupil of Taskica Shadowdawn.

Keyesa Stormwolf: Female/Human

Keyesa is a druid studying the summoner path of druid life. It has always been tradition in her family to summon a pack of storm wolves, which get vicious during storms and have a natural resistance to lightning or electricity, and have strange bluish fur coats.

Kharious Bloodwing: Male/Obsidian gargoyle

Kharious is the leader of the gargoyle kingdom in the Obsidian Peaks of Mystasia. He has developed hatred for mankind and the alliance races. Kharious is a shadow knight, using shadow magic in combat. It is said that he was born in the Caverns of Fear. It is not known when he was born, but it was before the War of the Gods.

Khon'Tenn'Nul: Male/trow

Khon'Tenn'Nul is a cleric shaman, part of the Cleric Temple of Ku'Lee. His greatest skill is brewing potions, as he is very knowledgeable in advanced alchemy. He has his own shop where he sells potions.

Lacreth Irontomb: Male/Vampire

Lacreth is a head hunter, a vampire who stalks and kills vampire slayers.

Laronbac Redcrypt: Male/Vampire

Laronbac is a head hunter, a vampire who stalks and kills vampire slayers.

Llabarus Iceseason: Male/Vampire

Llabarus was an orc and a member of the twin assassin guilds, until Skyline destroyed them and randomly chose to turn him into a vampire, giving him the name Llabarus Iceseason. Llabarus seems to have a crazed appetite for blood and will even attack other vampires to get it. Admiring Llabarus's blood-crazed manner, Skyline became pleased with his choice to install him as a member of his own assassin guild.

Loamus Earthmend: Male/Human

Loamus is a druid who chose to become an evoker of the earth. His personality is described as earthy. He is tough like stone, and slow going and stubborn. He is very knowledgeable in preserving and healing the earth.

Ludacyn: Male/sprite

The only sprite to ever enlist himself as a ranger within Mystasia

Lure Vesper: Male/Vampire
Lure Vesper is nicknamed by mankind as the

"Prince of Darkness" because he is the leader of the vampires. Although the vampires have a castle in Bloodstone Forest, Lure has a house of candles in the Haunted Forest. Lure has no memory of being human, and believes he has always been a vampire. He is a blood lord of the Century of the Shades, making him the oldest of the blood lords, and he is also a self-proclaimed shadow mage.

Mornia Moonhaunt: Female/Vampire

An elementalist of fire, Mornia was originally born in Greensmith, Southguard Mystasia on Day 6 of Ciloshepu (month 14) in 1284 AG. She was transformed into a vampire by Skyline on Day 9 of Sistwarl (month 10) in 1304 AG in the Forest of Wounded Sands. Her specialty is fire mastery, and when she summons fire elementals, one elemental in particular named Charr always answers to her. Many believe there might be a romantic connection between the two. Her personality has very much the same characteristics as fire.

Myra Southstorm: Female/Human

Myra is a moon mage at the sorcerer of secrecy level. Myra was born with a rare but precious gift. She has advanced energy regeneration, which allows the energy needed to use magic to recharge quickly. She is a great researcher and the second highest mage of the Guild of the Blood Moon.

Nadja Kost: Female/Human

Nadja is a moon mage of the Guild of the Blood Moon, and ranks as a minister of magic. She is the most determined member of the Guild of the Blood Moon. She specializes in divinatory research and knows more spells than anyone else in the guild, even more than the arch mage himself. Concerning her powers, she relies on the blue moon, Shalamar. Her relationship with Sir Jermyia Braveblood is complex because of his lack of understanding of magic.

Nagh Shann: Male/ettin

Engineer and trap specialist hired by Taskica to secure Shade Deep with traps and other sources of security.

Nakon Dreamcaster: Male/gem mage

Twin to Tethus Dreamcaster, Nakon is the only gem mage in the mage guild

Namira: Female/Forest Fairy

Namira is a druid ranking as a guardian of nature, and is talented as both an evoker of the earth and a summoner. Although fairies are born with knowledge of nature-based magic, Namira decided to dedicate her life as a druid. Her greatest knowledge is on forest folklore.

Nario Pureheart: Male/Knight

Nario is the young brother of Riannon Pureheart, but did not follow the family tradition of becoming a paladin. Instead, he abandoned religion and became a knight. He attended Frost Beard's Academy, where he matched the education level of warlords in the philosophy of warfare. He is currently titled as the fourth of the Mystasian elite knights.

Olselg Alkeegg: Male/Common orc

Early in his life, Olsegg discovered a forgotten library that had sunk beneath the town in ancient times before the War of the Gods. There he discovered secrets and knowledge that led to his expertise in portal magic. He can open a portal almost anywhere, as long as he has knowledge the coordinates. Olselg can create different types of portals, including portals that cause pain, promote healing, and drain strength.

Ormela Bloodblend: Female/Human

Ormela is a cleric shaman, and the best in the temple when it comes to neutralizing poison. Ormela joined the temple to learn and exercise the healing arts, as well as for personal conflict. She hopes that by joining the temple, she will rid herself of the emotional pain that seems to be shackled to her.

Packura Rageclaw: Female/Were tiger

Packura is a member of the Moonmuzon Barbarian tribe, which are all naga slayers. It is impossible to ambush Packura, but she is renowned and infamous for her ability to ambush enemies and surprise them.

Pibb-Cor-Dyn (Pibbcordyn): Male/trow

A storm brewer druid from the Agate Hedge Druid Keep.

Pontyia Slayskull: Female/Human

Pontyia is a Mystasian dame and older sister to Remko Slayskull. She was born inFort Bladeworth, where her father remains as a Mystasian Marshall. Pontyia has hatred toward werebeasts, because her mother was raped by a werebeast and later committed suicide, fearing that she had been affected by the disease lycanthropy. Pontyia fears that she herself may be part werebeast, but no indication giving proof of her fear have risen yet. Pontyia is an expert in basic ballsitics and instrumental when it comes to sieges or attacks on enemy strongholds. She is currently the fifth elite dame of Mystasia, and is actually a baronet.

Pyhon-Ash-Pree: Female/trow

Pyhon-Ash-Pree is a Mystasian noble lord ranking as a baroness. Nearly all the farming and fishing in Mystasia is done under her supervision.

Remko Slayskull: Male/Human

Remko is a moon mage currently practicing the magical sciences at the arcane alchemist level. He is the younger brother of Pontyia Slayskull and shares her dislike toward werebeasts, feeling they are the cause of their mother's death. Remko experiments with brewing potions and is educated particularly with academic-based magic.

Riannon Pureheart: Female/Human

Riannon is the paladin lord of the Holy Temple of the Golden Halo, and a Mystasian noble lord ranking as a duchess. She resides in Skull Moat Castle, which sits on one of the tallest peaks in the Icecrown Mountains in Northguard, Mystasia. It is tradition for members of her family to become paladins, and she has a pet pegacorn named Angelwing, who was a gift from an arch angel from the Elysium Kingdom of Alyshia. She has an obsession with gargoyles and hopes one day to be successful in rebuilding an alliance with them that was broken during the War of the Gods.

Sedor'Dyr: Male/Wood elf

Sedor'Dyr is a Mystasian noble lord ranking as a Count. He resides in Jasper Oath Castle and favors Sir Jermyia Braveblood out of all the Mystasian knights, admiring his views on the importance of defense.

Shael Fatalfang: Male/Vampire

Shael Fatalfang has many followers, but many of them remain in the Catacombs of Open Graves. The unsettling nature of the Frozen Fire and the possibility of an alliance with mankind has caused Shael great concern that perhaps it is time to overthrow Lure Vesper and become the oldest of the Blood Lords. Shael Fatalfang is a Blood Lord of the Century of Tombs, making his the second oldest of the blood lords. Shael, like Lure, believes he has always been a vampire and originally came from Shadowsia, a country where vampires are native.

Shardana Rubyclaw: Female/Emerald gargoyle

Shardana is a battle mage, but has a curiosity about mankind. She is attracted to magic and how one uses it. The talents of the arch mage Dranus have caused her to recently leave the Obsidian Peaks, where she watches him instruct the new arcane apprentices. Shardana was created and animated sometime shortly after the War of the Gods. She has four hatchlings.

Shorhez the Shade: shade

Shorhez was once human and known as the Cannibal King. Now he is a shade, lost in a dark depression within Shade Deep.

Skyline Shadowfrost: Male/Vampire

Skyline is a guild master assassin. His original birth date and birthplace is unknown, but Lure Vesper turned Skyline into a vampire in the eclipsing years just prior to the War of the Gods. Skyline respects Lure only because he feels Lure gave him the greatest gift of all, eternal life. Skyline is feared even among the vampires, and Lure knows he has limited control over him.

Taskica Shadowdawn: Female/Human

Taskica has lived in The Underworld for eighteen years, and is one of only five humans to be successful at it, and the only woman to do so. Taskica is the overlord of a dungeon known as Shade Deep, which sits near the edge of the Abyss of Terrible Things. She is also a dark druid eager to teach new apprentices the dark, unexplored way of magic. She now has control over three large areas of The Underworld and is obsessed with claiming the Mystasian throne for her own.

Tethus Dreamcaster: Male/Human

Tethus is an arcane apprentice of the Guild of the Blood Moon. He has chosen to become educated particularly in arcane philosophy. Arcane philosophy is difficult to understand, and the arch mage Dranus admires Tethus' choice of study.

Tilph Nightmourn: Male/Vampire

Tilph is a blood knight assigned to protecting Lure Vesper, but is secretly loyal to Shael Bloodfang.

Tolbren Duskshroad: Male/Vampire

Tolbren is a blood knight assigned with protecting Shael Bloodfang.

Tor'Arbus: Male/Wood elf

Tor'Arbus is a guard captain and comes from a family line where all the males have been ranked within the Mystasian army for the past three thousand years. He has exceptional scouting skills.

Tybiss Pylimdor: Male/beholder

Tybiss is a warlock that rules over the Infernolands of The Underworld, who has recently joined forces with Taskica Shadowdawn

Vadamar Oakfounder: Male/Human

Vadamar is an arch druid and the leader of the druids of the Agate Hedge Keep. Vadamar is highly knowledgeable in the philosophy of nature, and can speak the elf language as well as the language of all the woodland beings.

Vygoulia the Damned: Female/Green Hag

Vygoulia is a charged curser, which is a type of witch that specializes in cursing their enemies. She was the leader of her coven, which was completely composed of green hags. An unfortunate occurrence transformed her coven into 'the damned' and drained her completely of the energy she needs to use magic. Vygoulia joined Taskica with the promise of having her powers restored.

CPSIA information can be obtained at www.ICGtesting.com
Printed in the USA
LVOW06s0707011113

359324LV00001B/1/P